More praise for *A Fragile Hope*

"Five-star, award-winning author, Cynthia Ruchti, writes *A Fragile Hope* with the depth that leaves a lasting imprint. Ruchti delivers a heartwarming/heartrending drama filled with wisdom and inspiration closely in tune with God. A must read!" —**Dianne Burnett**, *Publishers Weekly* reviewer

"Books either grab you or they don't. *A Fragile Hope* grabbed me by the throat with the first line and never let go. Cynthia Ruchti always writes heart books, but I was not sure if this was going to end the way I wanted. I so feared for those characters. Try *A Fragile Hope* by Cynthia Ruchti and then go after her other books." —**Lauraine Snelling**, best-selling author

"This book grabs you in the first chapter, and never lets go. You'll care for the people on these pages, and you'll grow with them as their hidden hearts are exposed. Honest truth: as I read *A Fragile Hope*, I laughed, I cried, I prayed and pondered, and I stopped and forgave someone. This book exposed my heart too, and I am grateful. Reading this book will herd you toward change and hope. Although this is fiction, it is a story of truth—a sturdy story of redemption and answered prayer. Read this book and breathe in hope." —**Betsy A. Barber**, PsyD, Associate Director and Associate Professor, Institute for Spiritual Formation (Talbot School of Theology)

"Master storyteller Cynthia Ruchti demonstrates a unique ability to weave tenderness with life-changing truth in her novel *A Fragile Hope*. It offers more than a good read. It offers answers for those seeking the path to forgiveness and longing for hope in the midst of seeming impossibilities." —**Grace Fox**, international speaker and author of *Moving from Fear to Freedom: A Woman's Guide to Peace in Every Situation*

"Exquisite storyteller Cynthia Ruchti has accomplished the seemingly impossible feat of beautifully portraying the inner struggles of a man on the edge of decisions that will forever change reality for all those he loves. I simply could not put down *A Fragile Hope* because, after all, everyone is seeking hope in the end. Must read!" —**Lucinda Secrest McDowell**, author, *Dwelling Places*, EncouragingWords.net

"*A Fragile Hope* is like reading the intimate diary of a marriage in crisis. Without losing an ounce of impact, Cynthia Ruchti gently navigates through the heart-wrenching journey of one man's crash course in faith, hope, and everything his books and degrees tell him he knows about marriage. *A Fragile Hope* is a story of triumph through pain, even when the outcome looks nothing like you imagined it could. Well done!" —**Allison M. Wilson**, Lifepoint Church of Palm Bay, FL, Marriage Ministry Team

"Josiah Chamberlain's climb to success is interrupted by tragedy compounded by bewilderment. I disliked him but couldn't stop turning the pages because my heart empathized and identified. Ultimately, I cheered him forward. *A Fragile Hope* by Cynthia Ruchti takes you to depths and heights and ultimately to truth and hope. This book is your must-read this year." —**Karen Porter**, author, speaker, coach

"Captured by each nugget of wisdom in *A Fragile Hope*, I suddenly realized—this is more than a novel. While it is the gripping story of a self-absorbed, self-righteous man and his unexpected journey out of despair and crippling fears, it's also a powerful means to help us confront our own hypocrisy, insecurity, and struggles when we 'do life' in our own strength and with our own agenda. Cynthia calls readers to hope-filled choices today that will change their lives, homes, and ministries for years to come. She scattered seeds of hope in my own heart that are already taking root. And I am grateful." —**Dawn Wilson**, founder, Heart Choices Today, and writer at Crosswalk.com

"Transported into the lives of Cynthia's characters, it's as though I walked by their side through the pages. *A Fragile Hope* is filled with deep nuggets of faith, relationship, and love. I will never be the same." —**Martha Brangenberg**, co-host of iWork4Him Radio and marriage mentor

"*A Fragile Hope* is an emotionally gripping story of a man's realization of his own failure in his marriage. Through trauma and life's difficulties, lessons are learned regarding faith, hope, and love. This is another excellent story woven with life application by Cynthia Ruchti." —**Susan Titus Osborn**, author of more than 30 books

"For anyone who needs to know that the struggle is real, who feels fragile or flustered, who needs encouragement as you seek answers for yourself or your loved one: find, in this illuminating novel, a treasure of wisdom and light for the journey and a handhold of hope as you fill in the missing pieces." —**Marcie Gribbin**, MA, family/mental health therapist

"What a book! Cynthia Ruchti has done it again with *A Fragile Hope*. Don't miss this outstanding read." —**Gayle Roper**, *Special Delivery, A Fatal Arrangement*

a fragile hope

CYNTHIA RUCHTI

a novel

Abingdon Press

Nashville

A Fragile Hope

Copyright © 2016 by Cynthia Ruchti

All rights reserved.

Library of Congress Cataloging-in-Publication Data

Names: Ruchti, Cynthia, author.
Title: A fragile hope / Cynthia Ruchti.
Description: Nashville : Abingdon Press, [2017]
Identifiers: LCCN 2016037705| ISBN 9781426791505 (pbk.) | ISBN 9781501837449 (e-book)
Subjects: LCSH: Marriage—Fiction. | Marriage counselors—Fiction.
Classification: LCC PS3618.U3255 F73 2017 | DDC 813/.6—dc23
LC record available at https://lccn.loc.gov/2016037705

The persons and events portrayed in this work of fiction are the creations of the author, and any resemblance to persons living or dead is purely coincidental.

Published in association with Books & Such Literary Agency.

Macro editor: Jamie Chavez

Some Scripture quotations are from the Authorized (King James) Version of the Bible. Rights in the Authorized Version in the United Kingdom are vested in the Crown. Reproduced by permission of the Crown's patentee, Cambridge University Press. The rest are from the Common English Bible. Copyright © 2011 by the Common English Bible. All rights reserved. Used by permission. www.CommonEnglishBible.com.

Song lyric on page 172 from "Here I Am to Worship" by Tim Hughes, Copyright © 2001 Thankyou Music.

17 18 19 20 21 22 23—10 9 8 7 6 5 4 3 2 1

MANUFACTURED IN THE UNITED STATES OF AMERICA

*To those who have chosen to walk this
storytelling journey with me.
Thank you for your companionship.*

Chapter 1

This wave of pain will pass. So will the next.
Life's hard seasons rock us. Hold on.
Some years, spring comes early.

~ Seedlings & Sentiments
from the "When Sorry Isn't Enough" collection

She punched the blender's Off button hard enough to rock the unit. Not good. All she needed was for that slurpy mixture to go flying across the shop. Maybe Josiah had a point about the blender noise. She couldn't think with it whirring. How could she expect him to?

But thinking could be dangerous.

"I love this one."

The voice came from behind her. She had no trouble discerning who it belonged to. She gripped the handle tighter to override the slick of her sweating palms.

"Karin, did you hear me? I said I really like this one."

She lifted the blender pitcher from its base and held it close to her body. Not a traditional self-defense posture. With his work cap too far back on his head to hide the questioning crease in his forehead or the tuft of artificially bleached-blond hair that teased the crease, Wade Frambolt waited for her response.

"It's part of our 'When Sorry Isn't Enough' collection," she said as casually as she could manage. "Still so new, the ink isn't dry yet." She should turn, empty the contents of the blender onto the mold-and-deckle screen prepped for it. She should.

Wade's mouth drew up on one side. "I don't know how you two keep coming up with these things. You find a way to express what people are thinking but don't know how to say."

Karin's tension eased one notch on an emotional belt with its holes punched too close together. Not much help. "We'd better be able to do that, or we shouldn't have gotten into this business." Her nervous laugh belonged to a fourteen-year-old girl, not a business professional. With a husband.

Wade pulled at his lower lip. She followed the path of his gaze. The shop. Her shop. Seedlings & Sentiments.

"So, now what? What are you working on now?" Wade pointed to the blender she clutched like a security blanket.

"Mulberry paper. Hence the color." She held the pitcher to catch the light from the antique chandelier Leah had insisted would soften the glare from the ceiling's overhead lighting. The mulberry slush had already begun to settle out. It would need another pulse or two to remix.

"Do you have a plan?"

No. That was the problem. Every plan sounded like a prison break, admission of defeat, or certain death of what she cherished most. *Once* cherished most.

"For the mulberry paper. Do you have a plan for the mulberry paper?" Wade stepped closer. "Karin, are you okay? Your reaction time is way off normal."

That her best friend's life mate knew her response time better than her husband did underscored part of the need for a plan. "Not sure yet." No matter the question she'd been asked, that was a safe, all-purpose answer.

And it was the truth. She wasn't sure of anything.

ঙ্গ ঙ্গ ঙ্গ

"Refill on your coffee, Wade?"

Karin watched Leah stretch an extra length of packing tape across the address label on the last of the boxes, smooth the crinkles with her thumbnail as she always did—crinkles or not—and head for the coffeemaker without waiting for Wade's reply. "Miserable night like this one's promising to be, you might want to try the cardamom mocha." Leah hesitated. "Not the night for either of us to be gone from home. Hope you're okay with frozen pizza while I'm at the accountant's, shuffling through the business's tax maze. So..." Leah turned to face her husband. "Cardamom mocha?"

Karin caught his look—a cross between curiosity and disgust. "It's her own blend," Karin offered. As if that would help.

"Madagascan?" he asked, twisting the lid from his travel mug.

"Scandinavian. Smell." Leah held the coffee carafe toward him and fanned the aroma his direction.

"Mmm. Cookies."

"That's the cardamom." She poured. "Said to aid everything from digestion to depression."

Karin's stomach churned. *Don't believe it. On either count.*

"Your packages ready now?"

What must it be like to see your husband during the workday, and have him care about what you do? To have him involved in delivering what you create rather than dismissing it as "that little hobby of yours"?

Karin turned back to the task of leveling the paper pulp on the screen, distributing chunkier bits with her gloved fingers. Gloves—a concession to the natural dyes and the less-than-natural coloring from shredded junk mail for which the shop had become all of the town of Paxton's repository. She lifted the mold and watched pinkish liquid drip through the screen into the catch pan below. If the packages were ready, that meant Wade was leaving.

"Yes. Sorry about making you wait. Again." Leah smiled, winked, and dumped the last half-inch of coffee into the shop's splattered stainless steel work sink. "It's the efficiency in me. I can't stand the idea of having an order almost ready to send off and needing to wait until tomorrow."

Sometimes a person can wait too long.

"But," Leah added, "that's why Karin's the artist and I'm the business manager. Right, Karin?"

"Are we the last stop of the day?" Karin knew the answer, but all the other questions in her mind couldn't be answered as easily.

"As always," Wade said. "I like to end the day on a positive note."

"My coffee has that effect on people." Leah arched her hand and pressed three fingers to her chest, pinkie extended, eyebrows arched, head titled just so, her grin rolling into a giggle.

"Not denying the power of coffee, but it's"—he scanned the room.

Karin held her breath.

" 'It's the atmosphere. There's something in the air here. It feels like safety, looks like friendship. And it keeps me coming back.' "

"Aw. How sweet." Leah's expression could have revived the coffee resting in the crook of the drain pipe.

"He's reading the whiteboard." Karin pointed.

"What?"

"Failed brainstorming session." She set the paper mold on the flat pan and crossed to the whiteboard wall. She rubbed away everything except the word *atmosphere*. "I'll know to wait for inspiration next time."

Wait.

Josiah. We need to talk.

She knew what he'd say. "Can it wait?" And then he'd assume the answer was yes.

No. Not anymore.

❧ ❧ ❧

Leah closed the door behind package-laden Wade. "I chose well. He's one of the good guys."

"Uh-huh."

"He looks a little like a younger Tom Hanks, don't you think?"

"I guess so." Karin slipped the newborn mulberry paper onto the waiting sheet of kitchen parchment paper on the worktable. She sprinkled another few cornflower seeds onto the surface of the mulberry fibers and pressed them lightly into the still damp, but already beautiful pulp. Another layer of parchment. Then the sponge. The rhythm of pressing out more water—more of the unwanted—covering every inch of the sandwiched paper, helped slow her pulse.

❧ ❧ ❧

Not fit for man nor beast. Karin could hear her father's well-rehearsed assessment of nights like this one. Dark too soon. Rain threatening to become something solid if the temp dropped another degree or two. Wind intent on driving the precipitation through buttonholes or jackets merely resistant, not rainproof.

One more trip back into the store before she could turn out the rest of the lights. For the last time for a while. Maybe forever. Janelle insisted Josiah would fight for her. Karin had given him every chance. She texted Janelle then started her note to Leah.

"Leah, you don't deserve the mess I'm leaving you."

She stopped writing. Her hands shook from more than the cold. Rain dripped from her wet hair onto the sheet torn from her ever-present idea notebook. "Forgive me. Please."

A fist-sized rock the shop used as a doorstop in summer became a paperweight on Leah's pristine desk. A boulder-sized lump clogged Karin's airway as she turned toward the rear exit of the building, slapping at light switches along the way.

She stepped onto the back stoop, tried the door to make sure it was shut, keyed in the security code, and faced the night. The phone in her coat pocket played a familiar two-toned alert. Only an insane person would stop her current mission to look. So she did.

It was Josiah, technically speaking. But he wasn't answering her last text, the one that could stop her. Instead, his automation system had sent a preprogrammed text to his reader fans with his "Marriage Moments" wisdom of the day.

Mister Irony.

"'The path to your happiness,'" she read on the screen, "'lies in paying attention to your spouse's heartbeat.'"

Rain on its way to sleet slid down the back of her neck as she lifted the Dumpster lid to toss in her phone with its cutting message.

Her coat sleeve caught on something. She tugged against whatever it was lurking near the top but hidden in shadows. Numbing cold stiffened her fingers as she dug with her right hand to free her sleeve. Pain. There shouldn't be pain. *No. I have to go. Have to leave. Let me leave!*

A broad dagger of glass flew from the Dumpster and shattered at her feet as she extricated her arm. Sleeve ripped. Skin slashed. Blood. So much blood.

Sleet. Cold. Stop the blood. Stop it. Not in my escape plan. Can't hold pressure and unlock the door. Can't get in.

But help will come, won't it? He'll be here soon. In books, heroes always show up on time.

Sound behind her. Steel door slamming hard. "Karin?"

I knew you'd come.

Chapter 2

No one knows the work you've put into this project, the heart you've invested. Take a moment to celebrate. You won't be alone. I'm here.

~ Seedlings & Sentiments
from the "Celebrate" collection

Josiah Chamberlain's flat-tipped fingers—from the maternal side of the family—hovered over the keys. One moment. Two. He expelled the breath he'd held since page 249. Reaching his arms overhead, elbows toed in, he grabbed the back of his skull. Eyes pinched shut, he forced himself to swallow. The tennis ball in his throat refused to dislodge. Agony now ecstasy.

It. Is. Finished.

The low ceiling of heavy clouds had drafted his green library lamp into service earlier. Its light camouflaged the passage of time. Dark. But it had been dark all day.

What time was it? Six-thirty. Karin would have eaten an hour ago. Had she called him to the table? Probably. If he'd put her off, he'd done it unconsciously. That's what laser-like focus did when he was on deadline. She'd understand. What a trouper.

He pulled himself from his reverie, laid his hand over the still-warm curve of his wireless mouse, and clicked the X in the upper right-hand corner of the screen.

Save changes? Yes.

He e-mailed the file to himself then pushed away from the oak trestle table, whistling the Doxology. The space shuttle had nothing on his liftoff from his leather chair. For a non-dancer, he traced a respectable jig across the wide plank floorboards on his way to the door. Hand on the white porcelain doorknob, he paused.

Can't be too careful.

He scooted back to his laptop, inserted a thumb drive in the USB port, and saved the freshly minted file in triplicate.

This time when he turned his back on the project, he straightened the framed certificate that had allowed him five years as a marriage counselor before taking his show on the road. Highly touted seminars, sold-out weekend events, and—he glanced at the now quiet computer—perhaps another best seller to add to his growing collection. Who wouldn't enjoy a moment like this?

He left the room whistling "It's a beautiful day in the neighborhood."

Tomorrow night—thick steaks on the grill. No. We'll go out. Russell's. Karin deserves her bacon-wrapped scallops. And what she'll call a "guilt-drenched" dessert. And a little more of my time. Okay. A lot more.

What other woman would put up with his disappearing into his cave for weeks at a time for a deadline or spending so many long stretches on the road when he wasn't on deadline? The picture of grace. That's what she was.

He descended the steps like a teen late for football practice and slid into the kitchen like Cosmo Kramer from *Seinfeld*.

No Karin. No plate on the dark granite kitchen island or waiting by the microwave. No matter. She probably had another plan. He yanked at the pantry door. *A little bubbly would be nice.* He scanned for the sparkling pear juice Karin favored. He'd grab goblets out of the china cabinet on his way through the dining room to find her.

"Karin! Where are you?"

No answer.

"Karin? I'm done. Let's celebrate." Wait until he told her the brilliant idea he'd used to end the book.

She'd had a project or something. Was this the week she said she was going to paint the back bedroom? No. Work related, right? Or what she called *work*. Best decision he ever made was to get her that storefront downtown. All the mess and that incessant whirring noise of the blender was miles away now. Sure, it cost him money he shouldn't have had to spend. But it was either he rent an office or she did. And what she did with that homemade card place wasn't *completely* without value.

"Babe," he called into the silence. "Deadline week. You know it's always like this. But it's over now. I haven't sent it off to Morris. I can do that after we pop the cork on this vintage pear juice. Two thousand seventeen. It was a very good year." He held the bottle high, as if she could see it.

Sure, it was corny, but couldn't she crack an I'm-disgusted-with-you-but-you're-adorable smile? *Laundry room. She probably can't hear me because of the dryer.*

After his last successfully met deadline, he'd made the same suggestion. "How about we make reservations at Russell's for tomorrow night, Karin? An ocean-view table."

She'd quirked an eyebrow at him, her dimples trying not to materialize. "We live in Cheese Curd Central, you lunatic. Totally landlocked. How do you propose we'll find an ocean view?"

"The a-quar-i-um in the lobby?"

Considering how sequestered he'd had to be for the last couple of weeks, he should probably back off on the sarcasm this time. When he found her.

Josiah's word-weary brain formed a question that refused to take itself seriously. He could feel his pulse in his temples, neck, and behind his eyeballs. The chill of the travertine foyer floor seeped through his cushioned socks. "Karin? Not funny anymore."

His stomach rumbled. He was perfectly capable of fixing himself something to eat. But that wasn't the point. Where was she? She knew he was near his deadline.

Josiah pulled out his phone and checked for messages from her. Nothing. He unmuted the phone from deadline mode, and punched in her number. No answer. Good. Probably on the road. Probably almost home. Doubt dialed the phone again. The Seedlings & Sentiments landline. Answering machine. He called Karin's number and left a message this time, regretting his tone as soon as he ended the call. He was tired. She'd understand. She'd forgive him the small offense.

If not, I can slip her chapter 7 of the book I just finished.

The thought ricocheted through the empty house. *"Don't let the sun go down on your wrath" doesn't apply if sunset was more than an hour ago, does it?*

Not wrath. Something between disappointment and anger. Closer to disappointment. She should be here to help him celebrate. Like always. Her absence took some of the joy out of meeting his deadline. Who else did he want to tell? Even if his dad were alive, news like this would elicit anything but what Josiah needed.

"Couldn't get a real job, boy?"

"Dad, this is a real job. I graduated magna cum laude, for Pete's sake."

"And what's the level just above that? Oh, that's right. Summa. Kind of like coming in second in a two-person race, isn't it?"

Never enough. Never ever enough for the man.

Josiah set the goblets on the kitchen counter for the postponed celebration and dug into the refrigerator for leftovers. Not what he had in mind. Not at all.

❧ ❧ ❧

What just happened?

Finished the book. Came downstairs to tell Karin. Yada yada, she's gone.

Not the ending he'd written into this night. He actually thought the evening would end with a delicious drifting off to sleep, her body curled into his.

What an idiot.

No. That was his dad's voice. His dad's curse. Josiah mentally walked over to the garbage disposal, tossed the condemnatory phrase through its black rubber flaps, and flipped the switch to pulverize the thought.

Another round through the house to look for a note or something he might have overlooked. He'd overlooked too much lately. Time for a course correction.

He set the pear juice on the entry table, sans coaster, and opened the front door again. The street stood empty. And slick with sleet. *Now you have me worried, Karin.*

He called again. No answer. He tried Leah's number, too, digging it out of his contacts list. Straight to voice mail. He hung up and found Wade's contact info. Wade would know where Leah was. If Karin was with her business partner, Wade might know why and when Josiah could expect her home.

How hard would it have been for Karin to have left him a note? Or called before she left work? Even though he'd gone dark for the deadline, he would have gotten the message eventually. At least he'd know what was going on. She didn't have a meeting somewhere, did she? Had she talked about a meeting? The one thing he could count on is that she hadn't left him.

Working so intensely had side effects. The latest? His left eye twitched.

He'd wait another fifteen minutes and then he'd—

"Worry wrings all the fun out of a relationship." Chapter 3, wasn't it? A lot he knew. A shelf full of books—his books—and a nationally recognized reputation as the go-to guy for relationship maintenance and repair, and he couldn't think of one good reason not to worry.

❧ ❧ ❧

A serpent of concern slithered through his abdomen. It bit into the base of his lungs and drained them of air. The closed door whistled a dirge. Ah, something else he'd ignored. The door needed its weather stripping replaced. The winter had been hard on it, too. How fitting that the wind was picking up.

The pocket at his thigh vibrated. He reached for his cell phone and held it to his ear without moving the rest of his body. "Yeah?"

"Josiah, my boy."

Morris. Not now.

"You are going to flip over what I'm about to tell you."

"Morris, it's not the best time." *And I'm already flipping out.*

"For this kind of news, it is. Marketing handed you an award-winning, certain best-seller title for that book of yours."

"The book."

"Yes, the one I expect to see in my inbox by Monday morning."

Josiah removed the phone from his ear. Morris Lynch kept talking, but in a thin, distant voice.

"Are you ready for it? You're going to do cartwheels, it's so perfect."

Cartwheels? I can't remember how to walk. "Morris, can I call you back?"

"Are you sitting down, buddy? Picture this. Face out on the shelves wherever books are sold, as they say. Your book—*Love Him or Leave Him*."

❧ ❧ ❧

"I don't know what to do," Josiah told Sandi, his hands digging deep into her thick butterscotch tresses. *How dumb is that? Magna cum laude—and yes, Dad, that's a real thing—and I'm not sure what to do.*

Sandi leaned into his touch. Silent comfort. Her warm breath exhaled in short puffs of sympathy.

Foul breath. What had she been eating? Road kill?

"Get away from me, dog!"

Sandi scooted back a few feet, then dropped onto the rug in front of the cold fireplace. She'd get over the rejection. In minutes, maybe. A little harder for humans.

Karin was wrong about one thing: watching ESPN with the sound muted was not "just as good." But the sports commentator's voices grated on his raw nerve endings. One voice could change that. Hers.

I'm home. You wouldn't believe the traffic!

But traffic wasn't an issue in Wisconsin's version of Mayberry. And this far out of Paxton, the most pressing traffic issue this time of year was—

Interesting timing. A salt truck barreled past, sending Sandi to the window—more nose prints—and rattling the house's brittle bones. The sleet must have decided to stay. *Karin, you should be home.*

The furnace kicked in, growling like a disturbed bear a month from the conclusion of its hibernation. Would this winter never end? He leaned over the side of his recliner to grab the chenille throw from her chair. It smelled like Karin. Her personal blend— warm and soft and fresh. Like the smell of a sun-dried pillowcase.

Josiah rubbed his stubbled face and tamped the anger that fought for dominance against what had morphed from concern to worry to fear. Why wasn't anybody answering the phone? Had he missed a church deal? What night was it? Saturday. He opened the church app and scanned for activities that might have involved Karin and the Frambolts. Nothing. Empty.

Like the house.

He surrendered to fear, let it have its say. When Karin finally came to her senses and realized she should have let him know she'd be late, they couldn't afford a U-Haul of his anger trailing them into a healing future.

That sounded like a line from his last book. It probably was. Josiah threw the chenille over his feet. *Nothing like being nipped by your own words.*

Love Him or Leave Him. Better than the other five title ideas Josiah had presented. Catchy. Intriguing. But tonight it left an unpleasant aftertaste.

He called Karin's cell three more times. Left messages in decreasing length and increasing intensity. The last one—*Call me!*—stung his own ears when it reverberated off the empty walls of his hollow house. Should he get in the car and go look for her? Wherever she'd gone, it couldn't be good. The salt truck made a return trip.

He should call the police. Yeah. And admit the relationship counselor didn't remember where his wife said she was going. He had a reputation to uphold.

If he found her sipping a cappuccino at an Internet café as if he didn't exist, hadn't been waiting for her to come home...

No. That wasn't Karin. The closest she came to raising her voice at him was usually related to his not trusting her to be strong enough to take care of herself, make her own decisions, run her own business. She hadn't raised her voice in a long time. She'd perfected the silent treatment, though. And—God help him—he'd ignored it, grateful he didn't have to adjust his writing schedule so they could talk it out.

He yanked the remote off the end table at his elbow and clicked off the TV, righting his recliner as the dot of green light faded. Discarding the throw, he slid out of the chair and onto his knees. Not enough. Not low enough. He lay flat on the carpeting, arms spread eagle.

The carpet smelled a lot like Sandi, but he stayed there, groaning a semblance of prayer.

He'd paid to upload a worship song ringtone. Now when it broke the flow of his prayer, he considered volunteering an additional fee for the message of hope its welcome sound conveyed.

He rose to his knees and fumbled for the phone. His frenzied fingers dropped it, twice. It skated out of reach on its slick plastic back. Heart pounding, palms sweating, he dropped to all fours and reached under the couch where the music was coming from.

"Yes? Hello?"

"Is this the Chamberlain residence?"

"Yes, it is. Who is this?"

"Are you related in some way to Karin Chamberlain?"

"She's my wife." The simple words ripped through him. "Who is this?"

"I'm with the Timber County Sheriff's Department. Your wife?"

"That's right. What's this about?"

"Well, sir, we're sorting things out little by little. Your wife and another person were involved in a motor vehicle accident. The car is registered to your wife. We found this number on an unsent text. From the driver's phone."

Every muscle in him spasmed. "Is my wife all right?"

"Are you able to get yourself to Woodlands Regional Hospital?"

"Yes, of course." He headed for the kitchen where his keys hung on a peg near the back door.

"We'd send a deputy to accompany you, but with the roads such a mess, we're spread pretty thin on accident detail."

"Accompany me?" That only happened when—"She's gone?"

"No, sir. But it doesn't look good. I'd advise you to make your way there as soon as you can, but take extra care. It's nasty out there."

Chapter 3

Grace outdistances you. It runs ahead to meet you
at the intersection of your next need.
~ Seedlings & Sentiments
from the "Time of Need" collection

Quarter to eleven. It had taken him an hour and a half to make the thirty-five miles. All of it maneuvered hunched over the steering wheel, peering out at the slick night, fighting to keep the white line in sight. Woodlands? Why hadn't the ambulance taken her to Paxton's medical center? Sure it was small, understaffed, with limited hours of operation. Could that have been the reason? One of many unanswered questions. Like, who was driving Karin's car? It was Karin's car, the deputy said. But she was a passenger? Why?

The hospital parking lot, with a glaze of ice over the parked cars and security lights, looked as eerie as a Hitchcock film. He guessed where the lines of demarcation defined parking spaces. His foot slipped as he stepped out of his Camry. The lot was worse off than the highway.

Sliding the last few feet into the emergency room entrance, his breath heavy and inefficient, Josiah bit back a fist of fear. He ripped the boiled wool cap off his head and, twisting it in his hands, asked the woman at the "All visitors please check in here" desk where he could find his wife.

A question he'd asked himself all night.

"Please take a seat in one of the green chairs," she said. "I'll let them know you're here."

Was that sadness he read in her eyes? Sympathy? Had she recognized him as the face she'd seen on the back cover of innumerable books? That might explain the added layer of concern. Or did the thick slabs of eye shadow weigh her eyes down at the corners?

Green chairs. Retaining imprints of past sitters. He'd stand, thank you. A bearded guy slumped in one of the chairs in the corner brought Rip Van Winkle to mind. How many years had the man slept stretched out like that—legs crossed at the ankles, arms folded over his chest, hat brim low to shield him from fluorescence—waiting for the answer to *his* emergency room question?

He woke Karin's mom and dad before he left for the hospital. His phone call said little more than, "I don't know anything." A call to Morris could wait until he got some answers.

Josiah smelled coffee. Harsh, aged coffee. Better than nothing. *Complimentary*, the sign said. He took a waxed cup from a tilting stack and poured coffee from a quarter-full glass carafe. The cup warmed his stiff hands. In his hurry to leave the house, he'd forgotten gloves. His Columbia jacket hung open. Expelling breath and emotion through dry lips, he pressed the coffee cup to the frozen tundra around his heart.

What was he supposed to feel? Besides numb. In the whole long trip, he'd mastered one thing: numb.

Josiah made a living off his creative imagination. Tonight it was not his friend. What-ifs stung him like fire ants. Sting, pain, itch.

What if Karin didn't make it? How could he live with himself for not taking her absence more seriously, for not going out to look for her, or calling the authorities right away? He'd been miffed that she hadn't been waiting for him when he finished his project. She'd tried to hint that he'd become self-absorbed. He'd jotted a note to consider a section on the subject for an upcoming seminar.

The deputy said Karin and another person were in the accident. He said *person*, not woman. What did that mean? It was a man? A man was driving her car? That made no more sense than anything else in this muddle.

Karin must have had a flat. The guy—a good Samaritan—stopped to help her and then got behind the wheel to drive her home? No. No, that didn't add up. She ran out of gas and—No. It was her car. With some man other than Josiah behind the wheel. An unsent text message? What? The *person* had been texting and driving? In an ice storm?

Josiah needed answers. Right after he found out that Karin was going to be okay. She'd be okay. She had to.

What was taking so long? The deputy insinuated he'd had to sort through who to call, since the natural assumption would have been that she and the driver were friends. Or related. Involved. Together on purpose. Crazy talk. Maybe the staff was confused. He could clear it up if someone would let him speak.

His mind drafted the imaginary conversation going on somewhere beyond the visitor's desk:

Her husband's here.

Isn't that *her husband? The one she came in with?*

Uh, no. Must be boyfriend.

Ooh. Sticky.

Yup. Now what?

We ask one of them to leave?

Which one?

Flip a coin.

He shook the false assumption dialogue from his head. The first sip of coffee burned the taste buds off the front of his tongue and stripped the lining of his throat. The pain felt good.

The phone again. Worship song he'd once found soothing. He'd have to invest in a different ringtone.

"Josiah?" The female voice on the phone trembled with more than old age's vibrato.

"Mom." He sighed. This must be killing her.

"How's my daughter?"

Josiah flared his nostrils in search of a deep enough breath to support his words. "Still don't know yet."

"Where are you? At the hospital?"

"I got here a few minutes ago. They haven't told me anything." Saying it cemented it.

"What was Karin doing out alone on a night like this?"

Alone. If only. Josiah rubbed the back of his neck. "There'll be time for all that later. Right now, we just need to—"

"Did you say Woodlands Regional, dear?"

"Yes, Mom. But don't you and Dad try to make it tonight. The roads are slick as a hockey rink."

"No, I know we can't come tonight. They've closed the interstate, we heard. We're so grateful you made it." The woman's voice disappeared into the abyss of distress with which Josiah was already familiar.

"Josiah, you'll call us when you hear something? Anything?"

"Of course. Don't worry." Fat chance. "Maybe I'll have her call you herself when they let me in to see her."

In the silence, Josiah heard the sound of Karin's mom's courage wrestling with fright. He pictured her bent in half over the phone. "I pray it's that simple."

Oh, this is so much more complicated than you'd ever imagine. "Try to get some rest."

"You know better than that."

Josiah allowed himself a faux chuckle. "Yes, I certainly do. Love you."

"Love you, too, dear. Give my daughter a kiss when you see her."

❧ ❧ ❧

A kiss? What would Josiah see in Karin's eyes if he tried? The idea lay crosswise in his throat, a fish bone of uncertainty. Too many unanswered questions.

The second hand on the emergency room wall clock ticked in spasms. The minute and hour hands seemed not to move at all. Twenty-four hour days. Double dark forty-eight hour nights. The math didn't work, but the truth of an unmoving clock overrides math.

Josiah cocked his head from side to side, stretching the tight cords in his neck. He leaned forward and rested his forearms on his knees. His hands hung useless. Some protector he turned out to be.

Words. He'd focused his life on teasing words into sentences, sentences into paragraphs. While he did, had another man whispered something in Karin's ear? Something she believed? Josiah wasn't a jealous man, or suspicious, but that one word choice—*person*—had sent him somewhere he'd never been. Not a good place.

"Mr. Chamberlain?"

Josiah bolted to his feet and faced the source of the voice. "Yes, that's me."

"I'm Lane Stephens." The gaunt man tugged at the v-neck of his shadow-blue scrubs. The fabric at that spot bore a permanent crease, as if Dr. Stephens often pinched his scrub top when about to dispense bad news. "Sorry to keep you waiting."

Josiah's response dug its claws into the muscles around his vocal cords and refused to move.

"Mr. Chamberlain, your wife sustained serious injuries in the accident. We've addressed the most life-threatening as best we can for the time being. I'll need you to sign this consent. She's not stable but we really have no choice. She's on her way to surgery now. We have to get the bleeding in her brain under control or—"

26

No. No, no, no, no—Josiah took the tablet and stared at the digital electronic consent form's swimming words.

"—there will be even less hope than there is now. I'm sorry. I wish I could have brought you more encouraging news."

A cloud of overworked deodorant followed Dr. Stephens down the hall. The man was sweating. Not a good sign.

What had he said after "Wish I could have brought you more encouraging news"? Did he tell Josiah to wait somewhere else? Was he supposed to follow? No. He said surgery. How soon? How long? How did a thing like this happen?

Horror-movie fog started at the top of his head and crept downward, engulfing every cell in its path. He stood where the doctor had left him, one more stone pillar around which the emergency room traffic flowed as if it had no eye for architectural detail. He heard sounds. But like all pillars worth their salt, he was not fazed by them.

His inattention or some other unnamed sin pushed Karin into the path of an oncoming car. Correction. Oncoming tree.

Somewhere behind a door or curtain Josiah's broken wife awaited rescue. And he couldn't do a thing to save her.

Broken wife. Broken life.

✤ ✤ ✤

"Mr. Chamberlain, I'll show you where to wait."

A spot of warmth on his shoulder. A woman's hand.

"I'll show you where you can wait for your wife while she's in surgery. You may want to take time now though to get something to eat. Would you like me to direct you to the cafeteria?"

What meal falls at half past disbelief? "No, thank you. Are you a nurse?" He took in her John Deere–green uniform top stretched over a belly so distended that her navel stood out like a conceited grape. "Can you tell me what happened to her?"

"I'm a unit clerk. You have more questions than we have answers right now. These initial hours are always distressing.

Through here." She slapped the flat, plate-sized disk on the wall and a door opened before them. "Take the elevator to the second floor. Once there, you'll see signs directing you to the surgery waiting room."

He must have hesitated a nanosecond too long. She reached to depress the Up button for him. Then, with a pat on his arm and a standard-issue "Don't worry," she was gone.

He should have asked her name. And thanked her. And said, "You told me where to wait. Now can you tell me how?"

❧ ❧ ❧

The surgery waiting room embraced him coolly, like a cursory hug from an estranged relative. It tried. He had to give it that. Tasteful couches and love seats. Low coffee tables built sturdy to support tired feet and tired magazines. An espresso machine. Nice touch. As if fancy coffee could erase pain better than plain.

Four hours into the wait, Josiah repented of letting all that coffee bean acid slosh around his stomach unaccompanied by real food to neutralize it. He found a vending machine and punched B-12 for the least offensive-looking sandwich. Turkey something on used whole wheat sponges. He remembered removing the cellophane and sticking it in his pocket for lack of a conveniently located wastebasket. He remembered because a faint, bordering-on-noxious onion odor accompanied him like a cloud of bad cologne as he paced. He didn't recall eating the sandwich, but his tongue worked to free a limp sliver of lettuce from between his teeth.

How sad was it that the stark aloneness he felt in the waiting room in the middle of the night appealed more than having to make conversation, even with a friend? He kept trying Leah's number. No response. While Karin fought for her life, Leah and Wade must have gotten away together, somewhere out of the reach of cyber connections. Josiah owed Karin a real vacation, some serious togetherness time.

His friends. Who could he have called at that hour to say, "Hey, buddy. Will you just sit with me here? Don't have to talk. Don't want to talk. Just sit here"? Maybe Nate. Some college friendships last forever, despite distance and the passage of time. And neglect. Josiah's and Nate's paths rarely crossed these days. But Nate was steady, solid as they came. And their history together bridged all gaps in time. *Does he still live in Baltimore? I should know a detail like that.*

He could think of only one person who would crawl out of bed in the middle of the night and drive across the country in this weather just because he needed a companion. Karin. That's what made all the suspicious part of her untold story so ludicrous. So impossible to consider.

His gut ached from stiffening against suspicion.

Near dawn, he slipped his fingers through the slats on the plastic blinds at the street-side window. The room faced east. He waited in the path of a rising sun chasing the night's storm into submission. This close to spring, the glazed-donut crust of ice wouldn't last long. It would soon mutate into puddles and clogged storm sewers. He could be out in that, scraping his windshield, checking his supply of wiper fluid, dodging ankle-deep potholes of icy slush.

Instead, he waited to hear if his wife would survive until the rooster's crow. If she did, would she deny she ever knew him? Would she offer an explanation that made sense out of all this?

He didn't need an explanation. He needed her to be alive.

Wrong. He needed an explanation, too. Something simple. Coincidental. Laughable. Anything but the thought that wormed its way deeper into his core—that she was with someone else on purpose.

About last night, Josiah.

Yes?

That's all the further he dared envision the conversation. Other men had been blindsided. He'd listened to their oblivion and disbelief. Counseled them. Brought them to reality and emotional breaking points so their marriage could start to rebuild. That's not what he and Karin needed. Couldn't be.

The temptation to search the hospital for a loser with a messed up face, maybe a broken leg or something, pressed strong. But Josiah couldn't afford to miss the moment Karin came out of surgery. Getting the driver's story would have to wait.

Okay, Karin. I do need an explanation.

Josiah's imagination argued pointlessly with a woman whose brain was leaking or swelling or whatever brains do when they've been shaken like a maraca.

His stomach churned. His turkey wanted out.

A hospital staff member with *Housekeeping* embroidered on her unisex polo breast pocket pushed a wheeled cart into the surgery waiting alcove. She bent to pick up a scrap of paper and deposited it in the waste receptacle on her cart. Josiah let the window slats rattle back into their resting position and met her at the cart with his sandwich cellophane. The offending odor now gone, his stomach could right itself. Unless the surgeon walking toward him had news to match his graveyard facial expression.

The soles of Josiah's feet itched, as if begging him to run before the surgeon started speaking. Josiah would have shaken his hand, but his palms had gone from bone dry to damp as a Brazilian jungle floor at the sight of the man with news. He crossed his arms and stuck his hands in his armpits. Swayed back and forth. *Yeah, that looks natural.* He stopped swaying and let his hands fall to his sides.

Focus, man. The good doctor's talking.

"Remarkably, we were able to save the child, for now at least."

The woman's thirty-four, Doc. Hardly a child.

"If your wife had been farther along, we might not have been so fortunate. Especially in light of all the pelvic trauma."

"Farther along?"

"The abdominal impact was absorbed by your wife's body, not the baby's."

A tremor shook Josiah's skeleton loose from its moorings. Freight train? Earthquake? "Karin?"

Dr. Whatshisname's plastic smile showed far less energy than it must have taken to produce it. "She's in recovery. I'm sorry I can't let you see her yet. As soon as we have her—"

"I want to know what happened to her." Josiah winced at the taste of bile his inflection produced.

The surgeon tugged at his v-neck and drew in a breath that when expelled smelled of Mentos and sadness. "Her brain injuries are by far our gravest concern." His eyes widened as if horrified at his use of the word *grave*. "In addition to the baby, of course."

Freight train. Definitely a freight train. "There was a child with her?"

"Let's find a place where we can talk in private." The doctor cupped Josiah's elbow and steered him toward an open door that led to the world's smallest conference room. Three chairs of the same ilk as those in the waiting alcove. An end table. A lamp. Not that it shed appreciable light.

The child was not in the car with Karin. It was inside her. Inside her.

And medical science told him it couldn't be his.

Chapter 4

No matter how high your problems mount, remember the One who scales mountains with the same elegance as when He walks on water.

~ Seedlings & Sentiments
from the "Challenges" collection

Severe internal injuries. Brain swelling. Intensive care unit. Critical. Ventilator. Intubation. Next forty-eight hours.

The words came to him in fragments, not complete sentences, though Josiah noted the doctor's lips moving among the dark shards. When the professional lips stopped, Josiah dumped the words accumulating in his own mouth. "I had no idea I'd be so worthless in an emergency."

"Excuse me?"

"You're going to have to repeat everything you just said. I can't process…"

The lips twisted into a much warmer plastic. "Mr. Chamberlain, I assure you I'm prepared to do that. Right now, I have another critical patient to attend to."

Critical.

"One of the ICU nurses will come get you when they have her settled enough to allow you a brief visit. They'll explain our intensive care family visitation policies. A strict ten minutes per hour. I know how much you want to be by her side, know how worried you must have been about both Karin and the baby, but it's important that the staff have the freedom to give her all the attention she needs to battle through these fragile hours."

Battle through this. Attention. *Yes, let's give her attention. Both of them. Don't forget about the baby.*

So, the driver wasn't a good Samaritan. He was—unlike Josiah—a sperm factory. And they were coupled. A couple.

No. Karin would never do that to him. Inconceiva—

Find a different word that doesn't have the word conceive *in it.*

Josiah swallowed a vile thought about a devil-child growing inside Karin, a fetus draining blood and oxygen and life from a woman who needed all of that and more to "battle through this."

She'd been unfaithful to him? Like, *seriously* unfaithful? How was that possible? Mistake. All of this—a mistake. Somehow.

He picked at the tissue he'd snatched from a lonely looking box on the lamp table. *I love her. I love her not. I love her. I love her not.*

A day earlier, not loving hadn't been an option. Now?

Even immutable truths had derailed. If he hadn't been exhausted, maybe it wouldn't feel as if he were watching that freight train plunge from a bridge into the water below, trying to tug it back onto the tracks with a frayed length of string.

❧ ❧ ❧

The room—her ICU room—did nothing to reassure him. Built for service, not aesthetics, it blinked and buzzed and clicked its equipment as if only the things with electrical cords deserved to be there. But a woman lay within the circle of wheezing machines.

If asked to identify the body lying on the bed before him, Josiah would have to say no. *No, that's not my wife.* Karin bought foundation in a color called "Flawless" and lipstick named "Perpetually Pink." Good husband that he was, he'd been with her on the color hunt too many times. Not enough times.

The pseudo person lying on the bed with a distorted, bloated face would—if called to match skin tones—have to tell the cosmetics counter lady she needed foundation and lipstick in "Napa Valley Purple."

But her hospital identification bracelet said her name was indeed Karin Alecia Chamberlain and he was her NOK—next of kin. The nurses hovering like dragonflies called her Karin. Repeatedly. As if she suffered from Alzheimer's.

"Karin, I'm going to check your vitals now."

"Karin, let's see if we can't adjust your pillow a little better."

"Karin, your husband is here."

Josiah half expected that the machine beeping her heartbeat—for all the world to hear—would have registered some reaction to that. *Your husband's here, beep-beep-beepbeepbeepbeep.* Code blue.

Nothing.

The ventilator sounded as if it had asthma. *Wheeze in, two, three, four. Wheeze out, two, three, four.* With a little hitch at the top and bottom of the rotation.

The rhythms. The seamless, flawless, inhuman, rhythmic patterns. No wonder Karin's pulse rate didn't subconsciously register a reaction to him. It wasn't her heartbeat but the machine's. Technology had no trouble remaining steady. *It* hadn't betrayed him.

"Mr. Chamberlain, would you step over here, please?"

Josiah turned his attention to one of an army of nurses in the room.

"You can get closer to her on this side. Fewer machines and stands and cords to tangle your feet."

Closer. That's what husbands do. He stepped farther into the glass-walled room, the cubed bubble. "Where?"

The high-chested Latina indicated a lone twelve-inch square of floor space not occupied by something that truly mattered. He stepped onto the tile as if finding his mark on a stage. "Can I—?"

"Touch her? Certainly. Just be careful not to jostle or startle her, and watch that IV line. She doesn't have the best veins."

Like a drawbridge slowly cranked into position, Josiah reached his hand toward Karin's as it lay unmoving and pale against the white sheet. The hand closest to him. Her left. Her rings were gone. She'd probably flung them out the car window just before the crash.

He slipped his hand under hers as if not wanting to disturb its sleep. With his thumb, he traced the indentation from her missing-in-action wedding ring set. The thin divot wrapped around her fourth finger like a scar, not a memory.

"If you're wondering about her rings," a nurse said, punctuating the public nature of the private moment, "we had to cut them off. Swollen fingers. Someone at the nurses' station can get them for you later. Standard practice. She won't need them here."

Karin insisted the set was perfect when they found it sitting among far more opulent engagement rings in the jewelry store display window at the mall. Perfect. She didn't need anything more than that plus Josiah's undying love, she'd said.

They were young then. What did they know?

When he slipped it on her finger a month later, a week before his graduation from college and her junior finals, she'd breathed that word again, "Perfect." Then she'd insisted on driving the two and a half hours from Madison to her folks' house to show them. Karin's mother spent a disposable camera on pictures of Karin's hand and the two lovebirds locking lips.

Karin's mom and dad. He hadn't called them back. Couldn't right now. What kind of slug would cheat a ten-minute visit by leaving at the eight-minute mark?

The nurse on the other side of the bed pulled back the thin sheet covering Karin's bloated, bruised, and, for all intents and purposes, naked body. A modest woman like Karin would be mortified if she were conscious. Leaning in, the nurse laid a stethoscope below the line of Karin's ribs. Listening for breath sounds? Pneumonia? Josiah knew that much about medicine—that pneumonia is always a risk. The nurse flipped her thick braid over her shoulder with her free hand and moved the stethoscope to a spot a few inches lower than the line of dark bruises arching across Karin's abdomen. Probably from the seatbelt. She repositioned three or four times, then removed the earpieces and held them out to Josiah. "Would you like to hear your baby's heartbeat?"

Three years ago, yes. When we'd been trying. Before we discovered most of my swimmers chose the sink option in sink-or-swim. Yes, I would have liked to hear my *baby's heartbeat. I refuse to listen to* his *child's, the man who stole Karin from me.*

That had to have been it. She wouldn't have left Josiah willingly. Sure, Josiah had been a little disengaged, distant. Okay, maybe Karin's word for it fit: *self-absorbed.* That's no reason to bail on a marriage. Or start a family with someone else.

Josiah palmed the lower half of his face like a seven-footer might palm a basketball. No, the shake of his head begged. *No, please no. I can't listen to that beating heart.*

He couldn't read the message the nurse's eyes communicated. Empathy, most likely. *The poor, traumatized father. Overcome with grief. Afraid that while listening to his son's or daughter's heartbeat, the strange pulsing thumps would stop. Forever. Poor man.*

Let her think that.

A child. Oh, Karin! What have you done? And where is the louse who did it with you? Had he walked away from the accident? The sheriff's department told him nothing. Was the guy in a room down the hall? Josiah leaned his elbows on the bed and propped his forehead on his fingertips.

How was it possible he could hear his blood cells clunking against one another in their rush? They banged against the interior walls of his veins and arteries, played bumper car, leaking oxygen with every collision. If he remembered correctly, breathing was supposed to be involuntary. Somewhere deep in the folds of his brain, the switch had been flipped. *Off. You're on your own, man.* Breathing takes such effort. Too much effort.

"We don't have her complete medical records yet. What were you given as a due date?" the woman's matter-of-fact voice asked.

"I guessed late August. Am I right? Thin thing like your wife, you'd think she'd be showing more. Ultrasound had her measuring at twelve weeks. But there's always leeway there. With my second baby, I measured forty-four weeks by the time that child was born. Forty-four weeks, if you can imagine. I expected my son would make the Guinness Book of World Records. What would you think, fourteen or fifteen pounds? He surprised us all. Eight pounds. Eight pounds! Just goes to show you."

Josiah coughed. And again. "I need a drink of water. Excuse me." The hall—antiseptic and clinical—welcomed him into its conversationless haven. He leaned against the wall outside Karin's glassy cell. A young woman looked up from the center nurses' station around which the ICU rooms circled like sterile covered wagons.

"It never seems enough, does it?" she asked him.

Enough?

"The ten minutes. A measly ten minutes every hour. Have you found the family waiting room yet? Someone left a plate of homemade cinnamon rolls in there. Make sure you try one before they're gone."

There are others like me? Other people with no clue what happened to ordinary life?

Josiah entertained a mental picture of all the king's horsemen on their knees, pawing through rubble, using giant tweezers to pick up pieces of eggshell and attempting to reassemble the bits. With duct tape and superglue.

Some people should not sit on walls. Period.

He told his legs to carry him out the building to his car. Home. Instead he found himself walking through the open door of a room marked Intensive Care Family Waiting. A foreigner, he crossed the border into unknown territory. The familiar scent of cinnamon grounded him, oddly enough, like finding a sign written in English in the heart of Darfur. Or Kosovo. Or some other desolate, ravaged place.

He picked one of several identical plum couches, the one facing the wall clock, and planted himself. Less than fifty minutes and he'd be expected to go back in there again. To sit with Karin Alecia "Gomer" Chamberlain—the Gomer of biblical Hosea and unfaithful Gomer fame—and the thing that grew inside her.

~❧ ~❧ ~❧

The plaintive cry of an unborn child woke him. A child who called him by name.

"Josiah?"

Karin's mother stood over him with her warm, satiny hand on his forearm. "We hate to wake you, dear, but—"

Eyes wider than necessary, Josiah shot upright, sharp slivers of pain tracing the pattern of nerve endings in his neck. "Catherine. Stan. I'm so glad you're here."

It seemed the right thing to say.

His mother-in-law sank onto the couch beside him. Stan stood, jingling change in his pants pocket, the lines in his face contorted into a topographical map Josiah hadn't seen before.

"How were the roads?"

"Good," Stan answered. "Almost clear now."

"Josiah, how is she?" Catherine's words cut through small talk with the efficiency and bloodlessness of a cauterizing scalpel.

He glanced at the clock. He'd slept through his opportunity. And theirs. He'd been asleep an hour and fifteen minutes. What kind of husband gambles away his chance to see his dying wife for the sake of a little sleep?

Dying? The word tasted like paint thinner.

He forced calmness he didn't feel. These people deserved hope. He didn't have any to spare but could fake it in brief spurts. He softened words like *internal injuries* and *critical* and *fragile* as if editing one of his lectures for an ultrasensitive audience. In their eyes, he read their efforts to translate what he said to what he really meant.

"You can see her in a little while. Top of the hour. For ten minutes."

Catherine's eyes glistened. "Will she recognize us?"

"She's not conscious."

For a moment, Josiah hated what his wife had done to her mother. The older woman's frame collapsed on itself, bone turned to limp pasta. He caught her from one side, Stan from the other.

"I'm okay," she insisted, lifting her chin and blinking back tears. "We have to be strong. For Karin."

Yes, let's all rally around the fallen woman. Let's whisper how sorry we are she had to go through all that misery. Married to Josiah Chamberlain. What a horrible tragedy. Good thing she found an escape route.

❧ ❧ ❧

No one had asked the "What happened?" question more often than Josiah. He owed it to these innocent parents to listen while they wondered aloud.

"I don't understand why they wouldn't have taken her to Paxton, Josiah." Stan hung his coat and Catherine's in a narrow locker designated for the purpose. "Perfectly good hospital there, isn't it?"

"For its size." Josiah moved a coffee table out of the way so his in-laws could navigate to the couch.

"Then . . . ?"

Catherine patted her husband's arm in a gesture Josiah had seen many times over the years. Correcting or calming, it always came across as loving. "Stan, we're asking the wrong person. I'm sure Josiah was as surprised as we were that the ambulance brought her here. Right?"

About that and a few dozen other things about your daughter. "Right. We'll get answers eventually. Right now the primary concern is—" His wife's name caught—unvoiced—in his throat.

"No sense worrying about that, I guess," Stan said. "The choice of hospitals, I mean. I found it curious, though. Maybe had something to do with insurance."

He'd heard of that before. Ambulances taking a longer route to the hospital with which it had a contract.

Would Karin rally enough to explain any of the curiosities? Josiah had written a family crisis manual that not only made the best-seller list but had become a staple at airport bookstores and bookstands. At the moment, he couldn't remember any of its sterling points.

Something, something, something, you'll get through this.

And readers bought that? Could his life's work be as meaningless as it sounded in an ICU family waiting room?

Chapter 5

Sometimes all hope needs is a little oxygen.

~ Seedlings & Sentiments
from the "Hope" collection

Karin's parents hadn't let him surrender his top-of-the-hour slot, despite his having snoozed through the last one. So he stood at her lifeless side. No change. No movement. Not even an eye twitch or a grimace. Josiah didn't want to know how they had surgically relieved the pressure building in her brain. The bulky bandage on the right half of her head gave a hint.

Seismologists in San Francisco could have measured the shift in his heart. Confusion and anger gave way to the breakdown he'd resisted for hours. He muffled his sobs with first one hand then the other, shudders racing through his body, unearthly moans rising and receding only to return stronger than the last wave. What if she didn't make it? How was he supposed to go on? She's the only woman he'd ever loved like that. Seeing her so utterly shattered erased all the questions. Nothing mattered. Nothing except keeping her alive.

Karin's battle lay in the physical realm. Josiah stared at the floor tiles at his feet as if he'd stepped onto a battleground full of mental and emotional landmines. One wrong step—

"Water?"

Blurred eyes saw a Styrofoam cup of ice water near his hands. He murmured his thanks and drank a sip before looking up. One of the nurses he'd seen before in the room. Her distinct Latin heritage made her memorable. "Thank you. And I apologize for that"—he gestured with one hand—"that scene."

She smiled. "Mr. Chamberlain, you call that a scene? This is a place where that would be considered not only normal, expected, but pretty healthy. And just so you know, it probably won't be your last." She handed him a cool, wet washcloth. "This might help. Or not. But it can't hurt."

He used the cloth to soothe his swollen eyes. No all-nighter for a tight deadline had done this kind of number on his eyes. Or the ligaments in his throat. Or the bands across his gut.

"You timed that well," the nurse said as she pushed a button to stop an alarm on one of the IV pumps. "I hate to be sticky about the ten minute rule, but—"

Josiah stood from the chair he hadn't remembered finding. "No. I understand."

"If you're nervous about finding a spot to kiss her, you can kiss her hand. Some people think that doesn't register in a patient's brain in cases like this. I disagree."

Nothing in the raw, lifeless shell that he once knew as his wife, knew intimately he thought, gave any clue that it would make a difference. But he bent over her, lifted her untethered hand, and pressed his lips lightly onto her too-cool skin. "See you later, hon."

He should say more. Something more. The one who wrestled with words for a living—and usually won—had none.

⟳

A spot of warm. And I'm so cold. So cold. Bring it back. Please.
Bring that kiss of warmth back. Comfortable. No.

He slid his cell phone from his pocket. Who could he call to check on Sandi? Sure, he was headed home, but in the time it took him to drive there, she could get pretty miserable. Or relieved. He had no heart to clean up after her.

What time was it? Most of their friends were at church, singing their hearts out, nodding and amening. Let them. He'd have to call someone not in church. How many heathens did he know? Only Morris. Doubtful he'd hop a plane to do a favor for his favorite client.

A lit sign marked Exit called to him.

Exit. Good idea.

"How is she?"

"What? Oh, Leah. What are you doing here?" Everything was off axis. He hadn't told anyone about the accident except Karin's parents and that quick voice mail to Morris. How did Leah find out? "I'm sorry." It might work in the movies, but shaking his head did nothing to clear his thoughts. "She's in intensive care. Hey, thanks for coming, but only family can visit. I'll let you know when she's well enough to—"

"You pompous—!" Leah freed one hand from the load she carried and punched Josiah's shoulder so hard he stumbled backward.

Was she insane? "Get a grip, Leah. My wife's fighting for her life!"

"My husband lost his. And it's Karin's fault. Or yours." She blinked back tears and fought to stop the quiver in her chin.

"What are you saying? Wade's dead?"

"You're as naive as you are pompous, Josiah. Who do you think was driving your wife's car?" Her words sounded more difficult to squeeze out than the last smear of toothpaste. "With an unsent text on his phone. 'Josiah, I'm taking Karin—' And her suitcase in the backseat."

"You're not making any sense. Where would they have been going?" Josiah caught sight of a hospital security officer approaching from behind Leah and lowered his voice. "Leah, I'm so sorry for your loss. But I don't understand what Karin—"

"You tell *me* where they were headed. He wasn't taking her home." Her anger seemed spent. It faded as disbelief and grief swallowed them both.

Josiah lifted his chin toward the security officer and put his arm around Leah. She didn't resist. The officer halted his approach and stepped to the desk but didn't stop watching. "This is such a mess," Josiah said, gesturing toward a conversation area not far from the exit that had seemed so appealing moments earlier. "I can't make sense of any of it. What do you mean that Wade wasn't bringing Karin home?"

She pulled back, a look of incredulity in her red-rimmed eyes. "You really don't know anything?"

"No one's talked to me except Karin's surgeon."

"Privacy Act." She sniffed and lowered herself into one of the chairs, her grip on the bundle in her arms as tight as ever.

Josiah reached for her bundle, intent on putting it in the third chair in the grouping. She clung to it, eyes pinched shut. Oh. Wade's belongings. Josiah was an idiot on so many levels he'd lost count. "Wade wasn't bringing Karin home? How do you know—?"

"The accident happened on Route 80. Six miles from here."

Not possible. "Why would they be heading this way?" But that would explain why the ambulance chose Woodlands. His thoughts stuttered as badly as the words he tried to spit out. Did Leah know more? Did she know about Karin's child? Karin and Wade's—? No. Impossible. Josiah wasn't going to be the one to tell Leah that her man was a slimeball. The woman had just lost her husband. Had Karin ever talked about Wade with anything more than friendship? What had he missed?

"Airport." She sighed into the plastic wrapped bundle. "It's the only thing I can think of. He wasn't taking her shopping at the mall, that's for sure." The sarcasm hung like stale smoke from a thousand cheap cigars.

"They were getting on a flight?"

"Not *them*, Josiah." She looked at him as if he'd lost all of his senses, not just the few he knew about. "Karin was leaving. I don't know how she talked Wade into taking her or why he wouldn't have let me know. I don't know why Karin didn't tell me she'd finally had enough."

"Enough?"

"Of you!"

The word-fists landed harder than her physical punch. She was delirious. Wracked with grief. Shock, maybe. Or completely delusional. They'd both been betrayed.

He wasn't alone in this. Was he?

Chapter 6

Grief doesn't know how to tell time.

~ Seedlings & Sentiments
from the "Grief" collection

*I*n less than twenty-four hours, he'd gone from elation to disappointment to concern to anger to fear to—betrayed. Everything except elation still churned inside, rising and abating like toxic, oil-slick tides.

Leah's husband, Wade, was driving the car? That made even less sense than the wild scenarios Josiah had concocted in the surgery waiting room. Leah's frame of mind couldn't be faulted, even if her reasoning was. She lost her husband. What a nightmare! But she of all people should know Karin wasn't capable of what poisoned Josiah's mind, what Leah insinuated. The two women worked together almost every day. Karin couldn't have been leaving Josiah. *One suitcase and unsubstantiated evidence do not add up to an affair.*

Wade always made Seedlings & Sentiments his last stop of the day, even on Saturdays, Leah said. Nothing suspicious there. Leah had showed Josiah Karin's note. "You don't deserve the mess I'm leaving you."

Josiah slapped his palm on the steering wheel. The overanalysis gene he'd inherited from his mom usually served him well, career-wise. Not now. Not in this shadowed labyrinth.

Morris waited for a phone call. And Josiah should call Karin's friends from church. If he tapped the domino named Janelle, the news of Karin's accident would tumble—tap, tap, tap—to the entire community. The whole world would know, and it would require only the one call. They didn't have to know the details that kept Josiah in a ping-pong match of concern versus anger.

Josiah mindlessly maneuvered the stretch of highway as if a steel rudder on the underside of his car were locked into a groove in the pavement. Inattentive driving? To say the least.

He punched the dash-mounted button for voice-activated dialing. "Call Morris." Blessed technology. As he waited for Morris to pick up, he designed and deleted three versions of how to tell his agent what happened.

Voice mail. Again. "You've reached Morris Lynch's machine. I'm not available right now. I'm golfing, gulping, or groveling. Leave a—Well, you know the routine."

Morris, you're a better agent than you are an author. Leave the writing to me, huh?

"I'll make this quick, Morris. Karin's been in an accident. It's pretty serious. I won't be available much for the next"—how long? how many days?—"for a while. I'll keep you updated as able. I'll take the laptop with me to the hospital and send you the manuscript from there."

A twinge shot across his collarbone. Disloyalty had nothing to do with his thinking about the book. He had responsibilities. Once it was sent off, he could focus a hundred percent on the crisis at hand.

He should jot that down. *Clear the Decks—Your Key to Crisis Management.*

The highway spit random remnants of melted ice as he committed the phrase to memory and contemplated what qualified as a "must do" once he got home. Pack an overnight bag.

Grab the laptop. See if the Wilson boy would mind feeding Sandi and letting her out a couple of times a day. Before and after school and once more before bedtime ought to do it. The kid might appreciate a chance to earn a few bucks.

Somebody'd better pray. Janelle would call the prayer chain thing from church. Right now Josiah couldn't think what came after the part about "Oh, Lord God."

Another chapter for another book. *Pray Like You Mean It.*

The car knew to turn right onto Peach Avenue. Then left on Hillcrest. The house never looked colder. Had it aged overnight? Had he? Josiah pulled into the garage, turned off the engine, and listened to the off-tune hum of the automatic garage door as it closed behind him.

Sandi's ADHD registered through the house's closed door. He thought golden retrievers were supposed to mellow by this age.

Josiah opened the car door and was startled to realize he'd neglected to fasten his seatbelt. And that somewhere in the trip, the seatbelt warning had stopped jangling without his noticing. Dumb. Dumbdumbdumb. *Karin, you didn't really intend to leave me, did you?*

I need my brain back if I'm going to survive this. Focus.

Beyond formality, Sandi shot past Josiah when he opened the door from garage to kitchen. The dog bolted through the doggie flap on the people door on the back wall of the garage. Freedom. It must feel good.

Sandi's stainless steel water and food dishes sparkled as if she'd run them through the doggie tongue dishwasher. He refilled both, in his mind writing notes of apology to man's best friend.

The answering machine boasted it had captured three messages. He fast-forwarded through two hang-ups then landed on a singsong message.

"Kaaarrriiin. Trudy, here. Where are you? We were counting on you to do nursery duty today, rememberrr? Don't worry. I grabbed one of the moms out of the worship service and drafted her to take over for you. If you're going to be out of town, you need to call and let someone knooow. Next time, 'kay? You're such a good one to call on since you don't have any kids. I mean, no offense."

Oh, I assure you, none taken, Trudy. Have you considered a job as a diplomat?

"But we have to know you'll be there when you say you will, Karin. Oh, you're forgiven, of course. Just give me a buzz and let me know when we can reschedule you. I have to get back to the service. My twins are playing the offertory today. Sorry you had to miss it."

Josiah formed a sizzling retort, but let it go and deleted all messages.

No kids? Slight misconception, Trudy. Mis-conception of the highest order.

How much did Leah really know about the "mess" Karin left her? Friends confided things like pregnancy, didn't they? Who was he kidding? Leah was married to the man whom Karin apparently found more appealing than Josiah. Leah must have lost her confidante status along the way.

A surge of sympathy washed through him for the other object of betrayal in this disaster. If that's what it was. It was a muddle no matter what. But if Karin—

A mind is a terrible thing to give counsel, Josiah remembered telling an audience in Houston. They'd laughed—oh, that felt good—then sobered as they caught onto not only the play on words from a long-ago college commercial but also the implication for the erratic thoughts that fuel the mind during a relationship crisis.

He needed patience. A raft of other explanations for the unanswered would float to the surface just as soon as Karin was talking again.

As Josiah walked through the house looking for Sandi puddles, he dialed another of Karin's friends. Voice mail. He might consider a lawsuit against the guy who invented voice mail.

Like a good girl, Janelle had turned off her cell phone during worship, no doubt. She'll probably forget to turn it back on.

Josiah left no message.

And Sandi left no puddles. Bless her. *Good dog.*

He grabbed the duffle bag he used for racquetball from the foyer closet. Just the right size for a couple days' worth of necessities. He dumped the racquet, hermetically sealed canisters of balls, and other paraphernalia onto the floor of the closet, knowing he'd pay a price if Karin found the pile before he had a chance to put them where they really belonged.

What were the odds she'd ever set foot in the house again? If she healed up, she was gone, apparently. If she didn't . . .

Low on logic, he stuffed a few clothing items and toiletries into the duffle without calculating their true usefulness, remembering his shaving kit at the last moment. On those rare occasions when he chose not to shave, Karin called him McScruffy. Shaving? Absolute necessity.

He unhooked and slipped his laptop and power cord into his wheeled laptop case. Then he began the search—admittedly halfhearted—for the kinds of things Karin might appreciate if she woke up. When.

He caught a whiff of something. Himself. He needed that shower. Leaving the half-packed bags on the floor near the door of their bedroom, he fought through the cloud of chaotic thoughts to the master bath. Any other day, a shower was a five-minute blip on the radar screen of his schedule. Today it was an Everest climb.

As the force of the water scraped off the top layer of his skin, he leaned into its scalding power. Eyes closed, palms braced against the smooth tile, he wept for the horror his life had become. And for his well-practiced stupidity. How had he not seen it coming?

The accident, no one could predict. But Karin's leaving him? What clues had he missed? He taught seminars on how to watch for clues.

Even his ability to process a thought slipped away, circled the drain, then plunged out of sight. He turned off the water, grabbed a towel from the rack, and buried his face in it. Josiah rubbed hard but couldn't erase the picture of Karin's broken body on the sterile hospital bed. Or the imaginary picture of a sweet-talk-spitting Wade bent over her, kissing lips that were now bloated and purple. Leah and Wade had been to their house for cookouts, the holidays. The four of them had considered vacationing together sometime. Josiah had almost agreed to it. Something about Leah got on his nerves.

Ironic. It's Wade he should have been worried about.

Josiah's natural instinct for revenge had nowhere to go. Wade hadn't made it through the accident. And Karin had come within a hair's breadth of that. It's where she still hovered—a thin hair away from not being here anymore.

The towel now tucked around his hips, he leaned on the sink and reached for his hair gel. Fog on the bathroom mirror reminded him he needed to take a look at the vent fan one of these days. The list of his neglects accordion-folded at his feet.

Clean clothes felt and smelled bracing and fortified his courage. Self-pity smelled rank. For the moment, he chose courage and determination. They'd get through this. Ironing out the wrinkles—however permanent they seemed—could come later. Sounded like logic for once.

Healing topped the list of priorities.

What an idiot he was! Karin begged him to let her opt for the Cadillac version of health care when they changed insurance providers. All Josiah could think about at the time was preferring a sky-high deductible rather than a hefty premium every month when they were obviously two strong, healthy adults with no major medical issues. And no children.

He won that battle. Lost the war.

He'd have to dig out their policy. Even if it contained a catastrophic need provision, it wouldn't pay off the mortgage.

The bed felt anything but welcoming when he sat on its edge to put on his socks and shoes. Tired as he was, he couldn't imagine lying there. Alone. Ever.

Do something. He had to do something. He'd call the Wilson kid. Todd. No, Tad. Twenty dollars a day. That seemed fair. If they didn't need Tad for long. Josiah didn't intend to foot the bill for the boy's college expenses. A few days. Maximum. By then Karin would be home, recuperating, apologetic, and eager to start their new life together. Sure, it would add to Josiah's stress level to haul ibuprofen and hot packs to Karin, care for the dog, and keep up with his writing deadlines. But it would be a good test of his theories on caregiving.

Who was he kidding? He pressed three fingers to each temple. She walked away from their marriage. She was never coming home.

Can I go home now? Take me home! How can you not hear me screaming?

Josiah's duffle had filled quickly with amenities he might need at the hospital. He'd traveled enough to have the list of essentials memorized. He rechecked the bag. Toothbrush and toothpaste. Hair gel. Disposable razor—smarter and lighter than his whole shaving kit, which he opted to leave at home. Deodorant. A change of clothes. Cell phone charger. Laptop. Earbuds.

He stood in the vacant bedroom, scanning for what he might have missed. Karin. He'd missed Karin. Somehow he'd missed signals that her irritation with him had slid into something far more dangerous. But none of that computed with the woman who'd been at his side for twelve years. Nobody would believe Karin Chamberlain would betray a telemarketer, much less her husband. She was the faithful, loving, uncomplaining, understanding wife other husbands envied.

And there it was.

Wade. The wife Wade not only envied but found a way to lure away from where she belonged.

Before Josiah's career took off, they'd golfed together a few times. Played on the same summer softball league. Wade was a decent pitcher. Not stellar, but decent. They'd worked together on a community project or two. Years ago. Before the worldwide community started clamoring for more of Josiah's time.

Josiah majored in confidence. On the surface. Wade had always seemed content.

Someday he'd have to sit down and think about why that would be an issue that nagged at Josiah when they were together. Right now, he needed to get the neighbor kid on the phone and Sandi back in the house.

And get that mental picture out of his mind—his wife and Wade intertwined.

The phone rang before he could find Tad's number on his contacts list.

"Mr. Chamberlain? This is Deputy Tuttle again. We spoke last night."

"Yes. I hoped we'd get a chance to talk. I have some questions for you."

"The accident is still under investigation. But I'll share the few details I know. Can you come to the sheriff's office during business hours tomorrow?"

Heat crept up the back of his neck. "My wife's still hospitalized, so I need to be with her."

"Oh. I'm grateful."

Grateful?

"I don't think any of us expected her to survive."

The heat turned instantly freezer-burn cold.

"Well, she did. So far." What do you say to someone who's surprised your wife is alive?

"If you'd prefer, I can meet you at the hospital to answer some of your questions tomorrow. Right now I need to let you know where your wife's car has been taken. We've finished that aspect of the investigation. It's routine to investigate even single-vehicle accidents with fatalities. I don't think there's any question that the car's totaled. You've called your insurance company, I assume."

Josiah bit the inside of his lower lip.

"Mr. Chamberlain?"

"No. I haven't taken care of that yet."

"You can give your agent my number for the report he'll need."

Why would Morris want to talk to—Oh. *Insurance* agent. Sleep deprivation and having your emotional guts ripped out made rational thought impossible, apparently. "Thanks."

"And you'll want to retrieve anything salvageable from the vehicle before long. Contents of the glove box. Your wife's suitcase."

Another gut punch.

Josiah lifted the front edge of his long-sleeved tee shirt, surprised he saw no bruises.

Chapter 7

Winter's tenacity has an expiration date. Hold onto that truth
when its biting winds seem to hold spring hostage.

~Seedlings & Sentiments
from the "Encouragement" collection

Sandi? Come here, girl."

Where was that old towel Karin used when Sandi's feet were muddy? With the yard in such rough shape, those paws would be caked after this length of time outside.

"Sandi! Food!" A surefire result-getter.

Josiah propped open the door to the backyard and scanned for a furry but happy animal. Nothing.

"Sandi, get your rear end in here!" He whistled like a junior high boy at a girl's volleyball game. Where was she? Come on. He did not need this. Not today.

Stupid, stupid phone. He yanked it out of his pocket, his eyes glued on the farthest corners of their half-acre lot, anticipating a tongue-flapping, tail-wagging reunion any second now. "Yes? What?"

"Josiah, do you have anger ish-ee-ooos?" Janelle asked.

"Oh, Janelle. You got my message."

"You didn't leave one. But I recognized your number. Hey, where were you guys this morning? We missed you in Sunday school. The Larsons tore up the class with their report on the 'In Love Forever' seminar they attended in the cities. You would have laughed your socks off at the ridiculous advice they were given. A hot tub filled with champagne? Those so-called marriage experts could have used a few lessons from you, Josiah."

She continued to talk. Josiah gulped back man tears.

"Janelle, I have to interrupt. Karin's in the hospital."

"What? Oh, no! After all she's been through?"

All she's been through? What did that mean? "She was in an accident last night."

"No! What happened? The roads were awful. They closed the interstate for a while."

"I know."

"How is she? Can I see her? What does she need?"

"Janelle, she's in intensive care."

"Intensive care? How bad is it?"

Josiah turned his back on the empty yard where Sandi should be and walked back toward the kitchen. "It's not good. I don't know much yet."

"What are the doctors saying?"

"When she came out of surgery, they said—"

Janelle's sharp intake of breath was loud enough for him to hear through the phone. "Surgery?"

"To relieve pressure in her brain." His throat was closing off again.

"I can't believe this. I just saw her yesterday morning. I stopped at Seedlings & Sentiments to pick up my order."

Josiah forced himself to ask, "Did you know about…about him?"

"It's a him? I thought it was too early to tell for sure."

"What?"

"I know technology has come a long way, even since my Megan was born."

She was talking about the baby. "So, you know about the child?"

"That's okay with you, isn't it? I mean, I know Karin wanted to keep everything quiet for a while."

Understatement.

"But, I mean, it was obvious she was pregnant. How could I not ask her?"

Obvious.

"Josiah?"

He reined in a stampede of thoughts. "What?"

"Is the baby okay?"

Was it okay a baby was involved? No. Was it acceptable that Karin's pummeled body would have that to cope with, too? Okay that his wife—his *wife*—would be a mother but he wouldn't be a father?

He cleared his throat. "So far, the baby's fine."

"Thank the Lord for that. Where are you now? At the hospital?"

"I'm home. Getting a few things."

"Ah. Karin's satin pillowcase. She hates regular ones. Me? I prefer Egyptian cotton."

Josiah headed for the bedroom to grab the satin pillowcase. He should have thought of it earlier.

"How are you holding up, Josiah? How are you feeling?"

Truthfully? Like a prisoner of war robbed of every trace of normalcy, every smidgen of joy. "I'm doing all right. Tired."

"I'll get the prayer team mobilized."

"Thanks. That means a lot."

"When do you think I can see her? Should I wait a day or two?"

Or six. Or a dozen. "I don't know, Janelle. I really don't know at this point. I'll stay in touch."

"Please do. Wow, what a mixture of joy and sadness, huh? The baby, but now this?"

She thinks the baby's mine, or she wouldn't say that. Karin didn't tell her friend everything. "About the child, Janelle."

"I understand. Keep it quiet for a while. You let me know when you and Karin have had a chance to talk about the right moment to share your news."

"Yeah. I'll do that."

She hesitated longer than her normal millisecond before filling the blank space with more words. "I'm so grieved over this."

"Me, too." *Deeper than you know.*

"You're heading back to the hospital then?"

"Yep. Woodlands. Did I mention that? As soon as I find Sandi. She bolted on me." *Seems to be a habit among my womenfolk.*

"Woodlands? Okay. Please know we're going to pray Karin through this."

"Thanks. I'm counting on it."

He ended the call before Janelle could invent something more to say. Where did he leave his coat? Time to locate that fool dog.

ಆ ಆ ಆ

If you'd told him a week earlier that both his wife and his dog would leave him—sounded like a sappy country-and-western ballad—he would have blasted both ideas out of the water. Faithful as the day is long, both of them.

Shows how much he knew. Perceptive. His counseling clients used the word *perceptive* to describe him. Boy, did he have them snowed.

Josiah knew he was rough around the edges. He hadn't known he was rough around his core. Deep inside breathed a monster that considered abandoning his wife's bedside to search for his dog.

The pain in his brain over driving away from the house without locating Sandi ran a ridiculously close second to the sensation he felt when he didn't find Karin waiting for him in the kitchen.

He'd made the tough calls to let the neighbors know he was looking for his dog and, oh, by the way, his wife was in the hospital. Sympathy on all fronts. Yes, they'd keep an eye out for Sandi. Did he need anything? Anything they could do?

Anyone know the name of a good lawyer?

He wrapped the vile thought in an imaginary paper towel and threw it in the garbage can.

Driving past the impound where Karin's car lay in state probably wasn't the smartest idea in his current string of dumb ideas. The sight crumpled him with creases deeper than those in the mangled steel. Her car looked like a public service announcement for not texting and driving. The driver's side took the hardest hit. Despite what Wade had done to steal Karin's heart, no one deserved to be pancaked like that. Josiah's stomach cramped as he stared, hands gripping the cold wire fencing that kept him from getting closer without permission. He didn't have to search for someone to blame. Wade had volunteered. Probably driving too fast for conditions. Or in the process of trying to text Josiah. But why? Wade wasn't the gloating kind on the golf course. Josiah couldn't see him gloating over this. Probably driving too fast.

But that didn't make any more sense than the rest of it. The man single-handedly ran a six-day-a-week delivery service. He'd logged more miles on the road in bad weather conditions than most. How could he have lost control?

Josiah pushed away from the fence. *The same way Wade lost control of his morals, it appeared. The same way he took his hands off of his marriage vows with Leah so he could convince Karin there was something better for her than Josiah. That's how.*

Leah. Josiah waited, bracing himself now against the roof of his completely intact vehicle while he said a prayer for the woman who'd lost her husband. Had she driven past this mangled steel? What must Leah be going through?

In professional mode, he would have called and offered to talk her through the early stages of loss. But Leah's friend and coworker Karin had apparently attempted to run off with her husband. And at the moment *Josiah* and *professional* didn't belong in the same sentence. Who does a marriage counselor call when his own marriage is in shambles?

No one. He couldn't let his father be right about him, that Josiah *created* shambles, not fixed them. That Josiah didn't measure up as a son worthy of respect, despite his accomplishments. That Josiah was an embarrassment as a man.

He couldn't let his father be right.

☙ ☙ ☙

Another of Karin's sins. She'd made Josiah paranoid. As he crawled his way back through the entrance of Woodlands Hospital, tugging a wheeled duffle behind him, he dodged the glances of visitors and medical personnel alike. When had he ever been afraid to look someone in the eye? Did that person know the Chamberlains' story? How many knew who he was? Did hospital gossip create its own version of why his wife lay broken and pregnant? The radio news reported the fatality and the fact that another injured party remained in critical condition. "No names released until family members are notified." That must mean Leah hadn't gotten to the end of her need-to-know call list.

Hey, Aunt Sally. Yeah, good to hear your voice, too. Just wanted to give you a quick call to let you know that Wade is deader than dead. We'll send word around when we know details about the funeral. Oh, and can you bring your hot potato salad for the meal after? It's always a hit at family gatherings. Love to Uncle Ross. Talk to you later.

Everything about this reeked. It stunk that Leah had to make calls like that—although no doubt with a lot more grace than Josiah's brain could muster. It reeked that when word got out about Karin's full story, Josiah's career might not survive.

He pushed the Up arrow on the elevator. Twelve times. "Jerk!"

"The elevator? It's slow sometimes, but…" A woman carrying a rack of lab specimens skirted around him and aimed for the stairwell.

Not the elevator. Me. I'm the jerk. My first thought wasn't Karin. Or that innocent baby. Babies in the womb don't ask to be put there.

The little thing was fighting to survive. It didn't deserve his resentment. Its father was somewhere between the morgue and the funeral home. Its mother lay unresponsive, unable to sustain her own breathing, much less its well-being. Someone was going to have to care about that baby. If it survived.

A shudder thundered through him. Had the little one felt the impact of the accident? It had to, didn't it?

The elevator doors opened for him. Its emptiness swallowed him whole. He couldn't afford the posture externally, but on the inside, he leaned against the wall, slid to the floor, and buried his face in his hands.

A mid-pitched *ding* announced his floor, although he couldn't remember having pressed the button. Look what Karin had done to him! He'd turned judgmental and skeptical and resentful and miserable. With one decision, she'd succeeded in changing his personality. The woman stepped around ants on the sidewalk and insisted he find a "humane" way to rid their basement of mice. How had she kept her ruthless nature hidden, the side of her that could rip a guy's heart out and rearrange his personality?

Josiah leaned one shoulder against the tiled wall of the corridor. *God, help me. I hate who I am. I hate what she's done. I hate what it will do to Catherine and Stan when they find out the truth about their daughter.*

As if summoned by the prayer, Stan approached from farther down the corridor. Josiah collected himself from the corners to which the pieces of his life had scattered.

"Any new word?" he asked as Stan drew near enough for conversation.

"No. Same. Did you get any rest?"

"I showered. Took care of a few things. Sandi's gone."

Stan's face registered an additional concern. "What? Where'd she go?"

Bad Josiah prepared to tell Stan what a stupid question that was. If he knew where she'd gone, he'd have found her. Good Josiah showed up and replied, "She took off when I let her out. No telling where. I alerted the neighbors."

"Oh, son, that's all you need."

Karin's father had already mastered the art of caring about others when his heart was breaking. How did he do that?

"Where's Catherine?"

Stan nodded toward the ICU beyond the double doors. "She's in with Karin. I have to pace myself. It's so hard to see her that way." His words dissolved into tears. The muscles in his jaw clenched and unclenched as if his python throat worked to swallow an antelope of grief.

Abandoning his duffle, Josiah closed the narrow gap between them and embraced his father-in-law. "It's going to be okay. She'll pull through this." Lies. All lies. He had no guarantees. And her survival, much as they all prayed for it, would introduce a whole new garbage pail of unpleasantries.

The men broke their embrace when an overhead speaker paged a code blue to ICU. That didn't sound good. Karin? How many other patients occupied ICU cells? Why hadn't he noticed before?

Stan rubbed his hands on the sides of his thighs. "We should be getting—"

"Right. Getting back." Josiah reclaimed his duffle and laptop case and followed Stan through the double doors. The halls had seemed colorless, lifeless in the middle of the night. By the light of day and distanced from the adrenaline overload of the previous hours, they boasted artwork and classy lighting. *Yeah, let's pretend this is a gallery.*

"Nice, huh?"

"What, Stan?"

"The art. Kind of nice to see something beautiful in a place where not much else is. Look at that one. Peaceful, isn't it?"

Josiah took in the gradient greens of the mountain meadow scene. Wildflowers. A stream so alive with reflective light he could almost hear the water bubble as it leapfrogged over the rocks in its way.

The sun, unseen but effective, must have been straight overhead in the artist's imagination. No shadows.

Surreal.

Josiah tore his gaze away from the scene to his reality. A few more feet and they'd cross into the family waiting room, the command post from which he would not command anything. He'd watch to see whether his life and marriage would live or die.

−❧ ❧ ❧−

Catherine had aged another ten years by the time her ten minutes of visitation expired. She worked up a wan smile as she greeted Stan and Josiah, but the slant of her shoulders and the way she fiddled with the hem of her jacket revealed it as counterfeit. Good intentioned, but false.

Stan rose from the couch he'd chosen as his favorite. "How is she?"

"Oh," Catherine said, "I think she has a little more color."

Is that the best she could do? Josiah envisioned Karin's previously flawless skin with an improved "warmer" shade of ghostly blue. "Has the doctor been in?"

"Not while I was there. Nurses in and out. They don't say much about her condition. I didn't realize until now how *small* small talk is." She lowered herself into a chair then popped up. "Josiah, did you eat? We should get you something to eat."

"Mama Catherine, you're too much. I should be asking that of you."

"We had a little something while you were gone."

Did they think he'd been gone too long? The look on her face didn't offer a hint of that. "Was Sandi happy to see you?"

With true vigor, Stan shook his head from side to side, lips pressed together, brows scrunched.

After that many years of marriage, it was no wonder Catherine picked up on his less-than-subtle signal. But something got lost in translation. Catherine slapped her hand over her heart. "Oh, dear. Did she make a mess?"

No. Your daughter did.

How vigorously would Stan shake his head once the truth came out?

Chapter 8

Take hope where you can find it. Hope isn't stingy.
But it is only visible to those who appreciate its presence.

~ Seedlings & Sentiments
from the "Hope" collection

*S*o pale. Karin's skin was now the color of sun-bleached bones. *More color, Catherine? Where?* Josiah smoothed the excessively laundered hospital gown over Karin's shoulder. Her body twitched.

He jerked back and sought out the attending nurse. Their eyes met. Hers registered nothing out of the ordinary. But she'd obviously noticed the movement. Why didn't she seem excited?

"That's a good sign, isn't it?"

"Mr. Chamberlain, your wife is experiencing involuntary muscle contractions."

"But isn't that a sign of—"

"Not necessarily." She smiled that pitiful oh-the-poor-man smile that gagged him. "I wish I could tell you differently. There's been little change. She's a three on the Glasgow Coma Scale."

"Three out of ten?"

"Three out of fifteen. There are three categories with numbered levels. The total score comes from her level in each category: stimuli, ability to communicate, and ability to move—intentionally."

"So, zero is the lowest in each of those categories?"

She looked away briefly. "One."

Three categories. Three ones. Three can't-get-any-worse scores. *Oh, Karin.*

"But, the curiosity is that her eyes are sometimes open. That's more indicative of DBT—deep brain trauma—than true, full-blown coma. Some rating systems—"

Josiah stared at the now motionless spot on his wife's shoulder. *Move, Karin. Do it again. Prove this Florence Nightingale wrong.*

"—use a little different scale to determine brain function."

Angie, was it? He waited until she addressed the IV pump and its annoying alarm then glanced at her identification badge.

"For instance, the Ranchos Los Amigos Scale," she said, "uses an eight-level system based on awareness, ability to think, behavior signals, and the way the patient interacts with his or her environment." She smiled. "And that probably sounds as if I just finished my final exam in neuropsychology, doesn't it?"

"A little bit."

"I know it's a lot to absorb right now. It's important. But it's not important for you to know today, at this stage."

She probably meant well with her smile, but it seemed completely inappropriate in that setting. "So, Angie, you nurses work pretty long hours, don't you?" Lame. But it qualified as conversation.

"The hospital's a little understaffed at the moment. Oh, don't worry. We have your wife's needs well-covered. But yes, it does require that we work extra-long shifts."

Her rubberized clogs squeaked with each step as she continued fussing with equipment and moving between the bed and the wheeled stand with its chest-high computer. Logging everything she did to his wife, Josiah assumed. Making sure the billing department knew about every needle, every change of sheets, every alcohol wipe.

"I don't mind." Her voice floated to him.

"What?"

She stopped, fingers hovering over the keyboard, and said, "I don't mind the extra hours. My husband and I are saving as much as we can before our baby comes. We're going to try to live on one income."

She's pregnant. He hadn't noticed. More than a little pregnant, in fact. What was with this place? Every bloomin' woman cradled a baby in her belly.

Including Karin.

You had to find someone else who could make that happen for you, huh, Karin? His eyes traced the line of her body under the thin sheet. The hollows on either side of her neck, the gentle rise of her breasts. He didn't recognize them. They looked fuller than he remembered. And the small mound where her empty womb should be.

Josiah cupped his hand over the mound. It just fit the curve of his palm. He rested his hand there, breathing, imagining, aching to change things so the little life could be his.

Karin, you've robbed me. I can't even ask you what I did that was so wrong, besides failing to make you a mother. When did you decide I wasn't worth forgiving for that?

He felt warmth growing under his palm, as if the life were responding to his touch. The baby probably would fit into his hand with hand to spare.

God, protect this child.

No more words came. He lifted his hand from the mound. His palm tingled. Stung. The room shook as Karin screamed.

⌒

Josiah? What are you doing? Why are you here? Why won't you talk to me? Need to talk. Need to—

⌒

He couldn't read too much into Karin's involuntary muscle movements. Involuntary screams. It wasn't a reaction to his touch.

Or his prayer. She wasn't demon-possessed. Just unfaithful. And broken.

Deep inside, on a level beyond recognition, her body railed against the pain, the nurse explained. A positive sign, in a way, she said.

Josiah cried the tears Karin couldn't. He understood soul-deep pain. His own screams died in his throat as he watched her writhe and thrash. Instinctively, he laid his torso over her flailing arms and convulsing chest while Angie tethered her lower extremities and called for help.

He heard a crack and prayed it was his watch crystal or the housing on one of the pieces of equipment, not yet another fragile bone. Karin wrenched, he countered, his weight holding her to the bed for her own good. Her own good.

Within one of those minutes that bloats into distended oblivion, a boost of medication drove Karin deeper into unconsciousness. Theirs. The one they shared.

Crisis averted, Josiah stumbled out of the room. His visiting time expired mid-writhe. He would have fought against leaving the room at all—ever—but the air in there rivaled Kilimanjaro for thinness and lack of oxygen. He felt his way out of the intensive care unit, down the hall, and toward the family waiting room. The door to the visitor restroom stood open. He slipped inside, locked it, and created his own scream. Muffled. Throat-burning. Scalp-tingling.

He leaned over the porcelain sink, his head unhinged at the neck. Unblinking, he reached to flip the chrome paddle faucet handle to the On position and waited while a stream of cold water grew colder. Then he cupped both hands, filled them with glacial runoff, and shocked his face back to reality. Out there in the plum-couched room, Catherine and Stan waited for his report.

It was time to let them know about the baby.

❧ ❧ ❧

Something was wrong. More than the obvious. Conscious of an irritant but disengaged as one might slap at a fly without reaching for the flyswatter, Josiah flicked the irritation away from his thoughts and took the last few strides toward the waiting room.

"Sharp dresser." Stan's eyes glinted with the mischief few knew lay hidden beneath his composed demeanor. "New fad in Paris? Milan? New York fashion district?"

What was Stan talking about? Josiah took a step closer to where his father-in-law sat at Catherine's side on an appropriately named love seat. He traced the path of Stan's gaze to the black long-sleeved tee shirt he'd pulled on after his shower. Backwards. And inside out. The label not only showed, it showed under his chin. And he hadn't even noticed in the restroom mirror.

"Leave the boy alone, Stanley." Catherine's smile radiated sympathy. "Just because you don't want to advertise what size *you* wear..." She jostled her husband with her elbow, then grabbed her arm as if she'd clunked her funny bone.

He let the two play, poking at each other with such good humor that a lump formed in Josiah's throat. He and Karin used to have interchanges like that—teasing but not really. Finding the comic side of their humanness. How many lifetimes ago?

Comedy and tragedy share office space, he reasoned. Either one might serve as receptionist and pick up the phone when it rings.

At the moment, his home-away-from-home ICU family waiting room served as the stage for the comic tragedy of the scene he could no longer avoid. Stan and Catherine didn't have to know about Wade. Not yet. But it wasn't fair to withhold the small matter of the child Karin carried.

How could he describe this child—the one he wanted but didn't? How does a person begin a story like that? The miracle of life conceived in betrayal? He begged for grace to construct a sentence he wouldn't trip over. *Ease into it, Josiah.*

"Karin's pregnant." *Yeah. Ease into it. Just like that.*

Catherine blanched and grabbed the neckline of her blouse with both fists. Stan clamped a hand onto her knee.

Say something, one of you. My words are gone. Catherine, come on. Stan?

"Oh, son. How...how wonderful." Stan's words sounded strained. Big surprise. "After thinking it wasn't possible. We'd given up hope of—" Whatever came next caught in the man's wrinkled neck.

Stan directed his attention to his speechless wife, as if urging a wise response from the one who normally oozed wisdom. Josiah joined him.

Catherine grimaced, rubbing her jaw on the left side. She obviously could only think of the additional threat to her daughter's broken body, not the wonder of a grandchild they thought they'd never have. Tears collected in the corners of her eyes and escaped down the folds of her face when she squeezed her eyes shut. Poor thing.

Stan turned his grip on her knee into loving pats. Pat-pat-pat, "No matter what, it's wonderful, isn't it, Catherine? Honey?"

Whatever else was happening in the room lost all importance when Catherine collapsed against the love seat's fat armrest. Out cold.

❧ ❧ ❧

Stan took the news of Karin's baby better than Josiah expected, his deepened concern for his daughter tempered by pride at the pending title—*Grandpa*.

Catherine, on the other hand, had a heart attack. Complete with chest pain, jaw pain, and an out-of-the-norm "code blue to the ICU family waiting room."

It wasn't funny at all. Not one bit. The sounds coming from Josiah weren't laughter. They claimed origins in the emotional word *hysteria*, not the amusing *hysterical*.

Nice one, God. What's next? Don't answer that.

Welcome to the Woodlands Regional Circus. The place should consider changing its logo and offer popcorn and soft drinks between acts.

Hours of chaos and two stents later, Catherine settled into a room in the cardiac wing, her pain under control for the time being, the rest of her medical protocol yet to be determined.

On the positive side, visiting Catherine on the third floor would make the waiting time between ICU visits more productive and focused.

Poor Stan. Stan, the Man. Strong as a barn timber externally but a pile of kittens on the inside. And Catherine stayed married to him for how many years to this point? Maybe the timber-kitty principle needed exploring by a marriage workshop expert. One who wrote books that changed lives. Books like the one Josiah still hadn't submitted to his agent. Morris would be on his case. The guy had a capacity for sympathy that would drown in the shadow of a kidney bean.

Assured that Catherine now rested comfortably, awaiting the cardiologist who would decide the next course of action for her, Josiah excused himself from her room and made his way through the maze of corridors to a quiet sitting area away from the flow of foot traffic. He slipped his laptop case strap off his shoulder and set up the computer on the low coffee table in front of the love seat. Within moments, he moved instead to one of the chairs closer to an outlet.

Free wireless access. Nice perk for the hospital to offer. Perk? Like anything about this place was a gift.

He checked his e-mail inbox first. Anything urgent? Reader mail—equivalent to writer food. Tempted as he was, he had to let it go for now.

A note from Nate. The distance between Josiah and his friend—half a continent—mattered. Now more than ever.

Ah, good friend. I've neglected you, too. Have to rectify a few things once we know where all this is headed.

True to form, Nate kept his message short. Never one to waste words—as opposed, said Nate, to Josiah's indiscriminate flinging them onto paper—or to waste an opportunity to create a chuckle, Nate had written:

"The church I grew up in was so conservative, we couldn't even raise our hands on a roller coaster! (I just made that up.)"

Clever. Pack your bags, Nate. You can audition for a comedy channel show with that one.

Josiah stared at the laptop screen. It didn't blink or beep or register respiration and heart rate. It didn't flash an alarm for a sudden drop in blood pressure or a spiked fever. Words on a blank background. His territory. A medium he understood.

So conservative. Roller coaster. Funny.

Two of the most important women in his life—other than his mother, God rest her weary soul—lay in separate corners of the building, fighting to breathe, hanging ten over eternity. And Josiah sat entranced by a lame, homemade joke.

He rested against the back of the chair. Retreating from the edge of insanity, he inched closer to the scarier option—reality. With a skeleton-rattling sigh, he leaned forward and starred Nate's post. He'd reply later, when he could think. When he'd formed a way to express the story of how his life had spun apart over the weekend—

No. He couldn't wait until the ability to think returned. He penned an e-mail to Nate that left out any detail that would make his friend drop everything and book a flight.

Before the last vestiges of energy drained from him, he composed a concise e-mail to Morris with a one-sentence, nonspecific update about Karin, attached his manuscript now dubbed *Love Him or Leave Him*, and hit Send.

His watchband pinched. To be more precise, time pinched. He shut down the laptop and stored it in its case.

His message to his agent might have held the last words he'd ever write.

Chapter 9

Some storms pass and leave the earth refreshed. Others leave
devastation in their path. Either way, you will go on.

~ Seedlings & Sentiments
from the "Life's Storms" collection

With his face pressed tight against a plate glass window at the end of the hospital corridor, Josiah gazed out at the parking lot and a world that had forgotten the storm fury of the weekend. If only he could. He let the coolness of the window iron out the lines on his forehead and closed his eyes against the pain that was at once foreign and familiar. It hadn't taken long for despair to become his "new normal."

He hated the cliché. He specialized in writing them. But this one—new normal—made his skin crawl. Which was also a cliché. Josiah could find few words that didn't seem like enemies. Dangerous for a man who made his living with them.

What if Wade had lived? What if Josiah's competition had suffered little more than a broken leg and bruised ribs? Discharged already. Recuperating at home with his devoted wife. Had Wade known about the baby? Could that have been why they were in the car together that night, resigned to finding a way to *take care of the matter* so their secret sin could stay secret?

Karin would never—would *never*—!

It was both a blessing and a curse that Josiah couldn't have a face-off with the man. Half the answers he needed died with Wade. But he also didn't have to walk the streets or golf course of Paxton wondering when their paths would cross.

Josiah pounded his temples with his fists. Leah's husband died in that accident! And Josiah felt relief? Relief! Was there a way he could wash his mind out with soap?

The man clearing his throat behind him turned out to be Dr. Stephens, sweaty from who knows what procedure. Stephens stumbled around the words, "Josiah, if you need to talk about anything..."

What was the good doctor going to do? Hug him? *Please, no.*

"If you need to talk, we have an excellent psychologist on staff."

I'm a psychologist, for Pete's sake. I paid attention in school, and believe me, Doc, this precise situation did not come up in class.

"Thank you," Josiah managed, "but I'm doing fine. My faith sustains me."

What? He hadn't planned to say that. Hadn't planned to feel it. Wondered if it were true.

Is it faithlessness to find prayer too exhausting to attempt? Is it offensive to the Almighty if Josiah felt nothing soothing, no *Presence.* He heard no low, molasses-like, James Earl Jones voice assuring him, "Lo, I am with you always."

Not that he'd been listening for it.

Proactive. He needed to be proactive. Josiah excused himself, reached for his cell phone, and punched a memory sequence. He'd get this over quickly. "Morris, I've wanted to connect with you. I sent the manuscript. But there's more we need to talk about. Give me a ring when you—"

"Josiah!"

He'd picked up. The one time Josiah hoped he could skate by with a voice-mail message.

"Talk to me. How's Karin? How are you? How soon can you get me the proposal for your next book?"

An electric twinge shot through the vein that skirted the hollow of his temple. He hadn't a clear answer to any of those questions. "Karin's hanging in there. I'm okay." The word scraped his tongue on the way out. "About the next book. Morris, I—"

"I can't imagine what you're going through. Tough string of luck, huh? It's not that I'm not sympathetic to your crisis, but the wave of your career is cresting, Josiah. Did I tell you I'm working on a deal to get you a guest appearance on Dr. Phil?"

"He's read my books?"

"One of his producers did. Saved her marriage, she said. Which, when you think about it, creates quite the story, doesn't it? She works for Dr. Phil, but *your* book was her saving grace. Cracks me up." Morris snorted and swallowed, ice clinking in a glass.

Josiah's thoughts scattered like beads of mercury. His attempts to rein them into some coherent focus forced them into chaos. Books, saving grace, Dr. Phil, television, career, wife, never writing again. Prozac.

"I need time." His exhale lasted too long and threatened to suffocate him if he couldn't convince his lungs that breathing would be worth it in the end. What's the opposite of sleep apnea? Awake apnea? "I have to have time to sort out what's happening here."

"At the hospital? You'll know something soon, won't you? Either way?"

Josiah's free hand formed a fist.

"I wish I could cut you some slack, but we're up against the wall here. Changes in the industry necessitate our being ahead of the game, Josiah, not apologizing for delays."

Mr. Warmth's approach sickened him. As if he hadn't been thinking the same thing.

"Morris, have I ever asked for an extension?"

His agent paused. Paused? How could he even wonder? Or have to think about it? Josiah was the consummate client. Prompt. Thorough. Incredibly easy to get along with, he'd been told.

"Strike while the printing press is hot, my boy. While the market's enamored with your marriage drivel."

The sharp intake of breath was his own, right? "Morris. Drivel?"

His agent's chuckle died too soon. "Oh, you know I'd never make fun of the client who's helping me save for beachfront property in Nicaragua."

"It's not about the money, Morris."

"Well, of course not. But then again, it is." Ice in the glass clinked again. "You and your code of honor. Honestly, Josiah, the day will come when you realize honor is overrated. It might net you a shiny badge, but it doesn't pay the bills. You're a phenomenon. But phenoms bear expiration dates. You don't want to finally find time to write and then discover the world's moved on to a new fad that doesn't include your brand of feel-good, can't-we-all-just-get-along writing. Harsh truth. You know the industry. More fickle than a woman with four lovers and a hundred pairs of shoes."

Yellow Pages. Literary agents. But Josiah wouldn't begin his search with the ones whose last names start with A. Everyone does that. He'd start in the middle of the list. The N's. His only requisite? An agent with heart.

What was that sound? Morris belching? How fitting.

"Josiah, listen. Forget I said all that. It's the businessman in me talking."

The evil-hearted, sulfur-snorting businessman?

"You need my support, not my cattle prod."

Amen.

"Tell you what. I'll go to the publisher and tell him it will be at least two weeks before he sees that next idea of yours. Multi-book contracts mean you don't have the luxury of breathing between projects, Josiah. You know that. Be grateful your publisher is enamored with your writing. He signed you before he knew what you'd hand him."

Josiah clenched the phone so tightly that he nudged the tiny volume button to full blast. "Two weeks?"

"Just a simple proposal. That's all I'm asking. Don't you have a bunch of time when you're waiting? Wouldn't it feel great to use the time productively?"

Josiah sensed the river of his stomach acid overflowing its banks, running like a green liquid surge to flood his internal organs.

"I'll do the groveling, Josiah. You do the praying."

Was it Nate who'd warned him that an agent who didn't share his beliefs would challenge him? Karin had ignited his faith. Nate threw gasoline on it. *Those were the days*. Who would have thought Morris, the belching agnostic, would lean on the power of prayer when Josiah couldn't?

Hadn't Josiah's beliefs stood him in good stead to this point? Oh, sure. "Before God and these witnesses" he'd vowed to love, honor, and cherish a woman who betrayed him but now needed him more than ever.

She did, didn't she? Need him?

What a ridiculous thought! Talk about a helpless hero. Superman without the power to fly. The Not-So-Incredible Hulk. Captain Didn't-Have-a-Clue. His father would have come up with a host of anti-hero labels that fit.

Which was more pathetic—that Josiah's mean-spirited, demeaning, make-everyone-miserable, high-school dropout father excelled at shaming his only son, or that Josiah let him? Small-minded men have to make others feel smaller. The smallest of all let them.

Morris rattled on about marketing plans and contract negotiations. Or so Josiah gathered from the snippets he heard that didn't sound like the wah-wah-wah drone of the off-screen teacher in Charlie Brown television specials.

When Morris put him on hold for another call, Josiah's thoughts wandered to a piece of reader mail he'd once dismissed—a woman six months into an eternity of grief over the loss of her husband to a wild strain of prostate cancer. She objected to Josiah's the-sun-will-come-out-tomorrow counsel about finding true love again.

True love. Josiah turned away from the window to face the hall that would lead him back to his wife's room at the top of the hour. *Karin, the operative word is true. What happened to the true part of true love?*

❧ ❧ ❧

Ten minutes every hour. Ten minutes to touch her hand and read the map of Karin's colorless face, the contours of her body, the rhythm of her breathing. Such a beautiful woman, even now. Heartbreakingly beautiful.

But the bruises, now yellowing even after these few days, revealed nothing of the condition of her heart or its angle—leaning toward him or away from him and toward a guy who lay stiller than still. Josiah cringed. When the tree loomed too close to avoid, who was on her mind? Had she been conscious after impact? What did she see or hear? Did she know—somewhere beyond consciousness—that Wade didn't make it?

Josiah fought the urge to let his eyes drift to the place where that man's child grew. He lost the battle.

The child had little hope of being born healthy. Maybe none. The doctors hadn't said so straight out, but Josiah was no dummy. Correction. He was no dummy on most issues. Between the trauma of the accident and the massive doses of medications Karin received around the clock, what chance did it have?

Josiah leaned his forearms on the coarse weave of the hospital-issue blanket draped over his wife. He loosely laced his fingers together. More pondering than praying. From his position in the chair beside her bed, he had a bird's-eye view of the baby bump. The kind Angelina Jolie's publicist would deny for months then, *Surprise!*

He supposed it had been easy for Karin to hide the small bump in the winter. Sweaters. Flannel nightgown. Book deadline. Brain-dead husband.

Brain-dead. Must delete that expression from my vocabulary.

A nurse asked him to slide back for a moment so she could check Karin's urine output from the collection bag hanging off the bed rail. The frown on the woman's—Angie's—face quickly morphed into a noncommittal expression, but the concern did not escape Josiah's attention. Sure, *now* he was observant.

Angie recorded her findings as Josiah scooted his chair back into vigil position.

"Did you see the ultrasound of your baby, Mr. Chamberlain?" She stepped to the rolling cart off to one side of the room and retrieved a piece of photo paper. "Beautiful child."

What now? Refuse to look? Spill the whole sordid story to someone who thought she was doing him a favor?

Like forcing his arm through cement drying too quickly, Josiah reached for the image.

As his eyes adjusted to the strange shapes and shadows in the picture, he recognized the bones of a tiny hand, splayed as if waving to him. The curve of a miniature spine. A disproportionately large head. Josiah touched his fingertip to the waving hand.

A tightness spread across his chest—a taut drum skin on which his pulse danced.

So that's what it felt like to be a father.

The cardiac wing offered a vast difference of sensory experiences compared to the pale, colorless, blinking but relatively odorless ICU. As he walked the corridor approach to Catherine's private room—321—Josiah noted the not entirely pleasant aroma of lunch trays. He guessed Salisbury steak, canned peas, and lime Jell-O with pineapple chunks. The cafeteria special of the day. The smell might not have been so bad—except for the unnaturally gray-green canned peas—had it not mixed with the antiseptic, alcohol, and oh-there's-a-bedpan-that-needs-attention odors on that floor.

The intensive care unit seemed stone-cold sober compared to the cardiac wing. Peopled with visitors and chatty medical personnel and flush with flower arrangements and Get Well Soon balloons—ah, that explained the difference in color. No flowers or balloons were allowed in ICU. Despite its unique version of life-and-death, this unit held more life. Cardiac patients lay in wait for healing. ICU patients? Not necessarily.

Stan greeted him with a wave from where he leaned against the window ledge in Catherine's room.

"How's she doing, Dad?"

"You can ask me. I'm not helpless." Catherine adjusted her bleached sheet closer to her chin, smiling as if proud of herself for having the strength.

He could get the full story from his mother-in-law. She was indeed far from helpless. Karin could tell him nothing. Not how she felt, where it hurt, what happened, or why she'd left him. What he wouldn't have given to walk into his wife's room and hear her chide Josiah for asking the nurse instead of her directly.

Stan said, "Now, Catherine. Don't get testy on us."

"I'm not an invalid, Stanley." She raised her arms and locked her fingers together behind her head as if to say, "See? Relaxed. All is well."

"Any news yet? How soon before they'll let you go home?"

Stan stepped to Catherine's side. "Did you know they have four doctors on her case already? The cardiologist who admitted her isn't the same one who did the angiogram, and now they're consulting yet another doctor who does pacemakers and things like that."

Josiah reasoned the more doctors involved, the more serious the case. *Please, Lord, not Catherine, too.*

"That's three."

"Oh, there's another one in there somewhere," Catherine said. "That foreign one. What was he, Stanley?"

A nurse in startlingly bright scrubs and blaze-orange rubberized clogs flew into the room. "Catherine! Arms down, please. Your heart rhythm is all over the place." She pulled down the neck of Catherine's hospital gown and checked the upper leads stuck to her patient's chest.

"So sorry. I don't have the rules down pat yet. Oh, where are my manners? Diane, this is my son-in-law, Josiah Chamberlain."

The nurse nodded his direction. "Pleased to meet you. Josiah Chamberlain, the writer?"

Not anymore. "I've written a few books."

"Your wife is—" She stopped herself, as if weighing sympathy versus a HIPAA violation.

"Here, too." So many possible endings to that sentence. *My wife is…disappointed in me. My wife is unfaithful. My wife is a betrayer. My wife is dying. She's broken. She's pregnant.*

"I'm so sorry." Diane touched Catherine's arm, now lying obediently at her side. "We'll get this one fixed up and back to you soon."

A hospital this size and the whole staff knew about the shattered woman in ICU and her semi-famous husband? He supposed that meant he had to stifle the screams that still clawed at him, begging to have their say. Bad publicity.

He turned to face the window Stan had vacated, ashamed again of who he'd become. Catherine's room was on the opposite side of the rectangular hospital building, so the view held a landscaped lawn rather than a concrete parking lot. Within a few weeks, it would blossom with spring color. The lawn would be lush and green—that deep, intoxicating, Midwest-jungle green residents spent most of their summer cursing from the seat of their riding mowers and tourists from the all-tan-all-the-time Southwest found so refreshing.

Perspective. It changed everything.

Where would Karin be when summer arrived? home? recuperating? sitting on the deck in white shorts and a clingy maternity top?

Or is that a sight Josiah would not be privy to?

The hand on Josiah's arm drew him back into the conversation. Stan's look asked the constant question: *Josiah, are you okay?* The answer was always the same: *No. How could I be?*

When the nurse exited, Stan asked Catherine's permission to be the storyteller regarding the pacemaker yet to come.

Catherine closed her eyes. "Go ahead."

"Once she's recuperated a little bit more, they're going to take my beloved back into surgery to install a pacemaker just under the skin on her chest. About here." He pointed. "It'll help make sure her heart doesn't go too long without beating on its own."

Josiah's face must have registered something Stan found unsettling. He was quick to add, "I know a lot of people with pacemakers, and they're doing just fine."

"Stan, he's heard of pacemakers before." Catherine's sweet spirit held a sharp edge that sounded awkward on her—barbed wire on velour. That would pass in time, wouldn't it? Catherine was an older version of Karin. Sweet spirit was their calling card.

Stan finished his storytelling with phrases like, "As soon as the surgery schedule allows. Maybe as soon as tomorrow." "Medication changes." "Monitor the stents' success." "More testing." "Cardiac rehab."

Whatever else his father-in-law said bounced off Josiah's eardrums. The voice he heard was his own, internally, chanting, *Out. Get out. Have to get out of here.*

After Catherine injected an artificially cheery half-joke about her body going "high tech," Josiah excused himself on pretense of needing a restroom break. He'd be back, he promised, after his next ICU visit.

In the hall outside Catherine's room it occurred to him that he hadn't said his visit *with Karin.* Or even *to* Karin. He said "his next ICU visit." Had he distanced himself that much from her? No. She's the one who walked away.

He merely slid.

Chapter 10

True friends don't shrink away when you
open the locked cupboards of your heart.

~ Seedlings & Sentiments
from the "Friendship" collection

$\mathcal{A}$ day and a night and another day and everything remained the same. Always the same. When it wasn't worse. Catherine's pacemaker installation had gone well. Her energy loss seemed only half physical. For all Josiah's internal World Wrestling Federation matches, for all his emotional bruising, numbness marked most of the waiting time. He missed Stan and Catherine's companionship when Karin had been the only one in trouble. Karin and her child.

"What are you in for?" A woman Josiah had seen before hunched over the game table in the family waiting room. She waited for his response.

Josiah had managed to avoid connecting with any of the other family-in-waiting people. "Hey, are you done with that magazine?" and "Coffee's fresh" served as his conversation depth finders. Now the late-fiftyish woman in a blue polyester jogging suit and well-worn Nikes wanted to punch holes in his barricade.

"Excuse me?"

"What are you in for? That sounds like one prisoner asking another, doesn't it?" she said, gray eyes sparkling. She closed the book of crossword puzzles on the table in front of her and focused her full attention on Josiah.

"My wife," he answered. Would that suffice? "Car accident."

"My son. About your age. Snowmobile accident. Hit a semi. He's been here three months."

Oh, Lord God. What this woman must have been through! And that poor young man. "I'm so sorry. How's he doing now?" *Chamberlain, you're an idiot. The boy's in intensive care. How do you suppose he's doing?*

"Better."

A gracious woman.

"There's talk of transferring him to a long-term facility if he can kick this latest setback."

Latest?

She leaned forward, toward him. "I'm not sure how I feel about that."

Was she kidding? To be discharged from this place? Wasn't that the goal? "I don't understand, ma'am."

"Nancy. Nancy Drew, and I know. My name always draws that expression on people's faces."

"Josiah. Josiah Chamberlain."

"My maiden name was Johnson. Nobody found that curious. Nice to meet you, Josiah."

"I'm sorry, I don't understand why you wouldn't be excited about your son leaving intensive care."

She leaned back, her gaze now fixed on a spot beyond where Josiah sat. "It's so final. While he's here, there's always hope he'll improve. Slim hope, maybe. But hope is hope. Can't survive without it. For my son, sending him to long-term care means he's come back as far as medical science can bring him."

Josiah felt something. Pain for someone else. He cared. There was hope for him yet.

"Is your son . . . ?"

"Blaine."

"Is Blaine conscious?"

"Off and on. He's so agitated when he's conscious that he's kept sedated for his sake and ours."

"My wife—Karin—has DTB, among other things."

"DBT," she corrected. "Deep Brain Trauma."

"You said 'for his sake and ours.' You and your husband?"

Nancy pressed her lips together. She fiddled with the bent corners of the crossword puzzle book. "No, the staff. My husband..." Her words faded like a cell phone conversation passing through a dead zone. "Chris finds this place depressing. Too depressing to push through and be here for his son."

The guileless smile and sigh that punctuated her sentence told Josiah she'd accepted the situation. She didn't like it but accepted it. Could she teach him that trick?

"Is your wife improving?" she asked, still fiddling with the book.

By what standard? "Too little progress to measure so far. She's alive. That's something." It was, wasn't it?

Thunder rumbled through the room. Its epicenter sat in his stomach.

Nancy laughed. Twenty-plus years more mature than his, her face turned into a starburst of tiny lines when she laughed. She stood, still chuckling, and reached out a hand like a teacher might to a reticent student. "Come with me, young man."

Against all reason, he stood and followed as she aimed for the waiting room door. "Where are we going?"

She spoke over her shoulder, "To get you something to eat. It's time you learned a few survival techniques."

"Like eating?"

She stopped her athlete pace, turned, and planted her hands on her hips. "Your last real meal was...?"

A flush of warmth crept from his neck to his forehead. "What day is it?"

Nancy lifted her chin. "As I thought. The hospital census is full enough, Joe."

He opened his mouth to correct her but couldn't think why.

"We don't want you occupying a bed needed for someone with a genuine problem."

A genuine problem? If you only knew. Josiah mimicked her hands-on-hips gesture. "I've seen the cafeteria food."

"Not going to the cafeteria. We're Dumpster diving. Grab your jacket."

Ah, the reason not to make quick friends. Half the world is crazy. The other half is medicated.

And she'd seemed so nice.

"Josiah, young man, please tell me that your sense of humor isn't completely gone. You will want to hang onto that too in order to survive this siege on your emotions. Dumpster diving? You thought I was serious?"

She shook her head and closed her eyes, lingering in that motionless position a tick longer than comfortable for Josiah. He shifted his weight and attempted to shift his concern about his self-appointed mentor. Before he'd decided whether or not to trust her, she mouthed "Amen" and turned to continue down the hallway. "We'll pick up a family pager at the nurses' station on our way."

"I need to tell my wife's folks where I am. They're on the third floor."

"You've got far more than your fair share of it, don't you? Can you call them? We won't be long. *Top-of-the-hour* rules the day. Tell them we'll be back sooner than soon."

Josiah obeyed.

"Okay, then. Let's go."

He hadn't given his feet permission to follow, but they did.

Around the corner. Into the elevator. Down to street level. Through the sliding doors of the front entrance. And a block west of the hospital complex to a storefront called "Ernie's."

He held the door for Nancy who was greeted with a *Cheers* welcome.

"Nance!"

"Nan-CEE!"

"Hey, Mrs. Drew. 'Bout time you showed up."

Nancy nodded to the welcoming committee—two men at the lunch counter and a young woman sporting a green apron and nose jewelry that looked like a drop of dew.

"Clyde. Robert. Steffie. Good to see you. This is a friend of mine, Joe Chamberlain."

"Josiah," he said, reaching to shake hands with all three.

"What's the special today, Steffie?" Nancy asked as she slid into one of the handful of booths along the exposed brick wall opposite the lunch counter. Josiah sat across from her, noting a sensation much like being swept along a river at flood stage.

"Bacon cheddar meatloaf with parmesan fries and coleslaw," the young woman answered.

Nancy scrunched her nose. "Sounds like an artery-clogging extravaganza. We'll have the cottage cheese plate."

Josiah leaned hard against the wooden booth back. *The cottage cheese plate?* His stomach rumbled again, not in protest of the *lack* of food this time but the *choice*.

"Now," Nancy said, as if the matter were settled, "I need to explain a few things."

A few?

"I'm not your mama."

What does a person say to that?

"But I'm old enough that I mighta been. And considering you seem like a nice enough young man, I figure you were taught to respect your elders. Right?"

His mother? Yes. His father? "That's what I was taught."

"You and I are going to have us a talk about how you're going to get through this."

Josiah pressed his hands onto the tabletop and leaned forward. "Nancy, my situation is different. It's so much more complicated than you know."

"Pain is pain. Waiting is waiting. Caring is caring. Sure, sure, everyone's story is a little different, but we all need hope and I only know one guaranteed place to find that."

"Ernie's?" Josiah offered.

Her face flattened, then erupted into the now familiar starburst of lines. Her laughter drew the attention of the two men at the counter, the dewy waitress, and a barrel-stomached man who emerged from the kitchen area with two mugs dangling from the fingers of one hand and a stainless steel thermal carafe in the other.

"Someone call my name?" the man asked.

Nancy held one hand to her chest as if putting a lid on her laughter. "Ernie, I'd like you to meet Joe Chamberlain."

"Josiah." Was it important to insist on that?

"Pleasure, Joe. I'd shake your hand, but as you can see, I'm loaded down with a little bit of heaven."

Nancy untangled the mugs from his fingers and set them on the table. Ernie poured from the carafe. The aroma of chocolate and coffee and something buttery and sweet rose from the mugs.

"Mmm," Nancy said. "What have we here?"

Josiah reached for the mug set before him and cupped his hands around its warmth. A small comfort, but significant in his comfortless week.

Ernie slid in beside Nancy. "Go ahead. Try it. A little something I threw together for the fun of it. Toffee Mocha Jolt."

Josiah thought about the cottage cheese and canned peach half on its way to the table and calculated that toffee in a mocha might help balance things out. He sipped, startled that it didn't scald him. The temp was perfect. Its smooth sweetness slid down his throat as if it had been waiting for just such a moment.

Karin often hounded him to try a specialty coffee when they ate out. He opted for straight, high-octane, Juan Valdez original.

Karin. Lying in immeasurable pain while he hobnobbed with the locals and sipped Ernie's experiment. He had to get back to the hospital.

"Joe," Nancy said, trapping his hand onto the table with one of hers. "I know that look. Get it out of your head, that notion that something horrible—more horrible than normal—will happen to your wife while you're eating and remembering what humor is like and enjoying yourself. Truth is, horrible things happen whether we're at their side or not. It's time to consider what your body and your mind and your spirit are going to need to keep you strong enough to endure it."

The look on her face—motherly, compassionate, all-knowing—scared him. It was the kind of counsel he should be handing out. Nancy was the flight attendant on this bizarre trip, instructing him to secure his own oxygen mask first before attempting to help someone else. Not natural. Not natural at all.

"Well, your order's here," Ernie said, prying his body out of the tight fit of the booth bench.

Steffie laid down two plates. Piled high with bacon cheeseburger meatloaf, parmesan fries, and a side of coleslaw on bubbled white china plates that looked like platters of cottage cheese. The cottage cheese plate. Perfect.

Josiah picked up his fork. Nancy slapped it out of his hand.

"Don't you be thinking about taking a biteful or a step or an hour in that waiting room without acknowledging gratitude for our only Hope."

Josiah bit the inside of his lip. Enough of this woman's interference and unsolicited advice. If it weren't for the magnetism of meatloaf wrapped in bacon, he'd leave right now.

"Josiah, fold your hands."

"Oh, for Pete's—"

The woman knew how to throw darts with her eyes. He folded his hands.

"You first," she said, closed her eyes, and bowed her head.

Josiah stared at the skunkish part in her hair—an inch of gray on either side of center abruptly morphing to light brown. This wasn't a woman who ditched her child in intensive care to spend the afternoon at the stylist's salon.

His throat closed off. He bowed his head but focused, open-eyed, on the rounded table edge. How far would the meatloaf cool before he could form anything that sounded like prayer?

"Go ahead, dear," Nancy whispered without looking up.

"I...I can't."

"Sure you can. Just start."

"All I can think to say is, 'Oh, Lord Jesus.'"

"Amen," she said. "Pass the ketchup."

Chapter 11

Alone. It's a feeling. Not a destination or condition.
God is especially near to those who think they're alone.

~ Seedlings & Sentiments
from the "Faith" collection

*B*acon cheeseburger meatloaf. Who knew such a thing existed? While life at Ernie's swirled around him, Josiah Chamberlain focused on his fork action. Half his slab of meatloaf was gone before he paused to take a drink of ice water.

Nancy seemed to enjoy watching him swoon over the meatloaf. "Eat, eat!" she said.

Could he bribe Ernie for the recipe? Karin would—

Karin.

He laid his fork on the edge of his plate.

"Eat, Joe." As if to punctuate her point, Nancy picked up a fry, swirled it through her pool of ketchup, then nibbled the end, rabbit-style.

Josiah pushed his cottage cheese–shaped plate toward the center of the table. Nancy pushed it back.

"It's not an affront to your wife if you eat a good lunch, Joe."

"Of course not. But—"

"You can't make her better by giving up coleslaw. Or a Brownie Thunder."

"We didn't order dessert."

She smiled again. "We will."

What percentage of his mind believed he not only deserved but needed to eat? It cowered in the shadow of the unseen bully who called him a selfish pig for breathing.

Eyes locked on Josiah's, Nancy called out, "Steffie, a Brownie Thunder, please?"

"Whipped cream, too, Nance?"

"Is there any other way?"

Josiah gripped the edge of the table. "Nancy, I appreciate your kindness, but I can't—"

"Can't share it with me? Did I ask you? It's all yours, my boy. I'm cutting back." She patted her stomach.

The dewdrop waitress stood at the end of the table. She held a bowl shaped like a melon half.

"Let me guess," Josiah said. "Fresh fruit?"

"Good for the heart," Steffie said and placed before him a tower of chocolate love. With whipped cream.

Josiah looked from the ice cream's moat of chocolate to Nancy's face. He wondered how many of those lines had appeared since her son's accident. Cringing and smiling use some of the same muscles. While he searched the map of her face for clues to more than the little he knew about his mentor, she reached for a spoon and slapped it into his palm like a nurse handing a surgeon a scalpel.

He let it clatter to the table.

"I don't have much of an appetite."

"Oh, it's still there," she said, picking up the discarded utensil and laying it neatly to the side of the bowl. "You've chosen to ignore it, mistakenly thinking that until your wife is well, you have no right to breathe, much less eat."

How did she do that? He would argue with her, but her wisdom must have come hard-earned. She recognized his symptoms because she'd fought the disease herself. Maybe still did.

Would she rally to help him if she knew how shallow was the pool of his faithfulness?

And that Karin's was a mirage?

Josiah scooped a partial spoonful of brownie, ice cream, and hot fudge. As if he'd majored in theatre, he took his time lifting it to his mouth. Savoring. Swallowing. Smacking. "Happy?"

Nancy's grin tilted. "Young man, neither one of us has time for you to dance around the issue."

The issue? The hospital grapevine couldn't have filtered that far yet. Oh, the food thing. The thunder concoction left a warm, sweet taste in his mouth. The meatloaf had wakened taste buds he'd let lapse in favor of flavorless anxiety. He'd *enjoyed* it. That was wrong on so many levels.

"My mother-in-law's in cardiac care," he said.

Nancy's face registered the concern Josiah expected from a woman like her. She could teach him a thing or two about compassion.

"Yes, you'd mentioned she was on the third floor."

"And it's my fault."

She blinked.

"Heart attack. I'm sure it wasn't the only factor, but she collapsed yesterday when I told her my wife's pregnant." That would get Nancy off Josiah's nutritional needs. The aftertaste soured.

She blinked twice. Three times. Tears fell anyway. "I haven't heard you mention children. Is this your first?"

Jack Nicholson's voice threatened to answer for him. *You can't handle the truth.*

"Joe?"

"First pregnancy." He stirred the soupy puddle, intent on the transient design his spoon created then erased.

"Is the baby okay?"

"So far."

"Your mother-in-law just found out? Must be early on. Did news of the baby come as a surprise?"

Josiah's laughter volcanoed into the room. Like a cough spasm, it refused to stop for propriety. "I'm s-sorry. Give me a . . . minute."

She gave him two.

The eruption over, he braced his elbows on the table, his head in his hands. With one quick exhale, he reentered the world where nothing, absolutely nothing, was funny.

⁂

A spiked rock bumped against the interior of his stomach. It started when the pager buzzed and picked up speed when Josiah returned to the ICU and heard the news. An infection of undetermined origin ripped through Karin's body, messing with her organs, threatening her tenuous hold on a filament of healing.

He should have been here, with her. His belch tasted of onions, bacon, and betrayal.

That word. Vile and slightly salty.

He should have been praying against infection, however one does that.

An undercurrent of resentment shot through his core. Why had he listened to Nancy? Divorcing himself from Karin's needs for the sake of lunch? Lunch? A cloud passed between Josiah and reason.

Wait a minute. Karin had left him for less.

Or was it? What had Wade promised her? What powers of persuasion had he used to lure her away from her home?

Josiah touched the skin of Karin's febrile forearm. It wasn't just abnormally warm. It felt clammy, sweaty. A medicinal odor hovered over her. Her lips were parted and parched. The flush to her cheeks would have made people think she'd been too long and vigorous on the treadmill if it weren't for her prone, immobile position.

Nurse Angie moved to the head of the bed. "Did you want to step out, Mr. Chamberlain?"

"I just got here."

"Some spouses find it difficult to be here when . . . I need to . . ."

Josiah couldn't imagine a medical indignity he hadn't already witnessed. "I'll be fine. Go ahead with whatever."

Angie fiddled with the object in her hands.

Tape?

"I need to tape her eyelids shut, Mr. Chamberlain."

She must have known he'd twitch at the thought.

"To prevent her eyes from drying. Her lids aren't fully closing. It's not all that unusual for victims of deep brain trauma."

DBT. *Keep talking, lady. Keeping trolling for a tidbit of comfort.* "I understand." *Liar.* He didn't understand anything after Karin's unspoken, "I'm leaving you." For that matter, everything he thought he understood before that moment was apparently bogus, too.

Twelve years. They'd just celebrated twelve years—what?— six weeks ago? Fancier restaurant than normal. Roses. She gave him a card. One of her homemade things. Had he read it? He remembered stuffing it in his suit jacket pocket at the restaurant. Karin's eyes clouded. Huh. They hadn't sparkled since. What was that supposed to mean? *Come on. It was just a card. What guy wants to read a mushy love note in the middle of a restaurant?* Or was it a Dear John letter he'd pocketed?

Angie waited—fabric tape in hand.

In the end, he couldn't watch, no matter how jaded he thought he'd become to the anything-but-sensual nakedness, the drooling, the urine bag hanging off a low railing of the bed, the asthmatic wheeze of the breathing machine. Josiah didn't look back to the form on the bed until he heard Angie move away to the other side of the room.

Flesh-colored tape. Nice touch. How thoughtful of the medical staff. At first glance, no one would know Karin's eyes were duct-taped shut.

"How will we know now?"

Angie turned toward his question. "Know what?"

"When she wakes up. How will we know if she can't open her eyes? Won't she...won't she panic if she tries?" *I would.*

I'm awake. Why can't you see that? Look at me.
No. No, please don't. I'm a...wreck.

Angie gave him that oh-you-poor-ignorant-man smile she probably thought seemed sympathetic. "We'll know. Other ways. Don't worry about that."

Ah. Okay. Done deal. I won't worry about that. Not a problem, Ange. Still plenty of entries left on my list of anxieties. He apologized internally for the sarcasm she hadn't heard him spew.

Angie adjusted something on the IV pump, punching buttons and chiding it when it rebelled against her instruction.

I can't do this. Can't feel. I feel too much.

The room sucked in its breath again. Its walls crept closer, threatening to push Josiah nearer than he wanted to be. Nearer his wife. And the child. And the improbability that either would survive. The heat of Karin's fever radiated to the rest of the room. Trickles of perspiration formed pools under his arms.

"Mr. Chamberlain?"

He leaned back to gain enough oxygen to speak. "Yes?"

Angie tilted her head toward the doorway. "The time. I dislike having to be strict about the visitations, but..."

What do you know? He hadn't looked at the clock. Hadn't counted down the moments, as with other visits. And he didn't want to leave. Maybe there was hope for him yet.

ॐ ॐ ॐ

Josiah and Stan traded places every couple of hours until the cardiac floor visiting hours ended for the night. Stan insisted he couldn't sleep but managed to pull off a good imitation of snoring in one of the ICU waiting room recliners. Josiah dozed off and on in the nest he'd built in a corner of the room.

Earlier than he ever did at home, Josiah woke to the smell of coffee. Fresh. Unexpected. Not that it mattered. He would have slugged it down cold, bitter, and cloudy. Stan's recliner had been righted. Who knew when he'd headed back to Catherine's side?

Poor Stan. Tenderhearted as he was, did Josiah's father-in-law have the emotional energy to deal with a sick wife? The irony of Josiah's thought pinched off his swallowing mechanism. Coffee splotches decorated the front of his shirt and the counter by the coffeemaker.

Did a man exist—young or old—with energy enough to deal with a sick wife? *This* sick?

Somebody ought to write a book.

How many days would look like this? Blinding nothingness interspersed with achingly hollow visits with a wife who looked more like a cadaver than the vibrant woman who'd stolen his heart with one glance more than twelve anniversaries ago. He stared at Karin for some sign of movement, some signal that she was still in there somewhere, and steeled himself for the moment her doctor would tell him hope no longer registered as a viable option in her case.

Late in the afternoon, Josiah left his waiting room cocoon to check on Catherine and Stan.

He opted for the stairs to the cardiac floor. Elevators were too passive. Too easy. Too kind. The echoing scuff and stomp of his footsteps on the stairs felt normal. Expected. Funny how the thrill of adventure had lost its appeal. Normal and ordinary were good, worthy goals.

Like running a gauntlet, Josiah dodged a third-floor corridor of supply carts, other visitors, volunteers with wheeled trays of flowers and magazines, and shuffling patients leaning on walkers or their companions.

He paused outside Catherine's room, as he always did, readjusting his facial expression as he might reposition the knot of his tie. How would Catherine's heart take the news of the latest downturn in Karin's condition? He knew enough to feel the weight of what a systemic infection could do to someone in Karin's shape. And the baby.

"Good news, Josiah," Catherine said, her eyes hope-brightened. "I'm going home."

Josiah caught the shadow on Stan's face. It disappeared when Catherine turned her head Stan's way, replaced by a look even an insensitive lout like Josiah could recognize.

"When?" he asked, digging deep for enthusiasm.

She lifted the neck of her hospital gown, as if a higher neckline could lend dignity to the ensemble. "Maybe tomorrow. One more test in the morning, I guess. Then we'll be released, just as soon as they get my discharge papers and forty-two prescriptions."

"Forty-two?" She'd used the words "we'll be released." She understood that both she and Stan had been chained to the cardiac ward.

Stan stepped closer to Catherine's bed, jingling change in his pocket. "Purt near. Thank the Lord for health insurance. One good thing came from all those years I gave to the post office." He took his hands out of his pockets and cupped his elbows. "How's yours holding out, son?"

Josiah waved off the question. *Can't think about that now.* "Home, Mom? They think you're ready?"

Stan's nostrils flared as he drew in a breath. The look that passed between the men said, "We need to talk."

"I need to go home, Josiah. It'll be...better there." More than hope seemed to glisten in her eyes now.

Stan cleared his throat. "We'll get m'lady all set up with a cardiologist back home. They'll take good care of her."

The first author interview Josiah did live for KTIS radio out of Minneapolis taught him about dead air. Anathema for broadcasters. The listening audience can't bear more than two seconds of silence over the air before squirming. It's worse in person. Josiah felt every nanosecond of the pregnant pause slithering its way through Catherine's hospital room.

"So..." He glanced out the window at an unbroken sky that defied all that clouded Josiah's life. Catherine and Stan—his support system—were not only limping, they were headed home.

Josiah bit his lip. It's not that he wasn't primarily concerned with his mother-in-law's health. Of course he was. But he already felt their absence from their corporate waiting room.

"Hey, Stan, you look like you could use something to eat. Something other than hospital cuisine. I know a place nearby where you can get a killer mocha and a slab of meatloaf that will sustain you until next Tuesday a year from now. Let me treat you. Is that all right with you, Catherine, if I snatch him away for an hour or so?"

Catherine reached for her husband's hand. "Good idea. You two men go off and have fun. I'll just be here waiting for my watery mashed potatoes and mystery meat." She winked.

Oh, to have the fortitude to wink.

The two were inches away from a clean exit from the room when Catherine called out, "Josiah, how's Karin today? And my grandchild?"

What's a word that means "worse than horrible"? A true thesaurus kind of crisis.

"Holding their own. See you in a bit, Mom."

As Stan matched strides down the corridor, Josiah slapped away the gnat of realization that neither Karin nor the child were holding anything, least of all "their own."

Chapter 12

When life threatens to topple you, hear two voices
inviting you to "Lean on me." Mine and God's.

~ Seedlings & Sentiments
from the "Faith" collection

*J*osiah and Stan avoided the inevitable questions until free of the hospital campus, as if discussing them could adversely affect a medical outcome if within earshot of a doctor. Once inside the protective embrace of Ernie's, Stan held out the pager that matched Josiah's. "We'll hear this if it rings, right?"

"It's just like the pagers at Olive Garden, Stan. It'll buzz and flash. We won't accidentally miss it." He knew that too well.

Josiah waited only long enough for Stan to order before probing. "Is Mom ready to go home, Stan?"

"Home with a capital *H*?"

Heaven? No! "Ready to leave the hospital."

Stan's thickly veined hands removed the napkin wrapped around his flatware. He put the fork and knife on the left of the spot where a plate would soon rest and the spoon on the right. Then he moved the fork to the right to join the spoon. The spoon to the left to join the fork. Wordless still, he bunched them together and laid the napkin over the top. Out of sight, out of confusion.

Hiding it doesn't help. It's not that simple, Josiah longed to tell him. "Is she strong enough?"

"Stronger in spirit than the two of us put together."

"No argument there. But her heart..."

Stan's fingers drummed the table in a pattern so arrhythmic, Josiah almost suggested Stan try again with the silverware.

"Son, I don't know what to tell you. It's all muddled. First the doctors tell us she'll have to have another surgery, then they change their minds and decide they'll try a bunch of medicines first. I'm..."

Another stretch of dead air, accompanied by the clink of glasses in the kitchen and the rumble of nondescript conversation three booths away.

"You're what?"

Stan's shoulders swallowed his neck. "I'm afraid to take her home."

Think, Josiah. The man needs a word of wisdom from you. "Won't you both be grateful to sleep in your own bed again?"

In slow motion, Stan let his gaze fall. "Sleep beside a woman I'm not sure will wake in the morning?"

Josiah reached across the table to grip Stan's forearm. "She'll be fine. You have a great medical facility there in Somerset. They'll take excellent care of her."

As if medical facilities and doctors ever have the last word.

Stan patted Josiah's hand resting on his arm. "Thanks, son. I know I shouldn't be worried. It's a trusting place. I was so sure I'd be the first to go. Statistically and all that."

"You still could be."

At that, Stan made eye contact again. A smile crept across his face as if breaking through ice. "Now, that's downright encouraging."

"It's not a race, you know."

The waitress slapped a plate in front of Stan and slid a diet cola toward Josiah. "Anything else, gents?"

Josiah answered for them. "No, thank you. This is great."

The focus of Stan's attention lay somewhere outside the window that fronted Ernie's. Josiah picked up Stan's fork and a purple-veined hand and guided Stan's fingers to close around the cold stainless. "Now, eat up. You'll need your strength."

ᴥ ᴥ ᴥ

"Was I wrong not to tell Catherine about Karin's infection?"

Stan laid his fork aside. A nugget of cheese clung to his upper lip. It danced as he spoke. "I don't like to keep secrets from her."

Josiah's stomach clenched.

"Learned that a long time ago," the older man said. "Did I tell you about the boat?"

The infamous boat incident. He'd heard. A fourteen-foot bass boat is a hard thing to disguise when you park it in the backyard. There was no disguising Catherine's displeasure when she found it sitting over her rhubarb patch. To Josiah's knowledge, she'd kept her promise that Stan would never again taste her strawberry rhubarb pie, except for the pieces he snitched at potlucks.

"Secrets can kill a relationship," Stan said.

Sir, you don't know the half of it.

"But," Stan added, "under the circumstances, we might could delay telling the truth."

"Delay." Josiah considered. "We'll still tell her everything."

"Oh, yes. Absolutely."

Josiah wiped condensation from the outside of his glass of cola. "News about the baby put her in the state she's in now."

"A grandchild. Never thought you two would grace us with a grandchild."

We two didn't. "A medical impossibility as far as we were concerned." Delay the whole truth. The only kind thing to do.

"But you can't hold to the thought that your telling Catherine about our grandbaby made her have a heart attack."

Josiah exhaled a practiced sigh. "The timing..."

"You heard the doctors. This was brewing for a while. We just didn't know it. I should have read the signs. I should have known."

"Stan..."

"She's my wife. How could I sit across from her at breakfast every day and not have noticed she was hurting?"

If Josiah still had tonsils, they would have touched. "We can't always know," he choked out.

"She always accused me of not paying attention."

Sorry. You can't be the king of that, Stan. I hold the world record.

"I'll deny it in a court of law," Stan said, "but she's probably right." He stabbed the last fry on the plate, sopped up meatloaf grease with it, and guided it to his mouth. "That just goes to show you," he said around chews.

"What?"

"I didn't even realize I was hungry." His sloped shoulders drooped farther.

"A refill, Joe?" The waitress snatched his glass before Josiah could answer.

"Breaks my heart, what's happened to Karin," Stan said, his gaze rooted to the tabletop.

Josiah forced himself to breathe.

"My daughter means the—" Stan's eyes pinched shut, and his mouth contorted. "She means the world to me, Josiah. After all Catherine's miscarriages, God gave us Karin."

All Catherine's miscarriages. The reason Karin was an only child. *Could that have been why Karin didn't tell me the truth sooner, ugly as that conversation would have been, given Wade's involvement? Did she assume her pregnancy would end in a miscarriage and no one would ever have to know? How could I have forgotten that Karin came from a long line of miscarriages? It had to have crossed her mind.*

"God gave us Karin," Stan repeated. "As far as I'm concerned, more than we ever longed for. I can't stand to"—he caught the sob before it found full voice—"to see her like this. I can't leave her, but I need to take Catherine home. No matter what I do, I'm letting down one or the other of the two women I love."

What does a person say to that? "Stan, Karin doesn't know we're here. She can't hear us or feel us. Catherine needs you more. She needs to know you're beside her." Josiah left a blank the space of two heartbeats. "I'll keep you informed. When Karin pulls out of this, Mom will be stronger. There will be plenty of time to visit Karin then and let her know how much she means to you."

"When she pulls out of this."

Josiah debated telling his father-in-law the truth—that he'd chosen the word *when* from a file drawer of wishful thinking rather than faith. "Right now, there's nothing we can do for her."

Stan raised his head and leaned toward Josiah. "Then why are *you* here?"

Obligation? Love? Because of all the unanswered questions?

Maybe all of the above. Love was in there somewhere. Buried under a pile of uncertainty.

The subject of insurance reared its ugly head again over the table at Ernie's. Did Josiah know how much of the hospitalization fees were covered by his insurance? No. Did he realize how much all that fancy equipment cost per day? No. Didn't he think he'd better check into it?

"Stan, that's the least of my concerns right now."

"I'd like to tell you I understand and let it go at that, son, but from past experience, I have to say it's not something you can ignore for long. When my neighbor had a foot nearly cut off when he dropped a chain saw on himself, he discovered mighty fast how little his insurance company was willing to pay."

Josiah hated to admit he'd had brief thoughts about the expense. He'd fought them back with a dagger named "how dare you think of money when your wife could be dying."

He needed to call his agents. His insurance agent. Then his literary agent. Repulsive as it seemed, he might have to write again to pay for IV fluid and canned oxygen and catheter tubing and ineffective antibiotics.

Josiah pulled his wallet from his pocket and slapped a twenty on top of the bill the waitress had left with the drink refill. "I guess we'd better get back."

Stan wiped his mouth with his napkin and followed Josiah from the booth. "You don't want to wait for your change? The little waitress was good, but..."

"I want to be generous. I want to not care about the money. I want to do something tangible for someone." Josiah hoped his tirade hadn't seemed directed at his father-in-law.

Stan nodded and laid a ten on top of Josiah's twenty.

ৼ৶ ৼ৶ ৼ৶

He forfeited two visitation slots to allow Stan time with his daughter. Josiah spent one of them with Catherine and the other in the hospital gift shop. He needed something to read or do or nibble on or flip through. He settled on Wild Cherry Lifesavers and a book—*What to Expect When You're Expecting*.

The checkout girl congratulated him. He almost responded, "It's not for me. It's for my wife," but realized the lid on that Pandora's Box had best stay closed.

He peeled back the top of the Lifesavers package and popped one into his mouth. The initial tartness soon turned sweet and soothing. When they were dating, Karin always gave him the red ones from the rainbow pack and kept the pale pineapple for herself. That's how marriage was supposed to work. Celebrate the differences. Share and share alike.

Marriage is a roll of Lifesavers.

Chapter title or a whole new book?

When he returned to the ICU waiting room, he found Nancy engaged in conversation with Morris Lynch.

Morris rushed to embrace Josiah. They'd never embraced. Not when Josiah's first book made the best-seller list. Not when Josiah's sales netted Morris the courage to break off from Neilson Literary and form his own agency. Not when *Love Handles: Getting a Grip on Your Marriage* went into its third printing.

The man smelled like sweat disguised—lightly—with Turkish spices. Either cheap deodorant or expensive cologne. Morris needed a hygiene makeover. No wonder he'd yet to marry.

Josiah pulled away from the suffocating hug and discretely sniffed his own armpit. Nothing right, left, or upside down guarded his sweat glands. No wonder Karin—

No. Foul smells were not irreconcilable differences.

She had some explaining to do.

Like, when did she have time for an affair? And why? For Pete's sake, why?

Josiah test-drove his relationship theories at home. They worked. He knew they did. She had no right, no reason, no excuse.

Shadows fell across Josiah's field of vision. Morris's hand.

"You in there somewhere?" Morris used his I-should-have-been-a-comedian voice.

"I'm here. What were you saying?"

"Not important. The point is we need to talk." Morris dug into the ostrich-skin briefcase at his feet. "Sit."

Josiah obeyed.

With a thespian flourish, Morris slapped a contract onto the table in front of them. "There it is. Your reason for living."

Not even close. Whatever the fine print said, it didn't come close to reason enough to keep breathing.

"And," the suited man added, "the reason you'll be eager to name your first child after me."

My first child. There's the hitch.

Nancy drifted from center stage to the magazine rack in the corner of the waiting room. She pressed her hands together—the international sign for "I'm praying for you."

A few minutes with his agent and she already knew conversation with him necessitated prayer. Wise woman.

"Morris, right now I can't even think about—"

"Where did you get the idea can't was an option? Not from me. This is huge, Chamberlain. Huge. This is lift-off."

"Lift-off?"

Morris pulled a stick of gum from his pocket, unwrapped the silver foil, and folded it into his cavernous mouth. Another attempt to quit smoking? Chewing, he said, "Until now (chomp), you've been spouting smoke and fumes (chomp) in ignition stage. It's time for lift-off."

Enough with the sappy metaphors, Morris. "What's the offer?"

Morris flipped past the first page to a point deeper into the contract. He traced a line with his index finger. "This is what will interest you most. A six-figure advance. Do you know how rare that is these days?"

Josiah looked at the number. The mid-range of six figures, but still . . .

It would cover a lot of bandages, catheter tubing, physical therapy—if Karin made it that far.

With a hand that trembled like a Chihuahua on speed, Josiah reached to flip the pages back to the contract's first page. "What would I have to give them?"

"The timing's perfect, don't you think? You've all this time here with nothing to do but wait. And write."

Where's a sharp object when you need one?

"I'm not heartless, Chamberlain. I feel for what you're going through. But think of the implications. You've been granted this block of time at the bedside of the woman you love. What better atmosphere for a project like this?"

"What project, Morris?"

The suit bunched around his shoulders as Morris leaned forward. "The one I'd almost given up on. The book you've been primed to write to help men figure out how to deal with caring for a sick wife. Publisher loves your title. The one I came up with."

Someone wanted to bite on that project? Now?

Nancy danced near the coffeemaker in a praise-the-Lord posture.

No. Impossible. Right now even the grace of God couldn't help him write a book titled *Lean on Me*.

Chapter 13

If all you hear is silence, welcome it.
Silence holds more wisdom than a rush of words.

~ Seedlings & Sentiments
from the "Comfort" collection

*N*ancy slapped him on the back as if trying to dislodge a piece of meat. "Congratulations! I didn't know you were an author. What a provision for you!"

"Yes. A provision."

Why can't I have one genuine, unadulterated emotion? I can't feel either joy or pain without interference from its opposite. I can't rejoice over a contract without the cement block of guilt and almost laughable inadequacy pulling me under. I can't fully mourn Karin's leaving me. She's still here. But I can't celebrate the fact that she's with me because she isn't. The baby should make me deliriously happy, but the baby's a threat to Karin's recovery. And it doesn't carry my genes. I have a new contract for a subject I know nothing about, a contract that will force me to find words—lots of them—at a time when they're more elusive and reclusive than ever.

Josiah put an asterisk by his thoughts: *Insert swear words here.*

"Kind of overwhelming?" Nancy asked.

"More than you know."

110

"I'm sure you can do it."

One of these days he'd have to sit her down and tell her how wrong she was. "I'm a little shy on confidence at the moment. And energy."

She sat in the chair recently vacated by jet-setting Morris. "People who write books amaze me."

"Don't waste any admiration on me, Nancy."

She pressed her lips together and lifted her chin. "You need a moment?"

A moment alone. Yes. "That would be great."

She pushed away from the table and headed out the waiting room door. "Come on, then."

"What?"

"Your moment. It's waiting for you."

By now he knew better than to question how her mind worked. Somewhere a *moment* waited for him and somehow she knew the way.

⁊ ⁊ ⁊

The hospital chapel lay no more than a few hundred feet from the waiting room. It's reverent double doors opened automatically to let them in.

"Good. No one else here right now. How perfect for you." Nancy's whisper barely rose above the undercurrent of flowing music. Surround sound.

"You aren't staying?"

"You need some alone time with the One who brought you here."

Here? To this chapel? That would be you, Nancy. Here to the hospital? That would be Karin and her beloved Wade, the world's worst winter-conditions driver. Here to the planet? Okay. Granted.

Nancy shooed him into the room, flapping her hands as if they were corners of an apron. "Go on. Have your time. He has a few things to say to you, if I'm not mistaken."

HE isn't doing all that much talking to me lately, my friend. It'll be a short conversation. "Thanks."

"You can find your way back?"

Back from the abyss? "I'll find it."

Nancy's eyes crinkled. "Good. I'm going to use the desktop computer in the waiting room to look up some books by Joe Chamberlain."

She'd left the room already when he answered, "It's Josiah."

How could an empty room feel so full? His eyes scanned the interior. No stained glass or fancy trappings. A simple room with rows of blue padded chairs arranged like pews. Artwork spotlighted with gallery lighting. Jesus and a lamb. Jesus at a heavy wooden door. Jesus with children on His lap. Jesus, Jesus, Jesus. An altar. A cross. That's all.

"It's Josiah," he said again, this time to the painting of Jesus with the children.

He knew that face wasn't the true face of Christ. It was an artist's interpretation. Josiah expected the true Jesus looked more like Corporal Klinger from *M*A*S*H*. And wouldn't that surprise everyone?

"No offense," he said aloud. He could have sworn he heard a voice say, "None taken."

He walked along the wall of artwork, noting other scenes familiar to him. Jesus at the well, offering Living Water to a thirsty woman who couldn't stick with one man. Jesus in Gethsemane, wrestling with the price He'd have to pay for love. Jesus at the last supper, feeding even the friend who would deny Him and the one who would betray Him.

Betrayed. Josiah knew the feeling. "Stinks, doesn't it, Jesus? Hurts like—"

The next picture caught his attention. A bloodied man on a crude cross. Thorns pressed into his skull. Whip marks snaked around from his back to the torn flesh on his sides. A look of terror in the divine eyes. Terror? Ah, the separation. The part about, "My

God, my God, why have you forsaken me?" A sensitive artist held the brush that painted terror shaded with pain.

He—Josiah Chamberlain, poor imitation that he was—had something in common with Jesus.

Who would have thought?

He tore his gaze away from the artwork and swiped at his eyes with the back of his hands. He needed to sit and think. Or not think. Better.

Josiah chose a spot on the aisle toward the back. No good. He rose and moved ahead four or five rows. Close enough. The quiet music resonated through to his marrow. He should pray or something. Or listen.

Silence has its own language. It chattered away while Josiah sat, shoulders hunched, eyes closed, heart imploding.

⚚ ⚚ ⚚

"Joe?"

Josiah startled at the weight of a hand on his shoulder. It couldn't be God calling. The Almighty would call him Josiah. Or Josiah Peter Chamberlain, if He were angry.

This voice was low but feminine. Nancy.

"Sorry. Were you deep in prayer or asleep?"

Hard to tell sometimes. "Asleep, I guess. What time is it?"

"It's the top of the hour. I didn't want to disturb you, but..."

Josiah took a deep breath and blinked "prayer" from his eyes. "Time to visit the loved ones."

On the way out of the room, he caught a glimpse of another painting hanging near the exit. Jesus in the background, leaning on a rock, eyes lifted to heaven, pain etched in His expression. The disciples in the foreground, asleep under a tree.

Before this trial was over, he'd need another moment.

⚚ ⚚ ⚚

Morning. The time had come. Josiah accompanied Stan, Catherine in her wheelchair, and the nursing assistant to the exit of the hospital. Catherine seemed to have weakened just from the ride through the hospital corridors. Maybe it was the fluorescent lighting. Or the fact that she was leaving her daughter for what might be the last time.

Stan trailed the wheelchair. He clutched the flower arrangement he'd gotten his wife the day before in the hospital gift shop. A spring bouquet that mocked the chill in the air outside the building. The plastic bag protecting the blooms looked as inadequate to keep them from frostbite as Josiah was to keep his marriage intact.

Elbow to elbow with his father-in-law, Josiah watched Stan's jaw muscles flex. He'd been assigned the task of transporting his fragile wife safely home. Would Josiah know the same frightening privilege one day?

At the curbside where their car waited, Josiah leaned down to kiss his mother-in-law's cheek. The car's heater already blasted, forming a warm, wheeled cocoon for the trip home. When she was settled in, Josiah followed Stan to the driver's side of the car, willing strength into his father-in-law through the layers of clothing.

"By the time I see you again," Josiah began, "Mom will be back to her old self."

Stan turned to look deep into Josiah's eyes. Was he waiting for a guarantee? A promise? "I hope you're right. You take care of that girl of ours." His eyes swam.

A gust of wind swept between them. Coatless, Josiah shivered. From the cold.

"Well," Stan said, climbing behind the wheel with a grunt, "I'd better get m'lady home."

Josiah leaned in with a brief, "Love you two." Then he backed out as Stan pulled the door closed. Had the air temperature dropped another few degrees? If the sun didn't come out soon, it promised to be a bitter day.

He tucked his hands under his armpits for warmth, but drew one out to answer their waves. The only people who loved Karin as much as he did pulled away from the curb.

Correction. He had to add one more to the list. Wade. The guy in a walking cast with a Tahitian tan and designer hair crossing the parking lot toward the hospital entrance bore such a startling resemblance to Wade Frambolt. Doppelganger-close resemblance. Rooted in place, Josiah watched the man maneuver the slush and curbs, limping and in obvious pain. If the tree hadn't been so efficient, that might have been Wade. On his way to see Karin.

In the crosswalk, the man looked up and caught Josiah's gaze. Imagination turned Josiah's stomach. Crazy. He was going crazy.

Had the guy recognized Josiah? The man abruptly turned and crutched his way back to his vehicle.

Mister, you can't have read my murderous thoughts just now. What's up with—?

The Wade lookalike reached into the SUV and pulled out enough Mylar helium balloons to launch a small child into space. Dinosaur shapes and giant mouse ears and teddy bears and cartoon cars. After navigating the puddles and curbs again, he entered the crosswalk, punching balloons out of his line of sight. He drew closer to where Josiah stood, an ice sculpture of indecision.

His face was flushed, not Tahitian. There's a difference. "Hey," the man said as he neared.

Josiah looked at his calf-high cast and raced to the door to assist.

"My son couldn't have waited to have an appendectomy until my hammertoe surgery healed. Oh, no." He smiled before, during, and after saying it.

"Sorry," Josiah choked out.

"He's doing fine now. Coming home today, but he insisted he had to let the nurses see the balloons his classmates sent to the house. That's my boy."

That's a good dad. A good dad would do stuff like that, right? Walk on nails to bring his son balloons. Josiah's dad hadn't walked on carpet to bring his son a bandage for a skinned knee. But good dads did things like that.

Josiah followed the helium parade into the building. He'd come dangerously close to vicariously punching a guy who just had his hammertoes straightened. Not the definition of a good person. Much less the makings of a good dad.

Wade had to have known about the baby. He had to. What might have appealed to Karin about Wade was that he wasn't as ignorant and unobservant as Josiah. Wade the Wonderful would have noticed. And no matter what he might have once had with Leah, he probably celebrated the idea of becoming a dad.

The thought exploded like a firecracker in Josiah's head, its still-hot embers drifting and burning through his brain cells.

"And I'm supposed to write through this?"

"Pardon me?"

The passing orderly who asked the question seemed unfazed by Josiah's quick rant. They must see that a lot in this place. People crazed by the waiting, the uncertainty, the concern, the pain.

The silence.

Doctors with no sure answers. Questions—so many questions—that dead people or those with DBT and their eyelids taped shut can't respond to. A God who had been as stingy with clues as He was with direction.

Imagination, though. That was anything but silent. Maybe he could find some kind of relief if he did what Morris suggested—write—odd and impossible as that sounded. Robinson Crusoe kept a journal when he was stranded without hope, didn't he?

Josiah's laptop waited for him upstairs in one of the family waiting room lockers. He had work to do.

Chapter 14

Hope and love find their deepest expression when paired.

~ Seedlings & Sentiments
from the "Hope" collection

*W*ords were his friends. They'd served him well, keeping him from a wordless life on a factory line or behind the business end of a bulldozer. Or a spreadsheet of accounts receivable.

But the words had deserted him. Abandoned him to a blank screen and now a blank imagination. As crazed as it had been before—incessantly chattering since the accident—imagination pressed its lips together and folded its arms across its chest like a petulant child, now that Josiah depended on it.

Words weren't like numbers. Numbers can be forced onto a page. Words have minds of their own. They must be coaxed, wooed, romanced so as not to frighten them away with the intensity of love for them.

Josiah possessed nothing with which to woo.

Fifty thousand blank spaces stared at him from his laptop screen. He wasn't attempting an epic-length book. Just a practical, stirring, fun read about caring for a sick spouse. Piece of cake.

While the minute hand crept toward the top of the hour, Josiah laid his inept fingers over the keys again, hoping the act itself would jump-start something. I-N-T-R-O-D-U-C-T-I-O-N. A word. A start.

> *I liked her, loved her, when she was strong. I liked her in the seat ahead of me in the canoe, trusting I'd match my paddle stroke to hers as we floated down Birch River. Liked her laughter that bubbled sweeter than the maple sap on our trip to the Sugar Farm last fall. Liked her energy for a new work project, her insistence that I'd appreciate the window display at Markum's as much as she did. I liked her swaying to the music from her headphones when she gardened. I liked her whole. Determined to lay the tile in the kitchen while I locked myself in the attic to write. I liked how she skipped with the kids in her Sunday school class. If they danced, she danced. If they bounced, she bounced.*

Josiah stopped writing. Karin's friend Janelle would have let the church know Karin wouldn't be available to teach or skip or bounce for a long, long time. Was that one of the messages waiting on his maxed-out voice mail?

God help me, I liked her better strong. And faithful.

He deleted the last two words. Not that they weren't true, but did the world have to know?

Why was he protecting her? If sympathy were what he wanted, he could generate enough to sustain him for the rest of his life by telling what she'd done to him. Her current inability to argue her own case, her *wordlessness*, worked to his advantage. No one would hear about his role, whatever that was. Sterility? Again, not a biblical basis for infidelity. Abram's Sarai could teach Karin a few things about consequences on that score.

He'd have to separate himself from his own reality if he were to write this book. The unknowns crippled his ability to think clearly. Separate or dive deeper in.

And . . . it was the top of the hour.

He closed the laptop and slipped it into its case, then into the locker along the interior wall of the waiting room. This could get old quickly. He worked best in his cozy office high above the world and away from all distractions but the rustle of oak leaves outside his window. His man-sized office chair. His trestle table desk that allowed him to prop his feet on the crossbar. His library lamp. The classical music drifting from the ancient boom box on the middle shelf of his bookcase. A room built for creativity.

He tossed another Styrofoam cup of bitter coffee dregs into the wastebasket at the door as he exited the room built for mourning.

ॐ ॐ ॐ

A foul odor assaulted Josiah when he entered Karin's ICU cell—medicinal and fecal. The nurse on duty—Lexie, not his favorite—shouted orders from her position on the left side of Karin's bed.

"Good. I can use you. She soiled herself again. Help me roll her enough that I can slide out the pad. Grab her here. Lift gently. Well, not that gently. I need room to work. What a mess."

Lexie. Not his favorite person.

Where to look? Karin's face. It registered no embarrassment. Nothing. If a spark of her real self throbbed within the DBT fog, she'd be weeping now. As he drew her frail body toward him, he focused on the curves of her throat. Untouched by the accident, it seemed, the symmetry of the cords and veins and hollows spoke of the beauty hidden by bruises and swelling, bandages and wires, tubes and tape and needles. Enamored by the throat hollow, he watched the ridges around it pulse as Lexie worked somewhere miles away.

An unnamed nurse-type person joined the scene. "Mr. Chamberlain, you don't have to do that. Here, let me help."

Returning his focus to the spot of smooth neck flesh to which his hopes clung, he said, "It's okay. I've got it."

119

Nurse Two assisted Lexie the Louse. Within minutes—his ten minutes—the "problem" was taken care of and Karin rested flat again. Josiah moved to the head of the bed. His "see you later" was his finger tracing the curve of her beautiful neck.

Her taped eyes leaked at the corners. She couldn't know—could she?—what happened to her. Josiah brushed the tears with his wordless thumbs. He wanted to stay. For reasons he couldn't articulate, he wanted to spit on the rules and stay.

Don't leave me here! I'm drowning in these tears—
the ones you don't see.

In the waiting room, Nancy hovered over a new family, showing them the coffeemaker, the rules, the magazines, the common computer, the family-only private restroom. He overheard her tell them about a great place to get a home-cooked meal and a wicked dessert.

The new family laughed in that pain-laced way they'd all adopted.

Josiah supposed that as an ICU veteran it was only proper for him to introduce himself and offer a nibble of comfort. Not now. People drained all the oxygen from the room. No. It wasn't fair to blame them. Oxygen had nothing to do with it.

He grabbed his jacket. Maybe he could walk off his misery over loving a woman who no longer loved him.

Four trips around the hospital complex and misery remained. But his lungs were cleansed and his head cleared. The sharp spring air hung in crystal contrast to the mud underfoot, mud that leaked onto the sidewalks and plugged the storm sewers. He completed the obstacle course and directed his steps toward the hospital entrance. In a bare brown flowerbed near the entrance, a single broad spike of green stood in the chilled soil. An early crocus? Karin would know. She knew flowers. Life, in the middle of all that lifelessness.

Josiah planted his shoe on top of it and flattened the unfairness of it all.

Then he glanced around to see if anyone had noticed his burst of insanity. The passing world had its own problems, apparently. No one looked his way. He wiped his feet on the industrial mat near the entrance and headed back upstairs to his personal drama, praying the hospital security cameras hadn't been trained on the flowerbed.

His jacket retained the crisp freshness of the outdoors. He buried his nose in it before hanging the jacket in the locker and retrieving his laptop. But his mind wandered to the last scene in Karin's room. She wouldn't want to live like that forever. If it came to it, would he have the courage to make the decision to pull the plug? And how would he ever know if he'd acted out of concern for his own convenience or for her sake? Or revenge? Revenge sat slightly offstage, waiting for its opportunity in the spotlight.

He mentally opened two folders: *The Book* and *My Life*. Separate. No shared files. It's the only way he'd ever get the proposal written.

Josiah pulled up the introduction on his computer. Select All. Delete.

Nancy tapped his shoulder on her way out of the room. "Did you eat?"

Josiah pain-laughed. "Not going out this time, Nancy."

"Want me to bring you something?" She finger-fluffed her faded bangs.

How long had it been since the woman had gone to a stylist? Or treated herself to a movie? Or taken a day off from her vigil? A mother's love . . .

He patted his belly. "I'm thinking of limiting my trips to Ernie's to once a day. This waiting isn't good for the figure."

Nancy pulled herself into a comedienne's version of a model's posture. "Anxiety. Cortisol. Depression. Way worse than the effects of butter and bacon. Trust me. I know." With a whoosh of air, she let her body sink into its normal stance. "I know."

Without further cajoling, she left Josiah to his mental gymnastics.

He retrieved what he'd deleted earlier, leaving it on the computer screen as a confessional. It stared at him with beady black *I*'s.

> I *liked her, loved her, when she was strong. I liked her laughter that bubbled sweeter than the maple sap.... I liked her energy for a new work project.... I liked her swaying to the music from her headphones when she gardened. I liked her whole.*

He opened the file of the book he'd sent Morris so few days ago. Beady black *I*'s everywhere on the pages. He'd filtered all of it through the *I*'s.

"Lost in thought?"

Josiah slapped the laptop lid shut. "Leah!"

"How is she? I know I can't get in to see her, but I . . . I want to know. I've tried calling." She stood with her hands clenched in front of her waist like an opera singer. The way she worked them, kneaded them, told Josiah she was no more comfortable with the conversation than he was.

"I haven't been listening to my messages." He stood and gestured toward an empty seat. "I'm sorry."

Leah hesitated, then took the offered chair. "Yeah. Me neither."

She looked like four-day-old leftover tuna casserole. He probably looked the part of her fraternal twin.

"Karin isn't responding to stimuli," he said. "Yet. We think the antibiotic is making progress on the infection." How much did Leah really want to know? "I heard Wade's funeral was standing room only."

Leah turned her head enough that she wouldn't have to look him in the eye. Better for both of them. "Yes. Lots of support. Lots of people thought highly of my husband."

The cords in Josiah's neck stiffened. It was true. He might be the only one in their community who no longer "thought highly" of her Wade. "I'd like to contribute something to the memorial fund, Leah." For her sake, not Wade's.

"That's not necessary. Or wanted." She faced him. "I came for two reasons." Her voice took on the timbre of no-nonsense businesswoman. "To find out about Karin. And to give you these." She retrieved a set of keys from her jacket pocket and extended them to him.

"These are . . . ?"

"Keys to the Seedlings & Sentiments shop. I'm not going back. I'm sure you can understand."

Karin's shop. He hadn't thought about it for days. He would have remembered when the rent came due. Probably another of the messages he'd ignored. "Sure, I understand."

"My paycheck was auto-deposited."

What was her point?

"I went in today and stopped mine. You'll have to be the one to get all Karin's end of the business taken care of with the bank and the landlord. You do have power of attorney, right?"

Power of attorney. He hadn't thought about that either. All Karin's business dealings were in her name, except for the rent. When she moved her craft project to the shop, it had seemed smart. It kept him from having to be involved. Had the business actually been making money? "I'll handle it."

"Good. There are some outstanding accounts receivable as well as a few bills coming in yet from our suppliers."

"Is there money enough in the business account to take care of the bills?"

The expression on Leah's face was half pity, half disgust. An odd but combustible mix. "I don't think you understand what I'm saying, Josiah. It's not my problem anymore. I don't care if you close the shop or keep it open or find someone to run it while you wait for Karin to recover. Or whatever." Her voice had dropped below whisper level. "I don't care about any of that. I can't care about any of that." She blinked back tears as if refusing to let them fall.

"I don't know anything about Karin's business, Leah." Shame inched up the back of his neck. He should have listened more.

"If you're as smart as you claim, you'll figure it out."

A retort died in his throat. Nancy and the new family returned from lunch. Supper. What time was it? What meal? What day?

"Leah, we should set up a time when we can talk. Not here."

"Do you have any concept"—her lips barely moved, her teeth stayed clenched—"of what this has done to me?"

"As a matter of fact, yes." *Keep it civil, Josiah.* "You're not the only one who was betrayed."

"Betrayed?" The red rimming her eyes turned fiery.

Josiah glanced around the room. The visitors had heard. "Leah, let's go to the cafeteria, okay? Or the chapel."

"The chapel? That's rich, coming from you."

He gritted his molars. Not here. Not like this. Not in front of these hurting people. He nodded toward the door. "Let's go somewhere we can talk." The pain on Leah's face pierced a crust Josiah felt crumbling. "Please?"

She stood. Waited, breathing. "Ten minutes."

"Agreed. Ten minutes." Josiah glanced at the clock. He was going to miss another top-of-the-hour.

Chapter 15

*A path that is arrow-straight eventually
leads you back where you started.
The winding, pulse-pounding path
leads to awe-inspiring vistas.*

~ Seedlings & Sentiments
from the "Challenge" collection

$\mathcal{I}$was not betrayed." Leah left the point of the four stabbing dagger words deep in the flesh of his heart. "Your wife may have left you"—*twist*—"but my husband was an honorable man."

Her laser stare seared his soul. "Leah"—he could manage little more than a coarse whisper—"how can you be sure of that? Neither one of us wants to believe something was going on between them, but the evidence is telling a different story."

"Evidence? You have assumptions. Nothing more. And they're built on lousy logic, to be frank. I know Wade. And I know Karin. She wouldn't do that to you. And she wouldn't do it to me." She slapped her palm against her heart.

It won't help keep your heart from breaking, Leah. I've tried it.

"Of all the"—her voice hitched—"people in the world who would be faithful no matter what, it's the two of them. You

125

know that. You *know* that." The bitter edge was gone, replaced by childlike pleading.

One piece of evidence remained. He couldn't share it without destroying her. The news about Karin's child.

Leah still clung to hope that her husband was innocent, loved her above all others, must have been performing some gallant act of service that night. Josiah could burst the grieving widow's bubble with a sentence or two.

And lose what little self-respect he still possessed.

And seal Karin's reputation.

There's no good answer here, is there, God?

Too weird for words. He could have sworn he heard a male version of a Jewish grandmother say, "So, *now* you're asking Me for advice?"

Leah dug a tissue from her purse.

"Did you have music?"

"What?" Incredulity lined Leah's forehead.

"Was there music at Wade's funeral?"

"Yes. Of course."

"Tell me about it."

"Josiah, what is wrong with you?"

He composed his thoughts as if creating an opening hook for a speech, choosing and discarding possibilities. Nothing would make the idea comfortable to express. "I may have to plan a funeral." None of the medical personnel would offer him as much as a "cautiously optimistic." A funeral was a logical possibility. "I don't know what to do about the music."

❧ ❧ ❧

"I'm dehydrated. That's all." Josiah grabbed bottled water from a vending machine after saying good-bye to Leah in a fragile truce of shared grief. He chugged half the bottle before turning his attention to his rogue emotions. So close to the edge. Teetering. Nancy's counsel about the need to take care of himself looped through his brain. He couldn't afford to lose his mind with this much at stake.

But that's what he'd been doing when Karin left him. Taking care of himself. *His* needs. *His* projects. *His* dream. And look where it got them.

"Don't try to hoard blame for your spouse's wrong choices." Last spring's seminar focus at his *Check Mate* events. Josiah drove his foot into the kick plate of the vending machine. *Nice theory, Chamberlain. Now tell me how that works in the real world.*

"Machine acting ornery again?"

Josiah's big toe throbbed, but he refused to limp as he stepped away from the vending machine and addressed the young man with the black-leather biker jacket and spotty attempt at a moustache. "Ornery human," Josiah admitted, tapping his fist on his forehead.

The young man's grin revealed the reason for dentists and orthodontists. "Yeah, we've all been there." He deposited a dollar bill in the slot. When it spit it back at him, he smoothed a crinkled corner and tried again.

It'll never work. Once wrinkled beyond acceptance, it'll always—

The machine swallowed the dollar and demanded another. Satisfied, it released its hold on a twenty-ounce bottle of yellow liquid sugar and caffeine. The young man guzzled faster than Josiah had downed his own drink minutes earlier.

He couldn't help it. Josiah flinched at the thought of liquid sugar racing over those bad teeth like toddlers on their favorite playground. *Choose the water for once.* No. Josiah couldn't advise anybody. He had no right.

He recapped his half-empty bottle of water and retreated toward the elevator, his gaze fixed on the repeated pattern in the floor tile. It looked like his father's frown.

Sooner or later, he was going to have to attack his nuclear reactor meltdown of voice mails. Unable to write or even talk to himself with any sense of reason, he snagged a pen and the small notepad he carried in his laptop case and started with the oldest message.

Reminder about his haircut. He tugged at the hair that had started to curl at the back of his neck. The least of his problems. And four days too late anyway. Delete.

A string of insistent messages from Morris. Also outdated. Delete. Delete. Delete. Delete.

Business calls he'd have to return, some of which would require apologies. He took notes and numbers.

An across-the-street neighbor curious about the lack of activity at Josiah and Karin's house. "Everything okay?" *Not even close.* Josiah returned Myrna's call, filled her in with a brief rehearsal of the situation, and asked her to keep an eye out for Sandi.

Myrna pressed for more details. What caring person wouldn't? He talked in generalities and canned responses. "Karin's going to recover, isn't she?"

Josiah's pause couldn't have been comforting, but it was a question without a solid answer. "We appreciate all the prayer we can get."

We. All three of us.

As he ended the call with Myrna, he jotted another note to himself: *Figure out how to word this.*

As if precise words could make a difference. As if words existed that would explain the unexplainable. As if "we appreciate your prayers" carried more weight than a grocery clerk's "Have a nice day."

Another note landed on the page: *Have a serious conversation with God.*

Next message? Michele from his speaker's bureau. Was he interested in serving on a panel addressing relationship issues for families of the incarcerated? No pay, but good PR. She needed an answer three days ago. He added the speaker's bureau to his list of people and places that needed a bulk e-mail explaining why he was currently out of pocket.

He deleted half a dozen calls from people he and Karin knew from church—likely responses to Janelle's exceptional news-spreading skills. He'd update her later this afternoon and let her handle their questions.

In the corner of the ICU family waiting room, a teen slumped, angled away from a woman who—by genetic similarities and the disgust on her face—must have been his mother. She alternately dabbed at her eyes with a tissue and used sign language to beg her son to get off his phone and talk to her. Or at least get in the waiting game. She glanced at Josiah, tapping away at his own phone.

This is different. Avoidance? Sure. But it's . . . unavoidable.

He turned his back toward the two and continued his voice-mail purge.

Another call from the sheriff's department, reminding him he needed to make arrangements about the car and its contents. Good grief! He hadn't called the car insurance guy. It's the kind of thing Karin would have handled for them. What did their policy provide regarding secondary drivers? That wasn't going to mess up getting their full amount for the totaled vehicle, was it?

A grunt escaped before he could stop it. Now he was worried about replacing a car for a woman who might never drive again, walk again, open her eyes. If he had a nickel for every ludicrous absurdity in all this, he could afford to replace the car.

The alarm on his phone signaled the approach of the top of the hour. He stuffed his belongings in his locker and made a routine trip to the restroom. As he washed his hands at the small sink, he chanced a look in the mirror. Probably wouldn't hurt to comb his hair. He had a date with his half-dead, cheating wife.

❧ ❧ ❧

The look on Karin's face confirmed the half-dead part. But nothing Josiah saw in those once-delicate features spoke of betrayal. What registered was the lingering shadow of her vows. Above the sound of equipment, he could almost hear her voice—that gentle, lyrical voice that had turned his head even before he saw the girl it belonged to, singing as she waited for the campus bookstore to open. He rounded the corner and found her—arms outstretched, palms turned up, face lifted toward what he soon discovered wasn't the ceiling but to the One no ceiling could separate from her.

His presence startled her. She'd stopped singing and opened her eyes. Her first words to him had been, "I'm sorry."

Ironic.

"Practicing for something?" he'd asked, failing even then to find the right words.

"Life," she'd answered. Her hair reached past her waist in those days. Burnt copper. Not quite brown. Not quite red. Straight as a highway through North Dakota. He didn't know she straightened it every morning until they were caught in a deluge on the way home from the coffee shop that night and it reclaimed its natural waves. She wore it shoulder-length now, with wisps around her perfect face and a swirl of bangs that seemed streaked with gold silk.

Life, she'd said. Practicing for life.

The half-bandage she wore on her head now reminded him of a gauzy, tissue-stuffed beret. He could see fine stubble where they'd had to shave part of her head. What was left of her hair lay stringy and sweat-soaked against the hospital pillow.

"Let me hear your voice," he whispered, leaning near her ear. "I need to hear your voice, Karin."

A high-pitched beep interrupted the moment. Not what he'd hoped to hear. Before he could pinpoint which machine had an issue, a male nurse Josiah had met briefly before entered the room, checked one of the monitors, then lifted the sheet to adjust a belt-like strap across Karin's belly. The nurse slid two fingers under the belt when he finished his adjustment, as if ensuring it wasn't too tight. "You woke her up, I guess," he said.

Josiah sat back in his chair. Karin's eyes hadn't fluttered. But he watched. Maybe he missed it.

"Your baby. She's doing some kind of happy dance in there." The nurse smoothed the sheet and pointed at a spot. "Here." He gestured for Josiah to lay his hand an inch below the belt monitor. "You have to be pretty sensitive to feel her movements this early," he said.

Sensitive. *You have the wrong dad for that.*

"I'm guessing it's a girl. It's a gift I have. I've only been wrong forty-nine percent of the time." His raised eyebrow and quirked mouth told Josiah he had more comedy in him than pride.

A little levity. Refreshing after so much that wasn't.

Josiah waited. Nothing moved beneath his hand. He felt the rise and fall of Karin's breaths. Shallow. But not as mechanical as they had been a day or two earlier. He glanced at the circus train of machines lined up in a wide arc around her bed. His pulse pounded at his throat. Where was the breathing machine? The one that wheezed and hitched?

He retraced the arc of those familiar machines. "Is my wife breathing on her own?"

"You hadn't been told? That's unfortunate."

"She's breathing on her own?" He measured his words in case the nurse hadn't heard him clearly.

"Yes, Mr. Chamberlain. We'd tried it in the night for a half hour, and she did pretty well, but we put her back on the machine when we could tell she tired. Another experiment today went so well, we're letting her handle it on her own. A big step. She's on oxygen, at least for a while. We're monitoring her pulse-ox level and respirations closely. You should be encouraged."

"I didn't know."

The nurse stopped his practiced routine and looked Josiah in the eye. "Except for emergency situations, we should never be too busy to keep family informed. It's inexcusable. I'll try to find out where the line of communication failed, Mr. Chamberlain."

Josiah braced himself on the bed with his free hand. What he wanted to say dragged its feet on the way out. "It's not about finding someone to blame."

It's all my—What's the word? All my—Josiah, I can't find the word. Fault! It's all my fault. Say something. Need you to say something.

He wasn't a heads-will-roll kind of guy. He coached others to lose that attitude and focus on the point of contention in their marriages rather than the contenders. Until a moment ago, he'd thought he needed to hear from Karin partly so he'd know who deserved the blame. As long as it wasn't him. How else could he know whom he had to work on forgiving so he could move on?

His mind scrolled through page after page of text he'd written, tips he'd outlined with memorable titles, sessions with couples he'd felt sorry for, faces of those who'd appeared starved for his wisdom. His pathetic wisdom.

This may have been among the few truly wise things he'd said. And he'd said it to a stranger as he braced himself over his wife's unresponsive body and the child that rumbled against his hand.

It's not about finding someone to blame.

Chapter 16

Forgiveness—though invisible—leaves its imprint
on every heart it touches.

~ Seedlings & Sentiments
from the "When Words Aren't Enough" collection

$\mathcal{W}$hen a person tells the story of caring for a loved one in their final days or while they heal from trauma—and why did his thoughts turn first to *final days?*—what do they write in their journals? "About the same as yesterday. Nothing new to report. A little weaker, if anything. Another minor crisis averted. On to the next one. Another day of waiting." He might ask Nancy if she kept a journal about her son's time in ICU. It seemed pointless. Josiah could write "About the same as yesterday" and photocopy that page or write "ditto" for the next month's worth of entries.

The next month? Weeks so far, now that Josiah thought about it. The only person marking time was the obstetrician. The longer the baby stayed where it was, the better its chances. Although Dr. Randall always coupled his week-counting with the reminder that because of Karin's condition, this particular baby's chances hadn't started at "good" or even "fair." A conundrum. The longer Karin remained unresponsive, "locked in" as some described it, the harder the child would have to fight to survive.

133

If Karin knew what she'd done to her child's chances...

Josiah watched her sleep phase, which looked a lot like her awake phase from the outside. How is it he'd seen threads of who she really was at her core when she couldn't say a word, when questions remained that she couldn't explain or apologize for or defend, when his touch brought no reaction and he saw no clues that she even knew he sat near her ten minutes of every hour almost all day every day?

He knew she'd be mortified to know her actions had threatened that child's life.

"I'm sorry, Karin. I'm so sorry." Josiah recalled the conversation from three years ago as if it had just happened.

"It's all right. It's not your fault." She'd briefly touched his forearm with her hand, then returned to her hands-clasped-together-in-a-faux-resting position in her lap.

"Of course it is. Of course it's my fault. And now we know for sure."

"We can adopt."

Josiah had slid his hands back and forth on the wooden arms of the chair that matched the one Karin occupied beside him. "Would you hate me if I said I didn't want to adopt?"

Of all the sentences he'd spoken or written, that's the one he now wished he could retrieve.

She'd postponed answering. Josiah remembered counting. One second. Two. Three. "What do you have against adoption?"

He'd leaned forward, forearms on his thighs. The fertility specialist needed to shell out for new carpeting in her office. The kind of salary she pulled down, surely she could afford carpeting with a little class. Karin could help her pick out something tasteful. Maybe the Chamberlains could barter for a discount on past fertility tests.

He righted himself. "I don't have anything against adoption, per se." *Per se.* These years later, those words echoed as hollow as they must have sounded to his wife.

She'd shifted in her chair to look at him rather than toward the empty office chair across Dr. Kayber's desk. "You obviously do."

"Nothing against it. I'm not sure how I feel."

Karin had tilted her head up as if her powers of persuasion hung from the ceiling and by reaching she could pluck a handful.

"And there's the expense." Four little words he wished he'd swallowed. How is it he couldn't remember the last conversation he'd had with Karin before the accident, but this scene was more vivid now than it ever had been?

Her jaw had tightened. A dentist would tsk-tsk over her grinding her molars like that.

"Not that money is the deciding factor, Karin." He reached to stroke her taut cheek. She'd drawn back. Not much. Enough. "Honey, can we talk about this later? My manhood's just been dealt a deathblow."

"Your . . . manhood."

Maybe that's when he'd first started talking to himself with any regularity. His self-talk started with, *Josiah, you're an idiot. Humor is not always welcome. Some situations call for a little more finesse. Apologize. Quick, before she—*

"Let's just go." Karin rose from her chair as if nine-months pregnant with disappointment.

"Dr. Doom-and-Gloom is coming back. We can't leave yet."

"Stay if you want. I'm going home."

And she had.

They'd talked it out. Worked it out. Within hours they were crying on each other's shoulders, aching together rather than alone. Josiah agreed to adopt. Karin said no. Not yet.

They revisited the subject every few months for three years. He'd changed his tactic, making sure she knew how much a baby would interfere with his career plans at this stage.

She stopped dropping hints about— Huh. Four months ago.

She and Wade? Already an item four months ago? Well, obviously. The now sixteen-week-old unborn child beneath his hand rumbled its presence again.

Josiah rewound. April to March is one, February, January, December . . .

Oh, Karin. The Christmas party? You can't fault me for staying home from your "company" Christmas party. That holiday book tour exhausted me. Did you expect me to come straight from the airport? After a string of TV appearances that would have choked Oprah? If you'll remember, you're the one who chose the party over picking me up at the airport. I guess that cost us a whole lot more than the taxi ride, didn't it?

Wait. April to March is one. To February, two. If the estimates are wrong, they could be talking November? The end of November?

Where was he the end of November? Where was Karin?

What did it matter?

There's no such thing as *rewind* in marriage.

The rebound effect of the staff-to-patient's-spouse communication breakdown almost made Josiah laugh, if there'd been anything funny in it. Crisis averted. Karin's latest infection responded to the high-powered antibiotics. Surprising them all, she was breathing on her own. Did he want to know her IV fluid intake and collected output or see the stitches in her head during dressing changes?

No.

A patient advocate arranged a confab among Josiah and all the key players in Karin's care. The obstetrician—the famed Dr. Randall—spent entirely too much time arguing with the neurologist for Josiah's taste. Whose judgment trumped the others'? *Way to reassure the loved ones, docs.*

Loved ones. Well, once-loved.

She'd loved him once. Sincerely. For almost ten of their twelve years together. He read it in her eyes, her touch, the way her smile broke open like a joy-filled piñata when he walked into the room.

He read it in her preference to turn off the electric blanket and curl herself into his body heat.

They tandemed well, worked in sync like few couples he knew. They shared coffee at the breakfast table, analyzing what went wrong with other peoples' marriages. They prayed together. Not so much lately, but—

The morning's revelation created a sense of urgency in his routine of getting ready to head back to the hospital from last night's break to check on the house and mail and sleep in a real bed for a change.

And Sandi had returned! Wet, thin, and sporting a scar near her right ear. Josiah gave her a bath, half of his supper, and a fatherly talking to. Sandi didn't leave his side the rest of the night.

"Where have you been, girl? Where have you been?"

It didn't escape his notice that he could reserve the same questions for Karin if—when—she recovered.

Sandi had been through something, and Josiah might never know what. But she was home. Josiah dragged her doggie bed to the master bedroom, his side, and woke frequently through the night to remind himself it was possible for someone he loved to come home for good.

The comfort of Sandi's return capped the wellspring of hope. The impossible wasn't.

The phone. Stan. Finally, some good news to tell him. Karin loved him once, and Sandi wasn't gone forever. No, the other news, about the infection and Karin's breathing on her own.

"Dad, good news."

"Yes. Me, too. In a way." Josiah heard Stan draw a quick breath. "Son, your mother-in-law has seen the face of Jesus."

Josiah shifted the phone to his other hand so he could finish shaving before heading back to the hospital. *What? In her toast? Pancakes?* He mentally choked on the last word. His razor rattled to the sink.

"Son, she died in her sleep. I woke up early. Don't know why. She was gone already."

"Stan! No!"

"It's okay. It's going to be okay. I have a feeling she talked God into taking her a little early so she didn't have to go through that next set of tests she dreaded." His chuckle sounded forced. "I wouldn't put it past her to have talked His ear off until He finally gave in."

"Oh, Stan." Josiah sat on the edge of the tub and propped his forehead with his free hand.

"Forty-eight years together. That's a good run."

"Not enough."

"It would never have been enough."

Josiah the Inadequate. Sitting on his bathtub, his face half-shaved, hours away from where his father-in-law sat in a house empty of Catherine's voice and steady presence. "You should have someone there with you, Stan."

"I do. And you know what? He doesn't look anything like His pictures in toast."

ৼৄ ৼৄ ৼৄ

So, does He look like Corporal Klinger, Mom?

That's what Josiah would have asked Catherine if the empty shell in the casket still held a remnant of her and if he could have attended the funeral.

The Novocain of pain to the tenth power kept him from falling apart at the news of Catherine's death. By phone, he'd stumbled through his consolations to Stan and listened as his father-in-law repeatedly shared the story of her Home-going. Catherine slept through the whole thing. Stan woke in the morning. She didn't. Stan immediately canceled her appointment with the hometown cardiologist for later that week. Her heart needed nothing more than what it had gained in that middle-of-the-night moment.

Josiah sensed his soul would look pale, anemic, if it stood side by side with Stan's. The man walked the delicate balance beam of grief and acceptance with the panache of an Olympic gymnast, recovering admirably when he wobbled, from what Josiah could see.

In the days immediately following the news of Catherine's death, the list of items to cover so Josiah could attend his mother-in-law's service grew. Unnamed phantom helpers—probably church people, aided by Myrna from across the street—had tended the lawn, taken out the garbage, planted flowers where Karin would have, and left an array of ready-to-thaw-and-heat meals in the freezer. Sandi was no longer a concern but a comfort. He stopped looking in ditches along the side of the road. She'd been on an adventure and had forgotten to ask him along. Hurting, Sandi spent her days healing and wandering the house as if wondering where Karin hid.

If he were to attend the funeral, Josiah's business had to get a little attention. His car needed its oil changed and a new tire or two. He'd rent or borrow a car for the trip to Somerset.

But the thought of asking someone else to take his place at Karin's side sickened him. So did the idea of leaving her alone for the two days the travel and funeral would take. A natural choice would have been Karin's friend, Leah, if it hadn't been for—

Josiah insisted on being kept informed about the funeral arrangements. In the end, he didn't need to know the time or location. Karin took a turn for the worse.

Or rather, her baby did.

The baby exhibited signs of being "stressed."

"What does that mean?" he asked Angie, one of the nurses he knew he could count on for straightforward information.

"Your little one is reacting adversely to Karin's pain."

"I thought you were keeping Karin sedated enough not to feel pain." Josiah's throbbing temples exhibited signs of being stressed.

Angie elevated the head of Karin's bed a few degrees. "No one is sure how much she's aware of. Brain injuries aren't always easy to read. With her breathing on her own, we assumed she'd work her way back to being more alert. That hasn't happened. But when the monitors show an increase in heart rate or blood pressure for Karin, the baby's heartbeat drops significantly."

"Can you do something?" Did Karin have some kind of sixth sense that her mother was gone? Is that why she was more agitated? How long would it be before Josiah was tasked with giving her that message?

Angie hooked a plastic syringe to the port near Karin's neck and slowly depressed the plunger. "We're doing everything we can. Believe me, we're not out of options yet."

Yet.

I remember the baby, Josiah. Sometimes remembering is harder than forgetting. Shh, child. Shh.

Josiah growled low in his throat.

"Is that a groan? Or are you angry, Mr. Chamberlain?" Angie tilted her motherly head as if she were asking a toddler.

"Groan. Frustration. I should be able to fix this. It's my life's work to fix broken people."

"And the sink at the plumber's house is always stopped up."

"What? Oh." So he wasn't the only professional with problems at home. Or thirty-five miles from home. "Especially true in my case."

"Maybe by your next visit, this little one will have decided to be less irritable."

That's my— That's Karin's child you're talking about. "Irritable?"

"Don't worry, Mr. Chamberlain. The feisty ones are the ones who survive."

Chapter 17

Strewn among the debris that washes up on the beach are bits of sea glass and remnants of grand things. Watch for them.

~ Seedlings & Sentiments
from the "Hope" collection

If he tried to divorce himself from the fact that the scene was happening to him, to Karin, to that too-small child, could Josiah record the journey? Could he commit to paper—or his computer files—the story of what it takes to care for a sick wife? He could devote an entire section to "Even When She Chooses Someone Other Than You." Might make for interesting reading. He wondered what conclusions he'd draw. At the moment, he was clueless.

He usually ignored the thrum of his phone, letting everything these days go to voice mail. But something about its insistence compelled him to answer this time.

The number on the screen threatened to stop his heart. Karin's number.

"Who is this?"

"Yeah, uh, this is Lyle."

"Lyle who?"

"Penderman. I think I have your phone." The man blew a breath that was all nostril.

"My wife's phone. How did you get it, Mr. Penderman?" It took everything in Josiah not to imagine a longer list of Karin's lovers than the single entry—Wade.

"Yeah, I found it." He made it sound like a question.

"You found it where?" Impatience might make the thief hang up. Josiah focused on slowing his heart rate and tempering his tone. "Near the accident site?"

"What accident?"

"Never mind. Can you tell me where you found my wife's phone?"

"I dig through the landfill sometimes. Look, it ain't got but a thin red line of battery left. You want it back? I may be a scavenger, but I like to do good things for people, too. If the phone still works, you might want it back, right?"

"Let me get your address before the phone dies, Mr. Penderman."

A Paxton address. Lyle had found the phone in their hometown. Discarded? How did it end up in the landfill? The Dumpster at Karin's shop?

"Lyle, how did you get my number?"

"Contacts. I figured it was okay to check. You're listed as ICE."

ICE. In Case of Emergency.

Fitting.

Josiah told Lyle he'd stop by the next time he was in Paxton. Would her phone hold any answers? The fact that it ended up in a Dumpster posed more questions. She wouldn't have intentionally thrown her phone away . . . unless she was desperate to keep Josiah from reaching her. Nothing else made sense. He could remove the word *else* and the sentence could still stand. She threw away her phone to keep him from finding her?

The possibility brought him as close to anger as he'd been in days.

If it weren't for the baby, he might have let the top-of-the-hour visit pass. But somebody had to care about that little one. The only people who knew were medical staff; Janelle, whom he avoided with Navy Seal stealth; Stan, who didn't need one more concern; and Josiah. He won by default.

He focused on the monitor that registered the baby's responses. To his untrained eye, it looked better than it had been. As soon as the thought formed, the pattern changed and an alarm sounded. Angie was at the bedside in seconds. She warmed a stethoscope disc between her hands, then laid it over the mound. Moved it. Listened. Moved it again. Listened.

Say something!

"That little stinker."

Not what Josiah expected.

"Swam under the radar, you might say." Angie readjusted the monitor belt. "That's better." She listened again with the stethoscope. "This should put you at ease." She pulled the earpieces out of her ears and handed them to Josiah. "See what you think."

Somebody had to care about that child.

He slid the earpieces into his ears and closed his eyes. A sloshing sound. And a heartbeat. Rapid. Rabbit-rapid. But steady. One of the most beautiful sounds in the universe. Angie had to tap him on the shoulder to get him to relinquish his audio connection to the heartbeat.

"Angie, do we know if it's a boy or a girl?"

"According to the latest ultrasound, which was"—she checked the computerized records—"this morning, it's a girl."

"I thought so." *I did?*

It's a girl? It's a girl. A girl. Oh, Josiah!

"Mr. Chamberlain?"

"What?"

"Look. Something's going on in there." Angie stood with her fists tucked under her chin, her gaze fixed on the head of the bed.

A tear dribbled down the side of Karin's face and onto her pillow.

Josiah reached to wipe it with his thumb. Instinct. That's what good husbands do.

Angie and Josiah watched for other signs. Per protocol, Angie tested for response to stimuli. Feet. Fingers. Light. Sound.

Nothing.

A random tear on a random day with no connection to the moment? No evidence Karin's brain functioned at a higher level than her limp body? Josiah didn't buy it. Didn't want to believe it.

He left the intensive care unit too few minutes later, hope and despair jockeying for the lead.

For so many days, his footsteps had taken him from that unit to the family waiting room or down the stairs or elevator for a soul-centering walk around the hospital grounds, or to Ernie's for breakfast, lunch, or supper—whichever meal landed at that imprecise hour.

This time, though, he detoured to the chapel. His hand lingered on the heavy bronze door latch.

What am I doing? He backed away from the door and dropped onto a slatted bench along the opposite wall. *I'm keeping watch over a woman who declared, with her words and her body, that she no longer loves me. I'm in a prayer vigil for another man's baby. I'm the definition of a fool. Who would love someone who intentionally left him? Who would choose to love a betrayer?*

It was time to walk away. Maybe past time.

Instead, he crossed the hall and took refuge in the chapel. As had become his custom, he walked past the artwork before looking for a place to settle in. He stopped at the painting of the Man on the cross.

The engraved title plate tapped into the bottom of the carved wood frame of the painting held three words: *With love, Jesus.*

The words buckled him.

People don't come to a hospital chapel to read a magazine or do crossword puzzles. They come for comfort, solace, and cleansing.

Or for the quiet, the music, the art.

How many hospital visitors, how many waiting family members—waiting, waiting, waiting—knew comfort and solace lay embedded in the threads of the quiet, the music, and the art?

Josiah contemplated the question as songs in the background washed over him and artwork surrounded him with the Undeniable.

A young couple huddled together in the front row. Her turban and IV stand told Josiah all he needed to know about the circumstances that drew them into the chapel's arms.

Josiah was a refrigerator in a summer garage, sweating with the effort of protecting the cold inside when the warmth outside tried so hard to get in. What was he doing here? He didn't need God to tell him he was a jerk for considering the unthinkable—abandoning his wife and her child because Karin had given up on their marriage. Josiah was the one who blasted the Beatles' "We Can Work It Out" through the event speakers as he took the stage. They could work it out. Eventually. Couldn't they?

How fortuitous that Wade no longer stood in the way.

He dug his fingernails into the flesh of his thighs, through his jeans, grateful for the pain. He deserved worse than that for entertaining a fragment of gratitude that his competition was dead.

God, I'm in worse shape than Karin is.

When the young couple left, their path took them close enough for confirmation of Josiah's suspicions. The woman had no eyebrows and her turban sat unnaturally loose on her head. How did they do it? How did that husband cope with watching his wife suffer and feeling utterly helpless to make a difference? How were they navigating the emotional component of all this? What chapters could they write for him? *To* him?

The woman stopped walking and reached out for the edge of the bench nearest her. Her husband tightened his grip on his wife and waited until she'd stabilized or the nausea had passed or she felt stronger. He'd tightened his grip and waited. Then he bent to kiss her sunken cheek before they continued their journey.

Josiah started a mental list of "Yeah, but" thoughts. "Yeah, but you're confident of your wife's love for you." "Yeah, but she didn't betray you."

The chair on which he sat creaked and dipped when someone slid into the one beside him. Close. Too close to be a stranger. Nancy.

"Did you get to see your son yet today?" he asked in a chapel-hushed voice. Her job kept her away from the hospital more than she wanted. Josiah's job might be portable, but creativity didn't appreciate hospital lighting.

"Just saw him a few minutes ago. Felt an irresistible pull toward this place afterward."

"How is Blaine?"

Nancy shrugged her shoulders. "Still this side of Glory. Any change with Karin?"

The tear. That single tear. Did it even count? He matched her shrug.

"How's Stan doing?"

"I haven't talked to him since yesterday. I think it was yesterday. The days and dates and times get muddied in this environment."

"Don't they though?"

Josiah shifted to face her more directly. She'd spared him from a conversation he didn't relish with the Almighty. "The service was nice, Stan said. Packed church. Beautiful tribute."

"Do you think he'll be back here soon?"

Josiah wondered how long a man needed to be ready to transition from his wife's funeral to the bedside of a dying daughter. "He still has family staying at the house. I told him to take all the time he needed. That I'd keep him informed."

"One of the blessing/curse mash-ups of prolonged hospitaliza-tion. Or any tragedy, I suppose." Nancy picked at a loose thread on the hem of her work shirt. "Keeping people informed. We love it that they care, but it can be a chore to make sure everyone is up to date. Especially when change is a long time coming. 'The same. Thanks for praying.'"

The veteran had so much to teach him. He'd relegated most of the updating to Janelle, whom he e-mailed sporadically. But he still found evidence of how much people cared. In the mailbox, the refrigerator, his lawn, Karin's garden. When this was over or stabilized or whatever it was going to do, he'd need an assistant to help him send out thank-you notes.

Good, church-going people that they were, what would their response be if they knew the truth about Karin's affair?

Had he used that word to describe it before? He'd always deferred to the word *betrayal*.

Nancy gripped the back of the line of chairs in front of them, eyes forward. "Do you want to share communion?"

"What?"

She nodded toward the altar. He'd been there more than an hour and hadn't noticed the wine carafe, small plastic cups, and a plate of linen napkin–wrapped flatbread on the altar.

"Is there a chaplain or something?"

Nancy stood up. "Sometimes. Not today. We serve one another. We'll see if those women who just walked in want to join us."

Serve each other? Josiah followed as if communion in a hospital with strangers were an everyday occurrence for him.

Karin, the things you've gotten me into . . .

His heart twisted. The veins and arteries knotted. Maybe this would serve as his confession starting point.

Nancy stopped to talk to the newcomers while Josiah waited at the altar. Left at the altar. Story of his life these days.

With her arm around the younger of the two women, Nancy brought the mother and daughter to the altar with her. "Josiah," she said, "why don't you read the Scripture for us?"

What Scripture? Oh, the traditional one. Where was it? He should know. The "This is My body, broken for you" verses. New Testament, obviously. As he pulled out file drawers in his brain in search of the answer, Nancy slid an open Bible across the altar table toward where he stood. It was open to 1 Corinthians 11. Verse 23 was underlined.

Nancy poured four small cups of wine or juice—he didn't know yet—and set them before the four members of their makeshift congregation. She held the broken loaf of flatbread and let each person break off a small chunk, which they held in their hands with reverence. Then Nancy—her work shirt smelling of hard labor—nodded toward Josiah.

An unseen hand switched the music playing in the background. As Josiah balanced the Bible in one hand and his portion of bread in the other, he heard a whisper of lyrics that said something like, "I was carried to the table of the Lord."

He blinked to clear his vision, then read, "'On the night on which he was betrayed, the Lord Jesus took bread—'"

Three sets of eyes trained on him. Anticipating.

"'On the night on which he was—'"

Nancy's hand felt warm and motherly on his trembling arm. "Josiah?"

"'—betrayed.'"

Wordless again, Josiah laid the Bible on the table, picked up his portion of wine, and walked to the depiction of the meal he held in his hand. He lifted the elements to the artist's rendition of the meal's central figure.

Details of the room in which Josiah stood, the people gathered with him, the abandonment that brought him to that place—all faded. Son-bleached.

The Man in the painting breaking the bread, lifting the chalice, offered His greatest demonstration of love on the night He was betrayed.

Chapter 18

When the morning dawns, it holds no promise of smooth seas.
But it does promise light by which to navigate.

~ Seedlings & Sentiments
from the "Guidance" collection

Care to explain that?" Nancy asked. She limped a little as she matched his pace down the hospital corridor. Josiah hadn't noticed her limp before. But then, not noticing rang as a recent theme for him.

"Care to explain the limp?" he countered.

"Touch of arthritis. I complain that arthritis in the hip is the worst location. Don't ask me to trade for a knee or shoulder, though. And quit changing the subject. I'd like to hear about what the Lord did in your heart back there in the chapel. You were having a moment, I'd say."

Josiah's throat tightened. He wasn't accustomed to people holding him accountable. If he told the truth about what he experienced, he'd have to connect it to Karin's betrayal. He was oblivious, but he was no squealer.

If people knew...

Was it Karin's reputation he worried about or still his own?

Wonder what Josiah did to make her leave him like that?

We never did figure out what she saw in him.

Sure, he can claim his wife left him, but she can't exactly defend her honor, can she? It's his word against—

Decent people, friends, even Stan would question *him*, not her. Was he ready for that?

Nancy stopped. He kept walking. Two steps. Three. He turned and erased the distance he'd put between them.

"Josiah," she said, her voice only a shadow of its former self, "do *you* know what it's like to choose to love someone who betrayed you?"

A fake and false and entirely untrue answer gathered itself in his throat. Before he could work it out of his mouth she added, "I do. It was no small thing what you taught me in there."

Taught *her?*

"No wonder you're the world famous go-to guy for relationships. I didn't realize you were so deeply spiritual."

I may have thought I was an accomplished swimmer, but I'm still wading in the shallow end on that count, Nancy.

The word jigsaw puzzle lying on the floor of his mind was missing the key pieces he needed. So he said nothing. What's the point of starting a puzzle you can't finish?

Josiah shrugged. A generic motion that could mean anything. *Multiple choice, Nancy. Pick one: I'm humble. I don't know. Isn't everyone deeply spiritual?*

Introspection sometimes feels like a colonoscopy. Josiah shook off the urge to think. "How's Blaine?" Wait. He'd asked that in the chapel. She'd know he was stalling.

Nancy's son hadn't shown any progress since one of the Bush administrations, it seemed. What did he expect the answer to be? The same.

"The same. Same as he was when you asked me fifteen minutes ago."

Figured. She'd remembered.

Nancy drew a sipping-through-a-straw breath and said, "I'm grateful."

"Grateful?"

"He's not losing ground. In this department, that's saying something."

Josiah stuffed his hands into his pants pockets. He toyed with a knot of lint tucked deep into the seam of the pocket pouch. "Are you…happy with his care?" What was he suggesting? Uncool.

Nancy cocked her head to the side. "Interesting question."

"Forget I asked."

"I'm happy with Blaine's care." She resumed walking. "The nurses are great, aren't they? And the doctors have done everything they can. Blaine's lack of progress isn't their fault."

Her pace, limp and all, quickly took them to the waiting room. The too-familiar carpet and furnishings. The overworked magazines. The overheated coffee.

Someone—a newcomer no doubt—had turned the television to a soap opera. As if Josiah weren't living melodrama. The dialogue banged against his eardrums. Dysfunction and discontent. Anger. Treachery. In the name of entertainment. What about adultery does the world find entertaining?

A vision of a Man in an olive grove flashed on the screen of his mind. A Man deciding—*choosing*—to love on the night He was betrayed.

Josiah chose an armchair, slipped off his shoes, and made himself at home. He wasn't ready to talk. He wasn't sure he'd ever be ready to listen the way he suspected he'd have to.

∙∙∙

It's not that Janelle wasn't a pleasant enough person, with everyone but him. Karin's friend could have won Miss Congeniality in any contest she entered. Bubbly. But the bubbles in Alka-Seltzer are different from those in champagne. For some reason, the sight of Janelle standing in the hall made Josiah's stomach churn.

Their last three or four phone conversations and e-mails—strained through an unspoken screen of "how much do you know?"—felt like work. It shouldn't be laborious to keep his wife's friend informed. Wasn't it supposed to lift his load to know someone else cared?

Janelle knew about the baby. Maybe more.

Time to find out what and how much and maybe a word or two about why.

But it was the top of the hour.

"Janelle, thanks for coming." He crossed the room to meet her in the hall, arms extended. She'd expect a hug. Didn't everyone in this setting?

She embraced him as you would a high-school classmate at a reunion, one you couldn't remember but trusted the name tag was accurate. Jefferson High School Class of 1990. There it was. Had they worked on the homecoming float together? No. Drama Club?

"Josiah, I know you said there was no point coming. I can't see her. But—"

He stepped back and to the side, skirting around her to deliver the necessary sentence on his way to ICU. "Do you have time to wait? Ten minutes? I'm allowed in now and have to..."

Her expression changed from too-sober-for-her-face to perky. "Oh, sure. No, you go. I'll wait. Here?"

He nodded. If Nancy chose to sit out this visitation period, she might work her magic and milk the story out of Janelle before he got back. She could slip it to him in an envelope, and he wouldn't have to face the truth head-on.

The ICU door collided with his shoulder. *Okay, I deserved that.*

His body found its way to Karin's room on automatic pilot. One of the nurses—the one with unnaturally midnight-black hair—stood at the foot of the bed, rubbing hospital lotion into Karin's right foot.

"Can I do that?" The words were out of his mouth before he could retrieve them.

The nurse turned. Darla. Thank the Lord for name tags.

"Do what? Rub lotion on her feet?"

"Yes. I thought if you had other things to do—"

"Be my guest." She held the tube of thick cream toward him. "The skin on her feet is so dry and cracked. Don't lift her foot more than an inch or two off the bed, though, Mr. Chamberlain. Slow, smooth motions."

Darla watched his first few strokes, then left the room. She left him alone with his wife. A wave of something that felt a lot like fear broke over him. Why would the nursing staff trust her into his care?

Dry friction signaled he needed more lotion. He squeezed a nickel-sized dollop into the palm of his hand, then rubbed his hands together to warm it. With Karin's bed elevated to a height that made it easier for the staff to tend to her needs, it wasn't necessary for Josiah to bend. He slipped one hand under her foot and cradled it like Prince Charming—his nemesis—might have when sliding the glass slipper onto Cinderella's size five.

Karin's foot lay limp in his hand. No tension. No urge to run. But no melting at his touch either.

He smoothed the cream across the top of her foot, between her toes, around her heel. He lotioned the sole of her foot, knowing the action would have sent her into a fit of laughter if she could feel anything at all.

"Janelle's here," he said. "I want to tell her you'll be all right."

No reaction from the foot. A vein pulsed, but nothing other than that.

As if rubbing his words deep into her skin, he said, "I want to tell her *we'll* be all right. I need a sign, Karin. Something. Anything. Kick me if you want to."

The foot warmed, involuntarily no doubt, in response to the massage, not the message.

⌒

Don't stop. Please don't stop. I . . . something to say.

⌒

He moved to the other foot. It didn't have the hip-to-ankle brace the other did, but he still held her small foot tenderly, as if the slightest jar would send her deeper into DBT rather than awaken her from it. *This, I can do. It may not help. For my sake, Karin, I'm going to pretend it does.*

They were alone. She was closely watched on monitors at the nurse's station. But it was one of the few moments no medical personnel hovered.

"Karin, I need to tell you something."

Can you hear me? Why can't . . . hear me?

Josiah warmed more of the lotion and rubbed it into the dry, cracked skin of her foot. He would have wiped it with his hair if he still wore it like he did in college. Only cleaner.

"I love you, Karin. Even now. More now. And I'm sorry I haven't been very good at showing it."

You're here! You came! Knew you would.

"How is she?"

Josiah had almost forgotten Janelle had been waiting. "The same." *There. We got that over with. She's the same. Always the same. And aren't we grateful?*

Janelle stood almost where Josiah left her. She held a gift bag by its twisted paper handle. Tissue paper shot out the top like a still picture of a wood fiber fountain. "For you," she said, holding the bag toward him.

"Thanks," he said, hoping passersby wouldn't make assumptions about a guy with a gift bag as they would a guy with a purse.

"To the future."

Was she proposing a toast? What future?

Rude to open the gift or rude not to? The tissue paper rustled as he bumped the bag against his thigh. Coarse laughter spilled out of the waiting room. The newcomers must have gotten over their initial crisis sadness. Josiah took Janelle's arm and directed her farther from the doorway. "Let's go find a quieter place to talk."

She winced as another burst of laughter shot out the door. "Good idea. Where?"

"Are you a fan of toffee mocha?"

❧ ❧ ❧

Hours earlier, he'd sipped communion wine. Healing wine. With strangers to whom he was forever bonded by the act. As he now watched Janelle use a coffee stirrer to draw fjords in the mountain of whipped cream atop her mocha, Josiah sipped tea he hoped would scald the fog out of his mouth and allow him to start the I'm-not-sure-I-want-to-hear-it part of the conversation. Tea. Coffee's medicinal cousin.

And the truth will set you free. Scripture, right? A promise. He could name a dozen other scenarios where that might be possible. But this one? He could tell himself it didn't matter anymore. He was going to love anyway. But how could a thing like infidelity not matter?

"Aren't you going to open it?" Janelle nodded toward the gift bag on the booth bench beside him.

"Here?"

"I want to see the look on your face."

155

Josiah reached instead for the tag on his tea bag and dunked the pocket of tea leaves once, twice, three times. In the name of the Father, Son, and Holy Spirit. Janelle's gaze didn't change. She waited.

He lifted the gift bag to the tabletop. The move drew the attention of Ernie's customers and the aproned man himself.

"Hey! Somebody's havin' a birthday!" Ernie crooned. "Free pie. On the house."

The announcement generated a chorus of congratulations. The customers congratulated each other on the good fortune of free pie. Oh, yes, and Joe's nonbirthday, which he opted to keep to himself.

"What'd the wife get ya?" Ernie asked, leaning his belly over the table to take a peek into the cloud of tissue paper. He winked at Janelle.

"She's not my wife," Josiah spouted. *Not even close.*

The look on Ernie's face would have made a great caricature. Eyes wide. Eyebrows disappearing into the folds of his forehead. Lips pursed. He held up his hands, palms out, and backed away from the table. "None of my business."

What? "No! No, this is Janelle, my wife's friend from church." Great. That sounded even sicker. "My wife's in the hospital." Sicker still. "Janelle brought me.... This is just..."

He dug into the bag, grabbed a handful of tissue paper, and tossed it onto the bench. His hand back in the bag again, he retrieved the small item nestled in the bottom. "See? It's—"

"Aren't they the tiniest moccasins you've ever seen? Doeskin. They're so soft. I ordered off the Internet. Nobody sells them by us. Aren't they adorable, Josiah?" Janelle's hopeful expression told him she had no idea what she'd just done.

His ears burned. Saliva pooled at the back of his throat.

"I know the baby's still in danger. I know it will be rough going. But we have to plan and act as if he's going to make it. He already survived the accident. That has to be a good sign, doesn't it? Josiah?"

Ten, maybe twelve feet from the booth to the door. Impossible for the "birthday boy" to sneak out and abandon the scene to crash on its own. He needed a pilot's ejector seat. *We're going down!* With a whoosh, he could break free of the doomed craft and let his parachute float him safely to earth, far out of reach of the flames and debris and Janelle.

Ernie turned his back on the scene. Smart man. The other customers in the too-small dining area returned to their patty melts, hot turkey sandwiches, and Belgian waffles with cinnamon apples. With one eye at least. The other they kept trained on the man with scarlet ears, a loudmouthed "girlfriend," and a baby on the way.

Bag of feathers, his grandmother would have said. You can no more retrieve a careless word or undo a wrong notion than you can gather a bag of feathers scattered to the wind.

"That's very kind of you, Janelle," he said ten decibels louder than the level of normal conversation. "Karin will love them. How thoughtful of you to think of *us* that way."

Bad acting. Bad, bad acting.

She leaned forward. "What is wrong with you?" Her eyes narrowed. "You're not still in denial about the baby, are you?"

He matched her lean. "Oh, I'm not denying there's a baby in there."

The physical sting of her slap left no imprint. The emotional sting threw him against the booth back. "What was that for?"

"Karin's right," Janelle answered. "You are being a total jerk about all this. That poor woman!"

She reached to stuff the infant moccasins back into the bag, which she shoved closer to him. "Would it kill you to show a little enthusiasm?" She punctuated her actions with fury as she pushed her mocha aside, sloshing most of it onto the table, and slid out of the booth.

Ah, lovers' quarrel. That's the look he got from the patrons as he exited the booth and followed Janelle out the door.

"*I'm* being a jerk?" When had Janelle started thinking that adultery was not only okay but sometimes, well, necessary and deserved? That having another man's baby was something to be proud of? That the jilted husband owed his ex-wife respect and "enthusiasm" for her lousy choices?

Ex-wife. That's not what he meant to think. Not at all. Freudian slip. *On the night He was betrayed. On the night He was betrayed...*

Janelle snapped around to face him. "If you had been there for her..." She was crying now. "If you'd paid attention or had gone to her that night, Karin would have stayed. And she wouldn't be fighting for her life. And that precious child's life wouldn't be in jeopardy." She swiped tears from her cheeks and left coal-miner smudges of mascara. "You self-centered, arrogant—"

Why was it he didn't like Janelle all that much?

She left her vindictive words hanging and sprinted down the sidewalk toward the hospital parking lot.

What did Karin see in her?

If he'd gone to her that night? *Sure, Janelle. Doesn't every husband offer to drive his wife to a rendezvous with her lover? It's the only polite thing to do. Wonder why he hadn't thought of that. Guess it wasn't covered in the premarital counseling sessions.*

Josiah stood in the spring sunshine but shivered with mid-January cold.

How much courage was it going to take to walk back into Ernie's and pay the bill for sloshed mocha and decidedly unhealing tea?

And besides. It's a girl.

Chapter 19

When you slide to the edge of "I can't do this anymore,"
open your eyes.
A handhold of hope is waiting in front of you.

~ Seedlings & Sentiments
from the "Hope" collection

The crocus he'd crushed in the flowerbed outside the hospital entrance now stood stiff-necked, an overcomer. How did it do that—bounce back after being ground into the dirt?

Josiah fought the urge to see if it could do it again.

The lawns boasted spring green. The air, no longer as cool, brushed kindly against his skin, as opposed to the biting revenge of winter. He pivoted away from the entrance and took the sidewalk that led the opposite direction of the route to Ernie's.

Another in a string of bad moves.

Isn't it China where it's considered good luck if a bird empties its intestines on your head? And isn't stepping to your ankle in a puddle a sign of divine favor in some cultures? Ah, spring.

He discarded his handkerchief, thick with bird refuse, in the concrete trash receptacle at the intersection of two stretches of sidewalk. Home called to him. A hot shower. Clean clothes. His own bed. Birds with manners.

What day was it?

What did it matter?

He glanced at his watch. If he went home now, it would only make sense to stay there until morning.

A slight course correction took him off the curb and across the parking lot toward his car. But a familiar form crossed the lot from the other direction. Stan.

Josiah prepared to greet him and made quick plans to wash his hair in the men's restroom.

"Interesting hair gel, son. Is that . . . ?"

"Yes. Welcome to my world."

Stan slapped Josiah on the back—hard—and laughed. His wife was less than two weeks in the grave, and he laughed. Stan had a lot of crocus in him.

"You're not heading home, are you?"

"No. Nope. Just stretching my legs."

Stan looked into Josiah's eyes as if peering through a microscope. "You sure? I should have called ahead. Just got it in my mind to come see how our girl's doing. And check on you."

Grace personified.

"Stan, I wish I could have been there for you. At the funeral. And after."

The two fell into a leisurely, even pace relatively undisturbed by the squish and squeak of Josiah's left shoe. Good news. He had a pair of infant-sized moccasins in the gift bag he carried. He discarded the thought and focused on staying emotionally in stride with his grieving father-in-law.

"I wasn't ready to live without her, son."

Josiah knew that feeling well.

"But God is good. His mercies are new every morning." He paused in conversation and step. "Sometimes in the middle of the night, it's all I have to cling to. A fresh batch of mercy will wait for me when the day dawns. I can count on it."

You're an amazing man of faith, Stan. No wonder your daughter had high expectations about good husbands. But sir, you threw off the curve. I didn't have a prayer.

"So, tell me about Karin," he said, picking up the pace again.

Same. She's—"Progress is slow."

"Understood. Understood."

They walked the rest of the way in silence. Brothers.

ও⅛ ও⅛ ও⅛

Stan took the next watch while Josiah cleaned up. He left his hair damp after shampooing with hand soap from the dispenser in the men's room. He wore out the button on the blow dryer trying to dry his sock and the lining of his shoe. Stan was back in the waiting room before Josiah got there.

"You look and smell a sight better, my boy."

Josiah affected a princely bow. "You should see me after I've showered in the drinking fountain."

Stan's smile left quickly. "Karin isn't breathing on her own yet. Thought for sure she would by now."

Josiah searched Stan's face for signs he was losing it. Understandable, considering his grief. "She's been breathing on her own for a while. I thought I told you that. I'm sorry if I didn't. It's a small step, but progress."

"They have her hooked up to that breathing machine."

The man wasn't as practiced at recognizing the equipment. Also understandable. "No, just oxygen."

"Josiah, it was that machine that wheezes. I saw it. Heard it. I thought it would be gone by now. Hoped."

He'd left the ever-present pager in his locker when he saw Karin. Ran into Janelle right after. Josiah snatched his phone from his pocket and checked recent messages. "Excuse me a minute, Stan."

It was true. Moments after Josiah left the hospital with Janelle, Karin's respirations dropped dangerously low. After several

161

noninvasive attempts to correct the downturn, they'd had no choice but to reintroduce the breathing machine. The nurse left a number he could call for more details.

Josiah knew words to recite, medical words meant to explain it all. He'd explored some on the Internet until the confusion factor imploded. He knew a few of the phrases the doctors used. He'd overheard the nurses. Everything was a guess. All that medical training and it was still anyone's guess how her DBT would progress and how deeply it had penetrated her ability to survive long-term.

"In the scheme of things, it's early yet," Josiah told him. "Patience is our greatest asset."

Straight out of the "How to manage your loved one's hospital stay" brochure.

"And my grandchild?"

"Resilient." A good word.

"He learned that from his daddy," Stan said, patting Josiah on the upper arm.

"Stan, I—"

His father-in-law held him by both shoulders. "Don't sell yourself short, son. You're stronger than you know."

Dare he? "It's the daddy part. I'm not—"

"Nonsense. No man feels ready to be a father. And in your case, with the little thing so fragile, it's only natural you'd feel it all the more. It'll come to you. Being a dad will come to you when you need it." Stan ducked his head. "Sorry. I snooped a little. Are these for him?" He picked up the moccasins from the bag on the end table and held them in one palm. They had room to spare.

Josiah had winced when Stan removed his grip, as if the scaffolding bracing him had fallen away. "It's a girl. So says the ultrasound." Josiah watched Stan's chin quiver. "Karin and I tried for so long. You and Catherine know how hard we prayed for a baby."

"No harder than we did *for* you." Stan slipped a perfectly folded handkerchief from his back pants pocket. Who would press them for him now that Catherine was gone? He swiped at his nose without unfolding it.

Josiah tiptoed on the crumbly part of the cliff edge. If he told Stan the whole story, he'd have an ally. One. But what would it do to the man's adoration of his only daughter? Neither of the men deserved what Karin had done to them. Ignorance is bliss? Sometimes.

"I guess I shut down the part of myself that wanted to be a parent," Josiah said. "Once we knew it was hopeless."

Stan flashed one of those Jesus-trumps-all smiles. "Hopeless, eh? Who got the last word on that one?"

I know his name. Wade. I call him Slick.

❧ ❧ ❧

Despite having to dance around the whole truth, Josiah found Stan's presence fortifying, sanity-saving.

Without warning, the square footage of the ICU family waiting room shrank periodically. Josiah pictured a scene from *Star Wars* and any number of James Bond or Indiana Jones movies when some outside force pushed a button or pulled a lever and the walls and ceiling crept inward.

With the Loud family still sprawled on the couches and using up all the oxygen, Josiah suggested he and Stan seek out another place to wait.

A sign on a wall of the main lobby indicated an atrium open to the public.

Perfect.

Amorphous music—melodic but indefinable—floated from the potted plants. Leafy surround sound. The furnishings in the atrium area hailed from a decade closer to the present. A recent addition? A continuous flow of windows on three sides and wide skylights in the ceiling gave the illusion of a greenhouse. Why those factors would dictate a lower decibel level of conversation, Josiah didn't know. But he was grateful.

A dozen other people occupied the room in tastefully decorated "conversation clumps." That wasn't the right phrase. Karin would know.

Stan and Josiah chose a pair of leather armchairs near the fireplace from which glowed a flame trying very hard to look natural. A for effort.

"Are you getting much writing done?"

Josiah's pregnant pause left the door open for interpretation, so he recovered enough to say, "Not as much as I should."

"Can't imagine forming one coherent thought much less write a whole book in a place like this."

Stan, how did you get so wise? And can you spare some of it?

The men fell into a comfortable pattern of words and silence.

"So, is your church still bringing in food for you, Stan?"

"You know how it is. I have enough Jell-O in my fridge to supply the school cafeteria."

Josiah chuckled. He'd e-mailed Janelle to call off the cadre of cooks who wanted so badly to stuff Josiah's fridge and freezer. Postponing their acts of kindness until Josiah could be home more seemed tantamount to blasphemy against the gift of mercy.

Even an unnatural fire is mesmerizing. He stared at the lick of flames. "Though you walk through the fire, you will not be consumed."

"What's that?" Stan leaned forward.

"The logs. Made of cement or something, I suppose. Blue-hot flame, but they're not consumed."

"Uh-huh."

"Guess that's the secret. You have to be made of cement."

The stretch of silence that followed lasted longer this time. Stan dozed off, his chin on his chest.

A fly buzzed the lamp on the glass-and-copper side table. It clunked against the inside of the shade, then stagger-flew in spastic spurts until it returned to thwap the shade again. Sluggish fly. First bird of spring, they say. A hospital shouldn't have flies.

It should be sterile and squeaky clean, with nothing to interest a pest or rodent or anything carrying diseases.

First, do no harm. The physicians' creed or motto or something. Or Scripture. One of those two.

He really needed to study his Bible more. More than zero.

❦ ❦ ❦

Almost the top of the hour. Josiah reached out to touch Stan's forearm. "Dad?"

"What? Yes. Uh-huh. I'm with you. Just resting my eyes."

"You'll want to see Karin one more time before you head home, won't you?"

Stan straightened in his chair, squawking the leather like a cowboy adjusting in his saddle. "I took a room at the Holiday Inn Express. I'm here for a couple of days. Thought you might appreciate a little break. Maybe go home for the night? I imagine there are a few things at home that need attention."

The man buried his wife so recently he could probably still smell the casket bouquet. Would Josiah's thoughts have been on someone else's need?

The weariness of constant vigil swept low to the ground through Josiah's body like the residue of a nuclear blast. Karin was back on the breathing machine. This was far from over. He'd take Stan's offer. Not because he deserved a break, but to honor the giver.

The Grace Giver, too.

Stan rubbed his hands on his knees. "I know I'm no substitute for you."

"An improvement. Like that favorite substitute teacher whom the kids all like better than their permanent one. The fun one."

"Nonsense. But I can sit with the best of them, and I may even take the opportunity to give that girl of mine a talking to."

Josiah studied the enigmatic man sitting across from him— the crevassed face and glacier-blue eyes that had witnessed such extremes of joy and pain in their lifetime. Talk to an unresponsive daughter? "Good luck with that." The last time Josiah tried, Karin took a dramatic turn for the worse.

"Unlike my lectures when she was a teen," Stan said, eyes focused on the glass ceiling, "she won't try to squirm out of it." His gaze returned to reconnect with Josiah. "And we'll celebrate if she does."

Karin wasn't the type to yell. Or claw. Case in point: Her leaving was the first he knew she was unhappy.

Well, *pathologically* unhappy. Sure, he understood that he disappointed her. Daily. What husband didn't? He misread what she wanted for her birthday. Forgot to tell her Catherine called. Left whiskers in the sink. Repeatedly.

What man didn't feel a sense of ownership over the remote? And was it his fault he could work at home and she couldn't? Or that most football games are played on her day off? Or that his peripheral vision stopped short of the garbage can that needed attention?

It stopped short of a wife who needed attention, too.

"Stan, I'm not sure I can go home."

The older man laced his fingers together over his stomach. "I need you to prove that you can."

Josiah searched Stan's face for a clue to what he meant.

"When I'm finished here, I need to go home to a life without my Catherine. Show me it can be done."

Chapter 20

The same wind that topples seedlings fills the schooner's sails.
Don't let the wind uproot you. Let it move you.

~ Seedlings & Sentiments
from the "Challenges" collection

*H*ome. *Ugly word.*

Josiah pushed the button on the visor that prompted the garage door to open. *Ugly door.* As he pulled the car into the cavern, he wondered why they'd fallen for the real estate agent's spiel. *Craftsman? Who really cared? Good bones? Big deal. Architectural integrity? Wide front porch perfect for traipsing across when you're in the mood to leave the person you married.*

Ugly place.

He pushed the button again and listened as the garage door mechanism ground and growled. The safety light—programmed to remain lit for three minutes—faded to darkness long before Josiah reached to unlatch his seatbelt.

His legs needed manual assistance to exit the vehicle. With one hand on the armrest and the other on the doorframe, he dragged himself to standing. His footsteps sounded hollow and harsh on the cement floor, like the shuffle of a man returning to his cell.

"Karin! You did this to me! You made me despise a building because it couldn't hold you."

Talk about melodrama. Blaming the house? He told himself to grow up and unlocked the door to the kitchen.

Ripe wastebasket. The inch of coffee in the coffeemaker sported a skim of mold. And the table boasted a mountain of mail on the verge of avalanche.

Who'd brought in the mail? Probably Janelle. She could have taken out the garbage while she was at it.

Josiah bypassed the table and the antiquated answering machine Karin insisted on retaining. Who else had a landline these days? He'd attend to the mail and messages. Eventually. First order of business? *Find out why it is so bloomin' cold in here. Someone leave a window open? Turn on the air-conditioning accidentally?* He checked the digital thermostat on the wall in the hall. *Seventy? Couldn't be.* He tapped it. Knocked on it. Slapped it. *Seventy. Doesn't feel like seventy.*

It would be another few weeks before he could count on the Upper Midwest weather passing the "threat of frost tonight" warnings on television. No sense heating the place with nobody there. But a cold house did not make for a warm welcome.

Nothing appealed to him in the foyer or family room, so he returned to the kitchen and yanked open the door to the refrigerator. That milk couldn't possibly be good. He pulled the carton off the shelf and set it in the sink. The latest version of church-lady lasagna. Dated eight days ago. He'd add it to the pile of rancid in the wastebasket. That half bottle of sparkling pear. Had to have lost its fizz two months ago.

Jar of olives. *They last forever. Unlike some things.* He removed the lid and popped three into his mouth. The salt tasted good on the front of his tongue but stung the back of his throat.

The sour sat heavy in his stomach. He should have known better than to do olives on a virtually empty stomach in a virtually empty house. Pretzels. Better choice. They had a neutralizing effect. He dug a bag out of the stash in the pantry. Snack size. For Lilliputians, maybe.

As he crunched, he directed his gaze through the window above the sink. The backyard showed a healthy start to what would become summer green. No sign of Sandi. The neighbor kid thought it would be easier to take care of her at his house, with no objection from his parents.

He supposed that was for the best, in a way. Having the dog to worry about right now added a complication he didn't need. Nope. No need for someone to come home to. Someone warm and unconditional. No need at all.

Tightness crawled across the ridge of his shoulders. Tension, no doubt. Not that he had any reason to be tense.

The last pretzel dragged its feet on the way down his throat. He grabbed a diet cola from the pantry and drank it warm. The carbonation formed some sort of foamy paste in his stomach when combined with olives and pretzels. He'd tackle some of the mail then make a real meal. Frozen pizza.

Like a Vegas dealer, he shuffled envelopes into four piles: bills, junk, reader mail, stuff Karin usually handles. He dug a rubber band from the utensil drawer and wrapped the bills into a thick packet he could haul with him to the hospital waiting room. The junk joined the rancid in the wastebasket, failing miserably to camouflage its odor, but succeeding quite nicely at the task of disguising its looks.

Reader mail never failed to inspire him. It seemed grossly out of place in his world at the moment. But an author doesn't dis reader mail. He'd deal with it. Later.

How long could he avoid addressing the Karin pile?

The tension in his shoulders crept up his neck and wrapped its tentacles around the sides of his skull. Wicked headache. A shower and a nap might have to take precedence over the ever popular mail-and-a-meal.

❧ ❧ ❧

A train rumbled past and shook the moorings of Josiah's bed. How many rail cars did that thing have? The shaking persisted. A brief flash of recognition told him there were no train tracks within ten miles of the house. And a couple of centuries had passed since that part of Wisconsin registered a significant earthquake.

He dragged himself another foot closer to wakefulness. It was his body shaking the bed. Chills. That wicked headache. Something sour in the back of his mouth.

He rolled onto his back. Wrong move. A kickboxer named nausea landed a punch.

I cannot have the flu.

A tsunami of saliva broke over the embankment of his teeth, propelling him out of bed and toward the toilet. He lifted the lid and fell to his knees in one panicked motion. So much for pretzels settling one's stomach.

❧ ❧ ❧

The first thought that formed in his heave-jostled brain when the heaves decided to leave was that it had been a long time since the toilet was cleaned. How long had Karin been gone? A smidgen shy of forever. And how often had she tackled the toilet cleaning?

He shoved the questions aside and pushed himself to a facsimile of standing. Hunched and limp, he stopped at the sink to splash his face with cold water and rinse his mouth—brushing would have churned up the dark forces of nausea again—before angling back toward his bed.

The sheets felt damp. Sweats must have preceded the chills. He eyed Karin's side of the bed. Untouched. Pristine. Dry. Smooth.

He couldn't do it. Couldn't lie where she should have been. He fell into the damp misery of his side, curled into a ball, and pulled the comforter to his chin.

What was that rule? Wait an hour then try a sip of water? Or was it a half hour? And who was going to venture all the way to the bathroom to get him a glass of water? No. He'd sleep through the bug. By morning he'd feel better.

Self pep talks lack a certain *je ne sais quoi*.

Josiah couldn't remember the last time he'd been sick. But he knew enough to appreciate the honeymoon period after his wrestling match with the porcelain throne. A brief respite from the wracking nausea. If he could fall asleep before . . .

No. The honeymoon was over.

What was that repulsive odor? And how had he managed to swallow his pillow?

Josiah pressed against the mattress to push himself upright, but the action alerted the talons of his headache to dig in. He would have taken ibuprofen if he thought for a minute his stomach wouldn't reject it. On one of his trips to the bathroom, he'd gotten a glass of water. It sat on the bedside table now, tepid, colorless, and mocking him.

Just try it, buddy.

"Another hour and I will. Maybe."

Or not.

He threw off the covers and hightailed it—in a rather low-tailed posture—to the bathroom.

His stomach no longer held anything of which it could divest itself. But it tried valiantly anyway. Had to give it credit for tenacity.

The episodes came less frequently. He longed for a hot bath or long, pulsating shower. And the odor, it turned out, was him. But he wasn't at all sure he could tolerate the pressure of water on his skin.

Josiah caught his reflection in the wide mirror above the sink. Clear evidence. A sick, sick man stared back at him. If he hadn't been so healthy to start with, this stupid bug might have killed him.

Oh, God. Oh, Lord God. Oh, God! Oh, God!

A few hours before it hit, he'd breathed on Karin. Touched her. Held her hand.

Oh, Lord God! What have I done?

He paced the bathroom tile, then the circumference of the master bedroom, clutching his stomach against the pain. *I didn't know! If I'd known, I never would have gotten near her! Lord, I didn't know this was coming.*

Drained and desperate, Josiah sat on the edge of the bed. He rocked back and forth, keening as if he held a bloodied knife in his hands and had no recollection of how it got there.

His one consolation lay in the fact that when the flu overtook her, Karin—fragile beyond comprehension—wouldn't be awake to notice. It would wring from her what little life she still possessed, but she wouldn't notice.

Little life.

The little one's life.

Double homicide.

The bedroom carpet cushioned his collapse and muffled his gut-born moans.

❦ ❦ ❦

Cold. Josiah was so cold he could register the chill in his marrow. Why couldn't he find the comforter? How far could it have—?

He lay on the floor where he'd fallen. Wearing only his shorts and T-shirt. Shivering. Only a portion of that could be blamed on the temperature.

His sinuses beat their fists against the back of his eyes and the bridge of his nose. He couldn't lie uncovered, exposed, uncomfortable any longer. He crawled back into bed, flipping his pillow to the fresher side and tucking the covers around him like a mummy sleeping bag. The discomfort remained and would for however long it takes a person to get over inadvertently snuffing out two lives. Three, if Stan didn't have the stamina to fight it or hadn't gotten his flu shot last fall.

Josiah's father had once labeled him a "worthless piece of humanity." Inadequate. Josiah believed him, despite his college, career, and public-persona attempts to shake the label. But he never dreamed he'd be an actual danger to someone he loved.

The bedside digital alarm clock told him it was 5:32. At night, he assumed, judging from the dim light.

He should call Stan. Warn him. Suggest he bulk up on vitamin C or echinacea or zinc or something. He'd have Stan break the news to the medical staff caring for Karin. Then he'd ask Stan what day of the week it was. What must that man be thinking? That Josiah had bailed on his dying wife?

As the minutes and his failures ticked past, Josiah's body warmed. The nausea had lifted. It hardly seemed fair, under the circumstances.

When had Karin painted the ceiling? He didn't remember it a slightly darker shade than the walls. She'd get on his case for tossing all those blessed throw pillows into the corner and for the way he'd abused the brocade comforter the last few hours or days or whatever. The least he could do was have it dry cleaned. In her honor.

He rolled onto his side, startled that the action didn't make his stomach beat a path to his mouth. He didn't feel human yet, but he was getting better.

"Josiah! What are you doing here?"

Josiah bolted upright and faced the doorway. "Janelle!"

"What happened?"

"Janelle, get away. You don't want to catch what hit me." His words sounded as if they'd been scraped over a vegetable grater. "What are you doing in my house?"

She eyed him as if judging whether he were covering for a binge of decadent fun while his wife's life hung from a piece of frayed floss. The smell of the room must have convinced her. She wrinkled her nose and backed another step into the hallway. "I came to bring in today's mail. The kitchen was a worse mess than before, and I heard a noise up here. A creaking sound. I didn't expect to find you here." She cupped her elbows with her hands. A defensive posture? Or was she cold, too?

"Janelle, really, you don't want to get this. It's a killer."

"What can I do? Do you want some soup?"

Had she forgotten they hadn't parted amicably the last time they spoke? She backed one more half-step into the hall.

"Thanks for bringing in the mail. There's nothing you can do for me. The worst is over. I think I just need to rest."

"Sure," she said. She took a breath and her lips parted as if she had more to say. Something significant. Nothing came out.

"We'll talk when I'm feeling a little better, okay?" Josiah lay his head back on the pillow, the international sign for "Now, leave me alone, please."

Janelle must have been fluent in international signs. She left without another word.

Chapter 21

Hope is relentless... unless we get in its way.

~ Seedlings & Sentiments
from the "Hope" collection

*A*nd evening and morning were the third day of his misery. If his calculations were correct. He'd left the hospital day before yesterday. Yes, according to *Good Morning America*, it was morning. Thursday morning.

Josiah managed time between "episodes" to call Stan and explain why he hadn't shown up as planned. Stan assured Josiah that Karin was unchanged—big surprise—and he could take his time getting better. Stan almost sounded grateful to be needed, more than happy to book another few nights at the Holiday Inn.

What a relief. And here Josiah had been hurrying.

His sarcasm served as a poor substitute for genuine humor. But he had little else at the moment. Energy? Not so much. Cleverness? *Nada*. Happy attitude? Right.

Did every flu bug carry a unique gestation period? How long before it would hit his wife?

He'd migrated from bed to couch. Progress. Karin would not have approved, but he dragged the comforter downstairs with him. He might have to burn the poor thing when the siege was over.

The morning show bounced along on the screen in front of him with its odd mix of gut-wrenching news, celebrity dishing, and what Morris would call puppies-and-butterflies human-interest pieces. Though disinterested in any of it, he kept it on, volume low but noticeable, because the silence in the house hurt his eardrums.

Within the last hour, he'd managed to down four oyster crackers, and that's where they stayed. Down. Major victory. He stared numbly at the screen and braved another sip of water. A fast-food hamburger commercial pulsed its fat-soaked message. He looked away.

Is this what a woman's morning sickness is like? A video picture of a burger is enough of a trigger? If Karin was pregnant for the past five and a half months or more, how had she hidden morning sickness?

Josiah rewound the brain tape of recent history. He couldn't recall her looking or acting the least bit green. What had she done? Stuffed it until she got to work so Josiah would never know? She'd had that lingering upset stomach a while back, the one she attributed to withdrawal when she dropped caffeine cold turkey.

She'd sworn off caffeine. Who does that if they don't have to?

He sneaked a peek at the screen. Foot-long meatball sub dripping with gooey cheese and marinara sauce. With lightning speed, he reached for the remote and clicked the power off.

Could he wipe out several hundred backed-up e-mails? He held the current title in destructive tendencies. World-class master at despair, depression, disillusionment, disgust, defeat, delete.

With his laptop propped on the couch beside him, he lifted the cover and booted up. While he waited, he tried to form a fitting apology to the medical staff who'd battled for weeks to keep Karin alive only to have a stray germ from her husband sound the death knell for her.

If she didn't catch his flu, it would be a miracle.

His life was full of miracles lately, wasn't it?

A book reviewer once called him the "Yay Rah Rah guy of marriages." A fist-pumping, back-flipping cheerleader for happily-ever-after-even-if-it-gets-rough-in-the-middle. In his professional role, he would have slapped a husband like himself who could only see the dark side of the situation.

It's not that he was ignoring the light. There was no light.

His laptop screen asked if he wanted to play the next song on his playlist. He meant to click Close but his index finger must have slipped. The music played.

"Light of the world, You stepped down into darkness."

He clicked the double bars and stopped the music.

The song spoke truth, but sometimes truth is more than a person can bear.

E-mails were safer. Within moments, he was connected to the Internet and deleting messages from humans with an intensity sufficient to drown out the Divine.

ᥱᏼ ᥱᏼ ᥱᏼ

By noon he'd cleared his e-mail inbox of outstanding communication debts. Morris was on his case, as always, warning that if savings accounts and unfulfilled contracts emptied at the same time, his career was over. Such an encourager. Josiah pacified him with teaser lines from the phantom book that defied its author like a wild mustang might buck against a bridle. "Don't worry, Morris. It's coming along," he responded and then hit Send before his conscience got the better of him.

The check from the car insurance company had arrived long ago. Josiah marked as Unread the survey from the company asking if he was satisfied with their response time. Theirs? Sure. His? Even when flu wasn't an issue, he'd moved too slowly on business matters for a motion sensor to even notice.

But Karin's car had been cleared out and turned into scrap metal. He had the replacement check in the bank. He also had no need for a second car. If it hadn't felt like an affront to his wife's condition, he would have changed his policy to one driver. Temporarily. Or permanently. Only God knew.

Turning his attention to the now almost-blank inbox, Josiah couldn't help noting the irony. In the mood to purge—as a tribute to what his body had been doing—he'd been ruthless in eliminating e-mails he once thought important. Speaking engagement requests. Radio interviews. Even notes from readers who found his work "fascinating," "life-changing," "miraculous."

That word again.

If you want miracles, don't look at me. Go to the One who—

His throat tightened. He pressed his eyes shut and leaned his head against the back cushion of the couch.

God, this has nothing to do with You and me. This is between me and Karin. So leave me alone, will You?

The thought tangled in the deep creases of his brain matter. Just as well. A person doesn't want to give a thought like that voice. It wasn't a real prayer.

Lord, don't count that as a prayer.

❧ ❧ ❧

Drool traced a path from the corner of his mouth, along the valley to the right of his chin and down his neck. He swiped at it with the back of his hand and sat upright. Awkward position for a cat nap—head back, chin up, mouth open, soul prostrate.

He shoved his idle laptop aside and walked to the kitchen. A piece of toast? How old was the bread in the cupboard? Karin insisted on healthy stuff with a hundred and two different kinds of grains and tree roots but no preservatives. He knew that plan would come back to bite them one day. Preservatives have their place.

The tap at the door startled him. He swirled too fast for a man so recently celebrating a barf fest. Janelle stood behind the glass. She opened the door, but only her hand and arm entered the room. Her hand held a plastic container of something. The arm guided it to the counter beside the door and set it there, then closed the door again and exited.

Odd woman.

Did he want to know what was in the container? He peeled off the lid. Homemade chicken soup.

Huh. *Janelle, you're a conundrum. How can you hate me but help me?* Ah. The divine factor.

🙚 🙚 🙚

The microwave dinged. Hot soup.

Josiah held the mug in his cupped hands, soothed by the warmth of the pottery and the kindness of a woman with whom he was not currently on speaking terms. *Janelle, what is up? You spit poison darts at me outside Ernie's. And now you bring. . .*

Wait a minute.

She wouldn't.

No, of course she wouldn't. Besides, where would she find colorless, odorless poison in Paxton? The soup smelled like soup. Its steam penetrated the fog. The first sip slipped down easily and landed politely in his grateful stomach. Good stuff.

Pace yourself, man.

Four spoonsful. I'll just have four. . . six spoonsful.

That sixth one was piled high with tender bits of carrot, potato, celery, and chicken, high enough to empty the mug except for the broth, which he drank because it didn't technically count as a spoonful. He tucked the remainder of Janelle's offering in the plastic container on the middle rack of the fridge and gave it a little pat before closing the door.

Half a cup of food. Felt like a feast.

Fortified, he plowed into the well-organized but still unwieldy stacks of mail. He and the bank account figured out which bills to put on hold and which to pay immediately. Their health insurance company meant well—giving the benefit of the doubt—but sent so much paperwork worded poorly that Josiah rarely knew exactly where they stood. *They need a writer on staff. But don't look at me.*

One random bill was overdue. Not his norm. Not much was his norm these days.

He owed the next month's rent on the storefront downtown. Karin's shop. Sooner rather than later, he'd have to decide what to do about that shop. If Karin recovered, would she even want to go back to it? Could he let the building go and keep whatever materials she had in storage until she could make the decision for herself? If it meant that much to her, they could find space here in the house. Leah was out of the picture. She'd made that clear. So Karin would be back to running her little hobby business on her own. How much space could she need?

Who was he kidding? She'd gone backward in the last week. More fragile than ever. And he hadn't been there for her. She might never come home again much less toy with her handmade paper.

How long would their savings hold out if Josiah defaulted on this next book contract? *Failure to produce.*

Medical bills were one thing. And he had help with that. Royalties were good but undependable and sporadic. Investments remained untouchable without creating a tax nightmare. No. He couldn't afford to cancel even one of his upcoming speaking events. The first was less than a month away.

Half the pile of envelopes addressed to Karin had the feel of get-well cards. Was it an invasion of privacy for him to open them? He could help her, pathetic as it sounded, by getting rid of all the envelopes. When/if she were moved to a normal room, she'd want to have the cards near her. She was a pushover for that sort of thing.

Nice time to notice, Josiah.

He slid his index finger under the loose edge of the flap of the top envelope. The envelope popped open, as did his finger. Nice. Paper cut. He dabbed at the minimal blood.

As he suspected. Get-well card. Flowers on the front. Rhymey verse inside. And a personal note.

Karin, our thoughts and prayers are with you. And we're lifting your precious husband in prayer, too. We can't imagine how a man who loves you that much could bear to see you in such distress. But we know the Lord will give him—and you—all the grace you need as you lean on Him.

Our heartfelt blessings,
John and Sylvette

Their neighbors from their first apartment building. How had they heard? And since when did they pray? And was his love for his wife "that much" back then?

He opened another.

He recognized the nubby paper. He turned it to the back first. As he suspected. *Seedlings & Sentiments.* Nice logo. When had Karin commissioned a logo?

The front of the card sounded like Karin. In neat, flowing letters, it read:

How high are your storm surges? They don't even reach the ankles of the One who walks on water for you.

Inside, the card sender had written:

I have to admit that I threw away the bookmark included with the Seedlings & Sentiments card a friend gave me when I was going through chemo earlier this spring. It landed in the compost pile. Imagine my surprise when the seedlings came up looking so familiar. They're blooming now. A small burst of colorful moss roses growing in untended compost. Hope grows here, your card told me. It does. Thank you.

Opening cards could wait.

Josiah reopened his paper cut when he rubbed a cracker crumb from his chin. Did he have the energy to shave? Maybe it was time to grow a beard. He'd passed the itchy stage a day or two ago. Who would complain about whisker burns interfering with a moment of passion anymore? His moments of passion were long gone.

On the heels of a prolonged sigh came the kind of clarity that rips the linings of organs on its way out. Life as he knew it was over.

Karin might never again care one way or another whether Josiah sported a beard or not. Her distaste for facial hair lost its argument when she smacked into a tree. No, sooner. When she got into the car with Wade.

Sooner. When she first *considered* leaving Josiah.

What day was that? How long ago did the thought first cross her mind?

He backpedaled through recent days, months, years. Where were the clues he missed? He pushed himself away from the table and stood. It took a handful of seconds for him to get his equilibrium. When it returned, he made his way to the family room to scroll through photos on Karin's phone. He still wouldn't have it if he hadn't retrieved it from the Dumpster-diving Lyle on his way to the house. Right before the flu hit. Yesterday, he'd found her phone charger. Today he turned it on. Still not ready for what it might hold

"Show me, God. Show me something here. How can I fix what I can't—?"

He sank to the couch and laid the phone on the coffee table in front of him. A new ache twisted in his stomach. He couldn't fix anything. Even if he discovered a moment that changed the course of their marriage, even if he could pinpoint the spot where they veered off course, what could he do about it now?

Contrary to the opinion of some of his reader fans, he was not a marriage healer. The best he could aim for was marriage suggester.

How much more obvious could it be that he didn't have the gift of healing? On any level?

The early days of their marriage were recorded in photo files. Their honeymoon. Vacations. Birthdays. Holidays. A record of their joys, their accomplishments, their friends and family and things that make a person smile. A photo essay of their life together. She must have copied all the photos every time she got a new phone.

The phone offered no clues to the mystery. If she'd talked often to Wade, she'd deleted every conversation. Nothing in her text messages or calls showed a hint of anything except Josiah's terse, almost businesslike answers to her messages.

Drafts. He hadn't looked in her drafts folder. His hand shook as he scrolled to find her drafts file. The tremors were a remnant of the flu, no doubt. Dehydration or something.

He tapped the screen then pulled back. She'd drafted a message on the night—

Maybe he should shave first.

Chapter 22

Scraps and bits are tools of the Artist's trade.
Hang on a little longer. A design is emerging.

~ Seedlings & Sentiments
from the "Hope" collection

Shaving would have gone better if he hadn't had to look at himself in the mirror. Number one, pallid did not become him. And number two, these days it was hard to make eye contact. He focused on the facial hair until it disappeared. Too soon it would return, like the questions that had no answers except the ones Karin kept locked inside a brain that couldn't communicate.

What had that drafted message meant? And why hadn't she sent it? Was that intentional? Or a glitch, a simple glitch? Phones didn't always respond as expected. Would it have made a difference?

> *Josiah, I can't come home. We need to talk before I leave. It's never been more important. Please answer.*

Would he have dropped everything? A couple of pages shy of his deadline, would he have answered her even if the message had gone through? "Before I leave." She intended to leave. But she was reaching out to Josiah. What did that mean?

He splashed aftershave into his palm, patted his hands together, then slapped Pacific Spice on his temporarily smooth cheeks as if it mattered.

On his way back through the bedroom, he yanked the sheets from the bed and stripped the pillowcases off the pillows. Arms loaded like a refugee fleeing a hostile government, Josiah hauled his bundle to the laundry chute along the wall in the hallway and stuffed the wad into the opening. The familiar shooshing sound of falling clothes stopped too soon. The wad of flu-putrid linens only made it a few feet down the chute, just beyond the reach of Josiah's arm.

He needed a stick or something.

His golf clubs lived in the garage. Broom was downstairs. Umbrella, likewise.

Did he have anything in his attic office? How many days had it been since he'd opened that door? *No. You can't unstick a wad of dirty laundry with a book. A book solves nothing.*

Dagger to the heart.

Bent over, he leaned one hand on the laundry chute door and stared at his problem while a world of possible solutions proved to him why they wouldn't work.

The back bedroom. Karin had been getting ready to paint that room, right? Maybe she had one of those roller extender handles in there. Better than a broom.

As he took the few steps to the closed room, he revisited the idea that burning the linens would have been smarter.

Josiah held the doorknob loosely. Karin's hand was the last to touch it. His heart rate quickened. Another remnant of the flu, no doubt.

Light from the south-facing window—odd expression, since windows by nature face both in and out—consumed the airspace. Josiah blinked. They'd need room-darkening shades if their guests were to—

A long box leaned against a chair in the middle of the room. Sample cans of baby soft paint colors sat on the drop cloth. A larger can had been opened.

She'd intended to bring the baby here to live. Something must have changed. "Before I leave." Or she expected Josiah to move out. What could she have been thinking?

A deeper deception. Not only had she planned to leave him, knowing she was pregnant and knowing it couldn't be his, but she'd expected Josiah to say, "Oh, no problem. I'll get a room downtown. You and Wade enjoy this house I paid for."

Why would she paint a nursery if she intended to leave him and stay gone?

How much deeper could her toxic game of hide-and-seek plunge—correction, hide-and-hide-some-more?

Toxic. Pregnant women weren't supposed to be exposed to paint fumes. Josiah bent to pick up a paint canister from the floor. "Nontoxic. No fumes. VOC-free paint, safe for children, pets, and the unborn."

That explained why he hadn't noticed the paint smell, why the odor hadn't drawn him into the room to see what on earth Karin was doing. Clandestine paint. His eyes surveyed what used to be a catch-all room. Almost done. One more wall and a little trim work yet. She'd been at it a while without his noticing.

"Come see," she'd said.

"Later, babe."

Four short words of interchange. He'd put her off for the sake of his deadline. Dead. Line.

What was in the box? Josiah cupped his hand over the top edge and leaned it toward him so he could read the label on the side hidden from view. "Lap of Lullaby Grow-With-Me Crib." He let it fall back against the chair. A rocking chair.

A scrap of cloth lay draped on an overturned bucket. He diverted his attention elsewhere. Outlets without switch plates. Nearly pristine paint cloths on the floor. How did Karin paint without slopping? The cloth drew him back.

Doeskin soft, it responded to Josiah as if grateful to be picked up, like a baby craving attention. The cloth boasted the same blush color as the walls. One of those skirt things for the crib?

He glanced at the unopened box then looked away before he suffocated. The swatch of fabric floated to the floor. He snatched it up before someone could step on it.

Someone? Nobody else was home.

ஒ ஒ ஒ

The sound of metal-on-metal woke him. The only evidence he'd actually slept.

Garbage day! From the decibel level of noise, the garbage truck was no more than a block away.

Josiah bounded from the bed and skipped most of the stairs on his way to the first floor. His bare feet slapped on hardwood and tile as he tore through the house to the door in the kitchen leading to the garage. He punched the button for the garage door opener, grabbed a wheeled garbage can with each hand, and slid with them—limbo-style—under the too-slow door.

The slant of the driveway threatened to encourage the cans to beat him to the curb as they accelerated.

Thunk. Thunk. Swish, thunk. A garbage collector flung three bags of the Horowitzes' trash into the business end of the truck as Josiah reined in his runaway receptacles. Laboring to catch his breath, he couldn't help smiling at his herculean effort. He'd made it. The day could boast at least one victory note.

"Nice," the garbage man said as the truck screeched and shuddered to a stop in front of his neatly aligned cans.

"Thanks," Josiah answered. So, his track-star skills hadn't gone unnoticed.

"Me?" the man continued, punctuating his short sentences with spit rather than grammatically correct periods and question marks, "I prefer briefs."

Briefs?

187

Spring morning chill seeped up through Josiah's feet. He sensed the day might be breezy. His boxers and T-shirt were little protection against the cool temperatures and the snickers of the garbage man. And neighbors.

"Good morning, Josiah."

"'Morning, Mrs. Lathrop."

"How's Karin?"

"I'll give you a call later. Okay?"

Josiah's now empty fig-leaf garbage cans guarded his front and rear as he chugged up the slope of his driveway and closed the garage door behind him. Did the neighbors have any idea what a wonder it was they were *clean* undies?

The consummate professional. Yessiree.

Time to head back to the safety of the hospital. Time to face Stan the Faithful and Karin the Anything But.

And Baby Girl the Innocent, Fatherless, Unprotected Endangered Species.

He'd show up, but he had nothing to offer any of them.

Maybe he'd stay in his shorts and tee. How much more exposed could a person get?

His primary act of heroism on this fine spring day would be to follow through on his word and call Mrs. Lathrop. One wisecrack about lily-white legs and he'd— He'd probably forgive her. What was happening to him?

The kitchen tile felt almost warm compared to the concrete driveway and garage floor. Sticky but warm. He should mop or something.

Nobody liked kitchen tile that felt like flypaper. He could be a hero and mop, then shower, then head for the hospital, fully dressed.

Unarmed but fully dressed.

⤙ ⤙ ⤙

Short detour. Karin's Seedlings & Sentiments building. He couldn't postpone it any longer. Electric and water bills. Rent. And now an annual business owner's liability insurance bill? She must have been paying these things from their savings without his knowing about it. No, he'd checked their balance two days ago. Could a handmade card hobby make enough money to handle these expenses? Had she racked up debt he also knew nothing about? One more betrayal?

On the night He was betrayed.

He couldn't even think about the word *betrayal* anymore without that phrase interrupting his thoughts.

Josiah turned onto the side street that would take him to the alley. He'd park in back. No sense stirring the curiosity of locals driving by. One of the keys Leah had practically thrown at him had to fit the back door lock.

The first key he tried worked. He let himself into the storage area at the back of the shop, feeling for a light switch before he closed the door. The shelves held enough boxes of supplies for thirty people's hobbies. How much did Karin have invested in inventory? How long would it take to clear those shelves? He had to start thinking practicalities. If Karin didn't return to the shop, Josiah would have to figure out what to do with all this stuff. Maybe it was already time.

How much could he return for a refund? He peeked into one neatly labeled box. Silk. It should have been more accurately labeled "silk garbage." Nothing but threads. A mass of clippings, as if the bag on a silk lawnmower had been emptied into the box.

"Karin, I do not understand anything about your fascination with junk like this."

Boxes of morning glory seeds, cosmos seeds, moss roses, lavender, alyssum—however it's pronounced. The woman stocked up on bulk seeds. Seedlings & Sentiments. Cellophane sleeves—hundreds, maybe thousands of them. Flats of new cardboard boxes yet to be assembled but already bearing the Seedlings &

Sentiments logo. Kind of classy. How much had that printing project cost her?

Leah excelled in business sense, Karin once told him. Was that a fabrication to keep him from poking his nose in the business? He should have gotten more involved. That was on him. He'd been happy to leave the two women to their venture without disturbing his world, which functioned in an entirely different orbit. Now he might be facing a keep-a-person-awake-in-the-middle-of-the-night level of debt. *Thanks a lot, Karin.*

His frustration dissipated as he stepped into the front of the shop—the work and display areas. Her touch lingered. He could almost smell the fragrance of her, pre-hospitalization, when she used to smell like citrus and sunshine rather than rubbing alcohol, antiseptic, and dried drool. He deleted the last example. It remained. The mental game was killing him. Who knew so much of the battle to get her well again would be waged in his attitude, his memories, his mind?

Josiah ran his hand along the edge of her desk, the one she'd hauled from the basement when furnishing the shop. It had been his during the early years of his marriage coaching and writing career. Cast off as soon as he received an advance that allowed him to invest in the sweet antique he now used. Used. Until the accident.

This early version of his workstation still bore evidence of his brainstorming sessions, long before she inherited the discarded relic. Karin had repainted it, but she hadn't sanded out the divots from his pencil tapping habit. He slid a piece of notepaper aside. Huh. She hadn't painted over his signature, either. With his first contract, he'd dug his signature into his desk with the tip of a screwdriver. Marking his territory, he supposed. Right now, it felt no more honorable than the way a stray dog marks his.

She'd encircled his intentionally flourished but unrecognizable signature with a dotted line—hemmed it. The only unpainted portion of the desktop. What was she thinking?

He picked through the papers and envelopes. Mostly sketches of ideas, scraps with notes, bits of phrases with which she must have been toying. He exhaled with enough force to ruffle the top papers. No note explaining that she was leaving him. Or why. Maybe it was this—the shop. Maybe she felt what he now recognized—that he'd dismissed what she did here as meaningless. A harmless way for her to stay occupied while he did the real work.

A nerve in his neck cramped, sending a jolt of needles down his right arm. He cupped his chin in his hands and twisted his head to the side. Better.

A project board occupied most of one short wall. The board sported two distinct sections. He gathered that one held examples of finished products. The other held works in progress. Josiah stood before the board longer than he intended. Among the postings were photos and child art. Pictures of class field trips?

Everything he read compelled him to read more until he'd at least skimmed everything posted.

How did Karin distill such large concepts into so few words? Every word weighty. Maybe he could get her to help him with—

He'd asked her to stuff and lick envelopes, to proofread his newsletters, to knead the knot that often formed under his right shoulder blade during marathon sessions when a book was due. To lick envelopes?

Heat crept up his neck and spread across his jaw. This woman—this one. The one who wrote one or two sentences of comfort that weighed more than the hardcover copies of books on his shelves. He removed an especially artistic card from the board, noting the nubby texture of the handcrafted paper, looking close enough to see threads of silk, a leaf—from an herb?—and a scattering of seeds embedded throughout. He opened it and read a hand-inked message: "Scraps and bits are tools of the Artist's trade. Hang on a little longer. A design is emerging."

He sank onto the wingback chair Karin had somehow converted into her office chair. It swiveled and scooted away from the desk as it responded to his weight. He grabbed the edge of the desk and pulled himself back. If only it were that easy to pull himself back from self-loathing. Eavesdropping on Karin's soul, Josiah found what he should have known resided there. Tenderness. Sensitivity. And a unique, put-his-efforts-to-shame way of communicating it.

The thank-you notes tucked into the wire basket on a corner of the desk confirmed it. Words addressed to her that he would have paid to hear said about him, about the impact of what he paraded before his readers and audiences. While he'd been on the fast track to fame, she'd been quietly making a difference in people's lives.

Sure, he had his own file of thank-you notes. Not that he could remember what any of them said.

Chapter 23

The beauty of your faithfulness through hardship shines bright,
piercing the fog of circumstances.

~ Seedlings & Sentiments
from the "Challenges" collection

For too long, four attic walls formed the edges of his world. The world wasn't flat. It was cubed. A square room with a porcelain doorknob and south and west windows with thermal glass that kept out the weather and the people. Thanks to technology, he could "touch" his public without having to touch them. He could strike business deals with his agent without having to smell Morris's stale-cigar-plus-cheap-deodorant-which-gave-up-trying-yesterday odor. Thanks to technology, he could e-mail or text Karin to tell her he had one more chapter to finish before he could break for the evening.

The accident—or was it her leaving?—propelled him into a different world. No well-worn, Josiah-shaped office chair, no library lamp, no glass-front bookshelves with his own titles facing out. The boundaries of his world now smelled like antiseptic and some nameless remnant from the hospital's microbiology lab that clung to the air molecules pouring out of the ventilation ducts. Or was that coming from the cafeteria?

Josiah noted that spring commanded a firm grip—spring on its way to summer—as he passed the groundskeeper's handiwork on his way to Woodlands Regional's wide glass-and-metal entrance. Shy as it was, spring had won the wrestling match with winter. A little sassy over the victory, it flashed its medals—lush lawns and well-dressed trees, worms on the sidewalk and bees poking their noses into the blossoms' business.

Automatic doors opened before him. Josiah stepped into the mouth of the lion and heard its teeth sliding against one another as the doors closed and the hospital swallowed him whole.

"Welcome back, Josiah."

Great. The security guard knew him on a first-name basis. That said something for his permanent status in Hospital World.

"Did you see the game yesterday?" the guard asked. His version of small talk.

Game? Another world, another lifetime. "No, Larry. I missed that one."

"New pitcher has some potential. Season's early yet, though."

"Right. Right."

"Time will tell."

Chatty thing, Time. It gossiped about their team's chances and whispered behind his back about Karin's hopes. Time would indeed tell, but it remained finicky about when it would spill its reservoir of wisdom.

Josiah took a step toward the elevator as he replied, "Indeed it will."

"Is your father-in-law doing better?"

Baby steps to the elevator. A couple more. "Stan?"

"Heard he took sick early this morning. Hope it ain't that flu. Nasty stuff, huh?"

Josiah bypassed the sluggish elevator and chose the stairs, a move he regretted at the first landing. How long before his energy level returned? He slogged the last section, pulling himself with the handy-dandy handrail and listening to the echo of his footfall shuffles on cement.

When had he talked to Stan? He'd sounded fine last night. *Sorry, Stan.* A headline streamed across the bottom of the screen of his thoughts: *Flu Epidemic Cripples Hospital. If Words Could Kill—Relationship Author to Blame.*

For everything.

The ICU nurses greeted him as if genuinely glad to see him, with reservations, as one might greet a long-lost family member who showed up at the reunion with leprosy or a prison record. He got no farther than the nurses' station, content with a "not much has changed" verbal report rather than a visual firsthand account. He'd wait until the top of the hour and settle in first.

The family waiting room revealed the normal turnover. Mostly new faces. ICU was supposed to be a temporary layover, not a destination. The narrow door to Nancy's locker stood ajar. Who wouldn't have looked? Empty. Another mystery for Nancy Johnson Drew. Had her son finally moved to a rehab unit? He should find out. Ask around. Call her. But he didn't know her number.

New book project—*How Not to Be a Friend. Don't call. If you care, don't show it. If you can, avoid caring.* The chapters collected themselves like iron filings to a magnet. Schwoop, there's another one. *Whatever you do, don't follow through to find out what happened.*

No one could accuse him of shoddy research on this one.

Josiah recognized the tall, artificially platinum woman engaged in discussion with a young man in one of the conversation areas of the waiting room. She glanced up and nodded to Josiah mid-sentence. The social worker. Jayne something. With a *y.* Her nod turned into a crook, as one might crook a finger to say, "Come here."

There? To the private conversation between the hospital social worker and a traumatized family member? Sure. Bring it on.

"Josiah Chamberlain, I'd like you to meet Brandon Gordall," Jayne Something said, pointing with her upturned palm from one to the other.

Josiah eyed the antibacterial gel dispenser at the room's entrance. How tacky would it be to run over there first before shaking hands with the young man, Brandon, who probably hadn't yet experienced the rabid properties of the current flu epidemic. Tacky. If prayers could irradiate his palm's germs...

He reached out to shake the young man's thin-fingered hand. Drug thin. Josiah recognized that gray/yellow skin color. His cousin Linc frequented the same cocaine untanning salon in the '90s. He'd kicked it, hadn't he? Turned himself around?

Next book: *How Not to Be a Family Member.*

"Brandon's girlfriend overdosed last night." Jayne purred as if announcing the spa's special of the day.

Josiah saw no cringe on the grayed face, nothing to indicate that her pronouncement embarrassed him. So much for privacy laws. Brandon must have given her permission to spill his story.

Jayne shifted in her chair, leaning a fraction of an inch closer to where Josiah stood. "He's worried about her, of course. I thought you could reassure him, from your perspective, about the staff of physicians caring for Meltonia."

Sounded like a disease. Meltonia. The melting disease.

Maybe that's what Karin had. She didn't so much choose to leave him. Her desire to stay melted. She couldn't help it. Meltonia.

What were the odds he could find the cure?

The young man squirmed, squiggled, squirreled in the upholstered chair. Twitchy eyes begged for the assurance that the bad trip would end.

How could Josiah promise that? Instead, he told the muscles around his mouth to smile and said, "The best medical staff in the county, Brandon." Was that reassuring? How big was the county, anyway? He should have said state, but that might have been an exaggeration.

The young man dropped his gaze to his hands, pretzeled appendages he twisted into new, fascinating shapes like a clown might worry a balloon doggy into a giraffe with a goiter.

"Thanks, man."

"It takes a while to get used to the ropes, here," Josiah said, "but the staff has been nothing but helpful. They know their stuff."

Josiah formed the words, "Can I pray for you?" but swallowed them. It wasn't the kind of thing he had to announce in order for it to work. Prayer was a personal gift—like lingerie at a bridal shower. (That's the *last* couples' shower he'd ever attend.) You couldn't just open a thing like prayer out there in public in front of a perfect stranger. Could you?

With a hint of the clandestine, Josiah silently prayed for the young man whose girlfriend was in danger because of his own sick habits. Seemed fitting. A three-word prayer: *Mercy, Lord. Mercy!*

"I'll let you two talk," Jayne said.

Josiah's imagination grabbed her arm to make her stay, but she slipped off to some other good deed. He should have been a social worker. They get to walk away.

Brandon excused himself to visit the restroom. Well, not visit it, but use it, Josiah assumed. He'd grown antsy when Josiah asked questions. Tough questions, like, "How long have you known Meltonia? Where did you meet? Does she have family we can call?"

In his normal frame of mind, Josiah would have been repulsed by the whole scene—scrawny druggie and his trip partner. But lousy choices no longer seemed reason enough to give up on someone.

Lousy, potentially lethal choices.

Almost time to visit Karin.

But first, he had to find out what happened to Stan. The call to Stan's cell phone went straight to voice mail. Not a good sign.

Now what? Josiah used the mirror on the wall opposite the waiting room coffeemaker to tame his hair into submission. He popped a breath mint and tested his stubble. The kind of things a man would do if his wife could see, smell, touch.

Lily of the Valley. Karin loved the smell of Lily of the Valley. He'd often find her sitting on the front steps at Stan and Catherine's house when they visited—Karin's childhood home—if she and Josiah were there during the precise two- or three-week stretch of spring when the foundation-hugging flowers bloomed and offered their sweet, thick fragrance gift to the world.

Hugging her knees to her chest, she'd breathe deep and exhale slowly, as if waiting until that fragrance had permeated every cell. She bathed her soul in it.

And here he'd thought her hard to please.

She wouldn't like the gown they had her in today. Not her best color. Or design. The pattern looked like men's pajamas—from the '50s—washed way beyond too many times. Why should that make him tear up? Things fade. It happens.

Josiah turned away from Karin's hospital bed, the machines, the noise, and focused his gaze on the speckled gray of the cupboard fronts along the wall. Evaporation took care of his tears.

She hadn't apologized, hadn't explained. She couldn't. But he ached for her anyway. Where was the logic in that?

Logic and love had little in common at a time like this. If it depended on logic alone, Josiah might be in a condo on Maui, text messaging Morris and his lawyer.

Lawyer.

Logic would have hired a lawyer to plaster a letter *A* on Karin's shoulder and slap her with divorce papers that would milk her 401K dry, if she'd had a 401K.

Logic would have sent him to church solo to ask for prayer for his fallen wife.

He turned back toward Karin and stepped closer. A mechanism in the mattress wheezed like an asthmatic in a room full of cigar fog. Still, he drew nearer, placing his hand on the growing mound of her belly.

Logic would have considered her child a symbol of her unfaithfulness—an adultery icon—and might have missed its beating heart.

The mound moved beneath his hand. It moved!

This time he let the tears fall all over that pathetic, faded hospital gown. They formed damp constellations on the heaven under which the baby girl kicked.

What's logic got to do with it?

If it had been up to logic, would Jesus have given His life?

How many minutes passed? He kept his eyes from checking the clock, kept his left hand on the mound, and moved his right to the spot where Karin's lay limp on the wheezing mattress. He guided her hand, untethered by tubes or wires, to the middle of her body and let it rest against the movement. "You're going to want to feel this, Karin. I hope you can feel this."

Karin's face registered nothing. But she had to know. Deep inside she had to know she cradled a miracle.

Thank you, Josiah.

"Talk to her," the staff kept telling him. "Sing to her. It doesn't matter what. Keep trying to make a connection."

He cleared his throat. The mound movement stopped. "So, I went to Seedlings & Sentiments today. I like what you've done with the place."

The shop. Ache. Deep ache.

He lifted her hand and laid it gently on the sheet at her side. Its normal position. Someone had put a rolled washcloth there. And another under her other hand. Josiah bit the inside of his cheek to distract himself from what that probably meant. The staff needed to keep her fingers from curling and locking in that position. Nancy had told him about her meltdown the day they started treating her son as if he weren't coming back from his coma.

Nancy. Where had she gone? Did he dare ask the nurses? Or would HIPAA get in the way again? Likely.

Karin's primary physician insisted Karin's DBT didn't follow the path of a traditional coma. She should be able to respond. Why she couldn't remained a mystery with no expiration date.

"One of these days, we'll have to decide what to do about the shop, now that Leah's no longer involved."

Leah? Why—? Wade! Oh, Wade!

"What's going on?"

Josiah startled, then beat back the guilt that swept into the room with the nurse. He hadn't done anything wrong. The high-chested woman fiddled with a touch pad on one of the machines near the head of the bed. "Her blood pressure's rising. Not good."

She squinted at the machine, then Josiah.

"All I did was—" *Connect her to her child*, he wanted to say. But his ten minutes expired, and he needed to leave anyway. He directed Karin's hand back to neutral and waited for the nurse to say, "No, no, honey. It's not your doing."

She frowned and flicked the little bubble bulb on a piece of IV tubing.

"Don't worry," he said. "I'll let myself out."

He had patience for the woman who betrayed him and none for the angel of mercy trying to keep her alive. Logic. Highly overrated.

Chapter 24

Jesus wasn't afraid to get His feet wet—and His Hands—to rescue
Peter from the waves that overwhelmed him.
He offers to do the same for you.

~ Seedlings & Sentiments
from the "Faith" collection

Time to write. Time to make enough money to keep the house, enough words to keep his career. If only he had Karin's gift.

Yes, the thought really did enter his mind, stomp around a little, and plop into a cranial overstuffed chair. Karin's gift for words. Or rather, for getting to the heart of the matter. Would he have a chance to tell her he now understood why she spent so much time on what he'd too long considered her hobby?

"Talk to her as if she could hear you," the nursing staff repeated. Every day.

Josiah jotted a note on the pad next to him. He'd talked *at* her plenty before all this, when he knew she could hear. Why was it so hard to communicate now, when most or all of what he said might never reach past the fog in which she hovered between life and death, consciousness and oblivion? He'd never been uneasy about her responses before. Now he was? *Now?*

Talking with the person you love when communication is one-sided. That could occupy at least a whole chapter. How long would it be until he understood the secret to making that work? Rebuilding a relationship when your spouse isn't aware that's what you're doing. Cumbersome titles. Cumbersome concepts.

He'd seen others put their feet on the sleek composite coffee table in the waiting room. Who actually used coffee tables for coffee? Was that their original design intention? Could have been dubbed a magazine table. Or a junk-mail table. Or a footrest.

Josiah shook the worthless thoughts from his brain. He had an excess of worthless. Quality thoughts eluded him, easily outnumbered, outmatched, and outmuscled by the meaningless. That had to change.

He settled into a corner of one of the couches, booted up his computer, and waited to open the so-far-practically-empty file of his current project. *Just write something. Anything. Get your fingers moving. The creativity will come.* It always had in the past.

"If your wife has to ask for your help, you're doing it wrong."

Josiah scanned the room. He was alone. But the sentence resonated in his soul as if spoken aloud. And he hadn't been the one to say it. If that was God's voice, it wasn't at all what Josiah expected. Wasn't it supposed to come with thunder and window rattling and two octaves lower than James Earl Jones?

Ah. He'd overheard the sentence. At Ernie's, of all places. A fifty-something couple in their second marriages, discussing why the second time around worked for them. Josiah hadn't been in the mood to listen to homegrown marital advice, but they'd occupied the booth right in front of him. He couldn't avoid it.

Ernie had teased the husband about agreeing to take on the task of loading the dishwasher when his new wife asked him to and bringing her a cup of coffee while she got ready for work in the morning. The second-time-around husband had taken his wife's hand in his and said—quietly enough that Josiah had to watch his lips to make sure he was hearing correctly—"If she has to ask, I'm doing it wrong."

At the time, Josiah dismissed the concept as—the word rankled him now—*amateurish*. He'd dismissed it. But here it was again, invading his thoughts, demanding reassessment.

Doing it wrong if she has to ask? Men don't read minds. Marriage 101. Basic premise. His opening remarks at his first weekend marriage seminar years ago: "Ladies, don't expect your man to know what you want unless you tell him. He's not clairvoyant."

"He's oblivious," he should have added.

Not completely accurate. "*Some* are oblivious. Like the man standing on the platform in front of you right now."

Instead, he'd convinced his audience of hopeful couples—and himself—that he knew what he was talking about.

I'm doing it wrong if she has to ask. His palms itched. Unrelated, he was almost certain. Josiah argued with the memory of the moment at Ernie's. "That lays an impossible load on the man in the relationship."

But what if . . . ?

What if he explored the idea, tested the theory, examined it rather than dismissed it out of hand? "You can't test a theory like that on a woman who is incapable of responding."

A voice two octaves lower than low said, "Sure you can."

Or was that his imagination?

He had a good fifty minutes out of every sixty to devote to cranking out chapter after chapter of life-changing drivel. Sometimes it just doesn't matter what you feel like doing. You perform because it needs doing.

Fingers poised over the keyboard, he waited for the magic to begin. A word. A sentence. A paragraph.

Nothing.

Saved by the cell phone. Caller ID said it was Stan.

"Stan, where are you? How are you?"

"Sorry I bailed on you, Josiah. I'm in my hotel room. I've been indisposed. Thanks for sharing your flu."

Josiah's stomach muscles contracted in sympathy. "Oh, man. You sound horrible."

"I love you, too." His father-in-law's age-weakened voice had lost even more of its oomph.

"I'm so sorry, Stan. You don't deserve this."

"And you did?"

"It's temporary, if that helps at all."

"Doesn't feel temporary. I'll talk to you later, okay? Gotta go."

"Is there anything I can do for you? Bring over some food or—" He'd already hung up.

The poor guy. If Josiah let himself think about it, he could vicariously experience what Stan was going through. He felt a surge of aching ripple across his shoulders. The familiar headache threatened to return. No. Josiah straightened in his chair. He was over it. *Think happy thoughts.*

His father-in-law was okay, or was going to be in a couple of days.

It was a pretty safe bet that Josiah wouldn't get a chapter written before the top of the—

Impossible. All of it. Waiting for his wife to either die or not. Waiting to see if the child she carried would make it. Waiting to find out where he stood with Karin. Waiting to get his career back. Reformed, retooled, but his again.

Through his constricted throat, he pressed out three familiar words. "Oh Lord Jesus."

The perfect prayer, Nancy called it. The raw, real, soul-deep groan of *Oh!* The recognition of Him as *Lord.* And *Jesus,* the only Name that could make a difference. Even when Josiah's mind tried to push the reality aside, in his soul—beyond the reach of his carefully constructed facade of control—he knew he really had no other hope.

Anyone who found repetitive worship choruses disturbing would have squirmed at how many passes Josiah made over the words "Oh Lord Jesus."

He typed them onto the screen. Highlight. Copy. Paste. Paste. Paste. A page full of the so-called perfect prayer.

By the end of his writing session, he'd increased his word count by almost a thousand. He'd clicked Paste 333 times.

۞ ۞ ۞

How can a lifeless body seem agitated? Josiah stood in the doorway, walled off by whatever troubled her. The tenderhearted of the two of them. He'd once wondered if her tenderness were a weakness that was his responsibility to help her overcome. His father's nickname for him sailed in the air like a paper airplane. Silent. But paper airplanes could still poke out an eye.

Josiah turned to leave. The steady beep of the heart monitor increased its pace until it raced. He turned back and stepped into the room to wait for the nurse bound to respond to the rhythm change. The monitor resumed its hypnotizing normal pattern of beeps. It couldn't be that—He stepped toward the door again. And again, the monitor indicated Karin's pulse inched toward the "too rapid" zone.

"I'd stay, if I were you."

A nurse had watched him advance and retreat? "She seems... restless," he said. He'd stared at that limp, unmoving body long enough over the last weeks to recognize a difference. "Can I flip her pillow to the cooler side?" *If she has to ask, I'm doing something wrong.*

"Sure," the nurse said, checking the fluid level in the bag that hung near the foot of the bed. "You know the protocol. If it weren't for the baby, she'd be moved to a rehabilitation center soon for"— the nurse paused and looked up—"the rest of her recovery. At a rehab center, you may be participating significantly more in your wife's care."

She made it sound like a gift. Maybe it was.

Josiah slid one hand under Karin's head to support her neck while he pulled the pillow out and up, then slipped it back into place, the fresher side next to Karin's warm skin and matted hair. Holding her head like that, even for those few seconds, would have made him squirm earlier. Too few steps from her current state to the morgue. Instead, he allowed himself to experience the sensation of her head in his hand, the texture of her hair—despite how much it needed shampoo, the intimacy of bending that close, of serving her.

"She turned her head toward me!" Josiah's words escaped in a gush like steam often did from his grandmother's pressure cooker. "She did! Look."

The nurse ran through the familiar stimuli checks—pupils, feet, fingers. "I'm sorry, Mr. Chamberlain." She hesitated. "Gravity turned her head toward you."

No. No! Gravity helped. I don't know. But I wanted to turn my head. I'm here. I'm in here. Somebody, please see that!

"It wasn't gravity."

The nurse didn't correct him. God bless her.

Josiah searched for a happy thought. "The scar on her forearm is healing."

"It is." The woman seemed grateful to change the subject, judging by the lilt in her voice. "That one worried us."

Of all the injuries Karin sustained in the accident, *that* one worried them? "Why?" With one finger, Josiah traced a path near, but not on the pale pink scar.

"From all appearances, it happened before the accident. The trauma team talked to you about that, didn't they?"

No.

"Bruising in that area showed evidence of having gotten a head start before impact. And that explains some of the blood at the scene, more blood than you'd expect with mostly internal injuries, they said. I bet it was sobering to see the inside of the car the first time, wasn't it?"

Karin, talk to me. He traced a finger upward on the other side of the scar on the inside of her wrist. In his clinicals, he'd seen women with sleeves pulled down past a spot like this, desperate to hide how desperate they were, pushed to take a razor blade to fragile skin. Most of those scars were horizontal, not vertical, running across the wrist not up the arm. But desperation is never neat and tidy.

Karin, you wouldn't have.

The nurse left Josiah alone with his wife.

"Karin, why didn't you tell me how bad things had gotten?"

Would you have listened?

"I don't know what I'm supposed to do. I don't know if I'm supposed to keep hoping."

Hope doesn't have an expiration date.

He'd kept one of the cards from the Seedlings & Sentiments project board. Taped to the inside of his locker in the family waiting room, it greeted him multiple times a day. He spoke its message now over the woman he longed to understand, the woman he longed to have the opportunity to love again. "But you know what they say. 'Hope doesn't have an expiration date.'"

You heard me!

Chapter 25

If today's sun seems dim, know the clouds may clear
before the day's end.
And if not, tomorrow has a dawn of its own.

~ Seedlings & Sentiments
from the "Hope" collection

The last three times Josiah booted up his computer to check his e-mails, he'd stared at the screen until it slipped into its hibernation coma from inactivity. He couldn't "deal," as Nate would say.

Nate Lawrence—one of the people owed an e-mail, a phone call, an apology.

Josiah inserted the key into the simple lock threaded through the aligned holes on the locker door. Freed of its constraint, the door responded with a metallic "ah!" when he slid the latch upward. A slip of paper floated to the floor.

Josiah, I left something for you in the cupboard above the cof-feemaker. Use it to walk and keep on walking. My son is Home now. Please know I'm committed to praying for you and your wife and child as long as it takes. Blessings, Nancy.

Walk and keep on walking? Walk away? If anyone knew the cost of staying beside someone who doesn't deserve it, Nancy did.

How much was it now going to cost her to care for Blain? Physical therapy. Rearranging the house to accommodate his physical needs. The changes in—

The paper crinkled as Josiah smoothed it flat and reread Nancy's message. She'd capitalized the word *Home*.

❧ ❧ ❧

The cupboard held a small paper bag. White. The kind that would ordinarily cradle a couple of donuts.

Home. Blain wasn't discharged. He was Discharged.

Josiah unfolded the top of the bag. *Walk and keep on walking.* Odd counsel from a woman who'd stayed to the end.

The interior of the bag seemed lit, illuminated. Light from the windows a few feet away shone through the milky sides. Nancy's mp3 player? Josiah lifted it from the bottom of the bakery sack. Sleek and cool to the touch, it spoke of espionage and a television rerun message: *Your mission, should you decide to accept it…*

Walk and keep on walking.

This life will self-destruct in five, four, three, two…

Whatever pep talk Nancy left for him on her player would have to wait. He wrapped the earbud cord around the unit and stuck it in his breast pocket.

The hospital employees stayed annoyingly true to privacy-law policies. No patient information dissemination to anyone other than cleared immediate family. He wouldn't find out what he needed to know about Nancy and her son from them.

Drew. Her last name was Drew. What was her husband's name? Had she said? Josiah rewound their conversations.

"My husband doesn't come to visit our son."

"My husband is a good man, but he finds it difficult to deal with—"

"My husband…"

Had she ever used his name in Josiah's presence? Googling Nancy Drew was unlikely to net him her address or phone number. But he might find a good children's book or two.

Who could he ask who would know? Who had gotten close enough to his ICU mentor, other than tight-lipped hospital employees, to know where she lived or the name of the guy she'd married, so Josiah could narrow his search?

Time for a trip to Ernie's for a slice of humble pie. *A la mode.*

⊶ ⊶ ⊶

The obits. Why hadn't he thought of that? *Blain Drew, loving son of Nancy and (blank) Drew, died earlier this week at Woodlands Hospital. Services pending.*

If he couldn't get what he needed from Ernie, he'd check the online obituaries.

Gripping the brass handle of the door of the restaurant, Josiah stood with his feet glued to the cement sidewalk. His last visit had ended about as poorly as it could, with diner patrons and Ernie assuming he'd impregnated a woman who wasn't his wife, then abandoned her. Change a few details and that was Karin's story, not his.

Trauma-induced schizophrenia. That's what he had. Loving, caring, patient, forgiving, drawn to his wife's side one minute and mired in her betrayal the next. Which, if he took that to its natural conclusion, meant that he was anything but loving, caring, patient, forgiving. Each of those qualities demanded longevity, endurance, consistency.

Forgiveness lost its luster if it didn't last, if it decided to show up one day and play hooky the next. No fine print. No exemptions for the days he didn't feel it. One day he'd walk into her room or lay his head on his pillow the nights he got to sleep at home and not juggle the two truths—that she needed him and that she'd cheated on him.

210

He dropped his grip on the door latch and circled the block. He wasn't ready. For any of this.

Karin made it easy to love her, before the— Before.

He didn't fall in love with her like tripping over a log, but more like cliff diving into an exhilarating, turquoise Caribbean sea. One glance. One. That's all it took. Those huge, maple-syrup eyes, wide open as if surprised by life itself. He'd thought the blush on her cheeks the work of an expert makeup artist that first day. But it never faded. Even in a neutral position, her lips seemed caught in a perpetual smile. Swirls of copper silk framed her face. But it was her laughter that rose above every other wonderful thing about her. A pure crystal sound. Light. With an updraft that caught everyone around her and lifted them higher, too.

Karin found joy in everything—the smell of orange peels, the pattern of foamed milk waves in her coffee, old houses, new sheets, thick socks, a word choice discovery in her Bible reading. Her faith reeled him in. He'd lived on the fringes—decided about God, but not necessarily devoted to God—until Karin made everything, including faith, irresistible.

Socks. She liked thick socks.

He ducked into the clothing boutique on the back side of the block from Ernie's. He'd passed it dozens of times. Decidedly more suited to Karin's tastes than his. Summer items greeted him. Colors that looked like flavors of sherbet.

"May I help you?" Ah. School was out. Summer help. Teenagers.

"I need a pair of socks. Thick socks."

"We only carry women's items." A tiny faux diamond—Who knew? Maybe it was real—sparkled as she spoke.

"Women's socks. For my wife."

"Summer weight?" She started toward a display along one wall.

"The thicker the better," he said. *Yeah, I know. Sounds goofy to me, too. But it matters.* "And soft. They have to be soft."

"I'm sorry, sir. We only have our summer inventory on display now. Have you tried online?"

The young woman kept her distance. Josiah could feel the tension hovering. Her shoulders crept closer to her ears. She glanced toward the older woman—her supervisor?—who watched from near the checkout counter.

"I need them now. Today." *Tears? Over socks?* He really was losing it.

"Sir, I'm sure there's a way to resolve this." The girl put a tentative hand on his shoulder and steered them both toward the counter. "Ruby, we don't have any thick wool socks in the back room, do we?" Her voice betrayed her obvious certainty that the answer was not only no but "Are you kidding?"

"Not wool," Josiah said.

"Excuse me?"

"Not wool. Thick, but soft and ..."

"What color?" Ruby tapped her computer keyboard.

The girl stepped closer. "He doesn't want to order online."

"Ordinarily, I would have said coral. But color doesn't matter. She can't see." The words hacked their way out of his mouth with a machete.

The manager paused a moment, then continued without pursuing the deeper questions. "Size?"

Did it have to be this hard? Did every single thing have to be this hard? "Foot-sized. About like ..." He held his hands eight or nine inches apart. About the length of a certain fetus. He couldn't say that. It would lead to the traditional, "Oh, congratulations!" Words that drew concentric circles around his rejection. *She chose someone else. The child I love is fatherless.*

The boutique needed to have its air-conditioning unit looked at. It was spewing hot air, wasn't it? "I'll look elsewhere. Thanks for trying."

He should have grabbed a hat. The sun glared at him as if it knew his secrets, as if it could read his mood. The sun in a snit. How fitting.

How long would it be, or what would it take, for him to lock into one track? He either forgave her or he didn't. He would either do whatever it took to get Karin well again and let her know she was loved, or he wouldn't. Vacillating emotions weren't helping him cope. Which man would emerge from the crisis—the Hurt Husband or the Noble Husband?

Before life got a little too real, he would have answered without hesitating. And would have found a way to turn it into a line others would ask his permission to quote. Who knew his strongest asset was arrogance? Or that self-deprecation would become his addiction?

His father. His dad knew and gave him his vein's first hit.

If he'd had a chance to be a dad, he wouldn't have been like that. Not like his father.

Josiah changed his footfalls. He'd been jamming his feet into the sidewalk as if he were capable of making dents in hardened cement. Or a hardened heart. But he kept walking. Beyond the path he'd taken on other "have to get some air" trips outside the confines of the hospital.

He'd told Karin he wasn't keen on adopting. What was he afraid of? Nothing. It wasn't fear. He crossed to the other side of the street to take advantage of a stretch of shade. Fear would have seemed more honorable than his true motivation for dragging his feet on the adoption issue. He had something to prove. Not his manhood, although that had been damaged more than once, hadn't it? He had to prove he could be the one to break the chain of son-shaming.

Innovation would serve him well in his efforts to create a parenting role model from the scraps his father left him. Adoption would only prove it worked for one generation. His. Genetics could account for his son's or daughter's successes and emotional stability. The quest loomed larger than that—proving Josiah could undo the damage his father had done could chart a new course for Chamberlain men. Some called Josiah a relationship miracle worker. He brushed aside their comments. For the most part. One unfulfilled miracle remained.

Forever unfulfilled. He would never father his own child.

And the one he cherished didn't belong to him.

How many dreams did God expect Josiah to watch die and still walk upright? He turned to look behind him, looking for evidence of his footprints on hardened cement.

Walk and keep on walking, Nancy had advised. Josiah stopped where the sidewalk ended at a park with a creek running through it. He'd reached the end. Like Forrest Gump, he didn't know what else to do but head back from where he'd come.

He pulled Nancy's small mp3 player from his pocket, unwrapped the earbuds, and hit Play. *Walk and keep walking.* After a moment, he heard a British voice in his ears. Soothing. Slow. The opposite of what he expected for walking accompaniment.

The voice started, "Psalm one, verse one. 'Blessed is the man who walketh not in the counsel of the ungodly.'"

Good one, Nancy. Okay, here we go. Diving back in.

He'd gotten as far as Psalm 30 by the time he reached the hospital doors. They parted for him just as he heard "O Lord, thou hast brought up my soul from the grave: thou hast kept me alive, that I should not go down to the pit."

As soon as he got upstairs, he'd order thick socks online. In coral. Karin's favorite color.

Chapter 26

Nothing left to give? There's no shame in stopping at the filling station.

~ Seedlings & Sentiments
from the "Rest" collection

Karin? If you can hear me, squeeze my hand." How many times in the past three months had he asked her to show him a sign that she was still in there? Her child gave him plenty of evidence. If he didn't know better, Josiah would have said the baby enjoyed chatting with him, responding to the weight of his hand with exuberant kicks and jabs.

The pressure Josiah felt from Karin in response to his request was the weight of imagination, not his wife's determination. Today marked the beginning. Weaning. Like a two-year-old being coaxed to abandon its pacifier, Karin's still body would be weaned from the medications that kept her in a protective twilight. Her injuries were healing. Not a lot, but enough. And she was breathing on her own again.

"We don't like to keep a patient out of it any longer than necessary," Dr. Stephens explained. He'd formed air quotes with his fingers around the words "out of it."

I understand the words medically induced coma, Doc. You kept saying it was DBT—deep brain trauma—not a true coma. Or did I miss something?

After this long, he knew all the words, could distinguish the variety of beeps and wheezes from the equipment, felt at ease pronouncing the Latin labels for Karin's broken bones, the pharma-cute names of her medicines. He knew which nurses worked casual, which phlebotomists knew what they were doing, which fluorescent light tubes in the hall ceiling had bad baffles. He knew how far the maintenance crew had gotten in converting to LED.

Josiah understood the implications of blood pressure changes. He kept his own mental chart of Karin's temperature fluctuations.

Karin Chamberlain—Josiah Chamberlain's project. Like a mask of expression, hurt shadowed her still-blank face, a hint of a day many months earlier when she'd knocked on his office door and told him she was lonely.

Lonely? How could she be lonely? He worked at home. He was always around. She knew where she could find him if she needed him.

"I'm less your bride than I am your research subject, Josiah."

PMS. Give her a day or two.

His smile probably seemed condescending. He knew better, but she'd caught him in the middle of a heinous chapter revision. His research subject? Well, of course! What fool wouldn't test-drive his theories at home?

How could she say she was lonely? They'd just spent four days together at the book expo in New York. She sat not twenty feet away from him during the author panel. He wasn't the one who decided she should skip the last two sessions and go shopping or whatever. And didn't that put him in an awkward position when people wanted to meet the woman married to Josiah Chamberlain?

The muscles in his left eyelid twitched. He pressed a finger against it, but the twitch would not be denied.

In the past, he'd pulled forgotten sweat socks from his gym bag that smelled better than the stench his thoughts created.

Criminal neglect. For how long had he poured megawatts of energy into the theory of their marriage to the neglect of its practice? Smiling and signing autographs all the while.

After Karin returned from a two-week stay with her mom following Catherine's bunion-ectomies, they'd had to throw away the peace lily Karin and Josiah received as a housewarming gift. Josiah had forgotten to water it. A pattern with him.

His left hand found the spot under which the child floated within its mother's body. His palm no longer covered the mound completely, as it had when they'd first been introduced. Against all odds, the child grew. It pushed Karin's organs out of the way to make room for its exercise routine. Josiah felt the flutters of a mysterious telegraph code. Tap tap. Tap tap tap.

Josiah centered his hand over the kicks. *I'm here. Go ahead. Talk to me, little girl.*

No more movement. Someone must have told the little one the truth about him.

The truth. He wasn't her father. He wasn't the husband he'd claimed to be. Children can sense that, can't they? Even in the womb? Science showed—

There. Not a kick as much as a roll. As if the baby were turning over in her cramped quarters.

"Can you teach your mother that trick?" No. The answer was no.

Could Karin feel her little girl growing, stretching, hiccupping? Did Karin sense anything? Josiah alternated between reading everything he could find out about DBT and avoiding any mention of it. Reliable website information proved scarcer than lengthy conversations with the medical team. What he read gave reason to hold onto hope. Each day that passed cut another rope that kept hope tethered to earth. The longer Karin lay unresponsive, the more hope strained against its few remaining connections.

If the trauma to her brain eased, other questions remained. How far? Would she return to full function? to her former self? to him?

Would she ever hold her child, if it survived? Would she snap out of this with a jolt, as some did, aware, missing only bits of memory but otherwise whole? Or would she crawl partway back to reality and live the rest of her life caught between light and darkness?

What would happen to the little one then?

ৡ ৡ ৡ

Another face-to-face meeting with Karin's medical team? Finally. No more bits and twigs. Josiah would get solid information, an updated prognosis. Maybe the monitors were catching signs of her awakening that didn't show on the surface yet. That could be it.

The conference room—a few doors down from the family waiting room—could have used some warmth. Windowless. Charmless. Hollow. Josiah took a folding chair at the head of the narrow, convex hourglass-shaped table—narrow on the ends and wide in the middle. His chair faced the door through which the team would enter "momentarily," an aide had told him.

Josiah sang "Hey!" into the emptiness to see if his voice would echo. Nothing. Either the carpet muffled the sound or the room wasn't as hollow as it was intimidating. He switched to a chair along one side just as the door opened and four medical staff members he recognized and two he didn't entered.

Dr. Stephens made the introductions. "Josiah Chamberlain, I'd like you to meet our patient advocate and a new resident with our Mental Health Services unit."

Josiah shook hands with the two—a man and a woman. But processing the possible need for their presence at this meeting turned their names into vapor that disappeared as soon as Dr. Stephens voiced them. Name tags. Wasn't everyone required to wear name badges? The woman's swung from her waist. Big help. The man's had flipped backward. *Think. Gary? Jerry?*

"So, is it good news for once?" Josiah vowed to keep the edge from his voice with the next thing he said. He smiled. He was the only one smiling.

One of them smelled like the perfume Karin used to wear. He couldn't pinpoint which one, but it seemed the height of rudeness.

"Mr. Chamberlain, there's no real point in our not being blunt with you."

Yes, there is. It softens the blow of whatever you're about to say. Yes. That's the point. Don't be blunt. Be dull for a change. Try it.

"I'm afraid you are facing some very difficult decisions." That was the patient advocate.

"And we're here to help in any way we can." The mental health resident.

"What kind of decisions?" Josiah looked from face to face, searching for which one had drawn the short straw.

Dr. Stephens lowered his gaze, folded his hands, and tapped them on the table. "We're still not seeing any response to stimuli in your wife. Negative or positive."

"She's . . . brain dead?" The words tasted chalky.

"That remains a curiosity. We can't technically determine that, according to medical protocol. Her brain activity isn't"— the neurologist studied the wood grain of the odd-shaped table, then looked Josiah in the eye—"gone. It's not responding to any normal stimuli."

"So, there's still hope."

The medical team members glanced at each other. One checked his cell phone, turned it off, and turned it upside down on the table.

The smell of perfume threatened to choke him. "What *are* you saying, then?"

"The longer this pregnancy continues, the higher the risk to both your wife and your daughter."

Not the moment to correct that last label. "We've known all along it was risky. But we agreed—"

Dr. Stephens' eyebrows crept toward his receding hairline. His long inhale started with a smacking sound. "You insisted."

"That we should give them both a chance."

"Which we have. But with the increasing stressors on Karin's body, and with the new infection necessitating another round of high-powered antibiotics, we're quickly nearing a point when—" The obstetrics specialist, Dr. Randall, cleared his throat. "Josiah, you may need to decide which one of them you want to save. In all likelihood, we can't save both."

No one should wear that much perfume. And rooms like this should have windows. Or fans, at least. And no one should have to choose to sacrifice the life of the guilty to save the innocent, or the innocent to save the guilty.

On the night He was betrayed.

No longer rooted in the conference room, mentally he stood at the front of the chapel, bowed low by the reality that his soul had been rescued because the life of an Innocent Son had been sacrificed. He thought he knew the definition of love. His website's free download listed ten quotable quotes defining love. Trivial compared to making a decision to give up the innocent to allow the guilty a chance. Only God.

Maybe that was a point he'd been missing too long.

"Nobody told me she had another infection."

"Did you hear what we said, Josiah? We want you to be prepared for the time when you'll need to—"

He didn't knock the chair over. It fell on its own when Josiah stood. A little too fast. The blood in his head bee-lined it to his toes. "I heard"—he ground out—"what you said."

The doorknob felt like a ball of barbed wire to his touch. "When can I take her home? Take *them* home?"

"Mr. Chamberlain, you can't take them home. Neither one would make it as far as the parking lot without the medical interventions we're giving them. You must know that."

He spun to face them. "And you must know you're asking the humanly impossible." His final word sounded as if it belonged to a seventh-grade boy rather than a grown man.

"Go home. Think about it. Get some rest. If you're a praying man, that would be a good place to start." The mental-health-expert wannabe, fresh from his textbooks and medical journals, stood and approached. He put his hand on Josiah's shoulder.

In his mind, Josiah grabbed his patronizing hand by the wrist, bent it back until the young man screamed like a girl, and shoved him horizontally the length of the table, arms and feet taking out the medical professionals on either side.

In his mind.

❦ ❦ ❦

I'm stronger than this. I need to be stronger than this. Have to be.

The chapel carpet underfoot held up remarkably well to his pacing. Anyone watching the scene might have wondered about him, pacing across the back of the room, talking to himself, gesturing when necessary to make his point or support his argument. With himself.

I can do this. I have to do this. It's time to be who I know I am.

Inadequate.

Wrong answer. Try again.

Overwhelmed.

Not helping.

Needy.

Well, yes, but…

Needy.

The room kept moving when he stopped pacing. Once he regained his equilibrium, he found a spot on an outside aisle and took a seat. His prayer started out like a pep talk. "I'm good enough. I'm smart enough. And people like me." It might have worked if he hadn't recognized it as too close to a shtick from a late-night weekend comedy show.

"God, I need You."

Better place to start.

Chapter 27

The heart that serves mercy freely will never lack
when mercy is the heart's need.

~ Seedlings & Sentiments
from the "Mercy" collection

For days, he'd successfully dodged the decision the medical team insisted was imminent. When Lane Stephens approached him, Josiah assumed it was for an "Okay, buster. It's time" confrontation.

"I don't understand." Three words not uncommon to Josiah's recent vocabulary. "Why didn't you tell me this earlier?"

Dr. Stephens tugged at the fabric at his throat as Josiah had seen him do hundreds of times in the last months. "I wanted you to be assured that your wife has a whole team interested in her case."

Her case. The Curiosity of Karin Chamberlain. "You've been planning this move for some time, I assume."

"Mr. Chamberlain, in a hospital this size, you must know it's been unusual for your wife's surgeon to remain with her as her attending physician."

"I assumed that was because you—" *Cared?* Dr. Stephens could walk away. He had every right. "Because you felt invested."

"I do. Of course. With your permission, I'd like to be kept

informed of your decisions. But"—Dr. Stephens picked at a hang-nail—"I can't turn down this opportunity to teach."

Teach. Josiah's arena, in actual arenas. His event less than a month from now had been publicized for more than a year. Book sales depended on it. His career depended on it and, in turn, his ability to keep the house, provide for a dramatically disabled wife and her child. If either of them survived. He addressed the soon-to-exit Dr. Stephens. "No. I wouldn't expect you to."

"She'll have quality care as long as she needs it. Dr. Moore is a seasoned and highly respected physician. The transition to her leadership on your wife's case should be seamless."

Transitions are rarely seamless, Doc. You should know that. Hard as you try, not everything can be gained from glancing at Karin's chart and health history. "When will I meet her?"

"She starts on the eighth."

"I won't be back yet from my speaking event."

Dr. Stephens took a step toward the door, his mission, apparently, complete. "Are you thinking aloud or did you expect a response from me?"

Which was it? Disappointment or anger? Frustration? What was the catalyst that started his stomach churning? Maybe it was a more noble reaction. His protective nature, wanting to protect his wife. He hadn't always agreed with Dr. Stephens, but the man had been there. Faithful.

Ironic. Faithful to the unfaithful.

God, my mind returns to that wound in our story like a tongue that refuses to ignore the empty space where a tooth used to be. When will it stop? It has to stop! I'm doing this no matter what. But, if You don't mind, I'd like to keep my sanity in the process.

Pretty gutsy, asking something that big from the God he'd too long thought he could ignore and do quite well on his own, thank you.

Nancy once told him God leans forward with exceptional interest when He hears a gutsy prayer. Nancy, bless her. One of these days, he needed to follow that trail to find out where she was.

"Best wishes on your future endeavors, Dr. Stephens."

"Thank you. And"—the man seemed to fight for evenness—"on yours."

The handshake felt more perfunctory than congratulatory. The good doctor could walk away from the endless swirl of no progress. Josiah had to stay.

As soon as the doctor left the scene, Josiah found an empty chair at the end of the hall, pulled out Nancy's loaned mp3 player, and hit Play.

"When I was comfortable, I said, 'I will never stumble.'"

He hit Pause. Was this still the Psalms? Weren't they supposed to be soothing? He glanced at the tiny screen. Somehow, he'd flipped the audio rendition to a different translation, but there it was. Where he'd left off. Psalm 30. He pushed Play and kept listening. Eyes closed. Focused. Except for the part of his brain that never left his wife's room.

"I cried out to you, Lord. I begged my Lord for mercy." That was more like it.

When the narrator reached the early verses of Psalm 31, Josiah stopped the player, backed it up to verse one, and listened again. Four times.

"I take refuge in you, Lord. Please never let me be put to shame. Rescue me. . . . be a rock that protects me; be a strong fortress that saves me!. . . Guide me and lead me for the sake of your good name!. . . Lord, God of faithfulness—you have saved me."

God of faithfulness. King of the Faithfulness Club.

Josiah would have listened a fifth time, but it was the top of the hour.

❧ ❧ ❧

"Should her wrist curl in that severely?" Josiah took his traditional, neutral spot just inside the door where he usually waited when the medical staff engaged in procedures.

*I would stop it if I could, Josiah. Do you know how
hard I'm trying?*

Angie finished feeding his wife and pushing the last of the
formula-like liquid through the feeding tube in her stomach.
Gavage. A necessary but wholly unsatisfying way for his foodie
wife to eat. What would Karin say if she could talk? Would she
beg for a turkey, broccoli, Swiss cheese, and hollandaise crois-
sant, her favorite lunch? Would she ask—in that lyrical voice he
hadn't heard since the day of the accident—for a vanilla bean
crème brûlée? He would drive to Russell's that second if she
would just ask.

*I hate this part more than a lot of the other . . . things.
What's the word? More than the other things they do
to me. Even a toddler can shove food in her mouth.
Even a newborn can swallow. Thank You, God, that
some of the words are coming back. The baby. How
can she be right? Give me more of that stuff, if it
means the baby will have what she needs.*

"No, Mr. Chamberlain." Angie deposited the gavage equipment
in the waste container attached to her rolling cart. "We don't like
to see that. The contraction of muscles is natural in these cases,
but not at all what we want to see. Physical therapy will work on
that more intensely."

"Is there anything I can do? Without hurting her?" *Hurting her
more than I have?*

"Absolutely. Here. Let me show you."

Josiah dragged his chair close to Karin's thirty-inch by eighty-inch world.

"Fist your dominant hand," Angie instructed.

"My right hand."

"Then open her fingers over your fist as if your hand were her computer mouse. Good. Move slowly. Tense muscles need time and tenderness."

Magna cum laude, and he had to be taught how to hold his wife's hand. Yesterday, that might have shamed him. Today, it humbled him.

"Now, tip your wrist down to help stretch her fingers and hand into a straighter position. Just a few seconds at a time."

"Like this?"

"Great. Slide your other hand under her wrist for support. Our goal is twofold. We want to keep those muscles and tendons familiar with the neutral position. And we want to strengthen them so contraction is less likely."

Josiah rocked his fist in a slow rhythm. "Can we undo what's already started? And don't answer, 'Are you a praying man?'"

Angie could take his questions without flinching. Of all Karin's caregivers, Angie could take it.

She glanced over her shoulders before responding. "They've talked to you about making…decisions…about Karin and your daughter, haven't they?"

Of all her caregivers, Angie might be the one he could trust with the truth about the "your daughter" part. Josiah watched Karin's face for a twitch, a muscle spasm, a hint that she could hear what they were saying. Nothing.

"This is off the record, Mr. Chamberlain. But holding on is a decision. Just thought I'd point that out."

"You've seen people come back from a condition like this?"

The woman used the toe of her purple rubberized clog to unlock the brakes on her wheeled cart. "Have I seen it? No. Do I believe it's possible? Yes."

"Angie?"

"What?"

"Thank you."

⌐⌐

Yes. Thank you.

⌐⌐

"And Angie?"

She turned at the door.

"Her skin's so dry. May I use that lotion on her hands and arms? The parts that have healed?"

"Mr. Chamberlain, you don't have to ask about those things."

"I'm a caregiving rookie."

"You're a blessing to your wife."

Not a word he would have chosen for himself. From all appearances, he'd have plenty of time to practice.

"Oh," Angie added, "nice touch." She pointed to the coral socks embracing Karin's immobile feet.

His internal clock told him when his ten minutes were up. Every hour marked time by a ten-minute block followed by a fifty-minute block. Even on the days he was home, his brain registered that pattern. When he sat down to write, on those rare days when the words met him, they stayed no longer than fifty minutes before checking out.

The touch of Karin's hand on his—resting there, as if it belonged, as if it could think of no more comfortable position than to lean on him—messed with his internal clock. He looked up when his hand began to cramp. He'd been at her side a half hour. And no one had said he couldn't. Time to sneak out before—

"You're still here." Angie's voice didn't hint at surprise or reprimand.

"I lost track of time. Seriously. On my way out." He slid his left hand from under Karin's wrist and reached to lift her fingers from where they draped over his right fist. The fingers dug in.

"Angie!"

"What?"

"Look. She's grabbing my hand. She doesn't want me to go."

Angie sighed, then clamped her lips tight. Her face adopted the I'm-so-sorry expression he'd seen too often. She lifted Karin's hand from his and held it a foot or more off the surface of the bed. Karin's fingers curled down and her wrist inward.

"Reflexive."

"I didn't help at all."

"Don't say that." Angie's chiding felt more like balm than berating. "We don't know what registers in Karin's mind. If anything."

Almost all of it.

Josiah's fingers ached. Bone deep. What he imagined "crippling arthritis" would feel like.

"But," Angie said, "none of your care for her is ever wasted."

She shut the mouth of the lion. "I could say the same for all your acts of kindness toward her, too, Angie."

"Some people would respond, 'Just doing my job.'" She touched a wisp of fine hair in the regrowth area on Karin's head. "It's more than that."

"I can tell. And I'm grateful. I'm sure she'd tell you that if she could."

I say it every day. In here. Deep in here.

Chapter 28

You may feel alone, so alone. But tucked among the shadows is a God who cares, is watching, and is ready to intervene.

~ Seedlings & Sentiments
from the "Courage" collection

Stan's phone call came as Josiah reached the family waiting room.

"How is she?"

"About the same. I hope you're feeling better." Josiah didn't have to think hard to imagine what the last weeks had been like for his father-in-law. First the flu then bronchitis? And what was it they said? For every decade a person is over forty, add another day of recuperation for any illness?

"Think I kicked this. Finally."

"Good. Good." He poured himself a cup of coffee.

"Did Karin...did she get this?"

"We can be grateful for small blessings. No."

Stan exhaled as if he hadn't allowed himself to do so until that moment. "Prayed every day she'd be spared."

"Me, too. Are you coming up today?" Josiah needed to stop in at home again, but if Stan were coming, he'd wait.

"In the morning. And then I have to check out of this hotel and head back home, son. I'm still dealing with some paperwork about Catherine."

"Understood. What time do you think you'll get here in the morning? I'll make sure I'm here then, too. We have some catching up to do. I've missed you, man."

"Same here."

"Treat you to coffee and a piece of pie?"

"I have to check out before eleven. But I thought I'd better get to the hospital more like ten and then get on the road soon after that. Might be able to pick up my mail at the post office before it closes for the day."

"Maybe we can talk Ernie into making your lunch to go. If the weather's as nice as they're predicting"—not that it mattered much to Josiah these days—"you could stop and have your lunch at the picnic spot you and Catherine liked so much."

"Two things. Appetite's not back yet. And... I'm working my way up to revisiting places that meant a lot to the two of us."

Josiah had so much more in common with his father-in-law than he'd imagined.

"So, I'll see you around ten, then?" *And we can take two or three minutes to talk about "decisions."* Josiah swallowed the bitter pool that collected at the back of his throat.

"Son?"

"What is it?"

"I might forget to mention it tomorrow. Isn't your big speaking gig coming up fast?"

The one I didn't cancel. The one I thought I had to do. The one Morris insisted was non-negotiable. "Yes. Great memory."

"How long will you be gone?"

"Honestly, I wish the answer were not at all. But with travel time, set up, and media connections, it's going to take me four days. I don't like it, but there it is."

"I can come back for that." Stan sneezed. "Random," he said. "That sneeze was completely random. I don't like the industrial strength cleaning materials they use here, even though I've been one of the reasons the hotel needs them. Even stronger smelling than at the hospital."

Josiah smiled. What a contrast between the two fathers—his and Karin's. It had been a while, but he breathed a silent prayer of gratitude that he'd been gifted with a kind father-in-law. After expertly remembering every detailed injustice he'd suffered both in childhood and now, it was probably time Josiah started listing the unacknowledged compensations with which he'd been graced. Stan was one of them. "If you can be here while I'm gone, that would make me feel a lot better. Let me pay for your hotel this time, though."

"I might just let you do that. It costs a lot of money to die. No offense to your dearly departed mother-in-law."

Josiah could hear the tightness in Stan's throat. He waited until Stan ended the call before adding, "It costs a lot to stay alive, too."

Stan would head home in the morning. Dr. Stephens would be gone in a few days. Nancy was absent. He'd asked the church people to give them privacy. Most of the world didn't know what they were going through. And the other visitors at the hospital had their own problems.

The "fiercely independent" gene Josiah thought one of his strongest assets kept misfiring, like a generator that would have helped in the outage, if it could get started.

I was comfortable being independent as long as Karin stood beside me.

An oxymoron and an impossibility in the same breath.

∝∝ ∝∝ ∝∝

At the very least, he had to find Nancy Drew to return her mp3 player. Eventually. After he purchased that audio version of the Psalms. He couldn't listen to it while writing, but he wrote better if he listened first.

Interesting commentary on life. A growingly familiar zing of recognition zigzagged through the ditches in his brain. *Almost everything in life is better if we listen first.*

He could incorporate that into his upcoming speech. Josiah jotted the idea into his old-school notebook. Its pages were filling fast. Not long ago, he would have categorized them as *What People Need to Know.* Today, the print swam into new formations, all grouped under the heading *What I Need to Learn.*

What was happening to him? He'd built his career on dishing out expert counsel in bite-sized bits of clever quotes, distributing relationship advice like a generous benefactor who lived for the applause more than the good his words accomplished.

I didn't just admit that, did I?

Like a misshapen vessel, everything internal had been slammed to the potter's wheel for remolding. Karin's words were getting to him. And she couldn't even talk.

He'd planned to spend the night in his own bed. Home. Too far away. And utterly empty. He'd pulled all-nighters in the waiting room before. The stuffed chair in the corner folded out into a not-quite-single bed-like structure. Cot-like. No, not that fancy. But he'd made it work. Alone at home—home alone—held no appeal.

Eating dinner alone at Ernie's? Not much appeal there, either. He opened the phone app that would show him the nearest take-out pizza place.

"Excuse me, sir. May I see your phone?"

He knew that voice. But it couldn't be—"Nate? What are you doing here?" He crossed the room and bear-hugged his longtime friend.

"The security guy at the entrance said I could probably find you here. Dude! You're famous!"

"Nice one, Nate. Seriously, what are you doing here? Woodlands is not exactly on the way to any place special." All of six foot six, if not taller, Nate Lawrence instantly made the room less hollow.

"I'm here to fix your phone. It must not be working. You don't call. You don't text. I'm beginning to think it's your subtle method of breaking up with me." He jabbed Josiah in the ribs with a good-natured punch. "You could have at least announced it on social media." Nate's facial expression darkened slightly, as if on a dimmer switch turned just a few degrees to the left. "Some people do that."

Josiah tamed his laughter. "Man, it's good to see you. And I apologize a thousand times for neglecting you."

"Wasn't it you who wrote—and I quote—'Neglect rings a relationship death knell.' Yes, it was you. I remember having to look up the word *knell*."

Josiah sank to one corner of a couch and gestured for Nate to do the same. "I don't believe that for a moment."

"Sure you do. Neglect is a killer."

"Not that." *I believe that now more than ever.* "The part about the dictionary."

Nate crossed his arms. "I work hard to hide my loquaciousness."

"You do know loquacious means chatty, wordy, not necessarily possessing a broad vocabulary."

Nate propped his feet on the coffee table. "I pride myself in my skills as a macroverbumsciolist."

Josiah's smile muscles—all seventeen of them—hadn't gotten a workout like this in a long time. "Are you confident you're pronouncing that correctly?"

"Not in the least."

"What does it mean?"

"You'll have to look it up."

"Nate, I'm a little"—Josiah pointed to their surroundings and his open laptop—"overloaded here."

His friend clasped his hands together as if preparing for an operatic solo. "A macroverbumsciolist is someone who pretends to know big words, then secretly looks them up in a dictionary."

"For real?"

"For real. Have you eaten dinner?"

"Not yet. How long are you here?"

"If I said four months, how would that make you feel?"

"Great!" Josiah needed the name of a house-cleaning service. STAT!

"Sorry. Four days is all I can give you. You and I are, after all, estranged."

Josiah cringed at all the word meant, the word Nate thought a joke that applied to Josiah's neglect of their friendship. And he deserved it. Couldn't help cringing.

"Hey, no offense, Josiah. I get it."

Nate's face masked something. Josiah couldn't tell what.

"I understand why dealing with what's happened to Karin would put me on the back burner. She's your top priority. Bad joke on my part. I should have gotten on a plane and come here sooner. If anyone was neglectful, it was me."

You have no idea, Mr. Lawrence. No idea. "So, you're staying at our house, right?"

"Hoped you'd say that. I left my luggage in your garage. Good thing I have a flawless memory. Knowing your security code came in handy. Knowing you don't change your security code often enough also came in handy."

Scratch the cleaning lady. Nate would have to take the house as is. And scratch not going home. But he wouldn't be home alone.

"Dinner. We were on the subject of dinner," Nate said, patting his stomach.

Ernie's. "I know a place."

⁓ ⁓ ⁓

I owe You one, God. Josiah walked through the doors of Ernie's with a friend. Most of his hesitation about revisiting the restaurant disappeared because he and Nate conquered the hurdle together. And Nate could remain oblivious that there even was a hurdle.

"Great advertising," Nate said as the two settled into a booth.

"What is?"

"The smell of this place. Seared meat, onion rings, and"—he lifted his nose and squinted as if testing the air—"rosemary, if I'm not mistaken."

"To me, the predominant aroma is homemade bread."

"That, too. I have a feeling I can be very happy here." Nate leaned against the padded back of the booth bench. "Karin would love it."

A perfectly natural thing for him to say. Josiah waved off the mental plate of distress offered him. "She would. Ruthie, too."

"About that . . ."

A waitress—new to Josiah—slid a cup in front of him. "One toffee mocha. Ernie said this is what you'd want." She looked at Nate. "And for you?"

Nate shook his head, his smile flatlined. "Oh, my brother, how far you have fallen." To the waitress he said, "Give me coffee— black, strong, no frilly stuff added, okay? And a glass of water."

"Coming right up." She left them menus—a new version since Josiah had last visited—and turned to get Nate's coffee.

"I'm telling you, Nate. One sip of this and you'll change your mi-ind." He made two syllables out of his final pronouncement and made sure to keep his voice in the baritone range. Toffee mocha—the manly man's drink of choice. "You have a Ruthie story to tell me?"

Not for the first time since his arrival, Nate looked uncomfortable. He opened his menu, ignoring Josiah's question. "What do you recommend?"

Josiah leaned forward. "I recommend you start talking."

"I will. I will. Let's order first, okay?"

The waitress passed their table balancing three plates.

"They serve prime rib here?" Nate leaned out of the booth to keep the plates within his line of sight.

"Weekly special." Josiah recognized the schizophrenic swing from sober to elated. He'd seen it in himself. And it didn't always follow reason. Prime rib was a strong enough motivation for elation when life fell apart.

"I'll have that." Nate said.

"And I second the motion. Great minds and all that."

"Not always." Nate tapped the tips of his fingers on the edge of the table.

Their order placed, Josiah dove in. Small talk no longer held a position of honor in his arsenal of people skills. He'd brought Nate up to speed on Karin's condition—the physical part of it—on the walk from the ICU floor to Ernie's. "Out with it."

"I'm here for four days, Josiah. We could ease into this."

"Secrets have a way of complicating the digestive process. You want to enjoy that prime rib when it gets here, don't you? Start talking, my friend."

For once, it appeared Josiah wasn't the neediest person in the room. Nate's "tells"—his finger tapping, downcast eyes, the way he opened and closed his mouth three times before finally speaking—gave away more than he probably realized.

"I messed up, Josiah. Okay, this was a bad idea. You've got more than your fair share of things to worry about. I shouldn't even be here. Bad, bad idea. Let's just enjoy our meal. We'll talk about the weather and the Cubs—"

"Nate."

"Right. Not your team." Nate held his elbows and rocked back and forth. "Oh, so now it's a staring contest."

"I'm no one to judge anybody, Nate. Tell me how you messed up. Then we'll talk about how to fix it."

"There's no fixing this. Ruthie's gone."

A lot of that going around.

"And I don't blame her."

"What did you do?"

Nate stared now at the salt and pepper shakers he moved in opposing circles on the slick tabletop. "I don't think Ruthie would have found out if I hadn't used the wrong credit card for the motel that one time."

Chapter 29

Hand on your heart. Feel that pulse? The soul's cry
feels a lot like that—a repeated beat that remains relentless
until it's no longer needed.

~ Seedlings & Sentiments
from the "Strength" collection

How many gut punches could Josiah take and stay upright? The way his skeleton seemed to collapse under his muscles, he guessed he'd reached his limit one gut punch ago. "I may not be the right person to tell."

"Because you'll kill me?"

"An option. Always an option."

"Thanks for your support."

Josiah drew a deep breath and sorted his personal emotions from his concern for his friend. Maybe he could pull that off. "What do you want me to say?"

"Tell me how to make it right."

"You're asking a lot."

Nate leaned his elbows on the table and pressed his clenched fists against his chin. Then against his forehead. "I know."

"I assume it's over?"

"What, Ruthie and me?"

Josiah reached across the table and flicked Nate on his nose. "Ow!"

"The other woman." Josiah backspaced his list of reasons why he didn't deserve the pain of this conversation.

"Yes, of course. What do you take me for? Never mind. Don't answer that."

"I haven't heard any excuses from you. Your supposed reasons." Josiah thanked the waitress who brought their salads. Hadn't he asked for dressing on the side? A small thing like that seemed immensely insignificant at the moment.

"I thought I had excuses. Truth is, I don't. But I have enough regrets to fill a stadium." His knee bounced under the table, hard enough to make the water in the tall glasses form concentric ripples on the surface.

Josiah nodded his head. "That's worth something. A place to start."

"Regrets? They're crippling me. Suffocating."

"Good. For a while. Eventually, regrets can be converted to fuel." *Wait a minute. That actually makes sense.*

"You don't have to loathe me, Josiah. I loathe myself enough for both of us. I've begged Ruthie's forgiveness. I don't know what else to do."

The prime rib arrived, perfectly cooked, juicy, and inedible. Both men stared at their plates. Neither lifted a knife or fork. They stayed that way so long that the waitress returned to ask if something was wrong with their dinners.

"No," Josiah said. "Looks great. Thanks so much. We're"—he glanced at Nate—"praying."

Nate's eyes widened. "Right."

"Sorry," the waitress said, retreating. "Didn't mean to interrupt. Let me know if you need anything."

We'll take a heaping helping of forgiveness. Bring me one of those wisdom platters. And we could both use a refill of "What now?"

Josiah uncovered the homemade bread that came with their meal. He broke off a palm-sized piece and handed it to Nate. Then he took a chunk for himself and held it at eye level.

"What are you doing?" Nate asked.

"Contemplating."

"Contemplating what?"

"All that can emerge from betrayal."

And yet again, Josiah would have to move through his days pretending he didn't know what he knew, hadn't heard what he'd heard, wasn't heartbroken. With Nate settled into the guest room and the air conditioner working hard to compensate for having been set to "sweltering" when no one was home, Josiah stood in the master bedroom, staring at the bed. Was there any point? He doubted anyone he cared about would sleep well tonight. Except Karin.

Nate hadn't intended to confess so soon, he said. He'd landed on Josiah's doorstep without meaning to. An irresistible force— he said—compelled him to try honesty. The honest truth sliced them both open with the efficiency of a gut hook for dressing a deer. When Nate had exhausted the details of his story, with everything spilled out in a steaming, smelly pile on the ground between them, Josiah created a pile of his own. Not the story of the betrayer, but of the one betrayed.

He hadn't skirted around his regrets, his oblivion, his neglect. And he hadn't intended to use the story to add to Nate's guilt. He wanted his friend to see the fallout for what it was, to empathize with the betrayed, to recognize the far-reaching effects of unfaithfulness.

Josiah went through the motions of his end-of-the-day routine, the homegrown version that seemed almost foreign to him compared to the home-away-from-home hospital routine. Had his intentions included an unspoken plea for sympathy from the friend he'd retained longer than any other? On some level, yes. Before his writing and speaking career necessitated cutting back on his counseling practice, Josiah rarely ended a conversation with a client without a conclusion or plan of action. He couldn't pry open the "plan of action" file drawer in his brain. So the two men agreed to pick up the conversation in the morning.

Across the hall, two doors down from the half-finished nursery that had been on Josiah's let-me-show-you-what-fallout-looks-like tour, a broken friend—guilt-ridden for good reason—paced. Josiah recognized the pattern of squeaks in the old house's floorboards. Was there any point in waiting until morning?

They both needed time to think. Nate's remorse marked his face, his words, his posture. Josiah wondered if he was ready to turn remorse into commitment. Separating concern and resentment had consumed Josiah as he listened to his friend's confession. A good part of him wanted to throttle Nate. Throttle. Flagellate. Cream.

Ah. Creamed Nate on Toast for breakfast.

And a second helping for forcing a sleepless night.

Josiah flipped on the reading light and reached to pull his Bible from the nightstand. God help him, he thought it might lull him to sleep. But the drawer was empty. He kept his Bible in the locker at the hospital these days.

He rolled to Karin's side and tugged open the drawer she might never use again. Her Bible was decidedly more well-worn than his. And full of color. She'd underlined and marked notes in the margins. Some pages sported artwork illustrations of phrases or verses she must have found meaningful. This wasn't the Bible she took to church with her on Sundays, the one she'd tucked into that infernal suitcase he'd refused to open until just the other day.

The suitcase. Who packs a Bible when she's planning a tryst? For that matter, who packs pajamas modest enough for the Amish?

He opened Karin's artsy Bible—this one—to the place where he'd been listening on Nancy's mp3 player. Psalm 31. Every blank space, even between verses, held asterisks, exclamation points, lines connecting the thought to another verse elsewhere on the page. Blue ink. Yellow highlighter. Red. Thin green lines. He turned the page. Its margin was dotted with a line of artistic turquoise tears. Must have been colored pencil, judging from the careful shading. A trail of tears.

How badly did he want to investigate what it was that made his wife draw a line of tears on the page?

"I am forgotten, like I'm dead," he read. "Completely out of mind; I am like a piece of pottery, destroyed. Yes, I've heard all the gossiping, terror all around . . . they plan to take my life!"

How long before her accident had she read this? What would have moved her to draw tears when none of this had happened yet? Maybe she'd been thinking about someone else. Or about an idea for one of her cards. The connection rocked him, no matter when she'd done this.

His finger traced the line of tears. "Karin, I don't understand what happened to us. But I want to understand. And you're not forgotten. Somehow, I will make sure you know that."

He turned the pages, one after another, watching for clues to Karin's heart. The book read like a journal. She spoke to him through what she underlined—in some passages, almost every word. The bits of resentment he'd clung to despite his longing to live an "on the night" kind of selfless love turned to powder that floated away as he glimpsed her soul recorded on the pages. Despite the so-called evidence, despite what seemed indisputable, this is who she was. This woman. The one who drew her strength from ancient yet new-every-morning truths. The one who lived it out with others and with him, even when he was unaware. This Karin. This is who he married. This is who she was. Still.

In the verses at the end of that tear path lay one she'd circled multiple times. "But me? I trust you, Lord! I affirm, 'You are my God.' My future is in your hands."

He laid the book on her pillow, leaving it open to that page. He wouldn't be able to sleep, but lying on his side, he could look at that thought through the night.

Alarm clocks are bold-faced liars. It couldn't be morning already. And he couldn't have slept. But it was and he had. More than a few minutes? From the ache in his joints and eyes, the answer was no.

Josiah showered, dressed, and pulled the bed covers toward the pillows. Karin's open Bible stared at him. She might appreciate having it near her. He reached for it with one hand while pulling the comforter the rest of the way to the headboard. The featherweight pages rustled and a bookmark fell to the floor.

One of Karin's handcrafted bookmark flaps. Most of the Seedlings & Sentiment cards he'd seen at the shop before he'd put everything in the storage unit came with an attached bookmark flap, perforated so it could be torn free from the card and kept— like this one—or planted, according to the fine print on the back of the cards. He had to admit that was a clever value-added idea.

The bookmark read, "The WHY is less important than the WHAT NOW?"

A good place to start the day with Nate.

A good place for Josiah and Karin to restart.

He'd never find the exact spot where the bookmark had been, so he opened to a random page. It would take a minute to get his bearings again.

Isaiah 21:11-12—"'Guard, how long is the night? Guard, how long is the night?' The guard said, 'Morning has come, but it is still night.'"

There it is in a nutshell.

ᥢᥱᥲ ᥢᥱᥲ ᥢᥱᥲ

"Why did Karin start to get the nursery ready if she planned on leaving you, Josiah?"

"I thought I was the one asking the questions." Josiah punched the brew button on the coffeemaker.

"She intended to bring the baby back home. She wouldn't have made the nursery here if she expected to be living with that guy."

"Maybe she thought I'd be the one to leave." He hadn't taken a sip yet, but his throat reacted as if he'd gulped scalding hot liquid.

"Doesn't make any sense. Want to know what I think?"

Josiah slid a box of cereal across the island and pointed to the bowls he'd retrieved from the cupboard. "Because your thinking processes have been spot-on for the last few months?"

"Point taken."

"Yes. I want to know what you think."

Nate dug a spoon out of the silverware drawer. Josiah had remembered milk. He couldn't be expected to remember everything.

"I think she had no intention of taking off with that guy."

"Wade."

"Whatever."

Just as I suspected. As soon as someone knows the truth about what happened, they'll be all over me with their words of wisdom, theories, and what I should do. "He had a name. And a life. And a wife, by the way." Bitterness for breakfast. No. He'd sworn off of that. "He had a name."

"Yeah, doesn't matter for the point I'm trying to make." Nate chewed a spoonful of cereal. "How old is this stuff? Cereal isn't around long enough to grow stale at our—" He dropped the spoon into the bowl. "At our house. Anyway, did it look to you like Karin didn't expect to return to that nursery and finish the project?"

"Nate, she hadn't even told me about the baby. Now, why would that be? She hadn't left a note or called me. She hadn't even said she was going to be late. But her unsent text said we needed to talk before she 'left.' That seems pretty clear. And why was she heading the opposite direction of home? I'll tell you why. Because the airport is that direction."

"So's the hospital."

The gash on her forearm that the staff was convinced happened before the accident?

"Did you find any plane ticket? Any evidence on her computer or credit card that she'd booked a flight? Josiah?"

No. "Maybe he booked their flight."

"What's his wife's name?"

"Leah."

"So, ask her."

"I don't want to put her through any more than I already have. What if you're wrong and Wade did arrange their flights? It'll devastate her. As far as she's concerned, her husband is not only dead but innocent. At the very worst, duped by my desperate wife. He's gone. It wouldn't help anything. Besides, whether she's innocent or guilty doesn't matter anymore." *There. He said it aloud.* "It doesn't matter whether she was faithful or not. I need to be."

Nate returned to the stale cereal. "So, what now? What are you going to do now?"

"I'm already doing it. Walk and keep on walking. I'm walking this out, a step at a time, working on loving her until she tells me to stop."

"She can't talk."

"Then she's not telling me to stop, is she?"

Silence took over. Josiah filled a travel mug, then turned off the coffeemaker. He was about to remind Nate that he had to get to the hospital before ten to say good-bye to his father-in-law when his unexpected guest said, "I have to go home."

"Yes, you do."

"Today."

"From what you've said, Ruthie isn't ready for you to force your way back into her life."

"I know. I can't do that. I have to keep showing my love for her until she tells me to stop. I have to get serious about gluing the pieces back together. I did a pretty thorough job smashing our relationship into microscopic bits. Whether she responds or not, I have to try."

Whether she responds or not.

"Hey, Josiah, can I take a copy of your last book with me? I started reading it in the night when I couldn't sleep."

All the pride had gone out of a moment like this, replaced by a consciousness of how little Josiah had to offer. "Sure. If you get anything worthwhile out of it, know that came from God, not me. I'm beginning to think I'm His target audience."

"Is that why you autograph your books 'JC'?"

"What? They're my initials." He emptied the remnants of milk from Nate's cereal bowl into the sink. "To write 'Josiah Chamberlain' every time takes a lot of ink and slows things down when there's a line of people waiting."

Not that he'd ever experience that again. Except this last time—in too few days. The stadium event. Nerves and reluctance shared a lot of the same visceral responses.

Chapter 30

A flutter of gossamer wings makes us wonder
how such a fragile thing as hope can achieve flight.
Yet it does fly.

~ Seedlings & Sentiments
from the "Hope" collection

*S*inging. Stan was singing to Karin when Josiah entered the room.

"What's that tune, Dad?"

"Something Catherine used to sing to her when she was a baby. I don't have the best voice, but—"

"But it's yours. I'm sure that means a lot to her."

It does. Oh, Daddy, it does. Where's Mom? When's
she coming back?

"Wish I could hear that from Karin's mouth. Not that I don't believe you, Josiah."

"Your granddaughter appreciates your singing." Josiah pointed

246

to a spot where the mound moved like a dolphin preparing to breach the surface of the ocean-sheet.

Stan kept his gaze rooted to that spot. "A miracle."

That's one way of viewing it. It's also the product of misguided passion, Dad. And you will never need to know. "Certainly is a wonder to see movement somewhere, isn't it?"

"How big do you figure my granddaughter is right now?"

"Maybe as much as two and a half pounds." The voice—a female voice—came from behind them.

The squat older woman in a dress the color of a mango, her lab coat flapping open, lime leggings struggling to maintain their dignity, and a silver haircut shorter than Stan's swept into the room. "More than a little bit smaller than the ten pound boy Angie just had." The woman turned to Josiah. "Angie told me to tell you she was grateful for your encouragement."

He'd have to get her a card. And a gift. "You're her replacement?"

"No." She pulled a small electronic tablet from her pocket and swiped across the screen. "I'm Dr. Stephens's replacement. Priscilla Moore. I assume you're Josiah. And you must be Karin's father, Stanley."

"Stan," he said, extending his hand.

"Pleased to meet you."

Not what Josiah expected. "Should we leave you alone with my wife? I mean..."

"I've completed much of my initial exam. Studied her chart." She turned toward her patient. "Karin, you would have made a great addition to my last research project. But I'm sure you know that. And I'm sure you'd rather represent the 'post-recovery' aspect rather than the 'mid-stage' aspect, wouldn't you, dear?"

She bent over Karin, pushing the IV pump out of the way with her hip. Dr. Moore peered through half-glasses at Karin's face. She squeezed Karin's earlobes, ran the back of her fingers across Karin's forehead, then turned to Josiah. "Will you use some hand sanitizer and help me for a moment?"

"Me?"

Dr. Moore chuckled at his hesitation. "Thought you might want the privilege of participating in this. Any minute now, young man."

Josiah cupped his hands under the dispenser and watched as three dollops of foamed hand sanitizer landed in his palms. He rubbed them together as if prepping for surgery.

"That's a good plenty," the doctor said. "Now here. Put one hand on each side of your wife's face. Karin, can you feel your husband's touch? He's here because he loves you. And I'm here because I believe you're grasping more of what we say than you're letting on."

His touch. Yes.

Josiah's heart rate increased. According to the lights on her heart monitor, Karin's remained even. Stan had stepped to the foot of the bed to give them room. Josiah heard whispers coming from his direction. Prayer, no doubt.

"So here's what I'm going to do. Karin, you stay relaxed."

As if she's capable of anything more than that.

Dr. Moore depressed the button to lower the bed and scooted her backside onto it. "That's better. Okay, I'm going to remove the tape on your eyelids. And we're leaving the tape off. During the day. If we need to, we'll replace the tape at night so you can sleep more solidly."

I'm afraid. Not of what I'll see, but of what they'll see when they look in my eyes.

"Let me know if I'm hurting you, dear."

Josiah watched Karin's face for a hint of a reaction. Nothing. Priscilla Moore was either overconfident or misinformed, despite her statement about having "studied" Karin's chart. Or brilliant. One of the three. Josiah would play along until he knew which.

With the tenderest of touches, Dr. Moore's fingers plucked at the edges of the tape until it loosened. "Stan, do me a favor."

"Sure."

"Dim the lights, will you? The slider control by the door."

"Got it. Want me to draw the blinds?"

Dr. Moore nodded, but kept her focus on Karin's face.

Don't get your hopes up. Don't get your hopes up. Don't get your hopes up, Josiah.

The doctor took special care around Karin's doe-like eyelashes. With the tape gone, Dr. Moore dampened a gauze square and used it to wipe Karin's eyelids. "Now, sweetie. Nothing's preventing you from opening your eyes when you want to. Take your time. Josiah, stroke the sides of her face like you might if trying to calm a newborn."

"I've never calmed a newborn."

"That's it. Just like that. You'll make a good daddy."

The truth confession was on the tip of his tongue. He swallowed it. "Her eyes were open all the time before. For days. Why isn't she opening them now?"

"Don't ask me. Ask her."

"No, seriously."

"Ask. Her." The doctor's multicolored earrings jangled when she used her head to point to Karin.

Josiah drew the backs of his fingers across Karin's forehead as he'd seen Dr. Moore do. Touching Karin this intimately, in front of a relative stranger—to say nothing of Karin's father—made him feel like a junior-high boy caught in his first public display of affection. His palms sweated. Any minute now, someone was going to tell him, "Quit that!"

He traced the unique line of her petite nose and touched her lips. "Karin, honey. Open your eyes."

"Talk to her."

"I . . . I haven't seen your eyes, those beautiful eyes, for so long. I hope your . . . our . . . I hope the baby's eyes look just like yours."

I'd give anything if they looked like yours, Josiah.

Dr. Moore leaned closer to Karin's face, which meant closer to Josiah's face, too. Definitely more awkward than junior high. "Okay," she said. "You're not ready yet, are you, Karin? Understood. It's been a while since you had a view of this colorless room. We don't mind waiting. But if *you* don't mind, I'm going to whisk your husband and father away for a few minutes and fill them in on my approach. You and I have had a nice long, crack-of-dawn conversation about that, haven't we? Unless you'd like to tell them what I have planned? No? Okay, then, it's up to me. Gentlemen?"

Could Priscilla Moore be more different from Dr. Lane Stephens, the ill-at-ease, low-talking, always-play-by-the-rules physician they'd been dealing with since the accident? Stan and Josiah followed as Dr. Moore's lab coat wings glided out of the room and toward the family conference room. The lime leggings brushed against one another like an instrument in a reggae band.

"Josiah," Stan whispered midroute, "I'm going to have to get on the road soon."

"I know. If you need to leave now, I'll call you later and bring you up to speed."

"I'd rather witness this myself, if it doesn't take too long. Cover for me if I have to beat a hasty retreat?"

Stan served as a good companion for this journey. Josiah's head ached at the thought of having to say good-bye to him again.

"Have a seat, gentlemen." Dr. Moore kicked off her heels, dropping her height another two inches, and rubbed first one foot, then the other. "They let me wear flip-flops at my last gig."

"Where was that, Dr. Moore? Where did you practice before Woodlands?"

Stan. Ah, the innocence of advanced age. Josiah busied himself adjusting the distance of his chair from the conference table.

"Haiti."

Stan smiled but leaned closer to Josiah. "Did she say Hades?"

"Haiti, Dad. The country."

"Oh."

Josiah couldn't begin to think about caregiving for an aging father-in-law until they knew Karin's prognosis. From the color-coordinated charts on the whiteboard behind Dr. Moore, Josiah assumed they were about to know more than they ever had regarding that subject.

"I'm not here to disagree with any treatments or protocols previously established in regard to Karin's care," she began. "Oh, who are we kidding? Yes, I am. And I'll tell you why."

Apparently lime-green leggings make a person feisty. Or feisty makes a person choose lime leggings.

Dr. Moore spent the next few minutes outlining the basics of brain trauma, the difference between brain trauma caused by lack of oxygen and that caused by injury, as in Karin's case. Stan stopped checking his wristwatch shortly after the conversation moved to the means of measuring levels of consciousness, a clearer definition than Josiah had heard from any of the medical team to date, or any he'd found online when he'd dared search. Most of his online searching widened the fissures in his heart, so he hadn't kept at it long.

"Recently"—Dr. Moore sighed with all five feet of her stature—"you may have been told that Karin has moved into a persistent vegetative state."

Stan looked at Josiah for confirmation. Josiah nodded. He should have known trying to keep that nugget of information from his father-in-law would backfire. Stan's hope stayed solid, unlike Josiah's vacillating version. Josiah didn't want to be the one to mess with someone's hope.

"That's not all bad news." She used a marker to circle a handful of words on the board under the heading "Vegetative State (less than three on the Glasgow Coma Scale)." The words were, "Sleep/wake cycles, no interaction with environment, no localized response to pain."

"Does that mean Karin can't feel pain?"

Stan's question wasn't his alone. Josiah had received such a wide variety of answers—none definitive—that he'd stopped asking. If the answer were that she was aware of pain, he might have lost his mind. Assuming that she didn't helped him cope. How self-centered was that? Or protective? What he thought he knew—about life, love, himself—was in constant flux.

"It means she has no measurable response to pain or negative stimuli, Stan." Dr. Moore removed her earrings and set them on the table. "We might have looked at that as a positive benefit for her, right after the accident. It's no longer working in her favor now that most of her injuries have had time to heal. Except the brain trauma. And that brings us to—" She circled "Persistent Vegetative State." "This is where Karin is right now, by most traditional methods of measurement and assessment. A vegetative state lasting longer than one month."

"A lot longer," Josiah reminded her. "We're closing in on four months soon."

"Yes."

How could she muster a smile in a conversation this grave? And why is it Josiah found it comforting rather than annoying?

"But, I'm of the opinion," she said, "that Karin is not near, nor will she reach, this stage." She circled "Brain Death" and dropped the marker into its holder. "Her eyes were initially open, though she appeared to have no level of consciousness, from what I've read."

"That's correct." Eerily open. Unseeing.

"Her eyes were artificially, or intentionally, closed to prevent infection, to keep them from drying out."

Josiah nodded. The woman knew her stuff.

"Not a wrong move. But now she's gotten used to that eyes-closed state. I'm planning a course of treatment or techniques, if you will, to keep her from reaching this phase—*permanent* vegetative state." She reacted to Stan's intake of air with, "She's currently in persistent rather than permanent vegetative state. We don't want to see her move to that. I'm going to do everything in my power to see it doesn't happen. And I have hope."

"Hope" sounded a lot better than Dr. Stephens's "guardedly optimistic," a term he hadn't used since soon after the accident.

"I believe something is registering in there. A faint, faint ember that I intend—with your help—to fan into flame. Technically, she would have to remain this way for a year in order to earn the permanent status. So we have seven or eight months."

Hope. Josiah let the word saturate his soul.

Dr. Moore picked up the marker and wrote "false hope." "False hope can devastate a family. I am going to be honest with you about the process, the prospects, and Karin's prognosis. The rest of the team may want to move her to a maintenance facility. I would like to see evidence of progress so her next move can be rehabilitation, not maintenance. No guarantees. And you won't always like what I say. Including these next statements."

The back of Josiah's neck cramped.

"Yes, the medical community has seen a few documented cases where a patient will awaken from the kind of persistent vegetative state Karin's in right now. Those incidences are so rare that they usually make national news. So that will put things in perspective. I will consider it a victory—and trust you will, too—if we see Karin swallow, eat, hold a spoon, hold her head up, hold that baby should the baby survive. That, gentlemen, is practiced hope rather than false hope. And it will likely need to be enough for all of us."

Chapter 31

One-word prayers carry as much weight
as those most carefully constructed.

~ Seedlings & Sentiments
from the "Faith" collection

*W*ith Stan safely home, back into the swing of picking up the pieces following his wife's death, and with Nate reporting every few days from his apartment a mile away from the home he'd once shared with Ruthie, Josiah planted himself in the waiting room and alternated between half-heartedly prepping for his stadium event and wholeheartedly thanking God for the phenomenon named Priscilla Moore.

No guarantees, she said. But the woman acted like a hope factory. The more Josiah thought about it, the more he saw a connection between his curious mentor, Nancy, and Dr. Moore in that respect. Watching Dr. Moore treat Karin as if she were fully present in the room was transformative. Her contagious confidence spread.

Days before his trip, he found the good doctor leaning over the ICU nurses' station counter, one flip-flopped foot in the air for balance, at the top of the hour.

"Can I help you, Dr. Moore?" he asked, his voice low out of respect for the ICU patients who could hear and feel pain.

"Josiah! I was trying to get a— Got it!" She brandished a pen. "Pen," she said, "to leave you a note. And yet here you are, making the note unnecessary. Providential. I have something I want to show you. Come with me."

"Could I—?"

"Hmm?"

"May I ask you a question we haven't addressed yet?"

"Shoot."

"I'd rather not talk about it in front of..." Had he noticed before that Dr. Moore's eyebrows were so much darker than her hair? Her half-glasses sat at a disturbing angle on top of her head.

She looked around the ICU. "Census is down. Let's step in here."

She chose an unoccupied room. Absent even a bed. A fitting atmosphere for the conversation they needed to have.

"So, they relaxed the rules about footwear?" he said. *God, please let her have a sense of humor that matches her fashion sense.*

"Technically off-duty as of ninety seconds ago."

"I'm glad you're here already. Dr. Stephens said you weren't arriving for another couple of weeks." *Just get to the point, Josiah.*

"Frankly, it was your wife's case that made me adjust my schedule. She fascinates me. And I don't mean that purely clinically, I hope you understand."

"She fascinates me, too." He let the truth of the words have their moment.

"I don't play favorites with celebrities, Josiah."

So, she knew of his work. "I wouldn't want you to."

"But, I've been a fan of your wife's artistry for a long time."

Josiah stared at the woman's lips. Had he heard her wrong?

"Finding THE Karin Chamberlain here, the heart of Seedlings & Sentiments as one of my patients, in need of my services, added to the appeal of accepting this position. A woman with her gift? Silenced? I'm banking on something I can't prove medically, but

I would love to be proved right for her sake. And yours. And that child's."

His wife, the celebrity. The laughter he stifled held no resentment. Pure joy. "And that's at the root of my question. A couple of weeks ago, Karin's team told me we were reaching a point where I was going to have to make a difficult decision." He choked on the last two words.

"And by that they meant what?"

"Choosing between saving Karin or saving her child."

The line of Dr. Moore's jaw tightened. Pursed lips and narrowed eyes, she took a step closer. Despite his relationship savvy, Josiah's insides fluttered.

"Mr. Chamberlain"—she pressed her index finger into his breastbone—"you and I will never have this conversation again. Do you understand?"

"Yes, ma'am."

"Any other questions?"

"Not right now."

She holstered her index finger and stepped back. "Good. I have something to show you."

He followed as her flip-flopped feet led him to Karin's room. She extended her arm as if introducing a celebrity guest. "Do you remember the color of your wife's eyes, Josiah?"

"Yes. They're—" Open! Karin's eyes were open. Unmoving, but wide open!

☙ ☙ ☙

As beautiful as he'd remembered. Like strong tea or fresh-from-the-sugar-shack maple syrup. Was it the fact that her body was healing, or was it his imagination? Her eyes seemed less blank. They didn't respond, react, move, follow lights or sound. But light reflected differently from them than they had four months ago. He could see himself in her eyes if he stood directly over her.

When the two of them were alone, Josiah said the words that couldn't wait. "I have to be gone a couple of days next week, Karin. Morris booked this event close to two years ago. I can't get out of it. And he says—you know Morris—that if I don't show up, he's cutting me out of his will. I don't want to leave you." He bent to kiss her cheek. "I wish I knew how that made you feel, whether it matters at all if I'm here or you'd rather I weren't."

Matters. Hurts. Can't say what I want to say.

"Your dad will be here while I'm gone. He's such a great guy. You were lucky—blessed—to have him for a father. I'm blessed to have him for a father-in-law."

Daddy. I never see Mom. I won't see Mom, will I?

"When you get better, and can come home, what do you think about our inviting Stan to come live with us? You didn't say no. I'll take that to mean you'll think about it."

It killed his back to stand bent in that position for long, his eyes inches away from hers, as Dr. Moore recommended. He pulled the straight chair closer and worked on massaging her right hand, the one that contracted more than the other. The clenching seemed especially pronounced today. The harder he worked to open her hand flat against the back of his, the tighter her reflexes fought to close up.

Josiah pried open her grip and laid her fingers flat on the bed at her side. "Oh, honey. The protector pad underneath you is soaking wet. Your catheter connection must have come loose. I'll get the nurse. Be right back."

He kissed her on the opposite cheek this time, vowing never to leave her without that gesture, small as it seemed.

He didn't have to go far. Her nurse met him at the door, stepped around him without a word, and braced herself against the baby mound while studying one of the machines.

Josiah said, "I think her catheter connection came loose. The bed is damp under her. Sorry to make more work for you, but—"

The nurse swore.

With their medical bills now in the catastrophic category, she could have restrained her tongue over having to remake the bed and fix the catheter.

The woman repeated her curse word of choice three times. Then punched the call button. She didn't wait for the unit clerk to finish her "Nurses' station. How can I help you?" speech. "Get Dr. Moore back here. And call Dr. Randall and the neonatologist on call. Karin's water broke. She's contracting hard." One more swear word for emphasis. "Sorry, Mr. Chamberlain. We've got a situation here. Gonna have to ask you to leave. But don't go far, okay?"

"Can't I stay? Is there something I can do? I can hold her hand." Lame. All he had to offer.

"The room is going to be a madhouse in a few seconds. We need to be able to do what we do best. Please. . . . Oh, no! She's crashing! Get out of here!"

Against all instincts and on legs stripped of their muscle tone, he obeyed.

❧ ❧ ❧

Five rude truths smacked Josiah in the face as he stood in the purgatory between the ICU and the family waiting room.

He might lose his wife. He might lose the nameless, too-small baby girl. He might lose them both. Baby Girl didn't have a name because he didn't have a legal right to name her. And Josiah had control over none of the above.

The five points replayed on a continuous loop. *Karin. Baby Girl. Both. No name. No control. Karin. Baby Girl. Both. No name. No control. Call Janelle.*

He should call Janelle. Not that Janelle had any control either. But maybe she could put words to her prayers. Wasn't it important for someone to know how to figure out the words? All Josiah had was a deep groan that ricocheted loudly and incessantly inside. His ears heard nothing. Judging by the absence of flinching in the people who passed him in the hallway, they must not have heard anything either.

The nurse hadn't told him where to wait. Correction. She hadn't *barked* where to wait. Were they trying to stop the contractions? Didn't they have medicines now to—

Somewhere he'd heard that after a woman's water breaks, nothing will prevent the baby from coming. No matter how lousy the timing, how frail the mother, how underdone the child. He wasn't going to waste mental energy trying to remember where he'd heard it or if it was even true. If it was, they would have taken Karin to an operating room or a birthing center, wouldn't they? He should wait wherever she was, not here in hospital purgatory.

They should have told him.

"Mr. Chamberlain, what are you doing here?"

"I don't know." As honest an answer as he'd ever given. Who'd asked? Dr. Moore. "I don't know where they've taken her."

She adjusted the Hawaiian-print scarf around her neck. "I'm on my way to find out. Come on."

"They told me to get out of there."

"Out of the room, I imagine. Not out of Karin's life."

No. She's the one who said that, or would have if she could talk. Why couldn't water under the bridge stay under the bridge?

"We need to move, Mr. Chamberlain."

He matched her pace.

"Karin crashed." He knew what that meant and said the words as if well-practiced.

"Your wife's still alive."

"Are you operating on her, Dr. Moore? I don't know what I'm saying. Are they operating?"

"At-risk babies are not my area of expertise. Here. Through here." She held the door for him. "Over the phone, it sounded as if Karin's OB was prepping for a C-section. I won't be needed for delivering your daughter." She stopped walking. "You want me to tell it straight, don't you, Josiah?"

Did he? "Please."

"We don't know what this stressor of labor will do to your wife's condition. She may crash again. We're facing three possible outcomes."

"Five." *They both live. They both die. Karin lives, but the baby dies. Karin dies, but the baby lives. Karin and the baby live but want nothing to do with me.*

"Pardon?"

Six, then. No matter what happened, Josiah could do more than forgive Karin. He could pardon her. Pardon. As if the affair had never happened. "Go on."

"I'm here," Dr. Moore said, resuming her quickstep toward the nurses' station, "in the event the outcome is not what we hoped for your wife. It may drive her deeper into her locked-in state. She may stroke out. She may not survive. I'll do everything in my power to make sure that doesn't happen. But I know better than to promise."

New to Woodlands Regional, Dr. Moore still commanded authority while instilling an unexpected breath of confidence in Josiah. The woman had weathered crises before. She moved swiftly but without the panic that pulled the loose marionette strings attached to his limbs. If he stayed close to her, he might not fall completely apart.

Within minutes, the two stood before a double-door marked Authorized Personnel Only.

"You wait here." Dr. Moore pointed to a lounge he hadn't seen before. "If I can't bring you news myself, I'll send someone out as soon as we know anything—about either of them. Look at me," she said, chin lowered. She whipped her half-glasses from her face. "Don't you trust me. Don't trust the surgical team in there." She pointed upward. "You trust the only One who can make a difference for your family. He can pull off rescues beyond our abilities. You hear me?"

"Yes, ma'am."

Five foot nothing, and she could talk him into believing hope hadn't exhausted itself yet.

Chapter 32

Inhale. Exhale. Repeat as needed.

> ~ Seedlings & Sentiments
> from the "Hope" collection

The room smelled of stale cigarettes. An inexpensive variety. The hospital might have staked its claim as a smoke-free environment, but the clothes on the family in the room to which Josiah had been directed came from a smoke-saturated environment, Josiah guessed. The odor grew stronger when one of the family members paced close to where Josiah sat. And it didn't matter which one. All six of them seemed equally saturated.

He guessed they were prospective grandparents, two sets of them, and possibly younger siblings of the expectant mom. The presumed siblings—a young man and young woman—appeared to be in their late teens. Neither set of grandparents looked old enough for the position, or all that happy. Josiah hoped the siblings were younger than the about-to-be mother.

The answer arrived in the form of a young man—if all of eighteen, just barely—who burst into the room, his eyes wide. "Whoa, that was freaky."

The grandmas stood to their feet, their facial expressions animated at long last. "What happened?" Their question sounded as synchronized as twins.

"I almost passed out in there."

"What happened to Shauna and the baby?" Grandma #1, who bore a strong resemblance to the young man, emphasized each word.

"Oh, they're doing great. He's, like, eighteen pounds or something. I mean, the kid's enormous."

"Linus, eighteen pounds?"

"Might have been eight. Yeah, eight."

Linus? Josiah would have tuned out the conversation if he could have. A big, healthy baby born to a clueless father. Josiah shared the clueless part with the teen trying to spit out the details of his son's birth.

"Shauna was awake the whole time. But she's, like, tanked up on something they gave her so she's not feeling *anything* when they slice her open. She had the easy part. I had to watch it all."

The grandfathers restrained their wives. One glanced at Josiah as if wondering if he could get away with punching the new father's lights out. Josiah would have had no trouble giving his consent and ignoring his obligation to report the incident to the authorities.

Instead, the grandfather turned to Linus and said, "So, the baby's doing okay?"

"Yeah. They want to check to see if he has an extra chromerzone, or something like that. I said, 'How much is that going to cost?' You know how doctors are always looking to charge you for more tests."

Josiah pulled out his phone. Offering to scroll through his e-mails was the most privacy he could give the family, under the circumstances. *A suspicion of Down Syndrome? Oh, kids, you're going to need to grow up fast.*

"When can we see our grandson?"

"The nurse is going to let us know when they have Shauna settled in her room. She's already whining for a burger and fries. I didn't get any lunch, so..."

Fatherhood is sacrifice, buddy. Marriage is sacrifice. It's all sacrifice. All of it. But that's the beauty of it.

The female sibling asked, "What's his name, Linus?"

"We were thinking about Linus the Second."

A grandmother spoke up. "I named you, son. And even *I* hope that's not what you decided."

Our Father, who art in heaven, hallowed be Thy name. Thy kingdom come...

"Had you going there for a minute." The young dad sank onto the couch and stretched out. "We named the kid Bruiser. Shauna's spelling it Brewster, like brew pub. But I'm calling him Bruiser. Wait until you see the size of this kid."

God, if this is Your idea of a way to take my mind off what's going on in one of those operating rooms, I am not amused. And Linus, move your feet so your folks have a place to sit. You are so not ready to be a parent.

And neither am I. Stepparent. Whatever. Maybe there was no word for him. His heart lurched. He might not need to figure it out.

※ ※ ※

When the room emptied, Josiah embraced the aloneness like a long-lost friend. *Good to see you. Yeah, I missed you, too. Have a seat. Don't mind if I do.*

The appeal of aloneness disappeared with the realization that he might be on the cusp of a long, endless stretch of aloneness. He texted Janelle: "Details later. Just pray. Thanks."

Stan. He hadn't called Stan. The more he thought about it, the smarter Linus seemed. Josiah hadn't even remembered to call Karin's dad. He fumbled with the phone but eventually got through.

"Dad."

"Josiah? What is it?"

"Karin's in trouble. The baby's in trouble. Baby's coming. Or, I don't know."

"I'll be right there."

"No. No, you just got home not all that long ago. I just knew you needed to know." He took a breath and begged it to flush out his inability to communicate. "I'm here, waiting for news. We should know something before long. Oh, Stan."

"What? Son, let me close up here and get on the road."

"Stan, in all likelihood, it won't be necessary."

The older man's pause was peppered with shared pain. "I need to come. I need to be with you, son."

Every icy moment from childhood with his condemning father melted in the warmth of this man who enjoyed calling Josiah *son*. "I don't know what you'll find when you get here, but it would mean a lot to—"

"Say no more. I'm on my way. I'll leave my phone on, but I promise I'll pull over if you hear something and need to call. I'm coming no matter what, Josiah. Understood?"

"Yes. And thank you. Love you, Dad."

"Love you, too."

Where did you go to school to be a father, Stanley Vortman? You graduated with honors, didn't you? Karin, at least you knew one man who treated you well.

"Mr. Chamberlain?"

"Dr. Moore." He didn't remember standing, but there he was, less than two feet from the door, searching Dr. Moore's facial expression for a hint of what she was about to divulge.

She looked down briefly, shaking her head. When she looked up, she drew a weary breath before saying, "Your daughter's a fighter. She has that going for her."

The baby had lived through that? Josiah's throat tightened but he managed, "She gets it from her mother."

"Probably from both parents." Her smile barely registered. "There's a tenacity in you that is admirable."

I passed nothing on to this child, Dr. Moore. And that's probably a good thing. "I should ask how big she is."

"It could be worse. She's a fraction under three pounds. But of course, size is of less importance than lung development right now. That's one of our largest concerns. Her neonatologist will want to talk to you and fill in all those details from his perspective. She's in the neonatal intensive care unit. We call it the NICU, as if it's two words—nick you."

Nick you? Closer to "mangle, decimate, shred . . ."

"Will I get to see her?"

"After they get her stabilized, I'm sure they'll make arrangements for that. I don't know when that will be."

"And Karin?"

Dr. Moore walked to the narrow window. She rubbed the back of her neck. "I fought for your wife, Mr. Chamberlain. Fought hard. To be honest, I was in the minority." She turned back to him then. "Oh, not that the team didn't put their best effort into her care. It's just that with her condition the way it was, I could tell that the team wrestled with the ethics of how far to take this, how much to invest in prolonging her life, considering how her life has been defined these past months."

Josiah rocked one fist against his open palm as he had with Karin. Now, after all they'd been through, he understood what it felt like to be trapped in a paralyzing glacier of numbing cold. He locked his knees to keep them from buckling.

"I wish I could tell you I was a hundred percent sure it was the right thing, but I insisted they keep fighting for her. I insisted."

Air still smells like stale cigarettes. Need to breathe. "I appreciate everything you tried to do for her, Dr. Moore." *Can't draw a breath. Ever again.*

"So she is back on the ventilator. And"—Dr. Moore pointed heavenward with an open hand—"we'll see."

"Wait. She's alive. She's still alive." Incredulity added no question marks at the end of his sentences.

"Yes. The question is whether we've—whether I've—done her any favors."

"She lived through this? How could Karin live through this?"

"Isn't that what you were praying for?" She snatched a tissue from the box on the waiting room lamp table and handed it to Josiah.

"I didn't think He'd answer."

"Mr. Chamberlain, He always answers. 'Yes. No. Maybe. Wait.' And one of my personal favorites, 'You asked for *what*?'" She grabbed a second tissue and pressed it into his hand.

"What now?"

Down the hall, a newborn cried. It couldn't be his newborn. The cry had the strength to pierce eardrums. It probably sounded beautiful to the baby's exhausted but deliriously content mother.

Karin's baby girl didn't yet have the lung power to make an outburst like that.

"What now?" Dr. Moore ran her fingers through her stubbly hairdo. "We shift back into waiting mode. And you'll split your time between two intensive care units. Oh, that reminds me. They need you to sign the birth certificate. A nurse will be out in a few minutes to witness that process. So, stay here until you meet with him. And then he'll direct you where to wait to meet with the neonatologist. I'll check in with Karin frequently over the first few hours. So you and I will no doubt see each other later."

She stopped at the door. "Do you have a name for your daughter?"

He shook his head. Dr. Moore would have no way of knowing that the blank space for a name was not the most troubling portion of the birth certificate information.

"Josiah, she may be less than three pounds and impatient to get here. But she needs a name. Karin's not able to discuss it with you right now. Unless you two had decided ahead of time—"

"No. No, we hadn't."

"Then it's up to you, Daddy."

How could his hesitation not seem awkward? And who else could he talk to? It was time to man up and admit what he thought he might not have to face. The inevitable had come. Or had it?

"Can I see her first?"

"Karin? Josiah, they're transferring her back to ICU. It'll be a while before—"

"Not Karin. The baby."

"You can talk to the nurse about that. Not a bad idea. When my son was born, we thought we had a name picked out. But when we saw that face and that mop of dark hair, the name didn't fit at all." She smiled at the memory. "Maybe that little girl will tell you what she'd like to be named. Mr. Chamberlain, please know my prayers are joining yours for both your wife and your daughter."

Honesty. Soon. But he'd bought a little more time before he had to relinquish his claims to the baby with no name. Not that time would help.

≈ ≈ ≈

Karin's baby wasn't the smallest in the NICU. How sad was that? Dr. Bachchan, the neonatologist, assured Josiah she was doing better than expected. He had no explanation for how she'd managed to survive so well in what he called a hostile environment—the womb of a woman barely clinging to life.

Josiah listened hard when Dr. Bachchan spoke, his Indian accent strong and his vocabulary laced with unfamiliar, infant-related terms and medications. Some were *too* familiar. Oxygen levels. The importance of a feeding tube. Miniature versions of what the child's mother endured.

The baby lay spread-eagle, naked except for a playing-card-sized diaper. Josiah observed from his position at the foot of the Plexiglas unit that served as waist-high access for the staff and a platform with the tiny girl on display. Karin had started creating a nursery that would have been a soft haven for a child. The room at the end of the hall waiting for someone to assemble that comfortable crib, to finish painting the soothing colors, add soft blankets, sweet lullabies. How different that half-finished room seemed from this crisp-edged, sterile—and thank God for sterile—health factory.

The little one's chest heaved up and down in rhythm with the pump forcing it to do so. Both forearms were strapped to boards little bigger than tongue depressors.

One of the two nurses assigned to his daught—, to the little one, a woman named Eva, stuck her gloved hands through portals on the sides of the Plexiglas box. She opened tabs on the diaper, folded the front open, then quickly closed it up. "Daddy, your little girl has figured out one thing. Kudos to her. A wet diaper is a very good sign around here."

No pride he'd ever felt resonated as deeply as this. Little One knew how to wet.

"You can stand closer, Mr. Chamberlain. Right over here. What's her name?"

Josiah glanced at the pink card in the sheath at the head of the see-through box. "Baby Girl. Name: _____ Chamberlain. Height. Weight. DOB." "We haven't decided on a name yet." *And it only says Chamberlain because that's Karin's legal last name.*

Eva adjusted what looked like a hand-knit ski cap on the baby's head.

"Where did that come from?"

"The hat? Volunteers. These littlest ones lose so much heat through their heads. Some of the volunteers are moms who once had a preemie in this unit."

"And lost the child?"

Eva seemed startled. "No, Mr. Chamberlain. They took their children home when they were strong enough. But they remember. Some are grandmas of those preemies."

Josiah nodded as if any of the scene made sense.

"A few," Eva said, "knit in memory of a child who couldn't come home. When I get a minute, I'll show you our celebration board. Photographs of infants smaller than your daughter alongside pictures of them taking their first steps, heading off to kindergarten, graduating from high school..."

"Hard to imagine right now."

"I know. You can loan strength to your child, Mr. Chamberlain."

"Please call me Josiah. And if you knew how little I have to spare..."

"She's small. It won't take much." Eva's gentle voice belied her six-foot frame and broad shoulders. "The three best gifts you can give her right now are your fearless love, your voice, and your touch."

What would this little one look like without the surgical tape holding the tube in her nose, the tube in her mouth. All of what Josiah could see looked delicate and pale and like a stunning work of art. "I can touch her? Won't I—?"

"Joe—do they call you Joe?—her skin is fragile, but your voice and your touch are more important to this child's will to live than any of these medicines we're using and any of the machines helping her right now."

Eva's and the second nurse's ability to keep him informed without drawing attention away from the incessant needs of the baby-with-no-name lowered his respiration and heart rates closer to normal range. This child was in good hands.

Eva questioned him about his antibacterial hand washing, even though another nurse had not only instructed him thoroughly but monitored the process when he entered the unit. He held his hands to Eva for inspection—backs, palms, and nails. She nodded her approval with an appreciative smile and pointed to the box of purple surgical gloves. "You can use those if you're more comfortable. But your skin-to-skin contact with your daughter is important for bonding and for her development. More important than we knew even a dozen years ago."

He waved aside the gloves but pulled on a double layer of shame. What consequences would he bear for acting as if this really were his daughter?

"Slide your hands through the two portals on your side of the Isolette, Daddy."

When would that word stop making his nerve endings rebel?

"Good. Until we know how resilient she is and how she'll react, we'll move very slowly, okay? Step at a time. She's just come from an environment radically quieter and darker and more peaceful than this one. It will take her a while to adjust."

Josiah could envision Angie giving him the same lecture if Karin ever woke.

"Try sliding your pinkie finger under her little hand. But don't pull back if she startles. That's normal. In fact, it's a good response, at this point."

Josiah did as instructed. "The board her arm is tied to . . ."

"As long as you move slowly and don't dislodge any of the tubing, you'll be fine."

"You'll watch me?"

"Like a hawk." Her faux growl would have made him laugh if the baby-with-no-name hadn't curled her miniature fingers around his.

Chapter 33

Don't worry that your courage isn't enough.
Courage is measured in vibrancy, not quantity.

~ Seedlings & Sentiments
from the "Courage" collection

The only thing that could tear him away from the child's side was his devotion to the child's mother. He needed to see Karin, needed the reassurance that she'd somehow weathered what had happened to her. Had she felt the contractions? the incision? the pressure? the sutures? Had she felt any of it? Had the baby's birth sealed her locked-in state permanently? Had she exchanged *persistent* for the dreaded *permanent*?

"Josiah, before you leave..." Eva brought a clipboard from her side of the Isolette and extended a pen toward him. "We need to get this birth certificate filled out. Some of it has been completed already. We need information for these blank spaces."

He stared at the lines that seemed embossed, glossy, bold, raised above the surface of the page: *Father's name, age, and place of birth.*

The time had come. Integrity wouldn't let him falsify that information. It didn't matter that no one who cared would ever need to find out. Wade was gone. It would be a kindness to

Leah to keep the information from her. But Wade had parents. This child had grandparents who didn't know she existed. Even though it might decimate Leah to find out, those grandparents had a right to—

"Mr. Chamberlain? I know you've been on an emotional zip-line today, but . . ."

The second nurse moved to a storage cabinet near the windows.

"Eva, I need to talk to someone. I'm not sure what to do."

She nodded. "A priest? Minister?"

"No. Nothing like that." *Well, maybe.*

"I may have big feet, but I'm really all ears." Eva's voice didn't have the calming effect she probably intended.

Desert-dry throat. Burned-out bones. Prune-like lungs. How would he get these words out? And would they spell the end to his right to connect with the baby who chose that precise moment to open her eyes and turn her head toward him?

"I don't think I'm her father."

Eva's expression read more sober than startled. "You don't think you are?"

"I'm pretty sure I'm not." He wouldn't have to tell this almost-stranger how he'd failed the motility test, would he? And just about every other aspect of manhood? Like making sure his wife knew she was cherished?

"That"—the nurse checked over her shoulder—"will change your ability to fill out the birth record information, Mr. Chamberlain. Do you know where we can contact the baby's father? Has he been told that your wife was pregnant? Would he agree to a paternity test?" Had she backed away a step, or was that his imagination?

"He was killed in the car accident that brought my wife here."

Eva's soberness morphed to sympathy. "This must be difficult for you on so many levels."

I'm not the issue here. It's this baby who won't let go of my finger. Heart. Soul. "I don't know what's the right thing to do. I mean, how do we handle this? Karin can't give us this information. Please don't tell me I have to call the guy's wife."

"He was married."

No condemnation. She sounded vicariously heartbroken. "We may have to call in Social Services for clarification of how to proceed in this instance. But I know they will insist on having medical proof that you're not the father. Yeah, you don't have to tell me how cruel that must feel to you right now. I'm genuinely sorry, Mr. Chamberlain."

"Proof? Like, from my medical records?" Which humiliation would rate the strongest on the Richter scale?

"I assume you're willing to submit to a paternity test? Before you answer, I should tell you that it may buy you some time."

"What do you mean?"

She slid the pen into a holder on the clipboard. "As far as visitation rights here in the NICU, the natural assumption is that you're this little one's father until proved differently. With your wife in the condition you've explained, the baby needs some kind of surrogate parent connection."

A warning sounded on one of the machines. Eva reached into the Isolette and repositioned the pulse ox monitor. "Have you ever seen an infant version of a CPAP machine, Dad? Mr. Chamberlain?"

Her faux pas didn't escape his notice. "No."

"It will help her lungs expand more comfortably until they're stronger. Remarkably, she's breathing on her own. She needs a little extra help for a while."

Déjà vu. All over again. A miniature version of medical assessments he'd heard for the past four months.

"Are you okay, Mr. Chamberlain?"

"Josiah." *The woman knew more than most did about him. Vulnerability. It stinks.* "Some people call me Joe."

Eva narrowed her eyes as if thinking. "You look more like a Josiah to me. Are you okay? You can get through this. If you have half the determination of this little girl here—" She stopped.

Josiah saw it register on her face. She wasn't talking to the little girl's daddy.

"I have to do this right." He'd kept two sets of grandparents in the dark too long. "What do I have to do to prove she's not m—?"

The nurse raised her hand to prevent him from finishing his sentence. "Don't ask me how I know so much about paternity tests. Okay?"

The other nurse returned and appeared to have things well in hand. Eva turned her back to the activity in the room and indicated that Josiah should move closer to the NICU exit with her.

"We could do a blood test—a fairly simple blood type. But its accuracy isn't normally satisfactory. Not for custody issues and not for most who wonder if they're the father."

Josiah's eye twitch was back. She may not have noticed.

"Don't worry. DNA paternity testing is up to 99.9 percent accurate."

"So, zero point one percent doubt."

"I have a feeling you don't have much interest in the humor of that, Mr. Chamberlain."

"You're right."

Eva paused. She checked over her shoulder. "RFLP—Sorry. Laymen's terms. We can do a blood test—RFLP—or a simpler Buccal scrape. It's not as painful as it sounds. It's the swab on the inside of the cheek"—she pointed to a spot near her back molars—"you've probably seen on crime shows on TV."

"And that's accurate enough?"

"DNA is the same in every cell of the human body. The swab is as accurate as the blood test. We can compare your DNA to your daughter's. We'll use a cord blood sample from the baby. There's no adverse impact on you either, for the swab sampling."

"No *physically* adverse effect."

Eva hugged her arms across her middle. "You have no idea how much I sympathize with how difficult this is. With your permission, I'll relay the information you've told me to Dr. Bachchan."

So that's how the name is pronounced. As if the a's are u's and Bach rhymes with such. Name tags—names—don't tell everything.

"We'll get the process started as soon as possible," Eva said.

When he nodded, she returned to her duties.

He was going to have to walk away. The journey of a thousand miles starts with a single excruciating step.

"Josiah?"

He should have thanked her for her kindness. The other nurse moved to another Isolette. He walked back to the Baby Chamberlain area and waited for Eva to push the plunger on a syringe hooked to a length of tubing that snaked into the Isolette.

She laid her fingers at the base of her throat. Brow furrowed, she swallowed. "You wouldn't have had to say anything. She would have gone on record as your child. If your wife doesn't recover..." Eva drew a deep breath.

"Don't think I haven't considered that."

"You love your wife?"

"More than ever."

Activity swirled around them. Noises. Voices. Alarms. Eva glanced toward Karin's daughter's machines. The alarm belonged to another baby in trouble.

"You've forgiven your wife, and she doesn't even know it."

Josiah sighed. "It doesn't matter whether she knows or not. I do. And God does."

Eva shook her head. "That kind of love doesn't happen often enough."

"You're right. But the idea isn't original with me." *It started on the night He was betrayed.*

❧ ❧ ❧

Josiah again carried two pagers. He could have opted to have the NICU text him if he were needed—as if he had any power to make things better for that little one. He knew what they meant. If he were needed to say final good-byes. Or give consent for emergency surgery. He'd been through that gauntlet with Karin.

Receiving a text message from the NICU amid all his other inane text messages? How could he imagine them in the same category of urgency?

His leaden feet shuffled the corridors—the marathon route—between the NICU and the ICU where Karin had been taken. Same room? Likely. How empty that room would seem with the mound gone. It had been the only part of Karin that responded to him.

The elevator doors opened, but he couldn't move. He punched the button for the first floor and waited as the doors closed him in again.

He exited the elevator and turned right, toward the gift shop. Flowers weren't allowed in ICU. Would they let him bring in an "It's a girl!" Mylar balloon? He bypassed the packages of birth announcement cards. So little about this birth had followed a normal path. He purchased two items: a journal and a roll of Wild Cherry Lifesavers. Karin's favorite flavor. For him, not for her. He needed the reminder of who she'd been. Once upon a time.

Time. He should have paid closer attention. He'd missed the top of the hour by two minutes. What kind of husband misses twenty percent of the few minutes he's allowed with his wife? He popped a Lifesaver in his mouth and approached her bedside.

Most of the machines and tubes and wires and IVs looked the same as those that had formed her support system for the past four months. A flash of dark red drew his attention. A bag of red hung from one of the IV pole hooks. Karin must have lost too much blood during the C-section. That's all she needed.

"Karin, I'm glad you lived through all that." Not what he intended to say. "I'm glad you're still here." And he was. His heart apparently knew more than his brain did. Sometimes the heart is smarter than it's given credit for.

He leaned closer, his nose almost touching hers. "I love you and always will."

Her blank stare never failed to rattle him. He pressed on.

"You have a beautiful daughter." He held his phone screen where her eyes could see, if they could have seen. "This is her. Karin, her skin is so soft, with fine, fine hair all over her body, like the fuzz on a peach. I told her about you. I told her...how much you love her and that you can't wait to hold her."

The tear on Karin's cheek came from him. He brushed it away with his thumb. Another followed.

"The baby needs a name, hon. I figure if I pick one and you don't like it, we can get it legally changed sometime down the road." How easily words about their future slid from his mouth compared to how hard they fought to penetrate his soul.

"So"—he moved the Lifesaver to the inside of his left cheek from his right—"I was thinking about naming her after your mom."

Unless more registered deep in Karin's subconscious than any of them saw on the surface or in the testing, Karin wasn't aware her mother had died. *Choose your words carefully, Josiah.*

"What would you think about naming the baby Catherine? Catherine Alecia? Her middle name after your grandmother, your middle name?"

Karin's eyelids drifted shut as they sometimes did during her sleep cycles. Josiah bent to kiss her cheek. Her eyelashes brushed against the side of his face. She'd opened her eyes? So soon? Josiah held himself in check. He'd learned long ago he couldn't get excited over random involuntary movements.

But she did it again. Her eyes closed, then opened, as if blinking through molasses.

"Karin?" What was different about the way her eyes stared? Or was it his imagination? "Karin, did you do that on purpose? Did you blink your eyes?" He'd deal with himself later about pipedreams and wishful thinking.

Her eyes moved. Up and to her right. They froze there, as if waiting for something to appear. It was about the spot where he'd held his phone earlier so she could "see" her daughter.

Josiah retrieved his phone and showed her again. "This is your baby girl."

She blinked, a fraction faster this time.

"Is it okay with you if we name her Catherine?"

Another slow blink.

Random? Blinking was supposed to be an autonomic response. It seemed headline worthy at the moment in Karin's case.

"Karin, can you look at me?" Maybe the riskiest thing he'd asked in his life. Could she? Would she? Did she want to?

Her eyes didn't leave the phone image of her baby.

What now? He barely breathed, unwilling to disturb whatever was happening. "Are you okay with Mississippi for her middle name?"

She blinked twice.

"Alecia?"

Karin blinked once.

"You're there. You're in there."

One blink.

Man sobs. Dozens of them. Erratic. Convulsive. He squelched them as much as he could, but they escaped in unmanly squeaks and wild cherry exhales.

It took three tries for him to utter his next words. "Karin, welcome back." He risked adding, "I love you," knowing she would hear.

She blinked.

⁇ ⁇ ⁇

The team moved more slowly than Josiah expected when he told them what he'd observed. He expected chaos and got sloth. But as he watched the staff observe, test, and chart what looked to him like an awakening—every movement gentle, deliberate, and patient—he noted the caution in their smiles. Had they witnessed dawnings like this before and seen them regress into nothingness again? Were they protecting Josiah from even more devastation?

Dr. Moore arrived. The pace changed. As did the mood, as if the staff were waiting for her permission to celebrate. Josiah had to admit he had been, too.

"Well, young lady, you must be very proud of yourself. Giving birth and writing your own Rip Van Winkle story on the same day." She used the step stool she kept under Karin's bed for times when lowering the bed to a height she could manage well would take too long. Dr. Moore kept Karin's gaze while she reached to test reflexes—none—and negative stimuli responses—nothing. All Karin had was the ability to blink. But it was something.

"Two questions?" Tearing himself away from Karin's side pierced even deeper, knowing she was at least a little aware of her surroundings. He had two questions for Dr. Moore. Karin must have hundreds.

"I'll answer what I can, Mr. Chamberlain. In these cases, there's no such thing as a textbook pattern."

He followed her into the all-too-familiar corridor. "First question. Can you tell if this is . . . if this is all she'll regain?"

"No. I can't tell you that."

The confetti in his mind dropped like miniature bricks. The balloons hissed as they deflated.

"I can tell you my studied opinion. And that is, I believe we are seeing the bare, early beginnings of where Karin will be a year from now."

"A year?"

"Is that one of your two questions? We have empirical evidence and anecdotal evidence of a small number of locked in patients emerging rapidly to a remarkable level of consciousness, ability to communicate, movement. In those cases—especially those that have gone on for months, as your wife's has—we still face an extended recovery time. Regaining muscle tone. Relearning to walk. Recapturing bits of memory that are important to moving forward. Strengthening cognitive skills that have been on hiatus."

"Understood. Do you think it was the surgery that triggered this?"

"We may never know. It may have been the extreme hormonal upheaval of the birth. It could have been some subconscious level of concern for her child. That's part of what makes this field so fascinating. We know only a fraction of what transpires in the brain/intellect/neurotransmission/subconscious and conscious connections."

"Focus on being grateful?"

"Always a good option. Your wife will help increase our body of knowledge for other cases. Correction, other people." She smiled. "We'll monitor her very carefully at this stage. My prediction—take it for what it's worth—is that what she's exhibited in cognition—her yes/no blinks apparently being on target with what she intends to 'say'—is that we may be looking at a significant level of recovery on the horizon. Maybe not the near horizon. And, I must underscore, there are no guarantees."

Almost four months' worth of waiting escaped in a shuddering exhale.

"Was that your second question, Mr. Chamberlain?"

Elated. His wife remained in intensive care. The daughter he wished were his own lay in the NICU. And all he felt was elation. "I just wondered"—he pointed to her golf shoes—"how you did on the course. Big golfer, huh?"

"Caddy."

"Excuse me?"

"I caddy for other golfers. Keeps me from getting too full of myself and forces me outdoors. Fresh air. Sunshine. Exercise. And all the stress is someone else's. Do you golf?"

"I used to."

"Let's pray that life will settle down one day soon so you can get back on the golf course."

"I'll be a happy man when we're all home. That'll be enough entertainment for me."

"And your role is more caddy than golfer right now, isn't it?" Dr. Moore took a long sip from the drinking fountain. "I have a question for you, Mr. Chamberlain. Two, come to think of it."

"Yes?"

"Can I see a picture of that daughter of yours? And have you told the news to that man walking straight toward us?"

Josiah turned. Stan. He waved his father-in-law closer and held his phone screen so they both could see.

"So tiny," Stan said, in a voice equally small.

Dr. Moore sighed. "Beautiful child. She's in good hands. The NICU here has a stellar reputation. Stan, have you seen Karin yet?"

"No."

Dr. Moore's eyebrows danced. "Why don't you take him on in, Josiah? I'll text the nurses' station that you have permission to ignore the rules this time. Okay?"

Josiah owed it to his father-in-law to as quickly as possible dispel the confusion that masked his face. But not with words. Words wouldn't have the same impact. "Let's go see your daughter before I take you to see Catherine."

Stan's complexion drained of color.

"Catherine Alecia," Josiah hurried to add. "Your granddaughter."

Chapter 34

God never says, "Go away."
He beckons us nearer, no matter what we've done.

~ Seedlings & Sentiments
from the "Faith" collection

$\mathcal{K}$arin tired long before Stan and Josiah were ready to leave her. Although he witnessed it, Josiah couldn't imagine how it must feel from Karin's perspective—using all the stamina she had to raise and lower her eyelids. She seemed impatient with herself. Her nurse said that, too, was to be expected.

"Having a granddaughter waiting beyond the ICU doors softens the blow of leaving my daughter," Stan said, swiping at his eyes yet again.

Don't put away your handkerchief yet, Dad, Josiah wanted to tell him. *That little girl in the NICU is a heartbreaker. Your granddaughter. My wife's child.*

Josiah hadn't fallen in love with Catherine Alecia because she was tiny and beautiful. He hadn't fallen in love because she had Karin's wide eyes and long, delicate fingers. Or her sweet mouth that—before Karin's accident—had seemed perched in a perpetual pre-grin.

He hadn't lost his heart to baby Catherine because she was his. That would have been easy. He fell hard because she was Karin's and he *longed* for her to be his.

Stan had a natural link, a birthright to the child. He stared at her a long time before venturing to slide his hand through the portal to stroke her peach fuzz forehead. "Your grandmother would want me to tell you how beautiful you are, little girl. She'd want me to tell you she's honored you bear her name. I pray you grow up to be the kind of woman she was."

Josiah gave Stan time alone at Catherine's Isolette. He gravitated toward the celebration board where the nurses had posted photos of the success stories—children smaller and sicker than Catherine who'd grown into toddlers and preadolescents and teens.

And parents. This facility had a long history of success stories. His gaze drifted to a framed space labeled "Here's where your child's photo will be posted."

Hope. The medical team had hope.

Maybe he could borrow theirs.

❧ ❧ ❧

"Morris, I'm glad you picked up."

"I wondered if I'd hear from you today, Josiah. You are quickly becoming my problem-child client. Nobody keeps Morris Lynch hanging when he's waiting for answers. Not with an event of this magnitude at stake."

Guilt plunged deeper. "I apologize. For much more than not getting back to you about the town car confirmation."

"Moot point. I changed my flight. We now land in Dallas within minutes of each other. We'll share one town car to the hotel. Frankly, we'll need more than that amount of time for me to bring you up to speed on the protocol for the weekend. Glad we'll have the extra day. Your disappearing act these past months has my nerves as frayed as the hem of a pair of designer jeans."

"Morris, I'm done."

"Done packing? I would hope so."

"Done."

"You, young man, have an obligation. It's not an option. You *will* meet me in Dallas in a couple of days. You *will* be on your best behavior and offer that stadium full of people exactly what they paid to hear." Morris's words were spoken as if each one were a sentence unto itself. And laced with an emotion half a degree away from venom.

"I can't do it."

Grizzly bears growl with more panache than Josiah's agent's response. "You're not going to do this to me."

"To you?"

"And I won't let you do this to your career."

"Karin had her baby."

"Well, congratulations. Now get on that plane."

"Morris, Karin's on the verge of— I don't know. She's aware. She's starting to respond. Blinking, but it's something."

"And the staff at the hospital will continue to take good care of her for the time you'll be gone. Josiah, you're not her answer."

"I know. Believe me, I know. And the baby's so small. So frail."

In the volley of conversation, it was time for Morris to say something. He didn't. Not anything that wasn't under his breath and outlawed in schools and churches.

"Who wouldn't understand that I can't leave them right now?" Josiah squeezed out the next words. "What kind of person wouldn't understand that?"

One of the non-understanding finally spoke up. "The event planners who have invested tens of thousands of dollars. Scratch that. Hundreds of thousands that they won't recoup. Scratch that. They'll recoup it from us, my boy. Breach of contract. Where are you? You sound like you're in a tunnel."

"Men's room. Not a lot of privacy around here."

"How much does it cost to keep your wife and baby in diapers, Josiah?"

He was going to have to buy a new phone. Few can survive being flushed.

❧ ❧ ❧

"Dad, can I borrow your phone?" Josiah took the cup of coffee Stan offered. Stale. He could tell before he raised it to his lips.

Stan rolled his shoulders as he often did when stressors accumulated. "Sure, son. Yours lose its charge?"

"In a manner of speaking. I need to call my agent."

"Everything set for your big event?"

What? How could his father-in-law imagine he would leave at a time like this? Josiah checked the wall clock. Five minutes before the top of the hour. "Not only is my heart not in it—my heart's here—but I have nothing to say."

Stan ran his palm down his face. It did nothing to erase the weariness etched in deep lines. "Don't you think you have more to say now than you ever did?"

"I can't leave."

"Aren't you under contract, son? I don't understand all of the everythings, but the way I heard, this is a pretty big deal. People are counting on you."

"Stan, I expect that from Morris. Not from you. Karin and Catherine Alecia—"

"—will still need you a few days from now. Probably a great deal more than they have to date. I knew a guy who had a stroke and had to learn how to walk again, talk, swallow, hold a spoon. It's no small thing. No offense, Josiah, but you and I are going to have to pace ourselves if we're going to still have energy enough four months from now. A year. Two years."

"But I can't leave now. I've waited so long to know if Karin would ever be able to—" *To tell me what happened. What happened? I can't leave when I don't know if she even wants me in her life.*

"—talk again? Waited to know if she'd ever talk again?" Stan waited for an answer.

Let's go with that. "Among other things."

"How much of a mess will you create if you don't show up in Dallas?"

Stan's wisdom stung sometimes. "Almost incalculable."

"And"—the older man rolled his shoulders again—"how many crises will you be able to prevent if you're here for the next four days?"

"Three. I can make it three days if I take the red eye after the final event on Saturday night."

"How many medical crises can you resolve?"

"None. But too many times in the past I haven't put Karin first. I haven't put family first." The minute hand inched closer to the top of the hour.

Stan stood. "It's your business what you decide, Josiah. But what you're facing here is long-term. And I can do my best to love those two and be present for them for that little bit of time you're gone. Your event in Dallas is intense, and it'll take God Himself to get you through it, but it's short-term. And I have to believe what you're going to tell them is something they need to hear. And maybe it's something you need to say. Think about it?"

He tossed his coffee cup in the wastebasket and waited for Josiah to do the same before they took the well-worn path from the family waiting room to ICU.

❧ ❧ ❧

As if proving her father's point, Karin didn't bounce out of bed to greet them. She didn't wiggle three fingers to say hello. She'd seemed to have made no appreciable progress in the couple of days since baby Catherine's birth. Unless a person could count pain as progress.

And it was.

Pain, no doubt from the surgery, had made her fitful, though still with no more alertness than the ability to answer simple questions with eye blinks. The pain medication prescribed for her kept her on the fringes of—or deep in—sleep. Stan and Josiah talked to each other more than they were able to interact with Karin.

"She'll be here when I get back," Josiah said.

"Are you talking to me or to yourself, son?"

"Myself."

"Sometimes the hardest thing is letting someone else take care of the ones you love."

Josiah repositioned himself in his chair. "Have you been reading my notes?"

"I've been reading your life."

"Don't watch me. I'm watching *you*."

"Yours is far more interesting, Josiah. A page-turner."

The nurse on duty kindly suggested they take their conversation elsewhere since their visiting window had closed and Karin's sleep periods were important for her healing.

"When she's transferred to the rehabilitation unit," she said, "you can be in her room around the clock, if you want."

When. Not if. How could such a hard thing, such a small promise, hold so much hope?

⚜ ⚜ ⚜

"Remember when routine used to dictate mealtimes, Josiah?" Stan handed him his phone.

"Seems like eons ago." Josiah spotted an empty bench at the end of the hall.

"All the years Catherine and I lived together after I retired, we had breakfast first thing in the morning, lunch around noon, and supper at five thirty, whether we were hungry or not."

When had they last eaten? "You hungry, Stan?"

"I believe I could eat."

"Let me make this phone call. We'll check on Catherine Alecia real quick. Then we'll get something from Ernie's. How does that sound? Wait. It sounds awful. I can't do 'real quick' with that

child. Let's eat after this phone call. I need more time with that
little girl. While I can."

"So, you've decided?"

Decided? It's not up to me.

"What time's your flight?"

Oh. Decided to go to Dallas. "Early afternoon tomorrow. I'll pack
in the morning, spend some time here, then head to the airport."
Woodlands Regional and the airport. Almost equidistant from
the tree that started all this. "I wish I could tell Karin I'm going.
And why. I don't want her to think I'm abandoning her." Ironic.
But real. "I don't know what her memory's like, how much she's
really comprehending or retaining. It's too early to know all that.
But you're right. I have a short-term obligation that will help me
do a better job at fulfilling my long-term obligation."

"Not sure I understood all that, but God bless you, son."

"He'd better. Because it isn't going to happen without Him."

❧ ❧ ❧

"It's been almost four months since Karin ate anything." Not
the discussion Josiah ever thought he and his father-in-law would
have on their way to a restaurant.

"That could change." Stan's response seemed propelled from a
deep, bottomless cavern of hope.

"My appetite is so different from what it was before."

"Earlier today?"

"Before the accident." It was always safer to use that term
rather than *the betrayal.* He no longer had an urge to capitalize it.
The phrase was losing its power to cripple him.

"In what way?" Stan nodded his greeting to a vagrant they
often passed on their way to Ernie's. He stopped, leaned toward
the man sitting cross-legged in the doorway of a vacant storefront,
and asked him, "Sir, will you be here in an hour?"

"Most likely." The voice sounded younger than Josiah would
have guessed.

"See you later, then."

Josiah fell in step beside his wife's father, a man so unlike his own dad, every moment was a ping-pong game between renewed gratitude for the one and lifelong regret about the other.

"How's your appetite changed, Josiah?"

"I forget to eat. I eat because I have to or I'll fall over. I eat alone a lot now and find myself conscious of smells and tastes and textures I took for granted before."

"Nothing wrong with most of that. Except the forgetting part. But I hear you. Since my Catherine's been gone..." He didn't finish his sentence. From Josiah's perspective, he didn't need to.

The men took their favorite booth at Ernie's and settled in.

"The usual, Joe?"

"Nancy?" Josiah slid out of his side of the booth and gestured for her to join them. "What are you doing here? I've been intending to get in contact with you somehow."

"Should be easier now," she said. "I work here. Toffee mocha?"

"Wait. What?"

"You're Stanley, right? Karin's father?" Nancy extended her hand.

Had Josiah ever introduced them? He must have. More than one thing was a blur these days.

"Nancy, thank you for being a good friend for my son-in-law. Son-of-my-heart."

"For good reason," she said. "I learned a lot from him."

Josiah found his voice. "Nancy, that's rubbish. It's the other way around."

"How's your son doing, Nancy?" Stan asked before Josiah could stop him.

"A day at a time. Like all of us. Let me get your drink, Stanley. If I know you two, you're not going to stay long. But if you take your time ordering, we can fit in a sentence or two to catch up."

"You know what? Bring me a raspberry iced tea, please."

"On its way."

In stolen moments between ordering and refills, Josiah caught bits of Nancy's story. Capitalization wasn't Nancy's strong suit. Home with a capital *H* meant she was excited to get her son Blain back home to live out however long he had left. Her husband, Chris, didn't share her excitement and filed for divorce. Nancy got half the house, which meant she couldn't afford a whole house, so she moved to a first-floor one-bedroom apartment in Woodlands so she could wheel Blain's hospital bed out to the cement patio when the weather was nice.

That much she'd shared in one breath.

Respite Care would help her get out of the apartment two days a week. She decided to spend part of the free time working at Ernie's. She'd missed the ability to encourage someone else. Josiah explained a few details about Karin and Catherine Alecia's story that could use the encouragement.

"It'll be good to see you around, Nancy."

"It'll be good to keep my eye on your little family, Joe. It's harder to pray long distance. It can be done, but, you know."

"I feel the same way, Mrs. Drew." Stan slid his iced tea glass closer to the edge of the table.

"Another refill?"

"Please. And you can put in that extra order any time now."

"You got it."

Nancy's husband had not been in it for the long haul. How easily Josiah could have taken a similar path. How much he would have missed. How miserable he would have been.

Stan asked for a plastic fork and extra napkins for his to-go meal. As Nancy folded down the top of the paper bag, Stan said, "If you don't mind the extra trouble, let's put a piece of cherry pie in there, too."

"My pleasure," Nancy said. Convincingly.

Maybe Ernie's was right where she belonged at the moment. The two men, on the other hand, belonged back at the hospital. Josiah needed to wrap his mind around leaving for a couple of days, getting home in time to do a load or two of laundry, and composing his revised talks.

That left little time to compose *himself.* No matter how much time he had, it wouldn't be enough.

On the walk back to the hospital, Stan stopped to hand the vagrant the extra meal.

"I appreciate the leftovers, mister," the young man said. "Thank you."

Josiah started to tell him they weren't, leftovers, but Stan stopped him. "You stay safe, sir."

"I'll do that."

Half a block later, Josiah said, "The man would have been satisfied with leftovers, Stan."

"I wouldn't have been satisfied to *give* leftovers."

"Point taken."

"He needed to know he was worth more than that."

"And pie."

"Well, pie's a given." Stan nudged Josiah with his elbow.

"Crème brûlée."

Stan tilted his head. "Not for me. I prefer pie."

"Not for me, either. I think it'll be the first thing Karin asks for when she can eat. Seared scallops, roasted veggies, watercress salad, and crème brûlée for dessert."

Unless her tastes have changed.

Unless . . . her tastes have changed.

Chapter 35

No one wins a battle of wills. Or a battle of won'ts.
Both claim victory when they rush to out-surrender each other.

~ Seedlings & Sentiments
from the "Love" collection

In the world of mistakes, this one had to rank as one of the prizewinners.

Josiah tightened his seatbelt across his lap, less irritated than he'd been when he realized Morris had booked him in first class. What a waste. What an affront to the indignities of his wife and child—the indignities Karin and Catherine Alecia bore. He'd arrived at the airport too late to ask for a seating change, and he wasn't excited about stirring any more conflict in his relationship with his agent. So he'd sullenly plopped into his first-class seat before it hit him that the extra space and relative quiet were a gift for his rattled brain.

He pulled the complimentary noise-canceling headphones over his ears, grateful too that the other seat in his row remained unoccupied. But even high-tech headphones couldn't cancel the sound of condemnation. It was a mistake to have left Woodlands. A mistake to think he could hurry through his responsibilities, focus on something other than Karin and little Catherine.

On the other hand, his trip postponed two potential heartbreaks. He wouldn't get the lab results until he returned, so relinquishing his emotional hold on Catherine could wait a few more days. And he couldn't know why Karin had kept her affair and the baby—and her disappointment in him—to herself. Or whether she wanted him in her life now.

She'd been more alert but still tired so quickly when he'd said his temporary good-bye that morning.

"Karin, blink once if you can hear me."

She'd blinked.

"I have to fly to Dallas for that *Mend Your Marriage* weekend extravaganzzzzza." He'd mimicked the way Karin had been describing it for more than a year. "I don't want to leave. But I have to do this."

One blink.

"If you tell me not to go, I won't."

She'd blinked twice.

"No? Does that mean you don't want me to go?" Yes and no answers weren't always clear-cut.

She'd blinked twice again.

"You want me to go?"

Yes.

He'd swallowed his next question. *"Forever?"* They both needed time before they had that discussion.

He should have stayed. Love stays. If Karin had stayed . . .

He opened his laptop when the plane reached cruising altitude. At one time, he would have faked his way through this. Look where that had gotten him. He was going to have to tell the truth about how to mend a marriage.

And he hadn't yet moved past training wheels.

Morris Lynch? Speechless?

The man leaned against the town car, arms crossed, shaking his head. Josiah tipped the bellman who brought his luggage curbside for the trip back to the airport. The driver took the luggage and loaded it into the trunk of the vehicle. Almost midnight, and the Dallas air still hung heavy and at least twenty degrees warmer than comfortable. The look on Morris's face wasn't helping.

"For a while there, I thought we were in trouble, Josiah."

Me, too.

"Not your typical message or delivery. Not Josiah Chamberlain style, that's for sure." He removed his glasses and scrubbed his face with one hand. "I don't know how you did it, but you pulled it off. They loved you. The planning committee is thrilled. They're talking about revisiting the same theme in a recap event next year. I've got a lot of precise negotiating to do for that to work. But—"

"Morris, this was the finale." Josiah slid his laptop case across the backseat of the vehicle. "No more events. No more hype. I have responsibilities at home."

"You have a book contract, if you recall. And marketing for the one releasing in a few months. *Love Him or Leave Him.* You *do* remember those responsibilities, don't you?"

Release your fist, Josiah. It won't help if you're arrested for assault, no matter how much the man deserves it. "I can't deal with any of that until my wife is better. I can't write now. I have to live it. I don't know if I'll ever be able to write about it, but I need to find out how."

"I'm not waiting around for you to figure out how much you need me. How much you need all this."

"See, that's the thing. I thought I did. Worse, I thought people needed my wisdom."

"They do. Obviously. This weekend should have proved that."

The driver cleared his throat. Josiah apologized to him and indicated he'd only be another minute. "Morris, do you know when the crowd applauded loudest? When I used God's material or Karin's material. And I don't know enough about either to sustain that for long right now. I'm going home to study both."

Is that what he was doing? Yes. Funny that it would come to him not while he bent over his Bible but while standing outside a hotel lobby at midnight. His *avant-garde* Garden of Gethsemane.

"I need you to see if you can get me a year's extension on the *Caring* contract. I hope that will be enough. And if you can't, then get me out of it. And that will be the last of our working together."

The muscles stretched tighter along his agent's jawline. "You have to make a living. What are you going to do? Bus tables at that diner?"

Josiah slid into the town car and reached to pull the door closed after him. "If that's what it takes."

❧ ❧ ❧

In the world of mistakes, he may have just topped his old record.

What had he done? He was his own iceberg, busting a hole in the hull of his *Titanic* career. At a time when he and Karin and her child needed financial stability more than ever. While their medical outcomes remained uncertain. With the potential for a lifetime of full-time caregiving on his horizon. Only a fool would give up everything for someone he could only hope would love him.

On the night He was betrayed, Jesus . . .

It all came back to that. His doubts fled to that ancient scene for recalibration. *It won't be the last time, will it?* God didn't answer, but over the sound of the flight attendant's instructions and jet engines roaring to life, Josiah was pretty sure he heard divine applause.

❧ ❧ ❧

Josiah had walked the hospital halls predawn before. He'd never been accompanied by peace. And the weird thing? A change in circumstances didn't serve as a prerequisite. Peace didn't need proof of progress. It stood on its own merit.

Lights in Karin's room had been dimmed for the night. It would be another hour or more before any stray hints of the new day snuck around the edges of the honeycomb shade on the window. It almost felt like candlelight. But not quite.

She'd been turned onto her side, a pillow both in front and in back of her torso to brace her. Karin's right hand rested on the front pillow, the fingers less swollen. She opened her eyes when Josiah leaned over her to kiss her forehead.

"I didn't want to wake you. It's early, hon. Go back to sleep."

She stared at him with her signature wide eyes. Then she blinked twice.

"No? You don't want to go back to sleep?"

No.

He curled his fist under her warm hand, grateful for the touch point. That simple connection.

She blinked in rapid succession. A spasm? twitch? tic? The blinking stopped, then started again. What could that mean?

"Do you want to talk, Karin?"

One blink. *Yes.*

How? He'd have to guess at what she wanted to say so she could confirm or deny with a yes-or-no blink.

"Are you in pain?"

Yes.

"A lot?"

No.

His day had started almost twenty-four hours ago. He'd catnapped on the flight but not enough to count. Exhaustion had him believing he could feel slight pressure from her fingers that matched her blinks. One for yes. Two for no.

"Karin, are you doing that? Are you moving your fingers against my hand?"

Yes.

More than four months of emotion welled up.

Karin blinked fiercely.

"I'd talk if I could," he said.

Her eyes moved across his face as if her gaze could mop his tears.

"Can I just lay my head here beside you?"

Yes.

Yes. Oh, yes.

❧ ❧ ❧

He woke to a stiff neck and an unfamiliar sensation. Karin's hand on his cheek. Did she do that? He must have positioned her hand there. Unconsciously.

Josiah lifted it and laid it against the pillow. She slept on. He massaged the muscles at the back of his neck and used the arms of his chair as leverage to unkink his back.

"And a gracious good morning to you, Mr. Chamberlain."

"Good morning, Dr. Moore. Sorry, I didn't intend to stay so long."

"Red-eye flight? Nice suit."

"Had to get back here. What did I miss? Other than the fact that she's got some movement in her fingers."

Dr. Moore squirted hand cleaner from the dispenser at the door and rubbed her hands together as she approached the bedside. "Now, that's a beautiful way to start my morning."

"You didn't know?"

"New development since my rounds late yesterday. Unless she was saving that revelation for you." The lift in Priscilla Moore's voice brought its own light source to the room. "Are you awake, Karin? Good. If you think you can handle it, we're going to have the NICU send a live feed to my tablet later today so you can finally meet your daughter in more than a phone image, and she can finally meet you. We want her to know you when you finally get to hold her. Judging from what your husband says, that might be sooner than we thought. We'll see if we can't get Daddy holding that little one for the live feed."

Karin's eyebrows moved into a frown.

"An expression! Congratulations, Mrs. Chamberlain. What do you think of that new trick, Josiah?"

Heartbreaking. It's heartbreaking. They could play Twenty—or Two Hundred—Questions to find out what made her frown. Josiah knew. The baby daddy, as he'd heard them called on television, had been buried months ago. He rubbed the spot on his cheek where Karin's hand had rested a few minutes earlier. The action told him he needed to shave.

He tried to match Dr. Moore's ebullience. For Karin's sake. "You're making so much headway, hon. That's worth celebrating. I can't wait for you to see baby Catherine. She has your eyes. Definitely. I missed that little button when I was gone."

Too much. He'd gone too far. The top half of Karin's face frowned again.

Couldn't they work this out somehow? Baby Catherine might wind up with more grandparents than she could count, but with Karin's improvement, Wade's mom and dad wouldn't expect to fight for custody, would they?

It would take a whole lot more than breathing on her own, active eyebrows, and the ability to make a millimeter depression in the flesh of Josiah's hand before any court would let her win a custody battle. Maybe he should call Wade's parents and talk to them. No. Their grief was so fresh. Hearing news of their son's baby girl from the other woman's husband would not be appropriate, no matter how carefully Josiah chose his words.

Life wasn't supposed to be this complicated, was it? He blinked twice.

"Karin, I'm heading home for a couple of hours. I need to brush my teeth, for one thing. And change clothes." He tugged on the lapel of his suit jacket.

She agreed with him. What a curious way to dialogue.

"Your dad will be here sometime this morning."

The opposite of a frown lifted Karin's eyebrows.

The morning shift of lab people, nurses, physical and occupational therapists would soon start their journeys in and out of the room. Dr. Moore's laughter rang from the nurse's station. Josiah and Karin were alone again.

He leaned down until their faces were closer. He backed off, popped a wild cherry Lifesaver in his mouth, then leaned forward. "Karin, I'm here. No matter what. For however long you need me." He brushed back a curl that had fallen over her forehead on the side that hadn't been shaved for her postaccident surgery. Half her head sported two inches of new hair. The other, the shoulder-length he'd always known. "It doesn't matter what your answer is. I'm here. But I need to know..."

He had to ask. Didn't he? Yes. He had to ask. "Do you remember the accident?"

Yes.

"Did you intend to leave me that night?"

No response. How many seconds passed? four? ten? She blinked. He waited for a second blink.

It never came.

The fierce ache he'd felt that first night returned with a vengeance. He had one of the answers he needed. When the vise grip around his throat loosened enough to allow him to talk, he said, "Thank you for being honest. I love you, and I'll be back this afternoon."

He made it all the way to his car, key in ignition, seat belt fastened, before releasing a primal scream.

Chapter 36

Love shows up best against contrasting fabric. Let it shine.

~ Seedlings & Sentiments
from the "Faith" collection

He still had to win her back, even though the object of her affection was dead and buried. It wasn't fair or right, but Josiah had stopped using *fair* and *right* in connection with what it takes to sustain a marriage.

Karin's confession opened the wound he'd thought farther along in its healing. She meant to leave him that night. She *intended* to walk away, drive away, fly somewhere.

While heading home, Josiah passed Stan's vehicle heading toward the hospital. What kind of miracle would it take for Josiah to get a few hours of sleep before diving back into the Woodlands Regional environment? He hadn't taken time to stop in the NICU to see baby Catherine. Regret—and bone-deep exhaustion—almost made him miss his turnoff. He whispered a prayer to the One who kept him from driving off the edge of the universe.

He'd had the radio on—the station Karin preferred—to ensure he stayed awake for this last leg of his trip. He sat behind the wheel in the garage, engine off, forehead braced against his crossed hands on the top of the steering wheel while the current song finished playing. When the last note faded, he turned off the radio before anything new disrupted his thought.

"God, give me a chance to be a good, good father."

No. Too much to ask. Even from a good, good Father.

❧ ❧ ❧

The house smelled fresher than it had in weeks. Stan's note on the kitchen counter explained.

> *Josiah, a woman named Janelle—said she was a friend of Karin's—stopped by with four women from your church on Saturday. They came with buckets and sponges and wanted to do something to help. I hope it was all right that I let them clean. I told them your office was off-limits, but have at it anywhere else. I think they did a great job. If I did wrong by letting them clean, you can take it out of my next week's salary.*

He'd ended his note with a rudimentary smiley face.

Janelle and the crew from church deserved medals for being faithful when Josiah had been so unfaithful to keep them updated. One of these days, he'd have to—

The phone rang before he'd gotten his luggage as far as the stairs to the second floor. Stairs. When Karin came home, they'd need a master bedroom on the first floor. He shoved the additional distraction aside and answered. Stan.

"Son, I don't know what to do." His voice held panic foreign to Stan's normal steadiness.

"What's wrong, Dad?"

"Karin's a wreck. She's apparently been out of her mind—no that's not how to describe it. The nurses say that if they can't get her calmed down, they'll have to sedate her again. Son, that scares the liver out of me."

"What's going on?" Had hope left the stage again?

"Her blood pressure's rising, but they can't find any medical

302

reason for it. She's blinking almost constantly, but none of us can figure out why or what she's trying to tell us. We keep asking questions, but apparently we're not asking the right ones. The only thing we got any kind of response to was when we mentioned your name. She kept blinking *yes, yes, yes.* 'Do you want us to call him?' I asked. And she said *yes.* Over and over. Then she'd start in on *no, no, no.*"

Josiah used his thumb and forefinger to rub his eyes. "Stan, I don't know that I'd have any answers, either." The win-win concept never seemed to apply to their crises. "But I'll get there as soon as I can. Will you tell her that?"

"I'll have her nurse tell her. Thanks, son. You probably need sleep, don't you?"

"Eventually."

Josiah grabbed bottled water from the fridge and snatched his keys from the counter. He glanced at the sweet-smelling kitchen as he pulled the door shut behind him. *I might have to move to Woodlands. Whoa.*

❧ ❧ ❧

The staff waived the top of the hour protocol for Josiah. He popped another wild cherry Lifesaver—How many calories did that net him?—and pulled his chair to Karin's bedside.

Her eyes glistened. She'd been turned on her other side sometime after Josiah left. Tears ran from one eye into the other. No one standing more than a few feet away would know. He grabbed a tissue from the supply stand and dabbed at the tears.

"What's going on, Karin?"

She opened her mouth and closed it as if trying to form words. She could open her mouth at will? Her awakening from motionlessness came at a pace that underscored how little he'd appreciated small victories before now.

He leaned closer but could hear nothing. Her delicate, almost pixie-ish mouth moved so slow it made lip-reading impossible.

303

"You want to talk?"

She blinked *yes.*

He had to take the risk. "About what you told me before I left?"

Yes.

The movement of her lips looked like Helen Keller's first attempts at speech.

"Water?"

No.

"Walk?"

No. No. No.

"Why?" Was that the question she wanted him to ask?

Yes.

Josiah glanced at the nurse who had been watching Karin's blood pressure levels. The nurse nodded and busied himself elsewhere in the room.

"You want to explain why you wanted to leave me?"

Yes.

Every symptom of sleep deprivation hit him head-on. He couldn't think. Didn't want to think. Pain pulsed behind his eyeballs. She wanted to tell him why.

"I know about you and Wade."

Her brows furrowed.

"I... I forgive you."

No. No, no, no.

"I do. It's taken me a while."

No. Emphatically, which isn't easy for a person with so little facial expression and no sound production.

"I know he offered you something I couldn't give you."

Brows furrowed again.

"Among other things"—he looked over his shoulder for the nurse, who had left the room—"that baby in the NICU."

Eyes wide. Wider. *No.* A succession of two-blink patterns followed.

"Karin, Catherine can't be mine. You know that."

Yes.

"Yes, you know that?"

No.

They were going to have to find some other means of communicating. He'd heard of alphabet boards where family members could point to the word or letter they thought the patient intended until they got a yes-or-no answer, then would move to the next word or letter. Slow, torturously slow, but effective. He'd seen a documentary about a computerized version that could read where the patient's eyes landed. Karin could type with her eyes.

"I don't understand what you mean. It's Wade's baby."

No.

"How can you be sure?" Where could he get a blood pressure cuff for himself? "Are you telling me you weren't . . . intimate? Wait. Let me rephrase that so I can understand your answer. Were you and Wade intimate, like six or seven months ago?"

That emphatic *no.*

"Ever?"

No.

A blood pressure cuff and maybe an oxygen cannula, too?

She knew what she was saying. The questions were clear. She hadn't hesitated.

"Karin, you said you intended to leave me that night."

Yes. Tears again.

"Forever?"

No.

He dabbed her eyes dry. "And not with Wade?"

No.

"But he was driving your car, hon. You were taking off together."

No.

"He was driving your car."

Yes.

"He wasn't leaving with you?"

No.

How many questions would it take to get the details she was trying so hard to tell him? If she intended to leave him, but

305

not forever, did that mean separation? If separation is what she wanted, she got it. Four months of silence. How long before he'd know what she was trying to tell him now?

One detail loomed larger than the others. "Are you saying I could be...that I'm Catherine's father?"

A slow but beautiful *yes*. The tension in her face softened.

"You're sure?"

Yes.

"How can that be? I thought it was virtually impossible."

Yes.

"Like, 99.9 percent impossible."

Yes. The corners of her mouth teased a smile.

Elation battled a new betrayal deep in his gut. She'd known it was his child—a fact he could only embrace by trusting Karin's word—but she'd kept it a secret for close to three months before the accident. How could she do that to him? Who would do that?

Someone whose mom experienced one disappointing miscarriage after another.

Someone married to a self-absorbed man who'd justified neglecting her unless it suited his needs, who'd made too many things a higher priority than his wife, and who'd—

His stomach wrenched with the recognition. He'd justified his failed motility test by insisting a child would get in the way of his career goals. Repeatedly insisting.

Who knew forgiving himself was going to be harder than forgiving his wife?

❧ ❧ ❧

They left a thousand unanswered questions hanging when the respiratory therapist arrived. How long would it be before they could communicate freely? He couldn't help seeing the hint of humor in that. He craved the ability to talk to his wife and to listen to every word.

Stan met him in the hall. "How's she doing?"

"Better."

"Did you ever figure out the problem?"

"Self-absorption."

"What?"

Josiah gave his father-in-law a hug. "She's resting now. I'm going to see baby Catherine."

"Just came from there. She's doing well, all things considered."

"I need to see her."

"Don't blame you. The little bug is getting prettier every day. If you ask me. Not that I'm at all biased."

"I'll see you in a few minutes."

"Take your time, son."

Josiah's feet moved on autopilot. He completed the hand- and forearm-cleaning ritual with his suit jacket sleeves pushed up under the paper gown and without having to consult the laminated chart for recommended times on each step of the procedure. Eva stood near another baby's Isolette but met him before he'd crossed the room to Catherine's.

"Mr. Chamberlain, welcome back."

"Thanks. It's good to be back." Despite the setting. Despite the long road ahead for those he loved most.

"We have the results of the test."

"Please don't tell me. I have what I need to know. She's right over there."

"Yes. The feisty one who insists her small stature is not going to be a deterrent for her."

Josiah's heart raced ahead of his body to get to baby Catherine's side. "She has my ears."

Eva made it a point to examine them. "So she does. And, for the record, if you ever need a kidney, she could be your donor."

It took him a second, but he caught her meaning.

"Daddy, can we get you to finish filling out the rest of the birth record information? We've put that off too long."

"Yes. I have."

Chapter 37

The past has history but no breath. Today breathes.

~ Seedlings & Sentiments
from the "Hope" collection

One Year Later

Smells good, Stan."

"I call it 'Morning Magnificence.' A little corned beef hash, a perfect fried egg, and a slice of avocado."

"You've been watching the cooking channel again, haven't you?" Josiah took the plate Stan offered and poured a cup of coffee for each of them.

"Miss Catherine insists she can nap better when she hears a cooking show on in the next room."

"Oh, she does, does she?" Josiah bent to kiss the copper-haired beauty chasing Cheerios on her high-chair tray with one petite finger. "Stan, your breakfast smells wonderful. You, young lady, do not."

Stan turned from the stove and waved a spatula her direction. "I don't think she's completely done, if you know what I mean."

"Your mama will not be pleased if you show up smelling like anything other than sweetness, child."

"Do you want to leave her home with me today? I had plans, but..."

Josiah took a bite of Morning Magnificence. "Okay, this tastes so much better than it looks."

Stan polished his fingernails on his shirt pocket and snuck a bit of something to Sandi. The dog sat at his feet, muzzle pointed upward for more.

"Karin specifically asked me to bring baby Catherine along today. She has something to give her or show her. I think she might have made something in her occupational therapy session."

"It won't be long until she's home."

"Did you ever dream she'd come this far? I know we have a long way to go yet. But I'm so proud of her."

Stan turned off the stovetop and filled his plate. "I wondered about her stubbornness in the beginning, wanting everything recorded, even the hardest parts."

"That's a lot of footage."

"You were a saint to accommodate all that, son."

"Far from sainthood. You've seen me frustrated a time or two." Josiah sipped his coffee. "Do you think she'll like it here?"

"She's seen pictures. Liked them well enough, didn't she?"

"It doesn't have the hundred-year-old 'charm' of the house we bought together." Josiah took in the open floor plan, the wide walkways, the features that would make Karin's transition safer and more comfortable. "Maybe it was Karin who added the charm in the old place."

"Wait until she puts her decorating touches around here. And maybe, someday, she'll want to relaunch her business. She'll be glad you put all the inventory in storage for that possibility."

"I wouldn't put anything past my wife's tenacity."

Stan pulled a handkerchief from his pocket and wiped at his eyes. "Do you think Leah would ever want to be involved again, now that she knows her husband really was trying to be a hero that night?"

Josiah shook his head. "Her pain hasn't made the kind of progress Karin's has, Dad. My heart goes out to her."

"Mine, too."

"I don't know how we would have made it—Catherine and me—if you hadn't been here, Stan."

"You could have bought a place with one less bedroom."

"More than worth it, Dad."

Catherine jabbered her opinion, her joy turning to pint-sized wails when she lost a Cheerio between her chest and the high-chair tray. Stan stood, then sat again when Josiah shot him "the look."

"Catherine, you can find it. Find where you dropped it."

"Hard habit to break," Stan said, "running to fix things when they're capable of figuring it out themselves."

"Agonizingly hard with Karin. One of the toughest challenges this past year. Watching her learn how to dress herself, feed herself, drop something and have to figure out a creative way to get it back. I thought my role was going to be doing things for her, but that wasn't at all what she needed." Josiah dragged his fork through the corned beef—furrows in a mottled field.

"You think that battle's over, son?"

"Probably not. So what are your plans?"

Stan rolled his lower lip out. Catherine giggled—one of the most beautiful sounds on earth. Stan did it again. She giggled again, her pink plastic eyeglasses riding up higher on her nose.

"Your plans, Dad?"

"Having lunch with a friend."

"Oh. Good."

"Nancy's been a little lost since she's not caregiving anymore."

"You're having lunch with Nancy? The two of you?"

Stan huffed. "Don't read too much into it."

"Oh, I wasn't." Josiah busied himself with the fried egg. "Nope. Not reading anything into that. Two friends having lunch together.

Perfectly innocent"—he leaned in—"start to a relationship." He took a bite of avocado dipped in egg yolk.

"Not saying that."

"No. Me neither."

Stan's blush warmed the room. "Oh, there's a message on the machine. Nate called while you were on your romantic picnic date in the rehab center courtyard. He and Ruthie send their love."

Their love. Maybe Karin would feel up to a video visit with them one of these days. She'd prayed more diligently than anyone else for that restoration. Remarkable woman.

"Well, Miss Catherine and I plan to have lunch with Mama today, don't we?"

The little one said "Mama" as clear as day and clapped her hands together. The bond they shared seemed forged in conquering adversity as much as the traditional mother/daughter connection. Josiah read Karin's efforts as a mirror to Catherine's development. He could see Karin's arms and hands clapping like that a few months ago. Now more controlled, mother had bypassed many of her daughter's skills. The race was on. *Get out of their way, everybody.*

Physiatrist, neuropsychologist, rehabilitation nurses, physical therapists, occupational therapists all did their part. But it was a three-pound preemie who provided the strongest motivation.

That sounded about right.

Josiah put his plate and utensils in the dishwasher, poured a fresh cup of coffee, and set it aside with an unspoken promise to get back to it. "Okay, little one, let's get you a fresh diaper and pick out something stylish for you to wear to rehab today."

He'd never tire of the feel of her small arms around his neck, the weight of her on his hip, the way she laid her head on his shoulder or rubbed his cheek checking for stubble. He'd never tire of some of the things other dads found wearying. Her waking in the middle of the night because she wanted reassurance he was still there. Her insistence that he read her another book, or the same book. Her chatter.

He couldn't wait for Karin to live with all that, too, rather than experience their daughter's life in spurts of visits.

"Soon, little one. Soon," he said, looking into miniature versions of Karin's wide eyes, made wider by her toddler-sized prescription lenses.

Above the changing table, Josiah had secured a photo display of Catherine's life to date. Catherine lying on Karin's lap with a c-shaped pillow holding the child before Karin could do much more than look at the baby and stroke her fine hair with stiff, cupped fingers. Karin pointing out the Christmas decorations hanging above her bed. One of Josiah's favorites—Karin lying on her side, watching her daughter sleep curled next to her.

Josiah kept one hand on Catherine's tummy and with the other flipped open the card he'd fastened to the display. The card Karin made for their anniversary almost two years ago. "The past has history, but no breath. Today breathes." It had lived deep in the lining of his suit jacket pocket until he'd emptied the pockets the week after his arena event, readying the garment for the dry cleaner.

In the planter on the porch sat the Sweet Williams whose seeds had once been embedded in the bookmark attached to the card where Karin had announced she was pregnant. On their anniversary. He'd never read the card. Never reacted. Never mentioned the child growing within her. The card hung on the wall above Catherine's changing table as a reminder to take nothing for granted and to forgive big so forgiveness would be waiting when he needed it.

"Who's that?" he asked, pointing to one of his favorite pictures.

"Mama."

"Who am I?" He pointed to his chest.

"Dada."

No hesitation. No wondering. No question. No doubt.

For a guy who hadn't paid enough attention before, he'd grown adept at coordinating outfits for his daughter. He dressed Catherine in a soft green sundress, slipped a matching headband over her fine hair, adjusted the fabric flower on its side, and kissed her baby feet before sliding them into miniature sandals.

"Are you ready to go?"

She squirmed her answer.

Before they left the nursery with its faux picket fence and mural of flower and vegetable gardens, Josiah—as was his habit—read aloud the verse he'd had Janelle help him stencil near the ceiling: "Let your roots go down deep into the soil of God's love."

And above the door—the quote he took from one of Karin's *Seedlings & Sentiments* cards: "Hope grows here."

◦৺ ◦৺ ◦৺

So, maybe he wouldn't miss a few things about parenting an infant. Estimating how many bottles and how many diapers for any given outing. Car seats. Catherine agreed. Juggling a diaper bag, a baby, and a stroller—courtesy of the church baby shower—that the baby didn't want to sit in.

He parked in their favorite spot close to the rehabilitation center's wing of the hospital. Newer than the rest of the hospital by a couple of decades, it seemed separate from the hospital complex, but connected for ease of doctor access and emergency needs. The way the building was situated made Josiah a little less uncomfortable about bringing such a small child with him for the past year. It looked more like a hotel than part of the hospital, from the outside.

Inside the doors, he greeted the staff and turned right toward Karin's room. She'd texted a message to meet her in the physical therapy room farther down the hall. She'd *texted*. Josiah couldn't help smiling. How far they'd come.

"Ready to wow your mama, little girl?" He straightened Catherine's goggle glasses on her little bit of a nose. She wiggled her insistence on getting down on the floor. "In a minute."

The physical therapy room always appealed to baby Catherine. Plenty of visual stimulation for her inquisitive mind. He searched for his wife. There. In the wheelchair near the long bank of windows, surrounded by three of her favorite PT team members.

As they neared, Karin smiled and said, "Stay there. Don't come any closer."

Without the quirky look on her face, Josiah would have wondered if she'd caught a cold or something, warning them to keep their distance for the baby's sake.

Karin nodded to the women on either side of her who spotted her as Karin pushed hard on the armrests and raised herself to standing. She leaned her forearms on the waiting arms of her spotters, looked up once to see if Josiah was watching, and took four steps forward under her own steam.

When Josiah broke into applause, so did baby Catherine. Karin laughed so hard she wobbled. The young man holding the wheelchair closed the gap so Karin could lower herself into it.

Josiah shrugged off the diaper bag strap and set it in the stroller he'd been pushing with one hand. He let Catherine down, holding her hands while she stood between his feet. "This little one won't be far behind you, Karin." Daddy and daughter stepped together to get closer to where Karin sat.

"She's so steady on her feet, Josiah. I envy that."

God, thank you for restoring her mind, her body, her voice.

"Let go of her hands, Daddy. Let's see what she can do. Come here, baby. Come here." Karin held out her arms. Josiah let go. Catherine's baby steps didn't stop until she could cling to Karin's legs.

Karin bent to pick up her daughter, her spotters nearby but letting her figure it out. Which she did. "You knew she could do that, didn't you? Catherine's been taking steps at home?"

"It's only been the last day or so. We wanted to surprise you."

Karin snuggled the little one sitting on her lap, the one she'd carried just long enough to give her a fighting chance, the one who made him a good, good father...with a lot to learn.

"We have another surprise for you."

"Crème brûlée from Russell's?"

"They don't open until five."

Her fake pout morphed into her trademark impish grin when he pulled a book from the diaper bag. "My book? I mean, our book?"

The staff crowded around, then stepped back to allow Josiah and Karin some breathing space.

"Josiah, I love the cover."

"You should, honey. They used an image from one of your cards."

"*Hope for When She's Hurting*. By Dr. Josiah and Karin Chamberlain." She ran her hand over the satiny cover. Catherine reached in and played it like a drum. "Look at me," Karin said. "I'm crying like I've never seen a book before." She wiped her own tears. He hadn't minded that job.

"Open it." Josiah held his breath. The moment of truth.

She read, "'A quiet moment of gratitude is never wasted.' Seedlings & Sentiments, from the 'Gratitude' collection. Books always have a starting point. Ours begins in the muddy middle, where pain tried to swallow us, to suffocate us, to keep us from finding our way home. Where would we be if we hadn't discovered that seeds of hope can grow in mud?"

Gratitude

As an author, I owe a debt of gratitude to those who have lived through experiences like the story told in *A Fragile Hope*, including those betrayed, those who assume they were betrayed, those who forgave when it made no sense, and those who have experienced and emerged from DBT or a persistent vegetative state. Thank you for sharing your stories publicly so I could know hope was possible, even in those devastating circumstances.

Thank you, Dr. David Heegeman, for once again assisting with medical details that added depth and accuracy.

I sympathize with those whose stories have not transpired as this one did. Thank you for your patience and grace in allowing it to be told this way for its unique purposes.

Editor Ramona Richards gave me permission to take the risk of writing this novel, even though soon after, her career direction took a different path. I'm grateful for Ramona and for the Abingdon editorial staff who adopted this project as their own. Thank you, Jamie Chavez, for challenging me where I needed to be challenged. Thank you, Susan Cornell, for the fine-tuning that took the story even farther.

Jamie Nicole Hollins-Randolph mentioned an idea that led to the Seedlings & Sentiments concept. I can see it developing into a genuine business someday. Thanks, Jamie.

Wendy Lawton from Books & Such Literary Management, you have the heart of a champion and certainly graced my life with its overflow on this project.

Special thanks to my Wednesday morning study group. What would I do without your encouragement?

Becky Melby, these pages are marked with your tears as well as mine. Thank you.

Writing and reader friends who keep requesting more stories, please know that my gratitude for you is immeasurable.

To my husband, children, and grandchildren who not only love me but don't mind brainstorming with me when a plot point won't reveal itself, may you be extra blessed for your patience and thoughtfulness, especially during deadlines.

To my publishing team, marketing staff, sales team, retailers, librarians, book clubs, and the Storyteller to whom I owe my life and breath, know I am humbled by your kindness and consider myself the most grateful of authors.

Group Discussion Guide

1. How do you think Josiah's thoughts about Karin's disappearance—both physically and virtually—were different because of his career? Did you believe he reacted as a typical husband might? Or were his responses colored by his life's work? How?

2. Several characters served a mentor role in Josiah's life as the crisis progressed. How important were they to the decisions he made? In what way? Was it their words, their presence, or their attitudes that made the greatest difference?

3. Which of Josiah's character strengths served him well during the story? Which had to be weeded out or mature in order for the story to conclude the way it did?

4. The reader "heard" Karin's voice only in small snippets throughout *A Fragile Hope*—at the beginning of each chapter and sprinkled within the scenes. How did that storytelling technique add to the tension? Did you as a reader feel you "knew" Karin with only those few snippets?

5. Which scene in the book did you find the most compelling and why?

6. How did you personally connect with the moment(s) when Josiah discovered major revelations about the true nature of love, if you did?

7. Anyone familiar with long-term caregiving understands the unending nature of daily routines we take for granted. The bulk of the story takes place over the course of about

four months…and with relatively few scene changes. In what ways did that bring an air of reality to the crisis? Do you have a caregiving or recovering story of your own? Did anything in *A Fragile Hope* especially resonate with your experience?

8. The topic of betrayal is uncomfortable to read about, much less live through. Josiah's heartache took a sharp turn where an ancient tale of love and betrayal met on a collision course. We've been told love is a choice, a decision, not a feeling. In what way is that more true than ever when betrayal (friendship, coworker, marriage, family) is in the mix?

9. In what way was the Seedlings & Sentiments shop and what it produced a metaphor for the story's journey?

10. *A Fragile Hope* is not only a title but a concept with which many people wrestle. Each of the characters in this novel faced their own battles with hope's fragility. Nancy, Stan, Catherine, Nate, Josiah, even Karin. How were each impacted by the possibility of hope?

Want to learn more about Cynthia Ruchti
and check out other great fiction from
Abingdon Press?

Check out our website at
www.AbingdonFiction.com
to read interviews with your favorite authors,
find tips for starting a reading group,
and browse our other great titles.

Be sure to visit Cynthia online!
www.cynthiaruchti.com